W9-DDJ-011

DISCARD

from Here to Home

Center Point
Large Print

Also by Marie Bostwick and available from
Center Point Large Print:

Apart at the Seams
The Second Sister

**This Large Print Book carries the
Seal of Approval of N.A.V.H.**

From Here
to Home

MARIE
BOSTWICK

CENTER POINT LARGE PRINT
THORNDIKE, MAINE

This Center Point Large Print edition is published
in the year 2016 by arrangement with
Kensington Publishing Corp.

The text of this Large Print edition is unabridged.
In other aspects, this book may vary
from the original edition.
Printed in the United States of America
on permanent paper.
Set in 16-point Times New Roman type.

ISBN: 978-1-62899-969-3

Library of Congress Cataloging-in-Publication Data

Names: Bostwick, Marie, author.
Title: From here to home / Marie Bostwick.
Description: Center Point Large Print edition. | Thorndike, Maine :
Center Point Large Print, 2016. | ©2016
Identifiers: LCCN 2016008246 | ISBN 9781628999693
    (hardcover : alk. paper)
Subjects: LCSH: Large type books.
Classification: LCC PS3602.O838 F76 2005 | DDC 813/.6—dc23
LC record available at http://lccn.loc.gov/2016008246

from Here to Home

With Many Thanks to . . .

Martin Biro, my editor, for patience and encouragement above and beyond the call, his keen eye for the well-placed comma, and his ability to break up even the most convoluted of run-on sentences. Liza Dawson, literary agent, mother of dragons, and part-time border collie, for continual optimism, good humor, and wisdom, and her remarkable ability to steer me away from the cliff without letting me know I'm being herded. Donna Gomer, my sister, for her advice and counsel on all things equine. Scott Finley for insights into the world of television production. Jeff Turner for art project assistance. Betty and John Walsh, my sister and brother-in-law, for speedy, insightful, and accurate first-round reading and for getting me to listen when I don't want to. Lisa Sundell Olsen, my Sparkly Assistant, for enthusiasm, organization, and flexibility, and for being able to drive a recreational vehicle like a boss. Joyce and Sara Ely, for first inspiring me to want to give Howard and Mary Dell a bigger stage, for helping make sure this book is accurate and sensitive to the experiences, challenges, and triumphs of the Down syndrome community and their families, and for being an uplifting example to me and thousands of others whose lives have been enriched and expanded simply by crossing paths with you. Crystal Lynn Wagner, a talented young artist who happens to have Down syndrome, for inspiring me to imagine new vocational adventures for Howard and Jenna.

Marie Bostwick

Prologue

On a hot Tuesday afternoon, on the outskirts of Alpine, Texas, in the remote western region of the state, a man wearing dark denim jeans, a black Western shirt embroidered with horseshoes and flowers in turquoise thread, and a gray Stetson atop his gray head walked into a tavern.

The bartender stood at the tap drawing beers for his only other customers, three men in their early twenties who were sitting at a table in the corner. When he saw the cowboy come through the door, he jerked his chin and said, "Hey, Donny. How you doing?"

"Oh, about right. You?"

"Same."

The cowboy took a stool at the far end of the bar, directly in front of the TV set, which was tuned to a baseball game. After the bartender delivered three draft beers to his other customers, he brought a basket of tortilla chips and salsa and a bottle of Lone Star to the cowboy and set it on the counter in front of him.

"Anything else, Donny?"

The cowboy shook his head, dug a much-creased ten-dollar bill from his back pocket, and laid it on the bar.

"Keep the change."

"Thanks. Let me know if you want another."
The cowboy nodded.

Without further conversation, the bartender picked up the TV remote and started clicking through the channels, his action eliciting a chorus of complaints and cries of "Hey, we were watching that!" from the three guys sitting at the corner table. Groans of disappointment became howls of protest when his search ended on channel 46, which aired the House and Home Network.

"What? C'mon!"

"You gotta be kidding!"

"You turned off the game so that old geezer can watch a *quilting* show?"

The cowboy sat silently, dipping chips into salsa and ignoring the ruckus, his eyes glued to the screen and the faces of the two hosts: a tall, big-busted woman dressed in a blouse of scarlet sateen, with ash-blond hair of a shade commonly used to cover gray, and a musical, Texas twang to her speech, and a stocky young man in his late twenties wearing a pressed blue button-down shirt, with a wide smile, brown hair, blue eyes shaped like almonds, and a slight thickness of speech, as if he'd recently been to the dentist and the novocaine hadn't entirely worn off.

The bartender came out from behind the counter to deal with the trio of disgruntled barflies. One of the young men, who wore an

Arizona Diamondbacks baseball cap, got to his feet, intercepting his approach.

"What the hell, man? The Diamondbacks are playing. Turn the game back on!"

"I will in half an hour, when this is over," the bartender said, cocking his head toward the television set, where the young man in the blue button-down was pointing at different spaces on a color wheel. "You sit down and enjoy your beer until then. I'll get you a basket of chips. On the house."

"We don't want any chips. We want to watch the game. This isn't fair, man! There's three of us and only one of him."

"Good. You can count. So can I," the bartender said, his tone slipping from conciliatory to sarcastic. "Except things add up a little different, the way I see them.

"You boys are just passing through. You bought three beers and I appreciate your business. But Donny here's a regular; has been for the last seven years. Shows up every Tuesday afternoon, orders a beer and a basket of chips, watches his show, and leaves a four-dollar tip on a six-dollar order. Every week. That means that on Tuesdays, in my bar, from three to three-thirty, Donny gets to watch whatever he damn well pleases. You hear?"

The bartender, a bearded man in his middle forties who stood half a head taller and had twenty pounds on the Diamondbacks booster, took two steps forward, until he stood chest to chest with the kid in the cap.

"Come on, Kyle. Sit down. We're not missing anything. It's only the second inning and the D-backs are down three runs," one of the other guys at the table hissed.

The kid in the cap, Kyle, hesitated a moment, then curled his lip and took his seat. "Fine," he mumbled, slouching back into his chair.

"I'll get you those chips," the bartender said, coolly amiable again. "And a side of queso to go with 'em."

The half hour passed uneventfully.

Donny sat silently, watching his show and drinking his beer. The three out-of-towners ate their chips and ordered another round, the kid in the cap continuing to brood and drink while his two friends exchanged laughter that grew louder as the minutes ticked by.

At three twenty-nine, the big-busted woman and the almond-eyed man said good-bye to their viewers and waved as music played and credits rolled. The cowboy tipped the Lone Star to his lips, emptying the bottle, got up from his stool, and thanked the bartender, who tuned the television back to the game.

As the cowboy walked toward the door, the kid in the cap called out, "Hey! Nice shirt, man!

What kind of flowers are those, anyway? Pansies? Did you embroider it yourself?"

The cowboy paused, but briefly, then kept walking. The kid in the cap guffawed and punched one of his buddies in the shoulder.

"I bet he did, man. I bet he sewed it with his own little hands. Ha! Probably picked up some tips watching that crazy quilt broad with the big boobs and her retard sidekick."

Still laughing, the kid swiveled to the right to face his friends, so he didn't see the cowboy coming for him, nor the fury that blazed in those previously placid eyes. But he felt his collar choking him as the cowboy's big hand closed on the neckband of his T-shirt, hauling him to his feet, and heard the crack of bone against bone as a hammer-hard fist slammed into his jaw, knocking the cap from his head and sending him flying.

Lying flat on his back on the floor, the kid clamped his hand against his jaw. Angry, humiliated, and in no little pain, he rocked forward, attempting to get to his feet, but his friends ran to his side and pressed him back down to the ground.

The cowboy approached the crumpled form, planted his feet wide, and in a low, burred voice, said, "You need to watch your mouth, son." Then he turned and left the bar.

When he was gone, the kid shook off his friends and started to curse. "I'm gonna sue that

SOB! Somebody call a cop. I'm going to have him arrested for assault."

"I wouldn't try that if I were you."

The bartender walked back behind the counter, scooped ice from a bin, and wrapped it in a towel.

"I told you before, Donny's a regular. He's manager for a good-sized sheep ranch about eight miles north of town, lives here full-time. I don't think the sheriff will have a lot of sympathy for your side of the story," he said as he handed the ice pack to the kid. "Especially after I tell him what you said."

The kid sat up and pressed the ice to his jaw.

"What I said about what? The flowers on his shirt? It was just a joke."

"Not about the flowers; about the young man on the television."

"Who? You mean the retard?"

The bartender moved his head slowly from side to side.

"Now, that's a word Donny don't like. Come to think of it, neither do I. Because Donny's my friend.

"And that young man on the TV show? He's Donny's son."

Chapter 1

People often remarked on Holly Silva's resemblance to her mother. Considering her line of work, it was a fortunate inheritance.

But what people usually failed to recognize was that her father's features were equally in evidence. She had his sharper jaw and dark brown eyes flecked with gold, and his generous eyebrows, which Holly dyed dark and tweezed into a wide arch, providing stark contrast to her blond hair and the ivory and pink complexion she shared with her mother. The melding of these parental traits came together in a face that was lovely, arresting, and slightly exotic, like a warrior princess from an ancient land. But because her father, an Argentinian actor turned independent film director, had died of a drug overdose before his daughter's third birthday, most of the people Holly met had either never known Cristian or forgotten what he'd looked like years before, so the similarities between them went largely unnoticed.

Holly was introspective, too, like he had been, and sensitive, had unusual insight into and empathy for the feelings of other people, but was surprisingly obtuse when it came to her own emotional state. And, like her father, Holly was unfailingly kind and well liked by almost everyone, yet she constantly worried that people did not, in fact, like her or that they would come to dislike her before long. Cristian had been just the same. She had his addictive personality as well. But food, and not heroin, was Holly's painkiller of choice.

Unlike Cristian, Holly had managed to control her addiction, losing more than seventy pounds in her last two years of high school, which explained why few noticed how much she looked like her mom, which is to say how beautiful she was, until she was almost eighteen years old.

Besides her mother's good looks and in spite of the anxieties she'd inherited from her father, Holly had a kind of spark, an energy that made her stand out from the crowd. She was genuinely interested in other people and cared about and for others, and that trait shone through in all she did. When Holly applauded for a contestant who'd just won a new car she'd never dreamed she could afford, she did it with all her heart, as excited for her as if she'd been the one getting a new set of wheels. When she put her arm around the shoulders of another who'd embarrassed himself by having just given a bone-head answer to an obvious question on national television, then said she was sorry while escorting him off the stage, she really *was* sorry. If the contestant started to cry, sometimes she did too.

There were five other models on the game show with Holly, yet she was the model people on the street were most likely to recognize and want to take a picture with. But coming home from the gym on a Saturday afternoon, dressed in yoga pants and a gray T-shirt, with no makeup and her shining blond hair in a ponytail, Holly Silva looked like any other single twenty-five-year-old enjoying the weekend.

She pulled up in front of a big Tudor-style house in the Beverly Grove section of West LA, set the parking brake of her Jeep, then jumped out the door, ran across the lawn, and bounded up the stairs to her apartment, trying to extend the metabolic impact of her morning workout.

Still puffing, she unlocked the door and entered, bending down to greet Calypso, her calico cat, before filling and then gulping down a glass of water. When she was done, she opened the door of the refrigerator and surveyed the contents. Calypso got up from where he was sitting on the floor and started winding around her ankles, emitting a series of chirruping half meows.

Holly tilted her head to one side. "What do you think? Leftover moo shu pork and pancakes? Or coconut Greek yogurt and a pear?"

Calypso chirruped and bumped his head against her calf. Holly looked down at him and reached for the container of leftover Chinese food.

"Good idea. Leftover moo shu—no pancake—for you. Yogurt for me."

By the time Holly sat down with her food, Calypso had already wolfed down his shredded pork and was looking for second helpings. He hopped lightly onto the sofa, butting Holly's hand with his head, trying to push his face into her bowl of yogurt.

Holly pushed him away with one hand and hugged the bowl to her chest. "Knock it off. I swear, you're a bottomless pit."

The cat gave her a disgusted look, jumped off the couch, and slunk off to pout under the coffee table. Holly's cell phone buzzed. She glanced at the screen before putting it to her ear.

"Amanda? I thought you were supposed to be in Beijing."

"En route," said Amanda Grimes, Holly's agent. "Changing planes in Seattle. I've only got a minute before they make me turn off my cell, so this has to be quick. Remember that infomercial job I booked you for a few months back?"

Holly did.

Two years in, the luster had worn off her game show gig. Though she appreciated the security of a regular paycheck, she couldn't see spending the rest of her life grinning into a camera as she held up boxes of dishwasher detergent or bottles of furniture oil.

She was bored, trapped, and unhappy. When

18

Amanda asked what would make her happy, Holly wasn't sure. Sometimes she just wished she could wake up and be someone completely different, but she knew that kind of talk would just elicit an eye roll from Amanda, so she'd said, "Maybe . . . a talk show host? Something where I could talk but wouldn't have to act?"

Amanda got her a job hosting an infomercial for a juice machine—one of those things that looks like a talk show but is really just a long commercial with frequent entreaties for viewers to order now. It didn't seem like an upward career move to Holly, but when she voiced her doubts, Amanda said, "Trust me, okay?" So Holly did.

Now, apparently, something had come of it.

"I booked the infomercial to get some decent video of you actually speaking," Amanda said. "I didn't say anything because I didn't want to get your hopes up, but I've been using the tape to pitch you for real talk and information shows. It was a long shot, but I figured we might get lucky."

Hearing the smile in Amanda's voice, Holly felt her breath catch in her throat. If Amanda was calling her en route to China with the results of a pitch that she'd been keeping secret, that could only mean . . .

"And did we? Get lucky, I mean?"

"Maybe. Don't pop the champagne cork just yet. But if he likes you and things shake out the way I hope, it'd be an incredible break. You'd be the . . . co-hosting . . . House and . . . Network. It's . . . replacement . . . but if . . ."

Amanda's voice kept cutting in and out. Holly was getting only every third word, but enough to understand that, miraculously and unexpectedly, she was being considered as a co-host for a program on the House and Home Network, a national cable channel.

But what show? Before Holly could ask, Amanda's voice cut out completely. Holly pressed the phone closer to her ear. "Amanda? Can you hear me? Amanda?"

Apparently not. When the connection resumed a few seconds later, Amanda was speaking quickly and loudly, racing to finish the call before takeoff. ". . . issues, but that's my worry," Amanda said. "I'll work out the details with him. The only catch is, you've got to go out there to meet him on Monday."

"Meet *who?*"

"Jason Alvarez, the new VP for programming—or he will be, if the rumors about the reorganization are true. Don't say anything about that to anybody, okay? It's not supposed to be announced for a few weeks yet."

"But how am I . . ."

"Somebody from the office is reserving a flight for you first thing Monday morning. They'll e-mail you the confirmation number."

Holly sat up straight on the couch. "Flight? To

where? Amanda!" She held the phone directly in front of her mouth and shouted. "Amanda, what's the show?"

Amanda kept talking as though she didn't hear a word Holly said. "Listen, lovey, they closed the doors. I've gotta go. Call when you get to Texas, okay?"

"Texas? Amanda, do you . . ."

The line went dead. Amanda would be unreachable for the next twenty hours.

Holly barked out a frustrated yelp and threw the phone across the sofa and into a pile of throw pillows, startling Calypso, who skittered out from under the coffee table and into the kitchen. Holly grabbed her phone again, tapping words into a search engine until she found what she was looking for.

She was already familiar with some of the programming at House and Home Network, which, not surprisingly, focused on home, gardening, cooking, and lifestyle shows, with an emphasis on do-it-yourselfing. Holly was a semi-regular viewer of *Sizzle!*, a cooking show hosted by a celebrity chef who was pretty sizzling himself. She'd also seen several episodes of *Flippin' Fabulous*, hosted by three attractive sisters in their mid-twenties to early thirties who renovated old houses and sold them for a tidy profit. Perusing the Web site, Holly learned that even though the network was headquartered in

Los Angeles, many of the programs were filmed in Dallas. Holly guessed the production costs must be lower in Texas than in California.

The phone pinged to alert her to an incoming e-mail. There it was—a message from the network saying she was scheduled to meet with Jason Alvarez in their Dallas offices at one o'clock on Monday and that confirmations for her Monday flight were attached.

That was all.

Holly hit the "reply" button, asking for more information about what show she would be hosting and where it filmed. Within seconds, she got an out-of-office reply. The person who'd made her reservation was now on vacation and would not return until after the Thanksgiving holiday.

Great. Just great.

Now what was she supposed to do?

Holly put aside the phone, grabbed a throw pillow, and hugged it to her chest while chewing on her right thumbnail. Who could she talk to about the unsettling situation she found herself n? Who could help her understand all the up- and downsides to this potentially golden but still unconfirmed opportunity that was making her stomach clench and her head ache?

Only one person.

Holly picked up the phone but stopped mid-dial, remembering what day it was. Her mother wouldn't be home for hours. But Holly knew where to find her.

Chapter 2

Mary Dell Templeton voluntarily ended her short-lived career as a beauty queen at the age of thirteen, but like so many true daughters of the Lone Star State, she was still a devoted fan of pageants.

She loved the sparkle of them, the hot lights and rhinestones, the Lippizaner-like dance numbers with scores of grinning girls prancing and wheeling around the stage surrounded by plenty of flags and flash and shot at multiple camera angles to disguise the fact at least half of the contestants had never taken a dance class. But more than all that, Mary Dell loved the possibilities of pageants, the fact that on any given day any one of those girls—even those from the tiniest, most no-account, underdog towns that nobody had ever heard of—might suddenly have the best day of her life and, illuminated by an unprecedented and unexpected spark, shine as she never had before and, at the end of the night, be crowned the Queen of Every-thing.

That was what made pageants so exciting. Because you never knew what might happen or who might come out on top.

Of course, the downside was that the reign of a Queen of Everything was so short, limited to a single, flashbulb-fast year. Once it was over, the queen had to yield her crown and scepter to a new monarch and get off the stage. That part was sad, and the sort of thing that had been on Mary Dell's mind lately, especially after spending the afternoon reading figures on the slipping viewership for *Quintessential Quilting*, the HHN-TV show she co-hosted with her son, Howard. Those ratings would definitely be a topic of discussion during her meeting with Gary Beatty, the head of programming, who was flying to Dallas from Los Angeles on Monday.

It was time to renew her contract—or not. Gary forwarded the ratings to her late on Friday afternoon deliberately, Mary Dell was sure, so she'd spend the whole weekend stewing over them, softening her up so he could get more favorable terms. Gary always had been a tough negotiator. Usually, Mary Dell enjoyed the battle, but this year she wondered if she was up to the task. Was it time to get herself an agent? Maybe. But she couldn't hire one before Monday. She'd have to go it alone.

A swell of applause came from the television as Miss Nebraska, who had given a flawless performance of a Brahms piano sonata, rose from the keyboard and sank into a graceful curtsy. Next, the camera turned to Rachel McEnroe, a singer/actress whose star had burned brilliantly in the nineties but who was now rarely seen aside from appearances doing color commentary for pageants and parades, as well as the occasional mouthwash commercial.

Miss McEnroe flashed a smile and informed the viewers that, after a few messages from the sponsors and a musical interlude by herself, it would be nearly time to announce the top ten finalists. "So stay tuned, America! We'll be right back!"

Mary Dell lowered the sound and slid her feet into a pair of black marabou slippers, the heels adding another three inches to her nearly six-foot frame.

"Where are you going?" Howard asked, turning toward his mother. "Rachel McEnroe is next. She's your favorite."

"I'm going to get a Dr Pepper. You want one?"

Howard shook his head. "You okay, Momma?"

Mary Dell hadn't said a word about her worries or emitted so much as a sigh, but Howard, always so empathetic, had picked up on her mood. Worry gave way to pleasure, as it always did when she looked at her son's face.

Nearly thirty years before, when the doctor informed her that her baby had Down syndrome, Mary Dell had fallen into a deep but temporary despair. If only she could have known then that Howard would grow up to be such a capable young man, unfailingly honest and kind, and possessing not an atom of guile or meanness but more than a usual share of artistic inclination, color sensitivity, and showmanship.

But who could have predicted that? When Howard was a baby, who could have seen what a bright light he would grow up to be? How he would change the world's perceptions about people with Down syndrome? And who could have foreseen how the gift of being Howard's mother would define and enrich her, bringing her unspeakable joy, boundless love, and completion, filling the empty places in her heart? She wouldn't be who she was without Howard.

It was like she always said: You never knew what might happen or who might come out on top. The sun rose anew every morning, and when it did, you might be about to have the best day of your life. Even on days when it was too dark to see clearly, there was a plan, and if you just kept going, you were bound to find it.

Those few words pretty much summed up Mary Dell's approach to life. It wasn't a complicated or particularly profound philosophy, but it had gotten her through some very dark times, including years of infertility, the shock of being told that her baby had Down syndrome, the heartbreak of being abandoned by her husband, career derailments, financial woes, and more.

In short, like Hamlet, Mary Dell had suffered the heartaches and "thousand natural shocks that flesh is heir to," but unlike him, she had survived —perhaps because she was less philosophical and prone to introspection than the melancholy Dane. Through it all, Mary Dell endured, even when tragedies came on so relentlessly, one after another, as they had during that time she had named "the worst bad year."

In comparison to the worst bad year, her current career concerns were practically inconsequential. Things would work out in the end.

"I'm fine," she assured Howard. "I *am* a little worried about Miss Texas sliding off-key during her song," she said, "but I bet she made up points in the swimsuit competition. That girl has more curves than a Coke bottle."

Mary Dell tottered on feathered heels toward the door but was stopped by the sound of Howard's voice.

"Momma?" His question was strangely sharp, as though he had suddenly remembered something he'd been meaning to bring up for some time.

"Yes, baby? What is it?"

"Do I hafta . . ." Howard's voice became an indecipherable mumble, which was unusual. Years of speech therapy had ensured that Howard could speak with clarity. The only times he lapsed into mumbling was when he was ill, overtired, or upset.

Mary Dell frowned, examining his face to see if he looked pale or flushed, ultimately concluding that he must be tired. It was getting late.

"I'm sorry, baby. Could you say that again?"

Howard shook his head. "Not important."

"What?"

Howard licked his lips, hesitated, then spoke again. "I wanted to talk about . . ." He stopped in mid-sentence. "Never mind. Do you need me at the meeting on Monday?"

"Not if you've got something else to do."

"Jenna invited me for a sleepover so I could see her new painting and go out for barbecue. Mrs. Morris said she'll pick me up and bring me back Tuesday. Can I go?"

Mary Dell nodded. "Of course, baby. Sounds like fun."

Howard sighed and rolled his eyes. "Momma, when are you going to stop calling me baby? I'm almost thirty. Too old for that."

"Never." She walked toward him. "I'll always be your momma and you'll always be my baby. And don't you forget it."

She kissed him on top of the head.

"Call me when the commercials are done. I don't want to miss Rachel McEnroe. That lady can sing the paint off the walls. Don't you think, baby?"

Howard turned up the volume. "Yes, ma'am. She sure can."

Mary Dell was looking through the cupboard for a bag of tortilla chips when the phone rang. Jeb, her eldest nephew, was calling from North Dakota. He sounded upset.

"I can't stand for it anymore, Aunt Mary Dell. He shows up late, drunk, or not at all. He picks fights with the other members of the crew. So I fired him."

"Oh, Jeb, no! Think of all he's been through. Jeb, please. He's your brother."

"That's the reason I stuck out my neck, getting him this job," Jeb said. "Seeing as he's a veteran, my bosses were willing to give him a chance. But I won't tolerate that kind of crap from anybody else, and I sure can't put up with it from my little brother. Keeping him on is undermining my leadership. I waited five years to get promoted to crew chief. I can't afford to lose my job on account of Rob Lee.

"Aunt Mary Dell, you can't help somebody who doesn't want to be helped. If Rob Lee wants to ruin his life, there's nothing we can do to stop him."

"Maybe not," Mary Dell said, "but I have to try. I promised your mother—"

She was interrupted by the sound of Howard's voice, shouting from the TV room, "Momma! Commercial's over!"

Mary Dell pressed the phone to her big bosom and called out, "I'll be there in a minute, baby. I'm talking to your cousin Jeb."

She put the receiver back to her ear, her voice

stern. "Put Rob Lee on the line. I want to talk to him."

"He's not here."

"Where is he?"

"Don't know. Don't care," Jeb said testily. "He walked in the door, picked a fight, and threw the first punch. *That's* when I fired him. Right before I threw him out of the house."

Mary Dell gave an exasperated growl, befuddled as ever by men's preference for bashing out each other's brains over sitting down to talk. She wondered why God, surely having understood in advance the effects of testosterone, invented it in the first place. But that was a question for another day.

"I'm done," Jeb declared. "I've got my own family to consider. Cindy was real sweet about letting Rob Lee move in with us, crowded as it was. You can't find a decent room to rent for less than a thousand a week since the oil boom. But she's had it. So have I. My kids were watching when Rob Lee blacked my eye. Flannery is so upset, she's still crying. He can't stay here, Aunt Mary Dell. He flat can't. I'm only calling because I thought you ought to know what happened."

For a moment, Mary Dell was tempted to remind him of the tough times he'd been through, of the confused, angry, wounded little boy who had run away from home in the wake of his father's alcoholism and the ugly divorce that

30

followed, how he hid out in the barn and accidentally set it afire while smoking contraband cigarettes, and how she stood by him in all his terrors and troubles. But that wouldn't be fair.

Jeb had taken Rob Lee in at her request. He'd tried his best to help his brother, but he couldn't. Rob Lee was her problem. Twelve years before, she'd promised Lydia Dale she'd watch out for her children, including Rob Lee. Mary Dell never backed down from a promise, especially not a promise made to her sister.

"All right," she said, her voice weary. "But do one thing for me. Find your brother, sober him up, and put him on a bus back home."

"Home to Dallas?"

Mary Dell sucked her lower lip, thinking. "No. Home to Too Much."

"Is that a good idea? Having Cady and Rob Lee living in the same house?"

"You know your sister better than that," Mary Dell countered. "Cady doesn't blame Rob Lee."

"She doesn't have to. He's doing a real good job of blaming himself. Seeing Cady and Linne will only remind him—"

Jeb's words were interrupted by an electronic beep signaling an incoming call. Mary Dell glanced quickly at the telephone screen and noted the familiar area code. Who would be calling her from Too Much at this hour on a Saturday night?

"Jeb," she said, cutting him off, her sense of

being overwhelmed registering as irritation, "find your brother and put him on that bus. You hear me?"

"Yes, ma'am," he said, his quick acquiescence signaling he understood the discussion was over. Jeb, too, had spent some years in the Marines. He knew how to take orders. "I'll start looking for him."

"Thank you," she said, quickly but in a gentler tone. "Call me when you find him, all right? I've got to take this call."

Clicking over to the incoming line, Mary Dell was surprised to hear Pearl Dingus answer her greeting. Pearl, one of her very first quilting students, now worked part-time in Mary Dell's quilt shop, the Patchwork Palace, back in her hometown of Too Much, Texas. She wasn't the sort of friend to call up just to shoot the breeze after ten o'clock, not unless she had news, probably bad, to relay.

"What's wrong? Was there an accident? A fire? Has the shop burned down?"

"Everything at the shop is fine. I'm calling about your momma," Pearl said.

Mary Dell took in a sharp breath and held it, imagining the worst, not stopping to consider that had Taffy suddenly died, Cady, her niece, would likely be the one calling to tell her, not Pearl.

"Mary Dell, have you talked to Taffy lately?"

"Yes," she said slowly, wondering where this

was leading. "Last week. I call out to the ranch every Sunday. Pearl, what's this about?"

"Then you know Taffy's acting loopy."

"I don't know if I'd call her loopy," Mary Dell replied, her heartbeat slowing now that she knew her mother was still among the living. "She's forgetful, maybe. Scattered. Who isn't at eighty-five?"

"Mary Dell, this is more than being scattered. It's one thing for an old lady to forget her wedding anniversary or her coat. It's another thing to forget she ever was married. Or to put on clothes."

"*Clothes!* Pearl, what are you talking about?"

"I'm talking about Taffy losing what was left of her marbles. Your momma is under the impression that she is twenty-five, single, and the cutest little trick in shoe leather. She's been batting her eyelashes at every man in Too Much, eligible or otherwise. And this afternoon, I found her walking down the sidewalk, bold as you please, wearing nothing but pearls, high heels, and a slip!"

"Oh, good Lord." Mary Dell covered her face with one hand, trying to block out the mental image of her mother sashaying around town in her underwear. "Why didn't Cady call me?"

"Because Cady doesn't know about it. She called from the hospital early this morning and asked if I could open the shop for her. Moises had a stroke—"

"No! Is he all right?"

"Think so," Pearl reported. "But he won't be able to work for a while. You're going to need to find a new ranch manager until he recovers. Maybe permanently. Anyway, I was unlocking the store when I saw Taffy strolling down the block, half-naked and whistling. I brought her inside, wrapped her in three yards of calico, and drove her home to the F-Bar-T."

Mary Dell groaned. "Oh, Pearl. I'm so sorry. How did she even get to town? We sold her car after she ran it into the gate last year."

"She got hold of the keys to Moises's pickup. I found it parked on the square with the front wheels up on the curb. My Billy drove it back to the ranch. Taffy was very grateful," Pearl said wryly. "She kissed him on the lips and said they should go out and watch the sun set over Puny Pond sometime; then she sat down in your dad's old recliner and fell asleep. Guess all the excitement wore her out, thank heaven. I told the hands to keep an eye on her until Cady got home but not to say anything about Taffy's field trip. That poor girl has enough to worry about."

"What do you mean?" Mary Dell's brow pleated into lines of concern and she pressed the phone closer to her ear, as if increasing the volume of Pearl's words might help her make sense of them. "I talked to Cady the day before yesterday. She said everything was fine."

"Well, it's not," Pearl countered. "While you're

up there in Dallas, being famous full-time, your niece is all alone in Too Much trying to hold everything together with baling wire and spit. She has a daughter to raise, a quilt shop to run, a ranch to oversee, and a loopy grandmother to ride herd on!"

"Momma isn't loopy," Mary Dell insisted. "She's just confused. And Moises runs the ranch, not Cady. Well, he did. We'll find somebody to fill in for him until he's better. I'll try to get down there for a few days next week and—"

"Next week? Mary Dell Templeton, wake up and smell the coffee! Your momma is overdrawn at the memory bank and your niece is sick with grief. I know it's been three years, but the pain is still fresh. I can see it in her eyes."

Mary Dell was silent for a moment. She knew exactly what Pearl was talking about. She had seen that same look in her niece's eyes.

Cady's husband, Nick, had been a Marine stationed in Afghanistan, serving in the same unit as Rob Lee. In fact, it was Rob Lee who had introduced Cady and Nick. While on patrol with Rob Lee and two other Marines, Nick was killed in a roadside explosion. Rob Lee was the only one of the four who survived.

They say time heals all wounds, but in Mary Dell's opinion, whoever said that must not have been hurt that bad. Some things you never get over, not really, as Mary Dell knew from experience. Absent husbands were one of them.

It wasn't like Cady was just lying around in a dark room. She took care of her daughter, six-year-old Linne, managed the shop, and tended to all the family business that Mary Dell, in her absence, could not. She kept busy. Maybe too busy? Busy enough so she wouldn't have to feel?

Mary Dell knew what that was like too.

"Mary Dell Templeton, do you hear what I'm saying to you? Your family needs you. And not just for a few days. You've got to come home. For good."

"You don't think I want to?" Mary Dell barked in response, offended and angry that Pearl so misunderstood her motives. "I only moved up here *because* of the family. Don't you get it? My show shoots in Dallas. And the show is the only reason that the quilt shop has survived all these years—"

"That may be, but I'm telling you—"

"No," Mary Dell said firmly, interrupting Pearl's interruption. "That isn't what *may* be. That's what *is*."

The call didn't end well. Pearl was long on "should" but short on "how." And Mary Dell was tired.

It was easy for Pearl. She had a husband to lean on, whereas Mary Dell had to go it alone. She'd done so for a long, long time.

36

When Donny left, weeks after Howard was born, she'd had to figure out how to transform quilting from a hobby to a business, opening the Patchwork Palace with her sister, getting her patterns published in magazines, sometimes teaching at guilds, anything she could think of to keep the wolf from the door. And it had worked.

Later, during the worst bad year, when her dear grandma Silky and aunt Velvet had died within weeks of each other, followed three months later by the car accident that had instantly taken the lives of her father, Dutch, and her brother-in-law, Graydon, and then her beloved twin sister, Lydia Dale, three days later, Mary Dell had to reinvent herself yet again.

Economic downturns have no respect for private grief. With the quilt shop struggling and the responsibility of keeping the entire family together resting on her shoulders, Mary Dell moved to Dallas, where she could get more and bigger teaching jobs. She thought her banishment would last a year, two at most, until things turned around. Except they didn't. The quilt shop continued to struggle and so did the ranch.

Hoping it might bring in a little money and bring a little notoriety to the Patchwork Palace, Mary Dell brushed the dust off a book she'd written years before, based on her experiences teaching Howard to quilt and, later, using him as her "chief fabric consultant" and submitted it to a small publishing house. *Family Ties* didn't sell many copies, but it brought her to the attention of Gary Beatty, who offered her and Howard their own television show. The rest was history.

These days, Mary Dell spoke at a lot of trade shows and quilt conferences. During the Q&A someone would invariably ask her what the secret was to running a successful quilt shop. Mary Dell's answer never varied.

"Get yourself a show on a national cable network," she'd say.

After the laughter died down, she would go on to give a more serious answer, but, in a sense, she wasn't joking. It was the show that saved them, the shop, the ranch, and, in some ways, even Mary Dell herself. And all because of something nobody could have predicted, a lucky break.

Someone once said, "You can't get hit by lightning if you ain't standing in the rain."

Nobody could stand in the rain longer than Mary Dell Templeton.

By the time Howard came into the kitchen to inform her it was nearly time to announce the pageant winners, Mary Dell had a plan.

"I'll be right there, baby. I just need to make one more call. Howard, you're sure Mrs. Morris is fine with you sleeping over on Monday? Because if she is, I think I'm going to take a friend down to see the ranch. I'll only be gone one night."

Chapter 3

Holly's name wasn't on the list, but Bob had been working at the auditorium stage door since 2005, the same year Rachel McEnroe had started co-hosting the pageant, so he knew her daughter by sight and waved her in.

Holly stood in the stage-right wing of the auditorium, careful to stay out of the way, and listened to her mother sing.

The dusty smell that came from the red velvet curtains and the heat of the stage lights reminded her of the first time she'd been allowed to come and watch her mother work.

Rachel was booked for a four-month gig at the Desert Rose Hotel and Casino, but that was just the beginning, she had assured her little girl. Las Vegas was their new home and Mikey Grainger, who owned the casino, was Rachel's new husband.

Five-year-old Holly had been the flower girl at the wedding. The pink rose petals in the white basket were so pretty that she refused to scatter them on the ground. Rachel was annoyed, but Mikey just laughed. He held Holly's little hand through the whole ceremony, letting go only to put the ring on Rachel's finger.

After the wedding, they moved into the Desert Rose. Holly loved living in the hotel, riding the elevators, having the run of the house, ordering as many Shirley Temples and ice-cream sundaes as she wanted in the restaurants, and never having to pay a bill. Her mom said that was when Holly's weight problem started, but Holly didn't think so. Until high school, when she dropped all that weight, she almost couldn't remember a time when she wasn't, if not fat, at least chubby.

She did have one childhood picture that made her look skinny, a framed five-by-seven of her and her dad, taken just a few months before he died. It was a candid shot, taken from a slight distance. In it, Cristian sat astride a beautiful black thoroughbred, holding Holly in front of him on the saddle with one arm around her waist, his handsome head slightly bent, about to kiss the top of her head. Holly, at two years old, had her hair tied into two ponytails that stuck out almost straight from her head, her brown eyes were dancing, and her mouth was open, frozen in a squeal of delight. Her cheeks were chubby and dimpled, but her bare arms, stretched out wide as if she was trying to fly, were thin and delicate. Though Rachel said she was too young to remember that day, Holly knew she did.

They had gone to Argentina, visiting the ranch where Cristian's family bred fast, compact horses, a thoroughbred and criollo mix, prized by polo players. She didn't remember a lot about that trip, only the adults jabbering in Spanish and how they laughed when she took a bite of chorizo, a kind of spicy pork sausage, and pronounced it "muy bueno!" And she remembered riding across that field with her father's arm wrapped around her, feeling so light and happy and safe, feeling the wind rush past her open fingers, and shouting, "Faster! Faster!"

It was one of the few clear and happy memories she had of Cristian, and the photograph that captured it was one of two treasured mementos she took with her everywhere she went. The other was a present from Mikey, a souvenir of their "honeymoon" at the Desert Rose.

Those two weeks were among the happiest in her memory. Mikey treated her like his own daughter, called her "kiddo," gave her piggyback rides, and took her to play mini-golf. He made sure the hotel florist kept a vase in her bedroom filled with pink roses and even gave her a "wedding present," a small crystal figurine of a galloping horse that she still kept on her night-stand. Rachel said he was spoiling her and it was true, but Holly didn't mind.

Two weeks after the wedding, Mikey brought Holly with him to watch Rachel sing, and they stood in the wings, hidden behind the red velvet curtain, with Mikey's big hands resting on her shoulders. Holly thought her mother sounded like an angel and that the pink spotlight made her look like one too.

But the second Rachel bowed and exited the stage, her halo slipped. The brilliant smile disappeared, replaced by a scowl, and her eyes flashed with anger. Ignoring Holly, she stormed up to Mikey and poked a finger into his chest.

"A bar! You booked me into a bar to sing for a bunch of drunks? You promised me the big room! You said I'd be a headliner!"

"And you will be! Rachel, baby, don't be like that. It's a lounge, not a bar. The best in the hotel. You've never played Vegas. I'm trying to help you build a following. Next year you'll be a headliner, I swear."

Rachel wasn't appeased. She slapped him, hard, across the face. Mikey drew back, stared at her for a long moment, then turned and walked away.

When the run ended, the marriage did too.

Mikey drove them to the airport for the flight to LA. Standing at the curb, he ruffled Holly's hair with his big hand. "Listen, kiddo, you be happy. And take care of your mom."

Holly nodded. Mikey kissed Rachel on the cheek.

"Good luck with the movie audition. Not that you'll need it. You still got it, babe. You know that?"

Twenty years later, her mom still had it—the body, the pipes, the face the cameras loved. Though she couldn't hit the high notes quite the way she once had, Rachel still knew how to wring every drop of emotion from a song, handing the music and lyrics to the audience gently and sensuously, like she was delivering a love letter. Holly never ceased to be amazed by her mother's talent and determination. Hardly anyone but Holly knew how hard Rachel worked and that she continued to take weekly voice, dance, and acting lessons.

Still, at the core of all that effort was talent, a gift that you're either born with or not. Rachel had it; Holly didn't. She wished she did. But that didn't prevent Holly from being proud of her mom or from seeking her advice, at least on professional matters. Rachel's personal life was a train wreck, but when it came to the business of show, she had good instincts.

As the glow of the spotlights changed from pink to white and the camera moved in for a close-up, Rachel's left arm floated slowly, almost languor-ously, from her side, lifting over her head as the notes of the song rose and fell in volume and emotion until the end, as a single, softly sung note hovered in the air, then faded slowly, like the toll of a distant bell.

The applause was thunderous. If the stage managers hadn't started barking orders at the pageant contestants, telling them to get onstage *now,* Rachel might easily have taken a second or even third bow. Instead, as the beauty queens poured out of the wings, Rachel gave a wave and walked into the wings.

"Mom! That was great! You were amazing!"

"Thank you, punkin," she said as she unclipped the microphone from the neck of her dress. "But the tempo was too fast. We're running long."

"You got a standing ovation; did you see?"

Rachel handed the microphone to a waiting stagehand. "I saw. Twenty people in the first two rows. Not quite an ovation; more like the potential for one. But"—she smiled—"it was good. My last number. I wanted to go out with a bang."

"Mission accomplished," Holly said.

Rachel pressed a tissue against her brow to dab away the sheen of perspiration. "Hey, I've got to run back to the dressing room to touch up my makeup and change before it's time to announce the top ten. Come on. You can unzip me and help shoehorn me into some Spanx."

The dressing room was a mess. Gowns and stockings and scarves were thrown carelessly over the backs of chairs; high heels were abandoned in the middle of the floor. After unzipping her mother's dress, Holly started tidying up.

"Don't do that," Rachel said, looking up from the makeup mirror. "You make me feel like a slob."

"You *are* a slob," Holly said, shaking her head as she picked up a pair of red satin pumps and put them on a shelf. "Where are the wardrobe people anyway?"

"Attending to the needs of the beauty queens, I should think," Rachel said, peeling off a false eyelash. "Though why twenty-year-olds with flawless skin and figures that can stop traffic need help being gorgeous is beyond me." She frowned at her reflection. "Me, on the other hand . . ."

"Oh, stop it," Holly said as she hung a discarded gown on the rack and pulled up a chair near the makeup table. "You're gorgeous."

"I'm glad *you* think so." Rachel pressed the new lash onto her eyelid. "So, what's up? I bet you didn't drive through LA traffic just to help me change."

"My agent called. I've got an interview for a job co-hosting a cable show."

Rachel's face lit up. "Honey! That's great! Congratulations!"

"I'm not sure if I want to do it."

"Why not? Co-hosting your own show sounds a lot better than escorting contestants onstage or pointing at cars on that stupid game show."

"It's for the House and Home Network. I don't know the first thing about do-it-yourselfing." Holly started chewing on the nail of her pinkie finger.

"Not true," Rachel said, then reached up to bat Holly's finger away from her mouth. "Look how cute you fixed your place up. That coffee table you made? With the wooden crates and that old picture frame? It's darling. And what about those drapes you made out of the shower curtain? I'd never have thought of that."

"Those were ideas I got from a blog. It's not like I invented it on my own."

"So?" Rachel shrugged. "Look, if they needed somebody who can hammer nails, they'd be interviewing carpenters. Instead, they're interiewing you. Which means you're what they're looking for."

"But," Holly protested, "if you're going to host a show about a particular subject, I think you should know at least a *little* something about it."

Rachel put on some lipstick, frowned at her reflection, and wiped it off again. "You'll be fine. I played an astronaut once. And not only have I never traveled in space, I barely passed science. That's what acting is all about."

"But . . . I'm not an actress!"

Rachel sighed heavily and started talking to the ceiling. "Such a worrywart. I swear, sometimes I feel like I gave birth to my own mother." She picked up the powder puff again. "Holly, for once in your life, can't you just enjoy the moment? This is *good* news!"

She patted the powder across her décolletage. Holly started to put her hand to her mouth but pulled it back when Rachel shot her a look.

"I just don't want to end up looking stupid. I

don't want to come off like somebody they put in the chair just because she's pretty and her mother is famous."

"You don't even have the job yet. So quit worrying. Maybe they'll hate you."

Holly stuck out her tongue at her mother's reflection, then narrowed her eyes, suddenly suspicious.

"This isn't your doing, is it? You didn't call up one of your friends to get me this job, did you?"

"Punkin, is *this* the face of a woman who has friends at the House and Home Network?"

Holly saw her point. There was probably no one on the planet with fewer practical skills than Rachel. She couldn't so much as screw in a light bulb. Claudia, her housekeeper, handled all that, along with cleaning, laundry, and cooking—what there was of it. These days, Rachel subsisted mostly on salads and protein shakes.

Holly worried that Rachel wasn't eating enough. She worried about a lot of things where her mother was concerned. The antidepressants didn't seem to be working, but Holly wasn't surprised. The medicine Rachel really needed was work, the sound of applause. Lately, there hadn't been much of it.

Rachel swiveled in her chair, facing her daughter. "Listen to me. When you meet the programming people, your answer to every question is 'yes.' If they ask you if you know about carpentry, or gardening, or even small-engine repair, the answer is, 'Yes. Absolutely.' "

"But I don't. I can't lie to them."

Rachel rolled her eyes. "Gah! Don't be so nervous. Of course you can." She started sorting through a box filled with lipstick tubes. "Everybody in show business lies about their skills; it's practically part of the code. When I auditioned for my first movie, that Broadway biopic, the casting director asked if I could tap-dance. I looked right into her eyes and said, 'Yes. Absolutely. Started in the chorus.' " Rachel chuckled, enjoying the memory of her own audacity.

"By the time they figured out I couldn't dance, we were so far into filming that they couldn't afford to fire me. Instead, they added a subplot about a country girl who comes to New York, gets hired for a show because of her looks, sleeps with the director because she knows she's a terrible dancer and hopes that'll keep her from getting fired, then gets fired anyway."

Rachel turned back toward the mirror, traced a thin line of red on her lower lip, and then filled it in.

"That little lie got me twelve extra lines and a chance to cry on-camera. And *that* got me a mention in two reviews and a bigger part the next time."

Holly already knew this story, but since she'd read every magazine profile and feature ever written about her mother, she also knew this wasn't the whole story. Like the character she ended up playing, Rachel had also slept with her director, who was more humane than his celluloid counterpart. It was his humanity and not the cost of reshooting her scenes that kept her from getting fired after her lack of dance skills was revealed, and it was Rachel's ability to bewitch men—at least in the short term—that caused him to create a bigger role for her.

Rachel's tendency to cast herself as the heroine of every story and completely believe these myths of her own making was irritating but also impressive in its own way. Holly wished she could erase the memory of her own failures as easily.

"Remember that guest appearance I made on *Baywatch*?" Rachel asked as she blotted her lipstick. "When they asked me if I knew how to scuba dive and I—"

"You said, 'Yes. Absolutely.' Then you almost drowned. I remember."

"I *didn't* almost drown. The dive master got me out of the water about ten seconds after I lost consciousness. Everything worked out."

Rachel tossed a tissue into the wastepaper basket and looked toward her daughter once again.

"This could be *such* a big break for you. Don't take yourself out of the running before you even start. Oh, punkin. Life is so short. One minute you're twenty-two and beautiful, full of promise, impatient for your real life to begin. Then you blink and it's over. Or might as well be. AARP is sending you their magazine and the people who used to fight for a piece of you have suddenly lost your number."

Rachel stopped speaking and just sat there, staring vacantly at a spot somewhere over Holly's shoulder. A moment of silence stretched to two, then three.

"Mom? Are you okay?"

"What? Oh, yes. I'm fine. I was just thinking."

"About?"

"Missed opportunities." Her gaze met Holly's. "So listen to me, because nobody has missed more of them than me. When you get a chance to do what you really want to do, grab it! Don't let fear hold you back. Because those chances don't come around very often."

Holly knew it was true, especially in the entertainment industry.

When Holly had dropped out of college and announced her desire to act, it was Rachel's influence that got her the part of the daughter in a new sitcom. But her mother's influence didn't stretch far enough to keep her from being fired after the pilot aired. Without her, the show ran for four successful seasons.

Holly realized she wasn't an actress. Her agent, Amanda, insisted that with a face like hers, she didn't have to act, that they just needed to take another tack. The game show paid the bills, but it didn't exactly stretch her. She was a hanger, an object used to display other objects. But hosting a show would be different. It would give her a voice, a chance to share information and inspiration with the audience—that is, assuming she had any clue about what she was talking about.

Rachel was right. Her fear was holding her back. But it wasn't the only thing.

"Mom?" Holly looked down at her hands, clenched tight in her lap. "The network is head-quartered in Texas. Nearly all of their program-ming is filmed there." She lifted her gaze again. "If I get the job, I'm pretty sure I'll have to move there."

For a moment, Rachel looked a little stunned, but she recovered quickly.

"Oh? Well . . . what's wrong with that? Remember when we went to Houston that time? It was nice. Good weather."

Holly rolled her eyes and groaned. "Stop acting, okay. You know I'm not worried about the weather. I just . . . I don't want to leave you all alone in LA."

"All alone in LA?" Rachel laughed. "What are you talking about? I have a life, you know. I have friends. Things to do."

There was a knock on the door. A voice on the

other side said, "Five minutes, Miss McEnroe!"

"Thank you!" Rachel got up from the table, turned her backside toward the mirror, and looked over her shoulder at her reflection. "I don't know about this dress. All those bugle beads across the butt . . ."

"You look great," Holly said automatically, then got to her feet and raised the last half inch of Rachel's zipper. "What things?"

"Hmm?" Rachel murmured, still examining her posterior.

"These *things* you have to do? What are they?"

Rachel turned back toward the mirror, twisting her head from left to right, examining her profile from each side.

"I'm up for a part in some spy picture," she said absently and ran her hand over her hair. "If I get it, I'll be out of the country for at least a couple of months. Russia. Didn't I tell you? My agent called yesterday."

Holly wanted to believe her but didn't know if she should.

"Are you sure? Because you don't have to . . . ."

Rachel put a hand on her hip. "Punkin, can we possibly talk about this later? Because right now, Mommy has got to go to work!"

She opened her arms and gave Holly a very quick but very tight hug.

"And you," she said with a smile, cupping Holly's chin in her hand, "have got to fly to Texas.

So you'd better go home and pack. Call me when you get there, okay?"

"I will. Knock 'em dead, Mom."

Rachel tossed her hair over her shoulder.

"I plan to," she said, and swept out the door.

Chapter 4

Monday was a perfect Texas fall day. The sun was warm but not hot, and the sky was a clear bright blue.

Mary Dell put the convertible top down and drove out to the airport to pick up Gary Beatty. Walking to the baggage claim, she noticed a striking young woman with long blond hair and surprisingly dark eyebrows, the same deep brown as her eyes, standing near the door with a suitcase in her hand, frowning up at the array of directional signs.

Mary Dell approached and touched her lightly on the shoulder. "You look a little lost. Can I help you find something?"

"I was just trying to figure out where the taxis are."

"Lower level. Take a right at the bottom of the escalator."

The woman thanked her, turning to give Mary Dell a smile and a wave before stepping onto the escalator. Mary Dell waved back and then gasped, realizing why that woman's pretty face had seemed so familiar. She was a model on that game show Howard liked so much. Mary Dell didn't know her name, but she recognized her face.

For a moment, she thought about following her downstairs and asking for an autograph but decided against it. She didn't want to keep Gary waiting.

Today of all days, she needed to get on his good side. She wasn't entirely sure Gary had a good side. But if he did, she'd find it.

Having woken at four-thirty a.m. in order to catch his flight, Gary was far from cheerful when Mary Dell greeted him. But he perked up considerably once he got to the parking lot and saw their ride.

"My dad drove an Eldorado, a 'fifty-nine! What year is this?"

"A 'seventy-six. Isn't it cute?" Mary Dell grinned and took her place behind the wheel. "I thought about painting it pink—this ivory color, Phoenician I think they called it, is a little dull—but the dealer said that with the original paint in such good shape, it'd be a crime to cover it up. I just settled on new upholstery. Like it?"

Gary looked down at the seat. "I don't think I've ever seen cheetah-print upholstery in a car before."

"Oh, you have to order it special," she said solemnly.

• • •

Mary Dell chattered cheerfully as she drove, complimenting Gary's recent change of hairstyle, saying the gray at his temples brought out the blue in his eyes, admiring the cowboy boots he had worn for the occasion, doing her best to get him to loosen up. It worked. By the time they merged onto Highway 35W, Gary was telling her about the time he and his brother skipped class, "borrowed" their dad's convertible, drove it to Malibu, and picked up some off-duty flight attendants.

"They were gorgeous girls, absolute stunners," he said. "But there were *three* of them. That was where we made our mistake. I mean, I was barely eighteen and Billy was even younger. The odd number confused us, you know? We had no idea what to do with three beautiful women."

"So what did you do?"

"Spent my last thirty dollars buying them cheeseburgers and then dropped them off at their hotel." He laughed. "They kissed us good-bye, on the cheek, but that was it. Dad grounded us for a month. But you know something? It was worth it. I felt like a king, driving that car. It was a perfect day, just like this one."

He was quiet, smiling at the memory, but after a moment his smile faded. He swiveled his head from left to right and frowned.

"Where the hell are we? I thought we were going to the office."

"Nope. I'm kidnapping you."

"What?"

Mary Dell laughed. "Oh, relax. It's just for a day. I'm taking you out to see where I grew up. You've been to Texas on business—I don't know how many times—but I bet you've never set foot outside of Dallas. Honey, it is time you saw the real Texas. We'll see the town and ranch. My momma's going to make us chicken-fried steak for supper, and then later, we'll go out to the Ice House. Gary, I'm gonna take you honky-tonkin'," she declared, her Texas twang twanging a little more deeply than usual.

"Yeah, but our meeting . . ."

"We'll have it," she assured him. "Just not in the office."

"My flight . . ."

"Leaves at one-fifteen tomorrow," she interrupted again. "I know. I'll have you back in plenty of time. Too Much is less than a hundred miles from the airport."

Gary said nothing. Glancing to her right, Mary Dell saw his frown softening to a mixture of indecision and suspicion.

She grinned and punched him playfully in the shoulder. "Oh, come on, Gary. It's a perfect day! You don't want to be cooped up in an office on a day like this, do you? How long has it been since you played hooky?"

Gary's mouth bowed at the corners. He rested

his arm on the door, put his hand out into the warm wind, and opened his fingers. "Too long," he said, and let his head drop back against the seat, staring up at the bluebonnet sky. "Way too long."

Like a lot of small towns in Texas, Too Much was anchored by a large central block, the Square, which marked the location of the town's municipal building and was surrounded by a small park, one of the few green patches in town. Most of the town's commercial activity radiated outward from the Square, extending three blocks in all directions, everything from gift shops and auto repair joints to insurance brokers and dentist offices. But the busiest and most successful enterprises, including the Patchwork Palace, occupied the four blocks directly adjacent to the Square.

Mary Dell found two empty parking spots and pulled the Eldorado into the middle of them.

"I don't want anybody scratching the paint job," she explained as she turned off the ignition. "Come on. I'll give you the nickel tour."

They climbed out of the car and walked across the grass toward a bronze statue of a woman, a little bigger than life-sized, standing on a pedestal. She was dressed in pioneer garb, her feet wide under her skirts and her arms crossed defiantly over her bosom as her bronze visage scowled toward the horizon.

"Who's that?"

"Flagadine Tudmore, my great-great-great-grandmother. She founded the town."

"No kidding."

"No kidding," Mary Dell replied proudly, and proceeded to tell him the history of Flagadine Tudmore and Too Much, Texas, just the way her aunt Velvet had told it to her when she was a little girl.

"So you see," Mary Dell said as she finished, "I come from a very distinguished lineage." She stood at the base of the statue and struck a pose, crossing her arms over her chest and scowling toward the horizon.

Gary grinned. "Definitely a family resemblance."

Leaving Flagadine behind, they approached the courthouse, a two-and-a-half-story structure of red brick with tall, arched windows and wide granite steps. The basement, Mary Dell informed him, housed the Too Much, Texas, Historical Society.

"My aunt Velvet was the executive director here for over sixty years. Later in life, she had a beau, but she never married. Lived until she was ninety-one and went out with her boots on," Mary Dell said. "On the day she died, she worked a full day at the historical society, walked home, ate supper with my grandma Silky—they shared a little shotgun cottage in town—then went to bed and just never woke up. Grandma Silky passed two weeks later and just the same way. She was ninety-four."

Mary Dell smiled, remembering the two eccentric old women who had loved her so much and helped mold her into who she was. "They were a couple of characters. It was Aunt Velvet who came up with the theory of the Fatal Flaw."

"Fatal Flaw?"

Mary Dell nodded soberly. "It runs all through our family. On the female side, that is. Under normal circumstances, you won't find a more sensible, feet-on-the ground group of women in the world. But, every now and then, in the presence of a certain kind of man, we display an unfortunate tendency to let lust and biology trump morality and good sense.

"Laugh if you want," Mary Dell said in response to Gary's guffaw. "But Aunt Velvet was on to something. When the full moon sits just so in the sky, the Fatal Flaw can be a powerful thing. I should know. That's how I ended up marrying Donny."

"Your ex-husband? The one who left after Howard was born?"

"That's the fatal flaw of the Bebee men. When things get rough, they run." Mary Dell shrugged. "But I don't blame Donny. Not anymore. He just wasn't as strong as me; that's all."

"I doubt many men are," Gary said.

They crossed the street, returning to the commercial side, passing the Primp 'n' Perm Beauty Salon, Hilda's House of Pie, and Antoinette's Uptown Dress Shop. As they walked, Mary Dell told Gary more about the history of Too Much as well as the revitalization it had seen since *Quintessential Quilting* had come on the air, but they kept getting interrupted by people who stopped her, wanting to chat.

"You're quite the celebrity around here," Gary observed.

"What? You mean that?" Mary Dell asked, looking over her shoulder and waving good-bye to Pauline Dingus and her sister, Pearl, who had made a point of saying how happy she was to see Mary Dell had come home, repeating it several times during their brief conversation. "This is my hometown. They're just being neighborly. When you go for a walk in your neighborhood, don't people stop to talk?"

"I live in Beverly Hills," Gary replied.

Mary Dell gave him a pitying look.

A silver charter bus with red stripes pulled to a stop in front of the Patchwork Palace and let out a whooshing sigh as the driver opened the doors. Two score of excited, chattering women spilled onto the pavement.

Seeing them, Mary Dell let out a joyous whoop. "Well, well, well! What do we have here?" she shouted. "Quilters coming out to feed the habit! How you doin', girls? Welcome to Too Much!"

The gaggle of women let out a nearly simultaneous gasp, then started to hoot and clap. Within seconds, Mary Dell was surrounded.

She shook hands, gave hugs, and signed well-worn copies of *Family Ties* that some of the ladies pulled from their tote bags. She posed patiently for photos taken by older ladies who weren't quite sure how their cell phone cameras worked and took time to listen to their stories and admire fabric they purchased from other shops at earlier stops and to give advice on quilt projects in progress.

When everyone had been accommodated, she called out, "All right, girls. Y'all better get inside and get to shopping. There's only five hours till closing time."

The women laughed, then poured through the double doors and into the shop, with Mary Dell and Gary taking up the rear.

"Did you plan that?" Gary asked.

Mary Dell grinned. "No. But I should have."

The Patchwork Palace was housed in a historic, two-story wooden building that would have fit in on the set of any Western ever filmed.

Two big windows filled with an ever-changing display of the latest fabric flanked the double doors. Four rocking chairs arranged on the sidewalk provided a welcoming spot for customers to relax after the exertions of shopping. The top floor of the shop was divided into classrooms and storage rooms, but the bottom floor, the retail space, was one big, open room.

The oak floors, original to the building, were beautiful, darkened by age and scarred by the scuffling of centuries of feet. Most of the bolts of fabric were arranged by color and stored in simple white wall shelves, but some of the fabric, ribbons, and trim was displayed in or on pieces of antique furniture that Mary Dell had picked up at yard sales and thrift shops over the years, including an open-front china cabinet, an old wooden crib painted with soft blue and green pastels, a weathered white pine pie safe with tin door panels punched with a star design, and even an 1890s cast-iron stove with four black burners. The shop was charming and homey, with a touch of the Old West everywhere you looked, right down to the swinging saloon doors leading to a back office and an inoperable antique cash register with shining brass keys.

Mary Dell and Gary had to wend their way around the clusters of quilters, some of whom carried multiple fabric bolts stacked possessively in their arms, as if afraid that the shop might suddenly run out, though there were literally thousands of bolts in the store. Thirty-two hundred to be exact, Mary Dell informed Gary.

"That's twice what we carried before the show aired," Mary Dell said. "Not as many as some shops, but I've only got so much space. Howard picks most of the inventory, makes sure we are on top of the color trends. We focus on quality, variety, and education. See those?"

She gestured toward a long, high wall hung with nearly twenty different quilts of varying sizes, styles, and levels of complexity. "Those are samples for the classes we're offering this term. We've got five teachers on staff and another four gals who just help out in the shop, plus part-timers. It's a lot of schedules to coordinate and plates to keep spinning. That's where Cady comes in."

Mary Dell turned toward the back of the shop, where a woman in her middle thirties, who looked like a more petite version of Mary Dell but with sandy brown hair cropped short, was working the register. Next to her, a little girl of about six years of age with sandy brown braids was sitting perched on a stool, eyes cast down as she concentrated on a piece of cross-stitch.

Cady came out from behind the counter and gave her aunt a big hug.

"Mary Dell tells me you manage the store," Gary said warmly as he gripped Cady's hand. "Looks like you're doing a great job. The place is packed."

"Oh, well," Cady replied. "Aunt Mary Dell and

my mom were the ones who started it all. I'm just maintaining what they built. Of course, it helps if the owner is a great big quilting celebrity." She winked at her aunt.

"Don't listen to her," Mary Dell said. "She runs this place better than I ever did. Cady practically grew up in the shop. Just like this one," she said, tilting her head toward the little girl sitting on the stool.

"Linne? How's my sweet petunia? Don't you have a hug for me?"

Linne looked up, frowning in frustration. "There's a knot. Can you fix it?"

"Excuse me," Mary Dell said to Gary, "but I have been summoned." She tottered off, leaving Gary and Cady behind.

"Linne. Never heard that one before. Is it a family name?"

"Yes and no. The women in our family have always loved needlework. Somewhere along the way, we developed a tradition of naming our daughters after fabric—Silky, Velvet, Taffeta . . . It skipped a generation with my momma and Aunt Mary Dell. But my momma decided to bring it back and name me Brocade—Cady for short. And I kept it going."

She glanced across the room, smiling as Mary Dell slipped behind the counter, took charge of Linne's needle, and picked out the knot.

"Her real name in Linen, but we call her Linne."

"She's a doll. Going to break some hearts when she grows up."

"She's got her daddy's good looks," Cady replied softly, her gaze still fixed on her daughter.

"I've got two grown girls of my own. From the day they were born, they knew how to play me like a cheap violin. I bet Linne's the same. Your husband must be crazy about her."

Cady's smile faded. "Excuse me, Mr. Beatty, but I'd better get back to work. Nice to meet you."

"Of course," he said. "Nice meeting . . ."

He extended his arm for a good-bye handshake, but she was already gone.

Chapter 5

While Mary Dell was taking Gary Beatty on a tour of Too Much, Holly was sitting in a chair on the twenty-sixth floor of a glass office tower in downtown Dallas, talking with Jason Alvarez.

"Hang on," Holly said, not certain she'd heard him right. "You're considering me as co-host for a *quilting* show? Mr. Alvarez, I don't—"

"Jason," he interrupted. "I told you before, call me Jason."

"Jason," she replied. "Okay, Jason. Before we go any further . . . this show, *Quintessential Quilting*? I don't—"

"I know, I know," he said dismissively, interrupting her once again. "It's a terrible title. Almost as bad as the show. We'll be canceling it after this season."

"Why would I want to host a program you've decided to cancel?"

"Because as soon as the restructuring is announced and the deadwood is out the door, I've got big plans for this network. And if you play your cards right, you can be part of them."

He leaned back in his desk chair and ran his hand over his head. He had a habit of rocking his executive desk chair back and forth like a seven-year-old on a seesaw.

"But before I get into that," Jason asked, "do you know how to sew?"

Holly hesitated, thinking about Rachel. She licked her lips.

"Yes. Absolutely," she said, and felt her cheeks flush pink. But Jason was rocking so far back in his chair, which gave him a better view of himself in the mirror hanging on the opposite wall, that he didn't notice.

"Okay. Although, for my purposes, it might be better if you didn't. The sooner *Quintessential Quilting* is off the air, the happier I will be."

"I don't understand," Holly said, tilting her head to one side so she could see him better. "If you know you're going to cancel the show, why not just do it now?"

Jason, who was practically horizontal at this

point, folded his hands into a tent over his stomach and knocked his thumbs together.

"It's complicated. Some of it has to do with fending off possible lawsuits, but, truth is, some people around here actually *like* this show, despite the fact that it is"—Jason lifted a hand and began raising fingers one by one to list his objections— "A, about quilting, which is something that only old ladies wearing support hose and trifocals care about, definitely not a profitable audience demographic; B, hosted by Mary Dell Templeton, a crazy broad from Texas who is pushing sixt and way, way too old to be on TV; and C, co-hosted by Mary Dell's son, Howard. A retard."

Jason made an incredulous face and spread out his hands, failing to notice the way that Holly's jaw tightened as he spat out the last word.

"I mean . . . are they serious? A show like that has no place on television. Not on *my* network anyway. But the only way for me to be able to get rid of it quickly and forever is for the ratings to tank so bad that we *have* to cancel it."

His network? Who does he think he is?

Holly didn't like Jason. For a moment, she considered getting up and walking out the door. But then she remembered the e-mail that Amanda had sent her from Beijing, saying what an incredible break this could be for her, so she kept her seat and held her tongue.

"From here on out," Jason said, rocking

backward again and lacing his fingers behind his head, "we're going after a younger, hipper, more profitable audience demographic, the kind of people *you* can help us hook." He grinned. "I mean . . . look at you! Men will want you and women will want to be you!"

Holly crossed her arms over her chest. She understood that she was being hired for her looks—television was a visual medium—but she didn't appreciate being talked about as if she were bait in a trap. She didn't like the way he was leering at her either.

"*Quintessential Quilting* will be a placeholder for you, a way to get you a little more experience and raise your profile until I can get rid of Mary Dell Templeton. Once that's done, we'll get you a show of your own. Something sexier, more urban, with kind of a reality show feel to it. Something that will appeal to millennials."

He rocked forward, finally sitting with both feet on the floor. "Here's what I was thinking," he said, his face becoming animated as he pitched his idea. "We go to a different city every week, pick two young, fresh-out-of-school interior designers, and give them a limited budget to furnish and decorate a small apartment or condo for a couple of hipsters just starting out. The audience gets to meet the clients and the designers, hear their stories, then follow along during the design and construction phase until it's time for the big reveal!

"Hang on," he said, and held up his hands before Holly could speak. "I know what you're thinking; it's been done. But here's the catch. The work of each young designer will be judged by a panel of seasoned professionals. Each week they'll choose the winner, who will come back for the next episode, facing a new challenger. During the finale, the two designers with the most wins during the season will face off on a bigger project with a larger budget. Of course, there will be a lot of drama and suspense, a lot of things going wrong, a very close decision, a lot at stake. The winner will get his or her own spread in one of the big design magazines and a hundred thousand dollars to open his or her own design firm.

"So? What do you think?" he asked, even though the self-satisfied smirk on his face said he was sure of her answer. "It'll be the *Project Runway* of interior design."

"I love *Project Runway*," Holly said quietly.

"Who doesn't? How many seasons has it been running? And people are still watching. They can't get enough."

Holly chewed on her lower lip a moment. It was a good idea. A very good one. A show like that could run for years. She looked up at Jason.

"And I would be?"

"The Heidi Klum," he said, "but with more time on-camera. You'd interview the designers and the clients, drop in from time to time to talk to the construction crew, get their take on how things are or aren't progressing, and then you'd be back for the judging and announce the final verdict. If things work out the way I think they will, you'll be a household name by the end of the first season."

Jason tilted his chair back, not quite as far this time, waiting for her to speak. Holly clutched her hands in her lap, trying to fight off the urge to chew her nails.

Damn. She didn't like Jason. At. All.

But she knew she'd be a terrific host for a show like that and that Jason was right—after a year she'd be a household name. But to do *that* show, she had to co-host *this* one and help Jason make sure it failed. Damn!

But . . . if she didn't take the job, Jason would just find someone else. With her or without her, he'd have his way.

Someone else would help him bring down the curtain on *Quintessential Quilting.* Someone else would co-host the new design show, the show she would be so, so good on. Someone else would become a household word, a star, just like the girl who had replaced her on the sitcom.

It would happen, with her or without her. Right now, there were a million girls just as pretty and talented as she was who would do anything Jason asked them to, because chances like this didn't come along very often, not in this business.

When they did, you had to grab them. Everybody knew that.

She tipped her head sideways again.

"When do we start filming?"

Chapter 6

Wrapping up the tour of Too Much, Mary Dell drove Gary out to the ranch for a delicious meal of chicken-fried steak and peppery cream gravy, fried okra, green beans, jalapeño corn bread, and peach pie, all prepared by Taffy.

Mary Dell was relieved to see that her mother was kind and solicitous of their guest. This was something you couldn't always count on where Taffy was concerned. Nor was she acting "loopy," as Pearl had put it.

Of course, Taffy flirted with Gary, seemingly unfazed by the fact that he was twenty-five years her junior, but Taffy had always liked men more than women. She was more playful than predatory, in her right mind, and fully clothed. That was good enough for the moment.

After supper, Mary Dell took Gary to the Ice House, Too Much's favorite watering hole. Mary Dell nursed a single bottle of Lone Star. Gary, however, downed four beers in short order and soon became very chummy. And very handsy.

"Yer a helluva woman," he slurred, scooting his

chair closer to hers. "Ya know that, Mary Dell? A helluva woman."

"Why, thank you." Mary Dell smiled sweetly and pushed his hand off her thigh. "That's nice of you to say so."

"You sure you don't want another beer?"

"I'm good."

"I'll bet you are." Gary draped his arm over her shoulders. "Didja see that full moon when we came in? How's it lookin' to you tonight, Mary Dell?"

"Just like it always does. I've never seen a moon like the one I saw on the night I met Donny, which is lucky. A girl can only afford to make so many dumb mistakes."

Mary Dell scooted her chair to the right, out of groping distance.

Gary grinned and lifted the bottle to his lips. "Can't blame a guy for trying."

"And I'm flattered that you would," she said with good grace. "Also that you were kind enough to indulge me and come all the way out here."

"Did I have a choice? You kidnapped me, remember?"

"I'm sorry about that, but . . . it was necessary."

"Ah." He took another swig. "Wondered when we'd get to that. Much as I've enjoyed playing hooky, I'm pretty sure you didn't drag me out here because you thought I needed a break. I was kind of hoping it was because you'd finally realized how devastatingly handsome I am and were plotting to have your way with me, but"—he heaved a dramatic sigh—"guess not.

"So, what is it, Mary Dell? What do you want?"

She looked down at the gouged planks of the barroom floor, trying to think of a way to make him understand, wondering how much she should share.

"You remember the story I told you? About Flagadine Tudmore? She was pioneering with her husband, George," Mary Dell reminded him, "heading to Austin. They stopped here to camp, but the next morning, Flagadine told George that she'd had too much heat, too much wind, too much everything, and she wasn't going to move one more step. And she didn't. They stayed put, started the town, and named it Too Much. Flagadine founded my family's ranch, too, twelve hundred acres of the best grazing land in Limestone County. She was the one who scouted out and claimed that piece of ground and kept the place going after George died. Flagadine stipulated in her will that the ranch could only be inherited through the female line of the family. I'm not sure that'd hold up in court these days, but that's the way we've always done it. The title and responsibility of keeping the ranch together passes from mother to daughter, and all because of Flagadine. She's the reason it's called the

F-Bar-T too. Because she incorporated her own initials into the brand."

"A strong-willed woman," Gary observed. "The apple doesn't fall too far from the tree, does it?"

"Guess not," Mary Dell said. "But nobody can be strong all the time. Lately, I'm starting to feel like she did after she left Arkansas, like it's all too much. Too much noise. Too many miles. Too many nights spent among strangers. I want to come home. It's time."

Gary exhaled a long and thoughtful breath. "So what are you saying? You want to retire?"

"Lord, no! I still love doing the show. So does Howard."

"Oh. I wondered. I thought you might have heard the rumors about the show being canceled."

Mary Dell's eyes went wide. "Canceled! Why would they cancel us? I know the numbers are down a little . . ."

"They're down a *lot*," Gary corrected, his speech now clear of any insobriety. "In terms of pure viewership, you're still in the top fifteen, but even so, your audience . . . They just don't fall into a demographic category that attracts the big advertising dollars."

Mary Dell flattened her lips into a line. "They're too old. Is that it? Or do you mean *I'm* too old? That nobody wants what I have to offer?"

"I mean the network has changed. When I

signed you, HHN was practically a start-up, owned by a handful of private investors with a shared vision. Now it's a publically traded corporation owned by stockholders who demand bigger profits every quarter. They don't care about the message; they care about the money. I'm not saying you're irrelevant, Mary Dell; I'm saying you're unprofitable."

"That sounds worse."

"It is."

Gary knocked back the last of his beer, then lifted his eyebrows and jerked his chin at a passing waitress, signaling his desire for another.

"Advertisers aren't willing to shell out big bucks for an audience composed primarily of people over fifty-five. And with your audience shrinking, the price we can charge to the advertisers you have left is shrinking too. That situation is unacceptable to the shareholders. So, for the moment, we only have two options: reduce costs or cancel the show."

Gary reached into the pocket of his jacket, pulled out some papers, and handed them to Mary Dell. She unfolded the contract, scanned the "whereins" and "therefores" on the first page, and flipped to the second and then the third, until she found what she was looking for: the numbers. Reading them, her jaw dropped.

"A twenty-five percent pay cut? You can't be serious."

He shook his head and Mary Dell slammed the contract down on the table.

"If this is some kind of twisted negotiating tactic . . . if you think . . ."

"It's not a tactic. It's not even a negotiation. This is the best deal I can offer you, the only deal. Believe me, I had to fight like hell to get you this much. And that's not all," he said glumly. "Keep reading."

She frowned and picked up the contract again. While she was reading, the waitress returned and set an open bottle of Lone Star on the table. Gary took a long drink, waiting for Mary Dell to get to the relevant section.

"Wait . . . ," she said, her forehead creasing in confusion. "Last time, we had a two-year contract with an option for a third. Now they only want one year? And the option only kicks in if we increase our viewership by four percent overall and by eighteen percent in the under-fifty-five age demo-graphic?"

Gary gazed at her with flat eyes, his silence a confirmation. Mary Dell kept reading, noting other, smaller changes to the contract, none of which were favorable to her. But it wasn't until she got to the last page, the signature page, which had already been signed by the people at the network, with spaces for her and Gary, that she noted the absence of one signature line. The realization made her feel suddenly sick and a little weak, as if the blood had drained from her head.

"Howard's name . . . it's missing."

"I know. I'm sorry. You know how I feel about Howard and his contribution. He's one of the reasons I wanted to sign you in the first place. My niece, Charlotte, has Down syndrome. But there are people at the network who think that Howard is the reason for your ratings slide. Part of it, any-way."

"And the other part is?" She answered her own question. "Me. They think I'm too old."

Gary didn't deny her statement, just said, "They want to get you a new co-host, somebody to attract the under-fifty-five viewership."

"Let me guess—somebody young, blond, and brainless. Will she even know how to quilt? Or is that optional?"

Mary Dell opened her fingers, letting the contract drop from her grasp like a used tissue.

"Well, if they think I'm going to sign this . . . this"—she stammered, searching for a phrase that was more polite than the one that had popped into her head—"insulting piece of garbage, then they've got another think coming! You can take the next plane back to Disneyland and tell them that I would rather cut off my right arm and feed it to a pack of piranhas than cut my own son out of my show!"

"They know that," Gary said. "The only reason they're making an offer at all is to give themselves legal cover. This way, they can say they wanted to keep you on but you refused. They're afraid you and Howard might sue for discrimination."

"They ought to be! It *is* discrimination! My good friend Hub-Jay, the man who owns all the hotels, has a team of lawyers working for him. As soon as I get back to Dallas, I'm going to ask him to refer me to the meanest one he's got!"

"Don't. You'll lose. And it'll cost you a fortune."

Gary tilted his face toward the ceiling and blew out a long breath.

"Mary Dell, I hate this as much as you do. The only reason I flew out here was to tell you to tell them to shove their contract, that you didn't need their damned show. But now I can't say that."

He lowered his head again, looked her in the eye.

"Because you *do* need it—or at least a lot of people you care about do. You told me yourself, you've got nine full-time employees, including your own niece, and three more part-time. And how many of those women working for you are single mothers or the sole breadwinner?"

"Four."

Gary bobbed his head. "Four families who directly depend on paychecks from the Patchwork Palace to put food on the table. And remember what you were telling me about Too Much's renaissance and economic recovery? It's not the town or the times that caused that recovery, Mary

Dell. It's you! The great big quilting celebrity with the TV show that attracts busloads of tourists out here to the middle of nowhere! The tourists who come to buy fabric and stay to eat pie at Hilda's, or buy a scarf or dress from Antoinette's, or get their nails done at the Primp 'n' Perm. Mary Dell Templeton, you're a job creator. The ripples you make touch hundreds of lives.

"But if the show is canceled this year, tourist traffic will be down by half next year, and the year after that, and the year after that. Then it will stop completely. Even if it means Howard is off the show, you've got to keep *Quintessential Quilting* on the air for as long as you can. *If* you can. Furthermore, you've got to find a way to get those ratings back up where they used to be, and to attract those younger viewers. If not," he mused, "a year from now, it'll all be over."

Mary Dell was thinking, too, coming to the slow realization that everything Gary was saying was true. If the show went down, it wouldn't just be the quilt shop that suffered. The whole town would be affected.

Mary Dell felt as if the weight of the world were on her shoulders.

Maybe not the whole world, but *her* world, her home, the place her heart beat best and where she knew the names and faces and stories of everyone she met, her neighbors. She had to help them if she could. They depended on her. So did her family, her mother and Cady, and Rob Lee, already on a bus, heading home from North Dakota.

How could she help them all?

"There's this guy," Gary said after a moment, "Jason Alvarez. I can't stand him; he's a little weasel. But you need to set up a meeting, get on his good side. When you get back to Dallas . . ."

"But that's what I wanted to talk to you about," she said, her ears perking up at the mention of Big D. "Gary, I don't want to go back to Dallas. I want to come home. The reason I kidnapped you was to show you how picturesque the town and the shop are, what great locations they would make . . ."

As he figured out what she was trying to say, Gary's brows drew together into a single line.

"Mary Dell, the network isn't going to let you film all the way out here in Too Much. There's just no way, especially not now, with your ratings in a slump."

"There has to be a way. There has to! And you've got to help me find it, Gary, because this is personal. I have *got* to come home. My family needs me."

Opening up to him in a way she rarely opened up to anyone, Mary Dell told him about the call from Pearl, about her mother's growing instability and the weight of Cady's grief, the circumstances of Nick's death, as well as the injuries, physical and emotional, that Rob Lee was suffering in the aftermath of the explosion. When she finished, Gary's face fell.

"Oh God. That poor kid. And the little girl too. No wonder Cady ran off when I asked about Linne's dad. I feel terrible."

"You didn't know," Mary Dell said, and touched him lightly on the forearm.

"And your nephew too? Poor guy. My older cousin, Mark, was in Vietnam. Lost a couple of buddies and was never really the same. But losing your brother-in-law? Surviving the explosion that left your sister a widow and your niece fatherless?" He shook his head. "That's rough."

"Rob Lee needs me," Mary Dell said. "They all do. I've got to come home."

Gary covered her small hand with his bigger one and squeezed it. "You really are a helluva woman, Mary Dell."

"Thank you." She leaned closer, fixing him with her gaze. "Now will you help me talk the network into letting us film in Too Much?"

"They'll never go for it. But," he said after a long pause, "I'll still help you."

He picked up the contract, flipped through some pages, then took a pen out of his pocket and started crossing things out and writing things in.

"What are you doing?"

"Writing my own execution orders," he mumbled. He placed his initials next to the changes he'd made, then clicked his pen closed and looked up. "Sorry. Just a little gallows humor."

"Gallows humor? Gary, what are you talking about?"

"The gallows. The place they hang you. Which is where I will most surely be headed after I amend and sign this contract. Don't worry," he said calmly. "I was headed there anyway. I just hadn't been willing to admit it to myself until now."

He placed the beer bottle to his lips and tipped it high to get the final drops.

"I am fifty-eight years old, Mary Dell. In the television business, that means I have ten years on Methuselah. They brought in this young guy, this Jason . . ."

"The weasel?"

"That's him. Supposedly he works for me, but he's been nipping at my heels for months. Always talking in meetings without my permission, blabbing about how we can up our ad revenue by bringing in younger viewers, pitching shows without my input. He wants my job and, quite frankly, I'm ready to let him have it. I was going to try to hang on for a couple more years, then take early retirement. But there's been a rumor going on about restructuring that is sounding like more than a rumor.

"To borrow a line from a show that the little weasel is constantly holding up as the ideal, 'In this business, you're either in or you're out.' I am about to be out, and there's nothing I can do about it. Oh, well. I had a good run."

He turned to the signature page, signed his name, and then handed her the pen. "Your turn."

Mary Dell touched pen to paper, then hesitated. "Gary, are you sure? Really sure?"

"I'm getting the ax anyway. Might as well help out a friend before the blade falls. Though," he said, "I'm not sure if I'm really doing you a favor. The weasel is as bad as I've painted him, worse even. But you've got to find a way to either work with him or get around him. Otherwise . . ."

"I know. I'll be in this exact same place next year."

Mary Dell signed her name, put down the pen, and took Gary's hand.

"Thank you. I don't know what else to say. This is such a load off my mind."

"Yeah? Then why do you still look so worried?" Gary lifted his brows. "Afraid of the weasel? You can handle him."

Mary Dell shook her head. "Uh-uh. Afraid of telling Howard he's off the show. It's just going to break his heart."

"Sorry, Mary Dell. There's nothing I can do about that. Wish I could."

"I know."

Gary waved at the waitress. "Hey, can I get another round?" To Mary Dell, he said, "You have one too. We've got to toast my soon-to-be-announced departure from the House and Home Network."

"All right," she conceded. "One more."

Somebody dropped some money in the juke-box. George Strait started singing about all his exes in Texas.

Mary Dell grinned. "Gary, do you know how to do the two-step?"

Chapter 7

Hubbell James Hollander, called Hub-Jay, sat at his usual corner table near the window at Spurs, one of Dallas's most fashionable eateries, located in the Hollander Grand Hotel, waiting for Mary Dell to arrive for their weekly Friday lunch date.

She was late, which was unusual. In the four years since he'd known Mary Dell, he could count the number of times she'd been late to lunch on one hand. But because this was the first moment he'd had to himself all day, he didn't mind.

However, his peace and quiet was disturbed when Sallie Moffat spotted him from the other side of the dining room and started plowing her way through the maze of white-clothed tables with a stride that made him think of ice-breakers in the Antarctic. Cornered, Hub-Jay put aside his napkin, rose to his feet, and kissed her on the cheek.

"Nice to see you." He was stretching the truth, but good manners were Hub-Jay's default mode. "You're looking lovely. As always."

This part was true. People seeing her on the street might have taken Sallie Moffat for a retired cover model. She had perfect teeth, perfect hair, impeccable clothes, jewelry, and taste, and the finest plastic surgeon that money could buy. Several women in Dallas were nearly as beautiful, but none was quite as dull.

That was something Hub-Jay hadn't given much consideration when becoming briefly involved with her three years before. He'd been thinking with his eyes, among other body parts. Before a week was out, he realized that Sallie's conver-sation was limited to fashion, dieting, gossip, and her life goals of maintaining a size-zero figure and finding a wealthy husband. That was about the time he realized that the same could be said of nearly every woman he'd dated in the previous decade.

"Aren't you sweet," she murmured, returning his peck. "Haven't seen you at the club lately. You missed the gala too."

"Work has been keeping me pretty busy."

"So I've heard," she chirped, opening her eyes wider. "Breaking ground on another Hollander Grand in Fort Worth. How many hotels will you own now, Hub-Jay?"

"We've got seven Hollander House properties,

the smaller boutique hotels, but this will only be our third Hollander Grand."

"My goodness! Ten hotels! Hub-Jay Hollander, when you bought that first run-down motel in Abilene, did you ever imagine you'd be a *chain?*"

"Always."

She laughed softly and took a step toward him. "I just bet you did. I do admire a man who knows what he wants and how to get it," she said, making her voice a little breathy. "But don't you think you're working too hard? Isn't it time you settled down and had a home? Someone to take care of you?"

"I've got an entire staff of people taking care of me. Living in the hotel not only makes it easy to keep an eye on business, it makes for a short commute."

"But I worry about you, Hub-Jay—always working. And look at you." She clucked her tongue and gestured toward his empty table. "Eating all alone. That's just sad. You know what they say, all work and no play . . ."

"Makes Jack a *very* rich boy. Sorry I'm late, Hub-Jay. My meeting ran long." Mary Dell gave him a peck on the cheek before circling to the other side of the table and being seated by David, the handsome young manager of Spurs.

"That's all right. I hadn't ordered yet. Sallie, you've met Mary Dell?"

Sallie furrowed her brow, "Actually, I don't think I've . . ."

"Actually, you have. A couple of times," Mary Dell said with a smile. When David offered her a menu, she said, "Oh, I won't need that. I'll have my usual."

David nodded and recited from memory. "Large Dr Pepper, extra ice, jalapeño pulled-pork sliders, extra-crispy shoestring fries, and a side of steamed spinach."

"Because a girl can't keep her figure on pulled pork and fries alone. And isn't that too bad? On second thought, could you cancel the Dr Pepper and bring me a glass of white wine? Whatever kind is sweetest."

"Of course." He glanced quickly toward Hub-Jay. "The Trimbach 2012?"

Hub-Jay curled his lip and gave a short shake of his head. "Let's have a bottle of the Martin-borough Gewürztraminer 2006."

"Right away, Mr. Hollander," David replied, and walked away.

Sallie, who was still standing near the table, finally said, "Well. I'll just leave you two to enjoy your lunch. Nice to meet . . . to see you, Mary Dell. Hub-Jay."

She gave them a studied, slightly icy smile and walked away.

"Thank you for rescuing me," Hub-Jay said after she left.

Mary Dell took a corn muffin from the bread basket. "Hub-Jay, it wouldn't be Friday if I didn't rescue you from one of your girlfriends."

"Sallie Moffat isn't my girlfriend."

"No, but she wants to be. Along with half the other women in this town. I swear the only reason you keep me around is to serve as a human shield against all the gals who'd like to erase your name from the list of Dallas's Twenty Most Eligible Bachelors. When are you going to put them out of their misery and get hitched?"

"Why would I want to do that?"

"I see. Why buy a cow when milk is free; is that it?" Mary Dell shook her head disapprovingly as she buttered her muffin. "You are a scourge to womankind, you know that? If I had any loyalty to my sex, I'd quit hanging around with you."

Hub-Jay was used to Mary Dell's teasing. They'd met at an art museum gala during which a date with Hub-Jay, as well as dates with the other nineteen Most Eligible Bachelors, was auctioned off for charity.

Mary Dell didn't bid on him, but he called and invited her to the hotel for lunch the following week anyway.

When she countered that he'd better think twice if he thought she was going to pony up five thousand dollars just to eat a chicken sandwich with him, Hub-Jay laughed. She'd been making him laugh every Friday ever since. She had become Hub-Jay's best friend, probably his only friend.

Of course, he wouldn't have been lacking for female companionship if he'd wanted it, but that was the thing—he didn't want it. He hadn't for the last three years, after he'd woken up next to Sallie Moffat, looked at her sleeping form, and couldn't think of one single thing he wanted to say to her or to hear from her, except good-bye.

He hadn't woken up with a woman in his bed since.

At first, he'd chalked it up to his getting older— he'd turned sixty that year. Then to losing interest in the thrill of the chase, because these days, there wasn't any chase. Since making the Twenty Most Eligible list, inclusion on which required a hefty net worth, luring women to his bed required little more than a smile and maybe a round of drinks. Then he decided the problem was the women— they were all just like Sallie: beautiful, attentive, available, and boring. And maybe that was just as well. With nine hotels to run and another under construction, he had plenty to keep him busy.

He still went out with women because he still had social obligations; Dallas was a very social sort of town. But when the party, gala, or benefit was done, he escorted them home and kissed them good night at the door. The next day, he'd send a very nice bouquet of flowers. He never invited them home.

But Mary Dell didn't know that. There were some things a man just didn't discuss, not even with his friends, especially if the friend was female. Besides, she enjoyed teasing Hub-Jay about his playboy image, his "string of fillies," as she some-times called them, and he didn't dissuade her from doing so. Why spoil her fun? Or his image?

Except, today, it didn't seem like she was having fun. Today, Mary Dell seemed distressed. That wasn't like her. Neither was ordering wine at lunch.

After David uncorked the Gewürztraminer and made his silent exit, Hub-Jay topped up her glass. "Rough day?"

"Rough week, rough day, rough *hour*." She lifted the wineglass to her lips and drained it by a third.

"Want to talk about it?"

"No, sir, I do *not*," Mary Dell replied, and then started talking about it anyway. "You know, this *should* be a happy day. I'm finally getting what I've wanted for so long, the chance to move home to Too Much, but the way that this—"

"Hold on." Hub-Jay lifted his hand from the table. "Did you just say you're moving?"

Mary Dell winced and nodded. The jolt Hub-Jay had felt when she uttered those words became a clench in his stomach when she confirmed them.

"Sorry. I forgot I hadn't told you yet. I've been so crazy these last few days that I don't know if

I'm shucking or shelling. But then, I've hardly told anybody. When Gary grabbed the contract, started crossing things out and writing things in, I really wasn't sure it was legal.

"Truth to tell," she said, sounding a little astonished, "I'm still not sure about that. But it looks like the network is going to stand by it. I can't believe it. Neither can Jason. He was mad as a red ant!" She picked up her wineglass and took another large swallow. "He really *is* a weasel. You'd think he'd be satisfied to see Gary gone and himself made head of programming, but no. He's just bound and—"

"Mary Dell? I still have no idea what you're talking about."

She winced again. "Sorry. I forgot. Why don't I start over . . ."

She explained it from the beginning.

"Even though Gary sounded relieved, even happy, when he called to tell me how things had shaken out, it was still a brave thing for him to do," she said.

Then she went on to explain how the network had decided to honor his changes to her contract, partly because Gary agreed to go quietly without calling a lawyer if they did, but mostly because he'd convinced them that filming in Too Much would actually save the network money. "And money is everything to these people; the *only* thing," she declared.

Having supplied the background, she went on to tell Hub-Jay about her meeting with the odious and arrogant Jason, relating how he had made no effort to hide his contempt for her show and her audience, how he'd made it clear that he was rooting for *Quintessential Quilting*'s failure and subsequent cancelation, and that, if not for the financial penalties imposed by her contract, made steeper by a stroke of Gary's pen, he would have canceled the show immediately rather than wait until the end of the season, which he absolutely intended to do.

"He wants to cancel before he even sees if the new location will help your ratings? That's not just mean; it's stupid. It's bad business," Hub-Jay said.

"I haven't even gotten to the worst part yet." Recalling that worst part, Mary Dell's eyes brimmed with tears.

Hub-Jay had never seen Mary Dell cry. The prospect of her breaking down was unnerving. He didn't know what he'd do or say if she did.

He reached into the breast pocket of his suit jacket in search of a handkerchief. But then, thinking about mascara stains and remembering that this handkerchief cost seventy-five dollars at Neiman Marcus, he handed her the napkin from his lap instead.

She waved it away and blinked back her tears just as, thankfully, the food arrived. After the server left she gave Hub-Jay a sad but brave smile.

"Sorry."

"Here. Eat something."

He nudged the basket of extra-crispy shoe-string fries toward her. Mary Dell took a handful, laid them on her plate, then started dipping them into ketchup and eating them, one by one.

"So," Hub-Jay asked, "what was the worst part?"

"Actually, there are two worst parts. First, they're bringing in a new co-host, some young girl."

Hub-Jay furrowed his brow as he started slicing into a piece of chipotle-marinated skirt steak "I don't understand. You already have a co-host—Howard."

Mary Dell shook her head. "Howard is off the show. They're firing him. That's the *worst* worst part."

"But they can't do that. His name is in the title."

"Was. Come next season, *Quintessential Quilting with Mary Dell and Howard* will be *Quintessential Quilting with Mary Dell and Holly.*"

Hub-Jay put down his knife and fork. "Holly? Who the hell is Holly?"

"You tell me and we'll both know," Mary Dell said bitterly. "I can't believe it. After all the work I put in, creating a show out of nothing, building up an audience, bringing in new advertisers . . . Hub-Jay, I have never been treated so disrespectfully in my life. The way that man spoke to me! The things he said about Howard! If we hadn't been on the twenty-sixth floor I might have thrown him out the window."

"If I'd have been there," Hub-Jay said in a low rumble, "I'd have done it for you."

"Oh, Hub-Jay. How am I going to tell Howard that he's off the show? He loves being on TV." She paused a moment, staring vacantly out the plate-glass window. "And how am I supposed to do it without him? We're a team. I can't even imagine—"

Before she could finish her sentence, Hub-Jay barked out a short but descriptive string of oaths questioning Jason's legitimacy and probable destination in the afterlife.

"Quit! I mean it, Mary Dell! Just quit! Those SOBs at HHN don't deserve you!"

Mary Dell's eyes went wide, and with good reason. Hub-Jay never swore. Having grown up with a father who used profanity like punctuation and flew into a rage at the drop of a hat, Hub-Jay had made a habit of avoiding both.

"I wish I could quit," she said, her expression softening. "But the cancellation penalty in my contract cuts both ways. I can't cancel on HHN and they can't cancel on me, not unless one of us is willing to pay a pile of money. Unfortunately, my pile is gone. Building those new classrooms on the second floor of the shop ate up a big chunk of it. And even without that, there's the sheer number of mouths I have to feed—not just my family but all the people who work for me too. If the show ends, it'll hurt traffic at the shop. I have to keep going! If I can . . ." Her shoulders drooped. "But that snotty Jason is bound and determined to knock *Quintessential Quilting* off the lineup, no matter what I do."

Mary Dell buried her head in her hands. Her shoulders started to shake. Hub-Jay sat dumbstruck, staring at the top of her head, battling twin urges that caught him completely off guard.

The first was to track down this Jason character and knock him into next week; the second, to gather Mary Dell in his arms and stroke her hair.

What he did instead was toss back an enormous swig of Gewürztraminer, a wine he had always loathed, and smack his half-empty glass back down on the table.

"Marry me!"

Mary Dell looked up. Her eyes were wet.

"What?"

"Marry me," he repeated. "Then you won't have to worry about money."

"Oh, be serious."

He took another, smaller drink. After a long moment, in a voice that displayed just a hint of surprise, he said, "I am serious. Why shouldn't we get married? We're a good team. We understand each other, make each other laugh. We've never had an argument—how many people can say that after four years? Plus, Howard likes me. If you stop to think about it, it just makes sense."

Mary Dell's face broke into a grateful, albeit somewhat watery, smile.

"Hub-Jay Hollander, you really are as sweet as tea. But you don't need to worry about me. I'll be all right. After all, Jason doesn't *own* the network —the shareholders do. And just like Gary said, the only thing they care about is money. If I can bring the ratings and ad revenue up, Jason won't be able to touch me," she said, her eyes beginning to spark with their customary light.

"Of course," she mused, lowering her gaze and biting her lower lip, "I still have to tell Howard that he's off the show. But . . . that might just be temporary. Once the show is a success, I'll renegotiate my contract with HHN, tell them that if they want me, they've got to take Howard too. We are a package deal. End of story."

Mary Dell raised her head, smiling broadly now.

"Thank you, Hub-Jay. I feel so much better." She lifted herself halfway out of her chair, placed her hands on either side of Hub-Jay's face, and gave him a smacking kiss. "You are just the *best!*"

"You're welcome," he said. "But, Mary Dell, when I—"

"Darlin'," she said, getting to her feet, "forgive me, but I've got to scoot. A Realtor is coming to list the house at four, but I need to talk to Howard before that.

"Oh!" She snapped her fingers. "Almost forgot. I'm flying to Connecticut week after next, so I won't be here for lunch. We start filming in Too Much right after Christmas, and I know I'll be busier than a one-armed paperhanger getting ready for the move. But I'll see you before I leave town—promise."

She hung her purse over her shoulder and stood there for just a moment, looking at him. "Sweet as tea," she said again, and hurried off.

Hub-Jay watched her go, then reached for his glass, took a sip, made a face, and called for a waiter to bring him some bourbon.

For the next thirty minutes Hub-Jay stared out the window, nursing three fingers of Maker's Mark and trying to make sense of what had just happened.

Chapter 8

When she said it the first time, Howard thought it was a mistake.

Because he'd had a lot of ear infections when he was little, sometimes he didn't hear things quite right. He took a step closer to his momma and made sure his good ear was turned toward her.

"Did you say that they don't want me on the show anymore?"

"Not everyone," she said quickly. "Just that mean man I was telling you about, this Mr. Alvarez . . ."

"He's the new Mr. Beatty?"

"Yes . . . I mean, sort of. He's the man who took Mr. Beatty's job at the network."

"And he doesn't want me on the show."

"Oh, Howard. Baby . . . I just . . ." Mary Dell's face fell and she shook her head.

It wasn't very often that Howard saw his momma looking sad, or lacking for words, but he was so surprised by her words that he hardly noticed.

He couldn't believe it had been so easy.

His girlfriend, Jenna, had said it would be, that his momma would understand, but Howard had his doubts. Jenna didn't understand about the show and what it meant to Momma.

Remembering that, he asked, "But they aren't canceling the show, right? They're going to move the filming to Too Much and they still want you—just not me."

She confirmed his understanding of the situation with a nod.

"Oh, that's all right, then," he said, and sighed.

She paused for a minute, examining him closely.

"What are you saying, baby? Are you . . . ?"

"Happy," he answered, filling in the blank. "I was trying to think how to tell you about it. Now I don't have to!" His face split into a grin.

"Now you don't have to tell me what?"

"That I want to quit the show."

"Wait. You *want* to leave the show?" Mary Dell gave her head a quick shake. "But why? I thought you loved being on TV."

Howard rolled his eyes. "Momma, I've been doing it for *seven* years. It's time to do something else. I'll be thirty soon. I have other plans for my life."

She started to question him, trying to probe more deeply into what these other plans for his life might entail.

"Going to college," he said. "I heard about some special programs for people with Down syndrome. I found a link about it on the National Down Syndrome Society Web site and looked for programs in Texas."

"But, Howard. College is . . ."

He lifted his hands out flat to intercept her objections. "I'll work very hard," he said earnestly. "You always said that I could learn anything if I worked hard at it. Remember how nobody thought I could learn to use a sewing machine or make quilts? But we didn't listen to them, did we? You showed me what to do.

"Remember when you taught me to thread the machine? You made me practice over and over until I could do it all myself—about fifty times . . ."

"Not that many," she said. "You caught on quicker than that."

"But I had to practice and work hard," he said. "And now I can run the machine and make quilts all on my own. If I can do that, I can take college classes. Don't you think so, Momma?"

"Oh, I do, baby. I absolutely do," she assured him. "But I don't think they have those kinds of programs in Too Much. The nearest community college is in Waco, and that's a long drive. Maybe we could get—"

"That was the other part I was going to talk to you about," he interrupted, then rapped his knuckles twice against his forehead. "I forgot. I've decided to get my own apartment."

"Your own apartment? Where?" Mary Dell cocked her head a little to the side. An amused, indulgent little smile tugged at her lips.

"Here in Dallas. Jenna's next-door neighbors have a nice apartment over their garage. They already said they would rent it to me. It's right on the bus line, but if I need a ride someplace, Jenna's momma said she would drive me."

"But, baby, I don't understand . . . we've finally got a chance to go back to Too Much. Don't you want to go home?"

"I am home," he said simply. "My friends are here. My girl is here. What would I do in Too Much?"

Howard smiled wide, so relieved that he failed to notice how his mother's smile was fading or the way the muscles in her neck twitched, as if her throat had become suddenly sore and she was trying to swallow the pain.

"You know, I was really worried that you'd be upset when I told you I wanted to leave that show. But now that you've got a new co-host, you won't need me anymore. Isn't it great how everything worked out?"

Chapter 9

Rob Lee couldn't sleep anymore.

Bone tired, he'd get into bed and lie there for hours, sometimes turning on the lamp so he could look at the clock and see how many hours remained until morning, sometimes getting out of bed to pull a fifth of Jack Daniel's out of his boot and take a swig or a few, hoping it would help.

Sometimes it worked. Sometimes it didn't.

Even when it did, the images that filled his dreams were often more terrible and vivid than the ones that invaded his thoughts in the daylight. When the terrible dreams came, he would act out his part in his sleep, thrashing his arms and legs, fighting and fleeing the nocturnal enemy, crying warnings to his buddies, always to no avail.

He'd hoped that the oil-field job, and living with Jeb and his family, would work out. For a little while, it did.

But one day, while he was on the job, a load of

pipe accidentally dropped from the back of a truck, hitting the pavement with a resounding *boom*. Rob Lee hit the deck with his arms wrapped over his head and his heart pounding, waiting for shrapnel and blood, waiting for death. When it didn't come, he looked up and saw a ring of faces staring at him, some confused, others amused. A young guy, maybe nineteen or twenty years old and skinny, laughed out loud. Rob Lee threw him to the ground, straddling his shoulders, but somebody pulled him off before he could land a punch. Rob Lee walked off the job.

The next day, he was an hour late. Jeb pulled him aside, his face all serious and voice real low, and said he understood it was rough, but brother or not, he'd have to dock his pay if it happened again.

The day after that, Rob Lee arrived three hours late. And three sheets to the wind.

He wasn't trying to embarrass his brother . . . well, not much. And he knew Jeb was trying to help, but every time he said he understood, it made Rob Lee's blood boil, because he didn't. Jeb might have been a Marine, but he'd never been in combat, and unless you'd been there, you had no clue.

Rob Lee was sure the phrase "to hell and back" had been coined by a combat veteran. There was no other way to describe it and no way to imagine it short of personal experience. But the weird thing about hell was that, assuming you lived through it, after a while you could actually learn to live with it.

Every day you woke up and tried to stay alive until the next day. No matter what else you might be doing or who you might be talking to, your mind was constantly alert to danger, your muscles continually coiled for action, always tense, ready to fight or flee. That was your whole focus, your only job.

Because of that, living through hell had turned out to be easier than coming back from it. He had lost the knack of living like he had before, of dividing his attention among multiple pursuits and people, lowering his guard, pretending to be normal. No matter how hard he tried, he couldn't pull it off.

When Jeb suggested, not for the first time, that he ought to talk to somebody at the VA, Rob Lee told him to mind his own damned business and threw a punch, which Jeb returned. Rob Lee threw his brother to the ground and started pounding on him, just like he had that skinny kid on the oil crew, only this time, there was nobody to pull him off. The only thing that stopped him was the sobs of Jeb's little girl, Flannery.

It was the sight of Flannery, her little face buried in her mother's skirts, howling in fear, that propelled him out the door and on a bender, not the fury in Jeb's voice when he threw him out. He didn't blame him for that, or for firing him. That part was a relief, albeit a temporary one, prolonged by three days of drinking that came to a close when Jeb found him.

He wasn't anxious to return to Too Much, but he had to go someplace. When Jeb left him at the bus station, he briefly considered exchanging his ticket for one to Austin, maybe seeing if he could get his old bartending job back. But even he realized that wasn't a good idea. Besides, he'd already agreed to come home and take charge of the F-Bar-T Ranch for a while, at least until Moises recovered. He'd promised Aunt Mary Dell when they talked on the phone.

And though he hadn't given voice to it, not even to himself, he had an idea that by going home to Too Much, he might be able to help his sister and niece, stepping into the hole left by Nick's death and, in doing so, somehow making up for being the cause of it.

But when Cady met his bus, put her arms around him, and started to cry, his own arms hung useless at his sides, unable to respond, and he knew it was no good.

Some mistakes can't be forgiven or forgotten.

His mistake, the moment of hesitation that had cost the lives of three good men, was one of them.

On that terrible day, Rob Lee recognized the form of the man walking next to the road. He lived in one of the neighboring villages, spoke passable English, and had done some translating when they'd come around, trying to make connections with some of the local leaders. The man had invited them into his home, served them tea. Rob Lee gave balloons to his children, two dark-eyed boys and a little girl, who smiled shyly when accepting his gift.

Rob Lee had been trained to trust no one, but for an instant, no more than the space of a breath, his brain resisted the idea that this man could be his enemy. A breath was all it took. The man started walking quickly away, then turned his head toward the sound of the oncoming vehicle. Rob Lee saw the hatred in his eye and knew what he was, and called out to the others, but his warning came too late.

A split second after he cried out, they hit the IED. There was a *boom* and a brilliant orange flash, a fireball.

Rob Lee was thrown from the vehicle. His face was burned and so was his right arm. Three of his ribs were broken, along with his leg, but he didn't realize that until he tried to get to his feet to rescue his friends from the inferno and collapsed on the ground, unable to walk and writhing in pain, the sounds of his own screams registering as terrible silence because the explosive concussion had ruptured his eardrums.

Of all the awful memories he carried with him,

this was the most indelible: those long, terrible, helpless minutes of screaming as loud as he could, but not being heard, not even by himself.

Now, whether he was awake or asleep, he still felt that way.

Chapter 10

December

Holly pressed her foot gently on the brakes, slowing the car so she could read the numbers on the mailboxes.

"Nobody *made* you come," she reminded her mother.

Spending more than a few hours with Rachel under any circumstances was stressful, but after two days of enforced togetherness in a car stuffed with her clothes, shoes, cosmetics, bathroom and kitchen stuff, a new used sewing machine she'd bought on eBay, and Calypso, who had yowled piteously for the first three hundred miles, Holly's definition of stress had taken on a new dimension.

And even more than usual, something just didn't seem right between Holly and her mother. In spite of Rachel's insistence that she take this job, Holly wondered if her mother didn't resent her going off and leaving her alone in LA. Holly tried to bring up the issue once or twice during the trip, but Rachel kept saying everything was fine.

Maybe it was. Maybe she was just projecting her own anxieties onto the situation. The farther they'd gotten from California, the greater those anxieties became. What was she doing? Traveling so far from everyone she knew and everything that was familiar?

When they got to Waco, her spirits had lifted briefly. It seemed like an all-right sort of place, with tree-lined streets and a huge park sitting near a big lake. Not as bustling as LA, of course, but there seemed to be lots going on.

Too Much, however, was definitely not Waco.

When they drove into town, Rachel took off her sunglasses, gazed at the sparse collection of buildings, and said, "Wow. It's not a whole lot more than a wide spot in the road, is it? Why would anybody film a TV show here?"

Her observation had really irritated Holly, mostly because she'd been thinking the exact same thing. Rachel kept doing it as they drove, giving voice to the same silent doubts and disappointments that were going through Holly's mind, and at almost the same moment she was thinking them. It was kind of spooky. In another situation Holly might have been impressed, or at least intrigued. Today, it just made her want to scream.

"I know I didn't have to come," Rachel said, fanning herself with a piece of paper. "I wanted to. I want to help you get settled."

"Then *be* a help and quit complaining."

"I wasn't complaining. I was just making an observation. It *is* hot and the town *is* small. And isolated." She frowned, gazing out the car window. "I had no idea. Do they even have a grocery store? What are you going to eat? On the other hand, since I'm sure there's no gym," she mumbled, "maybe it'll be better if you don't."

Holly clenched the steering wheel. She hated it when Rachel made comments about her weight.

She never came right out and called Holly fat, not even when she had been. It was always these little asides and jabs, questions of supposed concern like "Are you *sure* you want to finish the rest of that?" that were really criticisms.

Holly was slim. She had been for years. But Rachel made her feel like none of that had ever happened, that she was still that same fat girl, inept and clumsy, incapable of controlling her impulses, or her life.

This is her problem, not yours. You don't have to take the bait. And she's leaving tomorrow. You've just got to keep it together for one more day.

"Why can't I find it? Mom, what's the address again?"

Rachel slid her sunglasses to the end of her nose and squinted at the piece of paper she'd been using as a fan. "One eighty-five North Mesquite."

"North?"

Rachel nodded a confirmation. Holly puffed with exasperation.

"And since I'm heading to Galveston anyway," Rachel said, returning to their previous conversation, "it wasn't that much of a detour."

Holly pulled into a driveway, backed out, and headed back in the direction she'd just come from. "Yeah. And why are you doing that?"

"Going to Galveston? I told you before."

"Tell me again."

"Because from there," Rachel said wearily, "I'm going to Mexico."

"Via cruise ship," Holly stated.

"I've decided that I don't like flying."

"Uh-huh. And," Holly continued, keeping her tone deliberately neutral, "you're going to Mexico to look for locations for the movie. The one you're still not sure you've got a part in. The movie that's gone back into development."

Holly pulled up to a stop sign and gave her mother a sideways glance before crossing through the intersection.

"That's right," Rachel said breezily. "I'll be gone for eight weeks."

Holly gave her head a small shake. None of this made sense.

Rachel had never said anything about not liking to fly before. Nor had she ever expressed any interest in taking a cruise. She wasn't the cruise type. Well, except maybe a transatlantic crossing on the *Queen Mary*, with flowers and champagne in her suite and dinner at the captain's table, surrounded by British accents. Rachel would be all over that.

But . . . Galveston to Mexico? Mariachis and margaritas and people taking video of the midnight buffet? No. And what business did she have searching out places to shoot? She was an actress, not a location scout. Plus, she hadn't gotten the part yet, nor was there any guarantee the film would ever be made. A lot of scripts that were sent "back into development" never again saw the light of day.

A kid on a bike was peddling toward the corner. Holly stopped the car to let him cross and turned to look at Rachel.

"And that's your story? Eight weeks in Mexico to scout locations? Not buying it. Seriously, Mom. What are you really up to?"

"Nothing."

Holly stared at her, eyebrows lifted. Rachel dropped her jaw, making a clucking sound with her tongue.

"It's true. Jared asked if I would come along and help him scout . . ."

"Jared?" Holly interrupted. "Jared Hoffman? Is he the director?"

"Well . . ." Rachel stopped, pressed her lips together, and lifted her chin to a challenging angle. "Yes. Assuming it makes it into production."

Holly let out a groan. She understood now but wished she didn't.

"Mom, Jared Hoffman is married. He's married! And he has two kids. Carson Hoffman and I were in the same grade, remember? And you're so desperate for this part that you agreed to go off to Mexico with him?" She made a face, like she'd just tasted something terrible. "Geez, Rachel . . ."

"Mom!" Rachel spat back, her eyes flashing, carefully enunciating her words. "I am your mother, Holly. Not your child or your girlfriend. Your mother."

"Then why don't you start acting like one? Or even like a grown-up? I'd settle for that. A responsible, caring human being instead of—"

A pickup truck came up behind them and gave a short tap on the horn. Holly pressed the accelerator. They drove in silence for five blocks before Holly spoke again.

"You could end up hurting a lot of people."

Rachel's head turned to the left, the movement so deliberate it seemed almost choreographed. "What I do with my life is none of your concern. So let's drop it, shall we?"

"Fine," Holly said.

"Fine," Rachel echoed. "I think you just passed the house."

Holly pulled into the gravel driveway.

The yard, surrounded by a waist-high chain-link

fence, was brown: brown grass, brown patches of dirt showing up where the grass was sparse, and brown, spindly weeds and vines, lots of them, clinging to and climbing up the chain link like prisoners desperate to make an escape. The only green was on the leaves of the pecan tree planted on the west side of the narrow lot, grown so large that it blocked much of the view of the house. Through the heavy branches, Holly could spot pink siding and white shutters, both peeling. The peaked roof, an oddly angled, half-story affair, appeared to be missing a few shingles.

Holly turned off the ignition. "Don't say it."

"Say what?"

"What I'm thinking. Don't say it."

"How would I know what you're thinking?" Rachel frowned, then lifted her hands, palms out. "I'm not saying a word."

"Fine," Holly said, reaching into the backseat for the cat carrier. "Don't."

"Fine," Rachel said, and got out of the car.

"The porch is nice," Rachel said as she opened the creaking metal gate and walked up the cracked cement sidewalk.

From the deliberately bright tone of her voice, Holly guessed that they were now supposed to move on and pretend the whole Jared Hoffman thing had never come up. Probably just as well.

Holly stood at the bottom of the porch steps,

Calypso's carrier in one hand, staring at the pink cottage, thinking it looked like an iced petit four, or would have if the paint hadn't been peeling quite so much.

"It's tiny. The ad said there were two bedrooms, but . . . how is that possible? It can't be more than fifteen feet across."

"It's a shotgun cottage. My uncle Kenny lived in one of these, in Baton Rouge. The rooms stack up in a line, one behind the other, like looking down the barrel of a gun. They're designed to fit on narrow lots." Rachel walked to the corner of the cottage and stuck her head around the side. "See? It goes way, way back."

"Hmm . . ." Holly mounted the steps to the porch. The bottom step was cracked across the middle and the railing wobbled when she grabbed it. "It's only for a few months. I don't need much space."

She set Calypso's carrier down, pulled her phone out of the back pocket of her jeans, and checked the time. Six minutes after two.

"What time did the landlord say to meet her?" Rachel asked.

"Two o'clock."

Rachel joined Holly on the porch. "Let's go in and take a look around until she gets here."

"I'm sure it's locked," Holly said without testing the knob. "Let's just wait on the porch. I'll call and try to find out where she is." She punched the number into her phone and waited. "No answer. And the voice-mail box is full."

"Oh, this is ridiculous! I am not going to just sit here!"

Rachel marched up to the door, turned the knob, and strode across the threshold. Holly followed more cautiously, craning her neck to the left and right before actually stepping inside. Once inside, she put down the cat carrier and unlatched the door. Calypso came out immediately and started walking around the room, sniffing the walls and floors.

"See? It's just like I told you," said Rachel, standing in the center of the room and turning in a circle. "The rooms are arranged one after another, in a single line. This must be the living-dining room."

Holly tilted her head back. "The tall ceilings are nice. From the outside, I thought it was a story and a half, but I guess not."

"The extra height lets the hot air rise so the house stays cooler," Rachel said, then walked across the room and bent down to peer into the sooty black of the brick fireplace. "I think it works." She sniffed. "Smells like it does."

"Why would you need a fireplace around here?" Holly asked. "It's the second week of December and still seventy degrees."

"Wait till the sun goes down. I bet it gets pretty chilly in here."

Holly cast her eyes around the room, taking in the scarred wooden floors, the grimy leaded windows, and the brass pendant chandelier festooned with cobwebs, trying to picture herself occupying this space.

Maybe this was a mistake. On the other hand, it was only for a few months. And when the story of Rachel's affair with Jared Hoffman hit the tabloids —not "if" but "when," as the press always found out about that stuff—Holly would rather be any-place on earth but Los Angeles. Hopefully, the whole thing would blow over by the time she got back. And if not? Maybe she'd just move to Texas permanently.

Yeah, right.

Holly chuckled at the thought. Rachel turned to look at her.

"I thought you said it came furnished."

"I thought so too. That's what Brocade said when I talked to her."

"The landlord's name is Brocade? You've got to be kidding." Rachel snorted. "She must be two hundred years old."

"She didn't sound old. She said everybody calls her Cady."

"I don't care what they call her; she's *late*." Rachel huffed and started walking toward the hallway that led to the back of the house. Holly hesitated a moment and then followed, the sound of her footsteps, not quite in sync with her mother's, echoing through the empty room.

There wasn't a lot more to see.

The long hallway led to a small kitchen with blue-and-white linoleum and white wooden cabinets that looked like they had been painted and repainted many times over, followed by two bedrooms with a small bathroom sandwiched between them. The bedrooms were equal in size, but the one at the back of the house had more windows, better light, and a larger closet. Holly decided that was the room she would sleep in.

"Assuming somebody gets you a bed," Rachel said.

Holly bit at her lower lip, stung by the inherent criticism in Rachel's tone and wishing she'd called Cady to confirm the meeting time and details the night before.

"I'll call again after I use the bathroom. Hey, where's Calypso?"

"I don't know. Around here somewhere," Rachel said, and sighed impatiently. "I'm going to check out the backyard."

Rachel went out the back door at the end of the hall and Holly headed into the bathroom. Calypso was inside, stretched out on his side on the tile floor, eyes closed. Holly squatted down to stroke his fur.

"So, what do you think? Should we stay? It's your call."

The cat opened one eye and started to purr.

"All right, then. We stay." Holly stood up. "But I sure hope you know what you're talking about."

There was no towel or soap in the bathroom, so Holly wiped her hands on the legs of her jeans after rinsing them, then pulled her phone out of her pocket and hit the "redial" button. Hearing a noise in the bedroom, she assumed Rachel had come back inside and went to find her.

"Still no answer," she called out, nudging the bedroom door open with her foot.

There was a loud metallic thud and the startled cry of a man's voice. Holly gasped as pieces from the window air conditioner the man had dropped scattered across the floor and he spun around to face her, shouting.

"Who the hell are you?! What are you doing here?!"

The booming sound of his voice, rapid-fire barrage of questions, and enraged expression startled her and made her pulse race. The man's hand clutched at his pant leg, as if he might be reaching for something.

For an instant, Holly thought—*Gun!* Her body tensed up, ready to flee, but then she looked into his eyes and saw fear lurking beneath the surface of his rage. She took a deep breath and opened her arms, fingers spread apart.

"I'm Holly Silva. The new tenant?"

Her declaration didn't seem to register any

recognition in his eyes. She wondered if they had somehow gotten the wrong address.

"Listen, I'm really sorry. I didn't mean to startle you. I'm renting a house and thought this was it. We were supposed to meet the landlord at two, but she's late." Her heartbeat slowed a little as the man relaxed his hands and the jumble of fear and fury faded from his dark brown eyes.

There was a noise at the back door and the sound of running footsteps. Rachel burst into the room, looking from Holly to the air conditioner lying in pieces on the floor to the stranger in the gray T-shirt, battered Stetson, and scuffed black boots.

"Are you okay? I thought there was an explosion!"

Holly shook her head. "I think we're at the wrong address. I barged in here unannounced, scared him, and—"

"You *scared* him?" Rachel looked at Holly, all five foot six, hundred and seventeen pounds of her, then at the tall man with the heavy shoulders and work-calloused hands, and let out a short, sharp laugh.

His skin was bronzed and roughened from weather, with the beginnings of creases at the eyes, a complexion that would someday be described as leathery. Even so, Holly detected the blush of embarrassment in response to Rachel's question. She felt sorry for him. She knew how Rachel's barbs could sting.

"I was trying to install a new air conditioner. Had my back to the door . . . ," he said. He bent down and started picking up the broken pieces. Holly squatted down to help.

"It was totally my fault," Holly said. "I'm really sorry, Mr. . . ."

"Rob Lee," he said, eyes on the floor. "Rob Lee Benton. You're at the right address. My sister, Cady, asked me to come help you get settled in."

Rachel, who was still standing near the door, crossed her arms over her chest. "We've been waiting for half an hour. Where is the furniture? My daughter was promised that this place would come completely furnished."

"Furniture's in my truck," he said, tilting his head toward the window. "The last tenant pretty well ruined everything, so I brought some better stuff in from the ranch. Sorry I'm late, ma'am. I lost track of the time."

Rachel looked him over from hat to heel.

"Boy, you're right out of central casting, aren't you? Cowboy hat, boots, faded jeans, and a big ol' belt buckle. And now you're 'ma'aming' me?" She shook her head. "Does everybody around here have two names? Jim-Bob? Billy-Joe? Rob Lee?"

"Mom!" Holly hissed.

Rob Lee stood up and faced Rachel, hooking a thumb over his belt.

"Some do. My daddy's name was Jack Benny. My momma's name was Lydia Dale. She raised me to be polite to every lady I meet." He stared at her for a long moment, looking her over, hat to heel. "Whether they deserve the title or not."

Rachel narrowed her eyes and glared at him with an expression that Holly knew well, the "cobra preparing to strike" face. But before she could speak, he turned his back on her and went back to work, talking as he did.

"As I was saying, here in Texas, some of us have two first names," he said, grunting slightly as he used his legs to lift the heavy air conditioner onto the windowsill. "Some don't. Most of us like Mexican food, country music, football, and minding our own business. But not everybody. Nobody's playing a part here. We don't apologize for who we are."

He straightened up, wiped the sheen of sweat from his brow with the back of his hand, and turned to face Rachel.

"So if you're thinking of staying here, you'll have to live with that. We're not planning to change."

"Oh, believe me!" Rachel spat. "I won't linger in this godforsaken town one minute more than I have to. Holly might have to stay, poor thing, but *I'll* be out of here first thing in the morning."

"Well, then . . . guess that'll be our loss."

He turned to Holly. "If you'll excuse me, ma'am, I'll start bringing in your furniture."

After he left, Rachel spun around to face her daughter.

"Have you ever in your life met anyone so incredibly arrogant? So rude?"

"Almost never," said Holly and clamped her lips tight to keep from smiling.

Chapter 11

Within two weeks of returning to the ranch, Rob Lee moved out of the house and into the barn. There were several reasons for this, nearly all having to do with his family.

First off, Grandma Taffy's grasp on reality was intermittent. Sometimes she was completely sane and knew exactly who he was; other times she was as crazy as a soup sandwich and thought he was one of her old boyfriends from back in the day. Sounded like there'd been a lot of them.

One night, after consuming a half-pint of whiskey and finally getting to sleep, he woke with a shout to find Grandma Taffy in his bed. That wasn't just creepy; it was dangerous. Before he realized what was going on, he had his hands around her throat. Thank God he came to himself before he'd hurt her. After that, he and Cady agreed that it'd be better and safer for everybody if he slept in the tack room.

The move came as a relief, and not just because

of the incident with Taffy. Sometimes, when she didn't think he was looking, he'd catch Cady staring at him. He was sure that she was looking at him, wondering why he was here and Nick wasn't. It made him feel guilty and sad and angry all at once.

And then there was Linne. She was a cute kid but needy. And horse-crazy.

She constantly talked about horses, drew pictures of horses, read books about horses, and watched movies about horses. Her favorite was *National Velvet*, the old Elizabeth Taylor version. She watched it so often that she wore out the DVD. What she didn't do was ride horses. There was no one to teach her how.

The ranch hands were too busy with their work to take Linne riding, and Taffy, even had she been in her right mind, was too old. Cady had been thrown when she was nine while trying to mount a horse that she'd been warned was far too wild for her and had been scared to ride ever after.

Apparently Nick, on a rare stretch home between deployments, had promised Linne that he'd teach her when she was older. She'd only been three at the time but she hadn't forgotten. Now that Nick was dead, she somehow expected Rob Lee to make good on that promise, to step into her dad's shoes.

Rob Lee couldn't do it. Nor could he explain to her why he couldn't. How just the sight of her made his heart close like a fist and his throat tighten to the point where he hardly dared speak or even breathe because, if he did, he might start to scream and the vibrations of those screams would become like shrapnel, tearing apart what he was trying so hard to hold together.

He couldn't say that to a six-year-old. He couldn't say that to anybody, because if he did, they'd think he was as crazy as Grandma Taffy. Who knew? Maybe he was.

It was better this way, living in the tack room, keeping to himself. Better for everyone. Safer for everyone. Himself most of all.

Another good reason for sleeping in the tack room was because he could hear people coming. The door and floors creaked and the chickens would cluck and flutter when people walked into the barn, which was good. He didn't like people sneaking up on him. His response could be embarrassing, like it had been when he dropped and broke the new tenant's air conditioner.

But even without a creaky door and floors, there was no chance of Linne and Howard sneaking up on him. Linne was too much of a chatterbox for that, and, like a lot of six-year-olds, she hadn't yet embraced the concept of an "inside voice," especially when she was excited about something. She seemed to be very excited at the moment, talking to Howard.

Rob Lee was sitting on the edge of his bed, buttoning up his shirt, when they came into his room.

"Hey, Joe! Whaddaya know?" Howard beamed and embraced him tightly.

"Not much," he said. "Cady told me you were coming down for the weekend. How you doin', Hoss?"

That was a joke between them. For their tenth birthday, their late grandpa Dutch had given them a boxed set of *Bonanza* episodes. They loved watching that show, especially in the company of their grandpa, who knew every episode by heart. Soon, they started calling each other by the character names, cracking each other up by calling Howard, who stood only five foot three, Hoss, after the beefy character played by Dan Blocker, and Rob Lee, who stood a head taller than his cousin, Little Joe, after the shorter character played by Michael Landon. After a while, Howard dropped the "Little" and called his cousin just "Joe."

"Fine." Howard shrugged, then frowned. "Miss my girlfriend. A *lot*. Momma wouldn't let me stay at Jenna's while she went to Connecticut. Made me come here instead."

"That's rough, Hoss. But it's just for a couple of days, right? And, anyway, I'm glad to see you."

"Me too," Howard said, his face suddenly somber. "I'm glad you didn't get blowed up in Afghanistan."

Rob Lee looked away, discomfited by the direct, guileless way Howard had of saying what was on his mind. He'd seen his cousin four or five times since returning from combat, and every time, Howard said the same thing. He wished Howard would forget about it.

"Yeah, well . . . I'm here." Rob Lee sat back down and pulled his boots out from underneath the bed.

Linne, who had been humming to herself and swishing her blue skirt from left to right while they talked, piped up, "Rob Lee, can you take us riding? Howard wants to go."

"Can't," Rob Lee said, looking down as he pulled on his boots. "I've got work to do."

"But that's what you said last Saturday," Linne moaned.

"And it's still true. I've got stock to feed and water. There's no days off on a ranch. Maybe next week."

Linne stuck out her lower lip and kicked the dirt floor with the toe of her blue boot. Howard frowned, looking from Linne to Rob Lee.

"We could help with the chores," Howard suggested. "Then you'd get done faster and have time for a ride."

Rob Lee gave a quick shake of his head. "Can't," he said again.

"Why not?" Linne demanded.

Rob Lee cleared his throat, sniffed, and stood

up. "Because. I've got to go into town and deliver some more furniture to the rental place, mow the lawn, and . . . stuff."

"Can I come?" Linne asked hopefully. "I like doing stuff."

"Sorry, kiddo. You'd be in the way. Anyway, aren't you supposed to go in and help your momma at the quilt shop?"

"Not until ten."

"I'll be gone before then. So you'd better get going."

Linne stuck out her lip even further. Rob Lee, feeling guilty, reached over to ruffle her hair, but she jerked her head away and skulked off toward the house.

"Can I come with you?" Howard asked. "I don't want to go to the quilt shop. Everybody will ask me about Momma and I don't want to talk about her. I'm mad at her."

Rob Lee was genuinely surprised by his cousin's statement. Mary Dell adored Howard and the feeling was mutual. But Howard's stormy expression made it clear that he meant what he said. Well, why not? Howard was normally pretty easygoing, but he was entitled to his feelings and frustrations, just like anybody else. And while Rob Lee had always loved his aunt, she could be a little smothering at times. No grown man wanted his mother telling him what he could and couldn't do.

"Sure, Hoss," Rob Lee said. "Help me feed the stock and then we'll get going."

Howard's customary smile returned. "Okay, Joe. You got it!"

During the drive, Howard poured out his complaints.

"She won't let me grow up. I'm almost thirty! I want to get on with my life."

"I hear that," Rob Lee said.

Rob Lee had been twenty-two years old when he enlisted. Back then, when he pictured himself as an old man of thirty, which wasn't often, he figured he'd have his life completely pulled together.

That was one of the reasons he'd joined the Marines, because he wanted to jump-start his life, grow up, and find a purpose. For a while, it felt like he had. He was proud to be part of something bigger than himself, to work shoulder to shoulder with men he respected, to face difficult, sometimes dangerous, challenges, proud to be part of something that mattered.

And now here he was, nearly thirty and completely rudderless. At least Howard had a plan. That was more than he could say.

"I don't want to live on the ranch," Howard declared. "And I don't want to leave my friends in Dallas."

"Especially Jenna?" Rob Lee asked.

Howard bobbed his head. "I love her. Someday, I might want to marry her."

"Really?"

"Uh-huh. That's what you do when you're in love. Don't tell Momma I said that. I don't think she likes Jenna anymore. Rob Lee, have you ever been in love?"

Rob Lee mentally cataloged his relationships up to this point.

"Not really. There's a lot of girls I've liked. And a few girls I've . . ." He shrugged. "Never mind."

"Slept with? Is that what you were going to say? I know about sex." Howard gave him a slightly chiding glance. "But if you feel that way about a girl, you ought to marry her."

"Is that why you want to marry Jenna?"

"Not just that. But I think about it a lot," Howard admitted.

"Most guys do."

"But it's not just because of that. I just like to be with Jenna," Howard said, a smile coming into his voice and eyes. "She is so beautiful and creative. She's a very good painter. We laugh all the time. Someday maybe we will get married. Not yet, though. I don't want to be alone forever, but right now, I want to be on my own."

"Makes sense," Rob Lee said.

"Momma doesn't think so," Howard said glumly.

"Give her some time," Rob Lee advised. "She

probably doesn't want to be alone forever either."

"I was thinking about that," Howard said in a practical tone. "Momma should get married. Hub-Jay likes her. She likes him too."

Rob Lee smiled. "Yeah. I don't think it's quite that easy, Hoss."

When they pulled up in front of the cottage, Rob Lee got out of the truck first.

"Howard, knock on the door and let her know we're going to do some work in the yard. I'll unload the mower."

"What's her name?"

Rob Lee shrugged. "I didn't ask. Just let her know we're here, then come back and give me a hand, okay?"

Howard went through the rusty garden gate, climbed the steps to the porch, and knocked on the door. Rob Lee, busy manhandling the mowing equipment and hauling it around to the side yard, didn't see him talking to the woman or going inside the cottage.

Ten minutes later, Rob Lee took a loop around the yard, looking for Howard. When he didn't find him, Rob Lee figured he must still be inside, talking to the renter. You couldn't fault him for that.

She was beautiful, the kind of girl who, a couple of years back, might have driven him to despair, knowing she was way out of his league. That was one good thing about life as it was now; having concluded that he was better off on his own, he didn't agonize about beautiful, unattainable women. Of course, that didn't mean he didn't notice them when they came along. He might not have gotten that girl's name, but he sure enough remembered what she looked like. A face and body like that were hard to forget. So was that mother of hers. What a piece of work! But the girl was fine. No two ways about it.

He smiled to himself as he mounted the porch steps. Yeah. No wonder Howard was taking his time.

Before Rob Lee had a chance to knock, Howard opened the door.

"I'm going to be a while," he said. "I've got to help this lady fix her sewing machine. She's got the bobbin so tangled up it made her cry."

Rob Lee rolled his eyes. "Another one? What is it about this town? Attracts quilters like flies."

"She's not a quilter," Howard informed him. "But she has to learn. Fast. Her name is Holly. She's my replacement."

"Your replacement?" Rob Lee frowned. It took a moment for Howard's meaning to register.

"You mean . . . on TV? But she doesn't know how to quilt?"

"Don't tell Momma," Howard said seriously. "If she finds out that Holly can't quilt, she might not let her take my place."

The woman, Holly, walked up to the door and stood behind Howard. His cousin was right; she'd been crying. There was mascara smeared under her eyes. Why did women wear that stuff any_way? A couple of tears and they ended up looking like a raccoon with a hangover. No, Holly Whatever-Her-Name definitely didn't look as good to him as she had the last time he'd seen her, which was kind of a relief.

"Hi again." She gave a sheepish little wave.

"Hi."

"So . . . Howard is Mary Dell Templeton's son? And you're her nephew? Oh. This is kind of awkward. Especially now that you know I can't quilt." She let out a little sputter of disgust. "Leave it to me. I could have rented any house in town, but no. I had to pick this one."

"Hey," Rob Lee replied, "there's only about five places for rent in the whole town, so it's not like you had long odds. I won't say anything to my aunt, but . . . you seriously don't know how to quilt? Not at all?"

Holly shook her head.

"Huh. Then why'd they hire you? Just because of your looks?"

Holly's lips became a line. A fiery little flash came into her eyes, a look that Rob Lee recognized from his encounter with her mother.

"None of my business," he said quickly. "Anyway . . . you start filming after the holidays, right? Howard, think you can teach her how to quilt by then?"

Howard shook his head. "I'm only here for the weekend. We need to find her a real quilt teacher."

Rob Lee pulled his phone out of the back pocket of his jeans.

Holly, who had started biting her nails during this exchange, pulled her fingers away from her mouth. "What are you doing?"

"Calling the quilt shop."

Holly swallowed hard. "Your aunt's quilt shop?"

"She's in Connecticut for the weekend. I'm calling my sister," he said, and then held the phone up to his ear.

"Cady? Yeah, I'm over at the rental. We've got ourselves kind of a situation. Any chance you can come over here?"

Chapter 12

Mary Dell lay flat on the bed in an upstairs suite at the Beecher Cottage Inn, a throw pillow clutched to her chest, staring at the ceiling and feeling despondent. It was an emotion that was almost entirely unfamiliar to her, especially considering her current surroundings.

Mary Dell had been looking forward to her pilgrimage to New Bern, Connecticut, for weeks. The annual quilting getaway was normally a highlight of her year, partly because she so rarely had time to simply quilt for her own pleasure instead of for business, but mostly because she got to spend time with her dear friend Evelyn Dixon.

Evelyn and Mary Dell had been neighbors in Dallas. Evelyn had helped Mary Dell adjust to life in the city, and Mary Dell had helped Evelyn through a painful divorce. When Evelyn left Dallas for Connecticut to begin a new life and open a quilt shop, the two women maintained their friendship through phone calls, e-mail, and occasional visits, including the annual Cobbled Court Quilt Circle retreat, always held at the Beecher Cottage Inn. Over the years, Mary Dell had fostered friendships with the members of the circle, but Evelyn was the real reason she returned to Connecticut year after year. Even though they lived so far apart, Evelyn was her best friend.

After the second knock, Mary Dell called out permission to come in. Evelyn stuck her head around the door.

"I wondered where you'd gone off to. Are you feeling okay?" Evelyn asked.

"I'm fine. Just decided to come up to my room for a while. I'm just not in the mood to quilt."

"Now, those are words I have never imagined coming from your mouth." Evelyn stepped into the room and sat down on the edge of the bed. "So, what's up? And don't say 'nothing,' " she directed, a no-nonsense edge coming into her voice.

"It's complicated."

Evelyn just sat there, waiting.

"It's Howard," Mary Dell finally said. "No . . . maybe not. Maybe it's me. Maybe I'm the complication."

They talked for close to an hour.

Mary Dell felt bad about keeping Evelyn from her quilting time, but each time she mentioned it, Evelyn would brush her off, telling her not to worry about it because this was more important. Then she would lead Mary Dell back to the story, helping her open up, listening for long stretches before asking questions.

What did he say? What did you say? What did it make you feel? Think? Question? Doubt? Cry?

Evelyn's questions helped Mary Dell to finally see the connections between her words and thoughts, actions and emotions, and realize that she really *was* the complication. There were no maybes about it.

"I'm going to remind you of something you told me a long time ago," Evelyn said, "about how right it felt after Howard was born. You were so worried about Howard. You wondered about his future, his chances of success or happiness. Would he ever be able to walk? To talk? Would he learn to read a book or ride a bicycle, hold a job, a conversation? Would he know happiness in life and find purpose? Do you remember?"

Mary Dell's eyes filled with tears, thinking back to that day, to the unfathomable tangle of questions that had filled her in the weeks, months, and years after Howard's birth, and how, in time, the answer to every one of them had been "yes."

"What struck me when you were telling that story," Evelyn continued, "was that those worries you had for Howard were the same worries I had for my son. I think those are the same questions every mother asks at some point.

"And a lot of the questions that you had about Howard's future then are the same ones he is asking himself now. He wants to know if he can make it on his own, if he has anything unique to offer the world. That's what everyone wants to know."

"But it's different with Howard."

"Because he happens to have Down syndrome? Howard faces challenges that other people don't. But he also has an advantage that most people don't—a mother who poured herself into him, who gave him an appetite for life and made him believe he could do anything he set his mind to, because she believed it too."

"I still do," Mary Dell said. "I always have."

"I know. So what are you really afraid of here? That Howard can't survive without you? Or that you can't survive without him?"

Mary Dell was silent for a long time after that. She didn't respond to her friend's question

135

because she knew she didn't have to. Evelyn already knew the answer. Now Mary Dell did too.

Mary Dell sat up and leaned over to give her friend a hug.

"Thank you."

"Don't mention it."

"You're right," Mary Dell said, sweeping her index finger beneath her now dry eyes, just to make certain no telltale mascara smears remained. "I shouldn't be sitting here feeling sorry for myself. I should be celebrating the fact that I've done my job and raised a kind, capable, and independent man.

"You know something?" Mary Dell said, her expression brightening. "That's exactly what I should do. Celebrate! Howard and Rob Lee are both turning thirty in February. I should throw them a birthday party."

"That's the spirit," Evelyn said with a grin.

"But it needs to be something big. Something elegant," Mary Dell said in a half-musing tone, the wheels already turning in her mind. She wanted to celebrate Rob Lee just as much as Howard, to let him know how much she and the whole family loved him. She would give him a beautiful party, the kind of celebration that Lydia Dale would have wanted to give him, had she been alive. Maybe it would help to lift him out of this funk.

"We should have it in Dallas," she declared after a moment's consideration. "At the Hollander Grand! With food and music and dancing. I'm sure Hub-Jay will help me with the planning."

"Sounds perfect," Evelyn replied, and got to her feet.

Mary Dell did the same, smoothing out her hair as she followed Evelyn through the door of the suite and down the stairs toward the sewing room to join the rest of the group. Now that the despondency had lifted, Mary Dell was eager to get back to quilting.

"Do you think you and Charlie can come?" she asked as they descended the stairs. "I'll have to decide on a date, but it would be sometime in mid-February."

"Wouldn't dream of missing it."

Chapter 13

It was a little past eight in the morning. Spurs wouldn't open for another three hours, but Hub-Jay was sitting at his usual corner table. Emerson, the restaurant's executive chef, and David, the manager, were sitting with him, going over menu options.

"I want something special. This will be my last chance to see Mary Dell before she moves to Too Much, so I need you to stretch yourself here, Em."

The chef, a stocky man with a beard and several piercings in his ears, crossed his arms over his chest. "I *always* stretch myself, Hub-Jay."

Hub-Jay lifted both hands and dipped his head forward, an insincere but necessary gesture of humility. Emerson was a pain and a prima donna, but he was also an artist and had to be coddled a bit.

"Forgive me, I misspoke. What I should have said is that I wanted to give you a free hand and room to let your imagination soar, to create something completely original, no holds barred, no expense spared. I want this to be an intimate and truly memorable occasion, a meal that she'll want to linger over, where every single bite is a . . ." Hub-Jay cast his eyes to the ceiling briefly, searching for the right words. "A discovery, a revelation."

Emerson sniffed. Uncrossed his arms. "How about a tasting menu? Say . . . eight courses?"

"Perfect. Genius." Hub-Jay turned to David. "I'll rely on you to select the wine pairings. It won't be easy. You know Miss Mary Dell prefers sweet wines."

"I was already thinking about that, Mr. Hollander. I suggest flutes of Veuve Clicquot to begin and later a New Zealand sauvignon blanc, Cloudy Bay 2009. With dessert, we'll serve a 2010 Le Clos, Vouvray."

David, unlike the truculent head chef, always

treated his employer with deference, but also without a trace of obsequiousness, being neither fawning nor familiar, just unfailingly polite. This was how he treated everyone, from the governor to the garbageman. It was a rare quality in any man, no matter how genteel his upbringing, and David's upbringing, like Hub-Jay's, was anything but.

Raised in the remotest regions of West Texas, David had moved to Houston in his teens and been hired as a busboy at one of the smaller Hollander properties. Hub-Jay noticed him early on and saw that he learned quickly and was eager to improve himself. In a matter of months, David's West Texas twang disappeared and his vocabulary expanded. His promotions had been quick and well deserved.

Hub-Jay liked David. They were very similar men, pulled-up-by-the-bootstraps sort of men. David didn't know it yet, but Hub-Jay was considering promoting him to manager of the property he was building in Fort Worth. There would be a learning curve, but Hub-Jay was confident David could handle it.

"Okay," Emerson said, pushing himself up from his seat, "if that's it, I'll get back to my kitchen. The pastry chef had a meltdown this morning."

"Vivian?" Hub-Jay's brow creased with concern. "Why? What's wrong?"

"Nothing. I said her madeleines had the texture of pre-chewed gummy bears and she burst into tears. Pfft." Emerson lumbered off.

"David, check on Vivian later, will you? Send her some flowers and sign my name. Good executive chefs are hard to find and keep, but so are good pastry chefs."

"Of course, Mr. Hollander."

"Also, I want a fresh arrangement on the table. Tell the florist to keep it simple. All white blooms. And can you check with Gene and see what suites we have open that night? Mary Dell's furniture will be on the moving truck, so I'd like to offer her a room in the hotel—the best we've got."

"Perhaps we can speed up the renovations on the Alvarado suite," David suggested. "If so, Miss Mary Dell could be the first guest to stay there."

"She'll love that. Good idea, David. I want it to be a very special evening."

"I'm sure it will be, Mr. Hollander—so special that she'll want to return very soon. Perhaps permanently?"

David smiled ever so slightly and looked his employer directly in the eye, holding his gaze a beat longer than he normally might. Hub-Jay returned his smile.

"Exactly."

Mary Dell had been too busy with the move to join Hub-Jay for their usual Friday lunches, but in the weeks that followed, he'd thought of little else but her.

They were an unlikely pair. Though they'd both built successful businesses with few resources besides desperation and diligence, Hub-Jay had worked hard to distance himself from his humble beginnings, transforming himself into the person he wanted to be, a man of elegance, discretion, and uncompromising taste.

Mary Dell, on the other hand, embraced, even reveled in, her country-girl roots. Her speech was laced with old-time Texas sayings—a capable man was described as "a three-jump cowboy," a similarly clever woman as having "some snap in her garters." Her taste in clothing and jewelry could best be described as Dolly Parton meets Madonna; Mary Dell had never met a plunging neckline, zebra print, or rhinestone she didn't love.

Hub-Jay thought her crow-like affinity for glittery objects had mellowed since he'd first met her, but perhaps he'd just gotten used to it. Either way, he had no desire to change her; she was perfect as she was. Mary Dell laughed easily, loudly, and often, and attacked her food the same way she attacked life, with gusto. And whether in spite of that or because of it, Hub-Jay had fallen in love with her.

Mary Dell didn't know that. But why would she? He hadn't known either, not until recently.

Because the truth was, until recently, he hadn't known what it meant to truly love a woman.

Sure, he'd had plenty of women. He'd indulged his appetites at will, perhaps overindulged, so much so that he'd lost interest. And why wouldn't he? Though the hair and eye colors were different, the scores of women he dated were all the same: as perfectly proportioned, coiffed, and clad as mannequins in a Neiman Marcus window, and nearly as hard to hold a conversation with.

The fault was his; he knew that now. Those were the women he'd sought out time and time again. As a young man, back when he didn't have two nickels to rub together, women didn't give him the time of day. Or if they did, he hadn't noticed. He was too busy working, trying to make himself into the man he wanted to be, to worry about women. But once he'd become that man, made some money and a reputation for himself, he was surrounded by women, each more beautiful than the last. He collected them like trophies, as symbols of his success, but the thrill he experienced in acquiring them was always temporary.

He'd treated them badly, used them. Hub-Jay had realized that long ago. Of course, they'd been trying to use him, too, as a meal ticket and a retirement plan, but that didn't make it right. That was another reason he'd sworn off any real relationships with women. As a boy and a young man, he'd had all kinds of ambitions, but womanizer wasn't on the list. He'd wanted to be a successful man, a wealthy man, but also a good man.

And Mary Dell made him want to be a better man, a man worthy of her love.

When she told him she was leaving Dallas, it was like being told that the sun would stop rising; he couldn't conceive of a world without that source of heat and light whose presence he'd come to take for granted. How would he survive in the void?

And when she'd told him how that guy, that Jason, had spoken to her, he'd proposed impulsively, the words spilling forth in an instinctive, almost primal compulsion to defend and protect her.

His declaration took them both by surprise. But when she got up and left him sitting alone at the table, he'd felt like the sun really had set forever, and he had realized he'd spoken truly and from his heart.

He didn't just want to defend Mary Dell; he wanted to protect and cherish and keep her, always. He wanted to marry her. He'd never felt that way about anyone before. He loved her.

He wanted her physically, too. Just the thought of her stirred up emotions and desires he'd believed were dead in him. And he thought about her all the time.

She didn't know, because he'd never told her.

Even now, if he did tell her, she probably wouldn't believe him. Having been hurt and betrayed before, Mary Dell had built walls to separate herself from the possibility of love so that no one could ever betray or hurt her again. Hub-Jay was certain of it. If not, someone would surely have claimed her heart long ago.

But Hub-Jay would climb those walls, or tear them down, brick by brick. No matter how long it took, he wouldn't take no for an answer.

Chapter 14

Christmas was a strange day for Holly. It was the first time she'd ever spent the holiday alone. Rachel had left a few gifts for her—a couple of new tops, a necklace, an iTunes gift card, and a vintage, hardbound copy of *Black Beauty*, which was really kind of sweet. After opening her presents, Holly tried calling Rachel to say thank you and wish her a merry Christmas but ended up leaving a message on her mother's voice mail. They hadn't parted on very good terms, and Holly knew how stubborn Rachel could be when she was mad about something. Even so, Holly really did think she'd call back, but she didn't and that hurt.

Holly couldn't say that she loved quilting, but on that day, she was glad for the distraction quilting provided. It helped keep her mind off Rachel, or at least helped focus her mind enough so she could think it through a little more rationally, finally concluding that Rachel was either having some kind of tantrum or so wrapped up in her new love affair that she had forgotten she had a daughter. Either way, Rachel would get over it eventually—she always had before.

In the meantime, Christmas or not, Holly had work to do, and that's what she did, work, on Christmas Day, and the next day, and the day after that, only stopping to sleep, eat, and go to the bathroom. But all those hours and all that effort didn't seem to be doing much to improve Holly's skill or confidence in quilting. With only a few days left until the start of filming, she was more anxious than ever.

Holly had a habit of talking to herself when nobody else was around. She did so now, talking herself through the steps required to insert a new bobbin into the sewing machine, something Cady had taught her how to do earlier in the week.

"Check the bobbin case for lint." Holly lowered her head and peered into an open compartment of the machine. "No lint," she announced. "Now hold the bobbin with the thread coming down on the left. Insert the bobbin into the case. Slide the thread between the doohickeys. Pull until it clicks into the thingamajig. Excellent!" she exclaimed, hearing the click.

"Going on. Thread the needle, which," she reminded herself in a tone meant to inspire confidence, "you *totally* have down at this point. Then push the"—her finger hovered searchingly over a computerized panel—" 'double arrow' button.

"Once." The threaded sewing needle tip dipped down into the machine. "And twice. Pull gently to bring up the bobbin thread, and . . . voilà! You are a genius!"

Eight minutes later, she was talking to herself again as she stabbed a seam ripper into a tangled nest of thread, calling herself names. She didn't hear Cady's knock or notice her come through the door of the second bedroom, which now served as Holly's sewing room. When Cady tapped her on the shoulder, Holly yelped so loudly that Cady nearly dropped the big cardboard box she was carrying.

"You're almost as jumpy as Rob Lee," Cady said, then set the box on the floor.

"Sorry," Holly said. "I was kind of . . . focused." She held up her mangled quilt block. "I can't understand it! I did everything just like you told me to—put the bobbin in like a 'p,' drew up the thread . . ."

Cady took the block from Holly's outstretched hand. "Computerized sewing machines can be temperamental. Why did you buy this model? It's got three hundred and fifty-six stitches. At this point, you need three—straight stitch, backstitch, and zigzag. That's it."

"I thought more stitches would make quilting easier."

"It might," Cady said, "if you had *any* idea what you were doing."

Holly, feeling foolish, felt her cheeks color.

"Oh, don't mind me," Cady said, picking up a strip of fabric Holly had left lying on the table. "I had a fight with Rob Lee and I'm still ticked."

Cady looked down at her hand as she wound the fabric strip around her palm, only to unwind it and begin again, like she was trying, unsuccessfully, to bandage an old wound.

"I can't run the ranch and the shop at the same time!" she exclaimed after a few moments of silence. "I can't do everything by myself. Even if I didn't have the shop to run, I still couldn't manage the ranch. I can do the business part, but when it comes to dealing with livestock, I'm definitely out of my comfort zone.

"But Rob Lee practically grew up in those barns. He used to tag along after Graydon, our stepdad, like a lovesick pup. Graydon was an expert on anything with hooves, and he passed it all on to my little brother. Rob Lee wasn't ever that wild about dealing with the cattle and sheep—I think he did that mostly to please Graydon—but he sure loved horses. And they loved him. It was like he could read their minds.

For a while, I thought he might grow up to be a competition rodeo rider, but after Momma and Graydon died, he seemed to lose interest in a lot of things that he'd loved before.

"I just really thought having Rob Lee home would be a help. If not for me"—she sighed—"at least for Linne."

Cady tossed aside the fabric strip, then picked up a seam ripper and started attacking the knotted thread on Holly's mangled quilt block, leaning against the table while she worked and talked.

"You know, Nick got sent on so many deployments that Linne barely knew him. It's kind of a blessing and a curse," Cady said, methodically tearing through the tangled threads. "On the one hand, I worry that she won't remember him at all when she gets older. On the other hand, not remembering him means she doesn't miss him so much. But Linne just wants a daddy. Or someone like a daddy."

Holly hadn't met Linne, but her heart hurt as Cady spoke. She knew how it felt to be fatherless, adrift and unclaimed, like a piece of lost luggage with no label, nothing to explain where and to whom you belonged.

Holly blinked, embarrassed in case Cady should see tears in her eyes. But Cady's eyes were on her work, her voice solid but soft, as if she, too, had fallen into the habit of talking to herself.

"I hoped Rob Lee would step into the void

when he came home," Cady said. "When Linne was born, he was so excited. He bought this huge stuffed giraffe for her nursery—four feet tall. Now he won't even look her in the eye."

Cady shoved the ripper hard along a long line of stitches. The severed threads made a popping sound, like buttons bursting off a fat man's shirt.

"She came into the house crying this morning, asking why Uncle Rob Lee hates her. Hates her!"

Cady looked up, and her eyes, far from tear filled, were snapping with anger.

"I stormed out to the barn to ask Rob Lee if it'd kill him to spend half an hour playing with his niece, but we just ended up in a shouting match. Which I actually kind of enjoyed," she said, lips bowing into a grim little smile, "seeing as he was hungover. That was his excuse for telling Linne to get lost, but it would have been the same even if he was sober—which is getting to be kind of a rare occurrence."

"He wasn't like that before, was he?"

"Before Nick died?" Cady shook her head. "No. Not even when he came home between the first deployment and the second."

"Sounds like he's depressed."

"Yeah. He's not the only one."

Holly felt her cheeks go hot again. *Genius. Next maybe you could tell her that the sky is blue.*

Holly had seen Rob Lee only twice, on that first day here at the house, and the day after, when he'd come to trim the hedges—well, more like hack the hedges. They were so overgrown. Even though it was December, it was hot, so she'd brought him a glass of ice water. After he drained it, Rob Lee handed her the empty glass, said thanks, and went back to work.

That was it—the sum total of their exchanges. Holly obviously couldn't claim to know him, but she was sure he'd never intentionally hurt anybody. He was suffering, drawing into himself and sometimes lashing out, like a wounded animal. He was in pain. So was Cady.

"I'm sorry," Holly said, "that was a stupid thing to—"

"No," Cady replied, brushing off Holly's apology. "I didn't mean to snark at you. I'm still mad. Seems like I always am these days," she said, and started picking tiny threads off Holly's quilt block.

"For the first three months after Nick died, I cried every day. Then I got mad and stayed that way. Sometimes I wonder if I'll ever just feel like . . . like me again."

Cady paused, fingers still, head lowered, staring at the bit of patchwork.

"Sometimes," she whispered, "I wish I'd never met Nick. Isn't that awful?"

Holly didn't know what to say to that. She really wanted to get up from her chair and give Cady a hug, tell her to go ahead and cry. But she didn't think she knew her well enough for that. Besides, Cady didn't look like she wanted to cry. She looked like she wanted to punch something.

"Sorry," Cady said, shaking off her reverie. "I don't know why I told you all that."

"Sometimes it's easier to talk to strangers."

"Maybe. Here you go." She handed Holly the fabric patches, now free of knots, tangles, and stray threads. "Give it another go. But *not* on that machine."

Cady bent down and opened the lid of the cardboard box she'd left on the floor and pulled out a white sewing machine, slightly smaller than Holly's, with two dials on the front.

"I brought you something, kind of a belated Christmas present. Although, it's just on loan, so it doesn't really qualify as a present. Anyway, this is one of our class machines. It has eighteen stitches," she said, pointing to the dials, "which is still fifteen more than you need at the moment, but it's a lot simpler to operate."

Cady thunked the machine down onto the table. Holly got up to investigate. "Thanks! Is the bobbin easier to load?" she asked hopefully.

"The bobbin's the same. You just need more practice. If you hear the machine making that *thunkety-thunking* sound, stop stitching and check the seam before you sew for ten miles. If it's tangled, rethread the bobbin and try again. If that doesn't work, rethread the whole thing, top and bottom thread. Nine times out of ten, that'll solve the problem."

"Really? Why?"

"No one knows. It's a mystery."

Holly pulled a chair up next to the table. She wished Cady had told her about rethreading the top thread before. But maybe she had and Holly forgot. She'd listened to so many instructions and read so many manuals that she was starting to feel fuzzy, like maybe there was lint in *her* bobbin case.

"Do you think I'll ever get the hang of this?"

"Absolutely. But it's going to take more than a few days."

"But I've only *got* a few days! Why did I take this job? I am going to end up looking like a complete idiot."

Cady walked over to the sewing table and stood frowning at Holly's pile of Snowball blocks—blocks that were supposed to be easy enough for a beginner. The first couple had turned out, but then it all went horribly wrong. They were all different sizes, and the triangles in the corner were so inconsistent that none of the seams matched up. Cady sorted through the pile of blocks, shaking her head.

"This is hopeless," Holly moaned, watching her. "I'm hopeless. Why did you even agree to take me on as a student?"

"Because you seemed nice. And a little desperate. Also because I want the show to be a success. Every time a new episode of *Quintessential Quilting* airs, our online sales quadruple. We can't make it with a local customer base. We need online sales and tourists to survive. Without the show, I'm not sure we could. If the quilt shop closed, I'd be out of a job. So would a lot of people."

The pebble of anxiety that had been with Holly ever since arriving in Too Much became a boulder. It was bad enough to risk her own career by taking on a job she was so superbly ill suited for; now the future and livelihood of other people were on the line too—Cady, and little Linne, and Mary Dell Templeton, whom she was sure must be a nice person. She had to be to inspire such loyalty in her niece.

But Mary Dell had no way of knowing that her own network was betting against her, setting her up with a clueless co-host precisely because they hoped the show would fail and had recruited Holly to actively assist in its demise.

Well, she wouldn't. That was all.

Jason could weave all the webs he wanted, but that didn't mean Holly was going to play spider to Mary Dell Templeton's fly, not even if it meant she never got the spot on that design show that Jason had bribed her with. No way. No matter what Rachel had advised, she couldn't do that to anyone.

Of course, the way things were going, she could probably sink *Quintessential Quilting* without even trying. Holly buried her face in her hands and groaned.

"Oh, c'mon," Cady said, clucking her tongue. "Don't give up now. Everything is going to be okay."

Holly looked up. "Do you really think so?"

"Sure. Absolutely," she said, in a tone that was only marginally convincing. "But I've got to ask you something: What happened there?"

She pointed at Holly's sleeve. Confused, Holly looked at her arm. Sure enough, she had somehow managed to stitch a Snowball block to her top.

"No idea," Holly said.

Cady laughed. Holly had never heard her laugh before.

"Girl, you are just one hawt mess." Cady picked up the seam ripper to detach the block from Holly's sleeve. "How late were you up sewing last night?"

"I don't know. Till around midnight, I guess."

"Uh-huh. And what time did you start up this morning?"

"Six."

Cady tossed the Snowball block into the pile. "At least you got a break during the holiday. What did you do for Christmas anyway?"

"I kept busy," Holly said casually, not wanting to lie. "You know."

"Oh, no." Cady smacked her palm against her forehead. "I forgot you don't have any family around here. Why didn't you say something? We'd have been happy to have you out to the ranch for Christmas. My grandma Taffy loves cooking for a crowd."

"It's okay. I wouldn't have wanted to impose. Besides, I've got so much to do. We start filming in another week, and look at me," Holly said, spreading her hands to take in the whole disorganized mess that was her sewing room, wonky blocks and all.

"Listen to me," Cady said. "You can't quilt for eighteen hours a day. I'll bet you ten bucks that the three good blocks you made were the first three. Am I right?"

Holly nodded.

"You need to take a break. Get out of this house and go have some fun."

Holly glanced at the pile of Snowball blocks—a hopeless cause if ever she'd seen one. Maybe Cady had a point.

"Okay. So what do people do for fun around here?"

"Not much," Cady admitted. She thought for a moment. "Especially two days after Christmas. But there's an auction over at the Finley farm this afternoon. Old Mr. Finley died last month. His wife wants to sell, but that could take a while. In the meantime, she's got to auction off their horses. She just can't take care of them at her age. Anyway, I promised Linne we'd go." She shrugged. "Not too exciting, but you're welcome to tag along if you want."

Chapter 15

Normally, Mary Dell and Howard would have gone home to Too Much for Christmas, but with the move coming up so quickly, they'd had a hurried holiday in Dallas with a few presents, no decorations besides a tabletop tree, and a simple meal of roast beef, potatoes, salad, and pie, served on stoneware instead of the good china, which was already packed away. As soon as the meal was done, Mary Dell washed the dishes while Howard dried, then wrapped them in newspaper and packed them as well.

On December twenty-seventh, the moving truck arrived.

"Ma'am?" A man dressed in blue coveralls carrying a sewing machine case put it down and wiped a bead of sweat from his brow. "Where does this one go?"

Mary Dell looked up from the cupboard she had just opened, pulled out a teapot and saucepan, and said, "The four big machines go into the truck. Put the small one in the van. It should go to Howard's apartment."

"Never met a lady who had four sewing machines before. What about the boxes of fabric? There's twenty-three of them," he reported. "You want all those in the big truck too?"

Mary Dell set the teapot down on the counter. "Leave that for last," she advised. "I'll sort it out."

The man picked up the machine and went off to the truck. Mary Dell placed the teapot and saucepan in a box marked "Howard—Kitchen," then added a few more items she thought Howard might need.

Howard would eat his dinners with the Morris family, so he would only have to prepare his own breakfasts and lunches and wouldn't need much in the way of kitchenware, but Mary Dell wanted to make sure he was properly equipped anyway. After packing two boxes with pots, pans, glasses, cutlery, and dinnerware, she went off to search for Howard. Though the house looked like it had been ransacked and the truck was already half-full, she was dismayed to see how much was yet to be loaded.

"Where did we collect all this junk anyway? When we moved in, everything we owned fit into a pickup truck," she muttered. "Howard! Where are you? I need you to help me sort through some fabric!"

"In here, Momma!"

She followed the sound of his voice into her office and found him sitting cross-legged on the floor, looking through a pile of old photo albums.

"Baby, we don't have time to look through pictures right now. We've still got to finish up here and get you moved into the apartment. And I've got to meet Hub-Jay for dinner in"—Mary Dell pulled up her sleeve and looked at her watch—"seven and a half hours. So come on and give me a hand, will you, please?"

"I will," he said absently, eyes still on the photo album. "Remember this one?"

The page was open to an eight-by-ten portrait that had been taken nearly thirty years before on the front porch of the ranch. Mary Dell was sitting in a rocker, holding baby Howard in her arms, and Donny was standing right next to her with his hand on her shoulder. She was looking into the camera and smiling. So was Donny.

It was a picture of a happy family.

Howard looked up at her. "Can I have this? For the wall in my apartment?"

Mary Dell glanced from Howard's face to the portrait. It was the only photograph she had of the three of them together. She kept it inside the album instead of putting it on the wall because seeing it always made her heart ache a little.

During all the years of infertility, the miscarriages and dashed hopes, this was the image she'd held on to, a picture of how she imagined life with Donny could be if they were ever fortunate enough to be blessed with a baby—happy, even joyful, and so very close. Close enough to touch.

When Donny abandoned them only weeks after Howard was born, going off to the market for milk and never coming back, Mary Dell had been so depressed she thought she'd die. A part of her had wanted to. After a week or so, Grandma Silky came to visit and, seeing what a state she was in, told her in no uncertain terms to pull herself together, because mommas *didn't* just lie down and die—no matter how badly they might want to.

"When your dreams turn to dust, maybe it's time to vacuum." That's what Grandma Silky had said, and she was right. Sometimes you just had to let things go.

"Of course. It's all yours if you want it. Do you want me to get it framed?"

"No, thank you, Momma." Howard got to his feet, moving a little slower than usual. It wasn't even noon, but he was looking a little tired. Mary Dell felt a brief twinge of concern but quickly dismissed it. Why wouldn't he be tired? It had already been a long day, for both of them.

"Mrs. Morris said she'd drive me to the mall on Saturday. I'll find a frame then. I want to buy some stuff for my groovy new bachelor pad." He snapped his fingers and struck a pose, then laughed.

Mary Dell smiled, but not very broadly. Howard

took a step toward her, laid his hand on her arm. "Momma? You going to be all right without me?" Mary Dell bobbed her head. "You sure?"

"Of course I'm sure." She smiled, more sincerely this time. "Your momma is *always* all right; don't you know that by now?"

"Me too," he said, and wrapped his arms around her.

Chapter 16

Hub-Jay was waiting for her in the lobby, looking especially handsome in a custom-tailored suit of black worsted wool, holding a ribbon-wrapped florist's box in his hands.

"You look beautiful," he said.

"Howard dressed me," she admitted. "Okay, that's not entirely true. I picked out the dress, but he did the accessories. He only let me wear one bracelet and made me get rid of my necklace—the gold choker with those big white urchin thingys on it—because he said it looked like I was being strangled by a sea monster. He made me change my shoes too, black peep-toe pumps instead of the gold sandals with the rhinestone straps. But the cocktail dress was my idea. Leopard prints are in right now," she informed him. "I know this because I've been waiting my whole life for them to *be* in."

"The dress is lovely," he said, and handed her the box. "And so are you."

"My!" she exclaimed as she opened the box and let Hub-Jay tie the ribbons of the sweetly scented gardenia corsage around her wrist, thinking how glad she was that Howard had made her take off those five extra bracelets. "I feel like I've been elected queen of the prom!"

"I wanted to make your last night in Dallas memorable," Hub-Jay said, lifting her hand to his lips, "so you'll remember to come back and see me."

Hub-Jay had never kissed her hand before. Mary Dell was surprised by the gesture, and by the little spark that ran up her arm and through her body as his lips brushed her skin. She laughed nervously and pulled back her hand.

"It's not like I'd forget. I'll be back soon for Howard's birthday party."

Hub-Jay heaved a melodramatic sigh. "Longest six weeks of my life."

Mary Dell rolled her eyes and thumped him on the shoulder with her evening clutch, feeling more comfortable now. He was just teasing her, playing the part.

Hub-Jay summoned a nearby bellboy and handed Mary Dell's bag over to him.

"You're already checked in. Jimmy will take your luggage to your room so we can go right into dinner."

"All right," Mary Dell said, "but first I want to call and check on Howard. He looked so tired when I left, said his back was bothering him a little bit too."

She clicked open the clasp on her evening bag and reached inside, searching for her phone. Hub-Jay clamped his big hand over hers.

"Howard is fine," he said, his voice deep and authoritative. "He probably strained a muscle while carrying a box. And who wouldn't be tired after a day of moving? Except you, of course. You look fresh as a daisy. And twice as lovely."

She smiled, enjoying the compliment, and closed the clutch.

"You're right. I'm sure he's fine. He said he was going to bed early. I'd probably just wake him if I call."

Hub-Jay offered his arm and Mary Dell took it, allowing him to guide her across the lobby and up the staircase.

"See how sensible I've become? How adept at untying the apron strings? I've been practicing."

"Very impressive. Are you hungry?" Hub-Jay asked as they approached the doors of the restaurant, where David was waiting to greet them.

"As a horse! I was thinking of ordering the whole left side of the menu."

"No menu tonight. I've asked the chef to prepare a few special dishes. And I reserved a private dining room. I hope that's all right."

"Oh, my! Now I really do feel like the queen of the ball."

"As far as I'm concerned, that's what you are."

The private dining room Hub-Jay had reserved really wasn't very private—but it was very elegant. All four walls were constructed from thick, soundproof glass, and two of them were lined, from floor to ceiling, with wine racks filled with expensive vintages. A wrought-iron chandelier with a dozen white pillar candles hung from the ceiling, and three more candles, in beautiful glass hurricane holders, sat on the table, casting a warm glow over the room, glinting on the rims of the crystal stemware and sterling silver cutlery.

As Hub-Jay helped her into her chair, Mary Dell started to crack a self-deprecating joke about how much she appreciated dim lighting at this stage of her life, but then David left the room, closing the door behind him, and Mary Dell thought better of it. It didn't seem like the right time for jokes.

The gleam of the candles, the sheen of the glass walls, the deep silence that engulfed them once the door was shut, the sight of other candles, other tables, other diners a few feet beyond the impervious crystal wall, their lips moving without making a sound, created a strange intimacy, a sense of being in the world but not of it, as if they were travelers in a transparent bubble, floating, untouched, above a troubled sea. It really was a beautiful room. And Mary Dell felt beautiful in it, like she truly was the queen of the ball.

No. Better than that.

Aloft in the silent glass bubble, amid the soft glow of the candles and with the faint scent of gardenias hanging in the air, she felt like the Queen of Everything.

The meal was long, relaxing, and incredibly delicious.

When she learned that dinner would be eight courses, Mary Dell felt a little anxious—worried about gaining back the five pounds she'd worked so hard to shed before getting in front of the cameras again. But her concerns were put to rest when she realized that each dish truly would be just a taste, a perfect little mouthful of something delectable.

The appetizer gave her pause, however. She couldn't imagine why anybody who wasn't in danger of starvation would voluntarily eat fish eggs. But when she popped that golden, beautifully crisp little pancake, topped with thick cream and a teaspoon of caviar, into her mouth, she understood the attraction. It was salty and briny and absolutely delicious, like tasting the ocean. And when she followed it up with a sip of champagne, she felt very elegant and more than a little spoiled. A feeling that failed to diminish as the evening wore on and the remaining courses were served, each more delectable than the last, and each accompanied by a different wine, but, again, it was just a taste—a few sips with each dish.

She'd been so busy with traveling, packing, and making arrangements for Howard's new, more independent life that she hadn't seen Hub-Jay since her meeting with Jason, so they spent the first three courses just catching up.

But then, for some reason, Mary Dell started telling Hub-Jay stories about growing up in Too Much. He returned the favor, telling her stories about growing up poor in a small town in Kansas with his mother, an amateur painter, who had done her best to bring beauty and art into their home and imbue her child with a love of both, and about his alcoholic father, who had belittled her efforts and taken out his frustrations on his son. With his mother's blessing, Hub-Jay broke away as soon as he could, landing in Dallas, because that was as far as he could afford to travel by bus, taking a job as a clerk in a cheap hotel, pinching his pennies, moving up to a better hotel, being promoted to concierge, then manager, all before his thirtieth birthday, at which point he got a loan to buy a run-down building in downtown Abilene and remodeled it into a twelve-room boutique hotel.

Of course, Mary Dell knew much of Hub-Jay's

history already. But he'd never shared the details and emotions with her so openly before. Both of them had a tendency to put the best face on every situation and to deflect hurt with humor, which wasn't at all a bad quality—neither of them would have gotten as far as they had without it. But Mary Dell was cognizant of the honor he did her by being so forthcoming, the trust he placed in her by laying his emotions bare.

She returned the favor in kind.

And as she talked—about Howard, about Cady, about Rob Lee, about herself, about the past and the future, the hopes and fears and doubts that accompanied and colored each facet of her life—she felt a peace settle upon her, a lightness of spirit, the pure happiness that comes from making a sympathetic connection with another human being.

It had been so long since a man had shared his heart with her or listened as she shared hers.

When the server cleared away the final course, a tiny portion of salted caramel crème brûlée served in a white porcelain bowl the size and shape of a sparrow egg, Mary Dell glanced at her watch and realized that nearly four hours had passed. It didn't seem possible.

She didn't feel especially tired, but surely Hub-Jay was, so she touched her napkin daintily to her lips, then laid it on the table.

"This has been the most wonderful evening,

Hub-Jay. The flowers, the food, the conversation
. . . I can't thank you enough."

"I wanted to give you a good send-off."

"Let's not think of it as a send-off. I'll be up
here all the time to check on Howard. Whether he
wants me to or not."

She pushed her chair back from the table. Hub-
Jay rose quickly to help her.

"And you know you're welcome to come down
to the ranch anytime," she said.

"I'd like that."

"Bet you'd look good sitting on a horse."

"I doubt that, but, for you, I'm willing to give it
a try."

He laid his hand on the pristine glass, ready to
open the door. Mary Dell rose on her toes and
kissed his cheek.

"Good night, Hub-Jay. Thank you again."

"Don't you want to know where your room is?"

"Oh, that's right!" She laughed. "I'd better go to
the front desk and get a key."

"I already did." He smiled and pulled a plastic
key card from the pocket of his suit. "Come on.
Let me walk you home."

The elevator opened on the top floor. There were
only six doors on the corridor. Hub-Jay turned to
the left and led her to the end of the hall to a door
with a polished gold plaque that said, "Alvarado
Suite."

When Mary Dell stepped across the threshold, her jaw dropped. "Oh, Hub-Jay," she breathed.

It was the biggest, most beautiful hotel suite she'd ever seen, with white wood floors polished to a sheen, walls covered in a subtly textured gray linen, and floor-to-ceiling windows flanked by silk pistachio-colored drapes that overlooked the twinkling city lights; it was furnished with cushy sofas, chairs, and a chaise longue upholstered in white leather as soft and supple as a pair of kid gloves.

"You didn't have to . . . Just a regular room would have been . . ."

Looking and feeling a little dazed, she wandered from the living room into a formal dining room, decorated in the same white, gray, and pistachio color scheme, peeked into a butler's pantry stocked with lead crystal stemware, then down a wide hallway hung with original oil paintings by renowned artists, and into an exquisite bedroom suite with still more floor-to-ceiling windows, an even more spectacular view of the city, and a real fireplace with an elaborately carved mahogany antique mantel that added a surprising yet harmonious note to the otherwise modern interior.

In the bedroom, wood floors gave way to thick oriental carpets in white and pistachio with just a touch of pale pink, muffling the sound of Mary Dell's footsteps.

As her eyes scanned the room, she noticed that

someone had built a fire in the fireplace, placed a silver champagne bucket, two crystal flutes, and a bowl of ripe strawberries on the table near the window, and left a vase filled with pale pink roses on the dresser. The Egyptian cotton duvet and sheets had been turned down on the king-sized bed, and a single pink rose lay on one of the pillows.

The wine pairings that had accompanied the meal had been very small, so Mary Dell wasn't drunk, but those accumulated sips had made her very relaxed and slowed her reactions just slightly. It took an extra beat or two for her to collect and interpret all the evidence. When she did, the feelings of warmth and tenderness she'd been experiencing all evening were joined by something else: panic.

Mary Dell turned to face the door and saw Hub-Jay standing in it without his jacket or his tie. She started to apologize, to explain that she hadn't meant to give him the wrong impression, but . . .

He didn't give her a chance to finish.

He took three long steps toward her, twined his arms around her body, pulled her close, arched his head and shoulders over her upturned face like a sheltering oak, and placed his lips against hers, silencing her apology and suspending her reason.

That sense of panic swelled within her, crowding against those other emotions, tensing her fingers and limbs. She lifted her arms and placed her hands against his shoulders, positioned in such a way so she could have pushed him away if she wanted to, but a second passed and then another with his lips on hers, tender but insistent, his hands warm between her shoulder blades and on the small of her back. Panic subsided, then disappeared entirely, leaving longing in its place, and she realized that pushing him away was the last thing she wanted to do.

She felt her fingertips relax and curve, cupping his shoulders, sliding down to his chest and then around the muscles of his arms to his back, caressing the sharp blades of his shoulders as she parted her lips and melted into his embrace. Hub-Jay spoke her name softly, then kissed her again, holding her even more tightly. He took a step forward and then another, guiding her gently backward, partnering her in a slow dance across the room. She clung to him and followed his lead, willing and thoughtless, until she felt the cool velvet brush of Egyptian cotton on the back of her knees and, beneath that, the yielding firmness of the mattress.

The touch of fabric on flesh jarred her, wakened her to the knowledge of where this dance was leading. She slid her hands to the front of his shoulders again.

This time, she did push him away—not far away, but far enough so she could see his face.

"Hub-Jay, we can't do this."

He looked at her, his breathing labored, as if he'd just run up a flight of stairs, then said, "I want you, Mary Dell. I want you very, very much."

"And I want you. But . . ." She licked her lower lip, trying to buy some time and summon her reason. "I can't. It would be wrong."

"Why? What's wrong about it? I love you."

He loved her?

And yet . . . she couldn't deny that, after tonight, after those intimate hours apart from the world during which they had opened themselves so fully, one to the other, the feelings she had for him were different and deeper than they'd been before.

She wanted to tell him that she needed time to think—about a lot of things—and that she hadn't done this in three decades, had never been with anyone but Donny, that she was afraid of disappointing him, or being disappointed herself, and that indulging the desires that flooded her went against the moral code she'd been raised to believe and had wholeheartedly embraced.

Instead she just said, "We're not married."

He laughed again, this time with joy, and said, "But I want to marry you! I asked you before you went out to Connecticut. Didn't you hear me? Or maybe you didn't think I meant it. It wasn't a very stylish proposal, I'll admit. But I can do better."

He dropped to one knee and took her hand in his. Mary Dell shook her head.

"Hub-Jay, stop. Please. I can't marry you."

"Yes, you can. I know this seems sudden, but . . ."

"Hub-Jay, I'm already married."

The smile fled his face, replaced by an expression of confusion and then of disbelief as her meaning became clear to him.

"Donny? You can't be serious. You mean . . . even after all these years?"

She pressed her lips together, feeling suddenly foolish. "I never divorced him. I thought about it a few times, but I guess a part of me hoped he would come back. At least for the first few years."

Hub-Jay dropped his head forward with a sigh, the weight of it resting against her stomach. Mary Dell laid her hand on his hair.

"And then life went on. I was a young mother, with no one to depend on but myself, busy taking care of Howard and my family, the ranch, and the shop. And then, about five minutes later, I was forty, then fifty, then sixty. At some point, I just figured that ship had sailed. I never divorced Donny. There was no reason to."

Hub-Jay lifted his head, got to his feet, and looked at her with a determination and desire that made her breath catch in her throat.

"Make me your reason." He reached for her.

"But . . . Donny," she said weakly.

172

"I don't care."

He kissed her again, pressed her close, and back, and down. And she let him. Her only thought was how much she didn't want to think, because, at that moment, she didn't care either.

Chapter 17

Holly couldn't stop thinking about the horse.

As they'd driven out to the Finley ranch, Cady had explained about auctions and why this one was unusual. "A lot of times, if people have horses to sell, they'll send them to the livestock auction. Some folks do buy saddle horses there, but a lot of those horses end up being sold to slaughterhouses."

Holly gasped. "You mean they eat them?"

"There are no horse slaughterhouses in the U.S., even though it is legal. A few years back, a couple of companies tried to open horsemeat-processing plants, but the public outcry was huge and it didn't happen. But a lot of horses bought at auction here in the states end up being shipped to processing plants in Mexico or Canada—from here, mostly to Mexico."

"That's terrible," Holly said. "Why would someone do that?"

"It is terrible, but horses are expensive to feed and stable, and they live a long time. People buy a young horse or pony, but they don't always consider the fact that they're signing up for a twenty-five- or thirty-year commitment. Sometimes, even when they do know what they're getting into, their circumstances change. That's what happened here. Mrs. Finley is older and her own health is failing. With her husband gone, she doesn't have the money or stamina to take care of thirteen horses. She's going to sell the farm and move to a retirement home in Waco. She didn't want to send the horses to auction, so she's trying to sell them off locally, to folks she knows will take care of them."

Linne's voice piped up hopefully from the backseat. "Momma, can we get one of Mrs. Finley's horses? I'd take real good care of it. Promise!"

"No," Cady said, her tone uncompromising. "I told you before; we're just looking, not buying."

Linne made a harrumphing noise and slumped in her seat, thumping her head back against it in protest. Holly twisted so she could see her, smiling when she saw the pout on Linne's lips. She was so darned cute! And Holly remembered just how she felt when she was little, how she'd begged and begged Rachel to get her a horse, how the answer had always been no, and how incredibly unfair she'd thought that was. In all fairness, Los Angeles wasn't an easy place to own a horse, not unless you were rich, but when she was a little girl, she didn't see that, or if she did, she didn't care. She'd wanted a horse—period.

Linne was clearly just as horse-crazy as she'd been at that age.

"Hey, Linne," Holly said over her shoulder, "I brought you something."

"What?"

The child's disgruntled expression gave way to bright-eyed curiosity as she watched Holly reach into her bag.

"It's a Breyer!" Linne exclaimed.

"Right," Holly confirmed, as she handed a plastic model horse over the seat. "And not just any Breyer. This is an Andalusian model, and it's retired. It was mine when I was little. Now I want you to have it."

"Really? Thanks!"

Cady glanced in the rearview mirror. Her eyes smiled when she saw Linne, grinning from ear to ear, examining the bay-colored coat and luxurious black mane and tail, tossed to one side, and the daintily lifted foreleg, as if the animal had been frozen in the middle of a dressage move.

Cady shifted her eyes toward Holly and mouthed a silent "thank you."

Eyes still glued on her gift, Linne called out, "Miss Holly? Do you want to sit with me at the auction?"

"Linne, I would *love* that."

The Finleys raised American quarter horses, the most popular breed in North America: hardy, handsome, gentle, and fast, these surefooted horses were the working breed of choice on cattle ranches in the Old West. In the ranch country of Texas, they were still valued for that purpose, as well as for competitive rodeo riding and short-distance racing, but they also made excellent family horses for trail and pleasure riding.

The bulk of those attending the auction were local families looking for a sweet-tempered and good-looking saddle horse. They'd come to the right place.

Each horse was more handsome than the last—roans, palominos, grays, buckskins, and one simply gorgeous pinto. Linne exclaimed over and fell in love with every single one of them, and every time a new horse was led into the ring, she reneged on her promise not to beg her mother to bid.

The first twelve horses went quickly amid spirited bidding, but even though the last one, number thirteen, was offered for an opening bid of only one hundred dollars, no hand rose to claim him.

The gelding, Stormy, a sixteen-year-old American Standardbred, wasn't as handsome as his stablemates. He stood fifteen hands. His coat was brown, his mane and tail were black—that was it. He had no special markings, no white blazes or stockings. He was just a dull brown horse in a very bad mood.

The other horses had followed the trainer calmly into the ring and stood quietly during the bidding, munching apples from the trainer's hand. Stormy, who had to be escorted into the ring alongside another horse, with the mounted trainer holding a lead attached to his halter, started to buck, rear, and writhe as soon as he spotted the crowd of spectators.

An older man standing next to Holly, who wanted to buy a horse for his teenaged grandson but hadn't been able to keep up with the bidding, shook his head firmly when the boy urged him to make a bid.

"No way, Clark. That horse is crazy. Look at him. He won't let anybody touch him, let alone ride him. Standardbreds are harness horses anyway."

"But, Gramps, I'd work with him. This is our last chance! Please. He's only a hundred dollars."

"And a bad bargain at half that price. Dangerous. No amount of working with him will change that. I'll get you another horse. Promise. One that won't kill you."

The old man walked off with his grandson trailing reluctantly behind.

The auctioneer, shouting to be heard over Stormy's frantic whinnies, lowered the starting bid to fifty dollars. When there were still no takers, he thanked everyone for coming and reminded those who'd made winning bids to settle up their payments and make arrangements to pick up their horses before departing.

The crowd dispersed.

As they walked back to the field where the car was parked, Holly glanced over her shoulder. Linne was trailing behind them, involved in an imaginary conversation with her model horse, but Holly kept her voice low just the same.

"Cady, that last horse, the one nobody bid on . . . Stormy? What will happen to him?"

"Well . . ." She, too, kept her voice low and looked over her shoulder, making sure Linne wasn't listening in. "Probably what I said. Old Mrs. Finley can't keep a horse like that. Nobody could."

"But that's terrible!"

"I agree, but you can't blame her. Nobody is going to take that horse off her hands; they'd be crazy to try. He's old, nothing much to look at, and so pissed off he could end up killing somebody. It's sad. Maybe something happened to him. Maybe he was born mean. Either way, what can you do about it?" Cady shrugged and opened the driver's side door. "Some poor creatures are just too broken to save."

Cady was probably right. But still, Holly couldn't stop thinking about the horse. She got into bed a little after midnight, but she couldn't shut down her brain. It was busy, sleepless through the night, thinking about Stormy.

Even though he'd been on one side of the fence and she was safe on the other, when Stormy started bucking and stomping, Holly was scared. But as the horse, living up to his name, stormed furiously around the paddock, snorting and pounding the ground with his hooves, Holly was able to look into his eyes. Not for long—it was no more than a breath—but long enough to see that he was scared too. He was terrified.

The other thing she'd seen that others had not was that, plain brown coloring or not, he was a handsome horse, a beautiful creature, and worth saving. But, like Cady said, a person would have to be crazy to take on a horse like that.

At five in the morning, before it was even light, Holly decided she was crazy.

Holly drove out to the Finley ranch, parked alongside the road, and waited. She saw a light turn on in the upstairs bedroom, and then, about twenty minutes later, just a little before seven, she saw the gray head of an old woman through the kitchen window. She got out of her car and knocked on the door.

The elderly woman, whom Holly recognized from the day before, was understandably cautious. Holly noticed that she kept the screen door closed.

"It's awful early to come calling."

"Yes, ma'am," Holly said, remembering to address her politely, the way Cady always spoke to older ladies. "I'm sorry to bother you. I was at the auction yesterday."

"Oh, that's right! I remember you! Pretty little thing. You're not from around here." Mrs. Finley smiled and opened the screen door. "What happened, honey? Car break down? Do you need to call somebody?"

Holly stepped over the threshold.

"No, ma'am. I came out to talk to you about Stormy. I'd like to buy him."

Chapter 18

In the wee hours of the morning, with the lights of the city still shining diamond bright in the night sky, Mary Dell slowly lifted Hub-Jay's arm from her shoulders, then propped herself up on one elbow, gazing at his sleeping face and form for some long minutes before slipping stealthily from beneath the covers.

As quietly as possible, she gathered her discarded shoes and clothing, lifted her overnight bag off the luggage stand, and padded down the hallway to the second bathroom so she wouldn't wake Hub-Jay.

She emerged ten minutes later wearing minimal makeup, dressed in black slacks and a purple-and-black-striped blouse, her hair combed and corralled by a gold clip. She opened and shut the door of the suite silently, took the elevator to the lobby, and asked a sleepy bellman to bring her car around.

Mary Dell's predawn departure did not stem from any sense of shame or regret. On the contrary, when she woke, drowsy and warm, with her head resting on Hub-Jay's chest and his arm still around her shoulders, the steady and soft whoosh of his breathing the only sound in the room, she felt better than she had in a long time. She felt happy. But it was more complicated than that.

She had tried to puzzle it out there in the bedroom, while studying Hub-Jay's sleeping face, regulating her breathing to his, as if this might help her find the answer and give a name to what she was feeling. At first, she couldn't put her finger on it, but then it dawned on her: this was what it felt like to be loved.

She had nearly forgotten.

That was why she slipped from Hub-Jay's bed without saying good-bye, and made certain that her phone was switched off before making her exit. Not because she was ashamed of what had passed between them, but because she wanted to preserve that feeling for as long as she could and she knew that if Hub-Jay woke he would want to talk about what came next, and she wasn't ready to talk about it.

Many, many years before Howard was born, she'd spent another night with another man who was not yet her husband, and it changed her whole life. Back then, barely more than a child, she'd been touched by a momentary madness, drawn to Donny as inexplicably and irresistibly as a moth is drawn to a flame, having no idea what she was getting herself into and why.

She wasn't a child now.

What had happened in the night, the awakening of passions she thought had passed her by, was not the result of an impulse beyond her control, a Fatal Flaw. It was a choice she had made. She understood that by every moral standard she'd ever set for herself, what she had done was wrong, but she wouldn't feign regret she didn't feel, heaping one transgression upon another.

Nor would she deny or forget what might have been the most beautiful night of her life, the kind of night she might never experience again. Because even before slipping from Hub-Jay's side, she knew she would never allow herself another such night, not for any reason, not unless they were joined as man and wife.

And that was something that might never happen. Or it might. She didn't know. What she did know, as her eighteen-year-old self had not, was that the decision she'd made in the passion of the night would require more decisions—

practical, sensible, well-considered decisions—made in the logical light of day.

But today was not that day.

Today she needed to go home, to tend to her family, her business, and her future. This was real life, not a movie. The night she had shared with Hub-Jay and the feelings they had discovered for each other had not solved her problems or become her happy ending.

Hub-Jay might love her and want to marry her, but that didn't change the fact that her family needed her, that she was responsible for the welfare and well-being of many. Right now, that was where her focus needed to be.

If the feelings Hub-Jay professed for her were true, they would wait and so would he. Wouldn't he?

That would be his decision. When she was ready and the time was right, she would make hers. But she would not be rushed, because this time, unlike the last, she understood exactly what she would be getting into. And she wasn't sure she was ready to have her life upended like that. Somewhere in the previous twenty-four hours, she had discovered feelings for Hub-Jay that surprised her, but she was old enough to know it took more than feelings to hold two people together, for better or worse, through the roller coaster of life. Donny's departure had shown her that.

And yet . . . how lovely last night had been.

With the convertible top down and the sun climbing warm into the blue, Mary Dell extended her arm into the air, stretched her fingers wide to catch the rushing wind, and smiled.

Eighty miles later, when the Eldorado passed through the gates with "F-Bar-T" sculpted from wrought iron and then bumped over the cattle guard and onto the long gravel driveway that led to the ranch, Mary Dell was seized with sudden giddy joy. Coming to the top of a little rise and seeing the house, she laughed out loud and smacked the horn, tapping out "shave and a haircut" with the heel of her hand.

By the time she turned off the engine and hopped out of the car, Taffy and Cady were spilling out the back door, whooping like cowboys on payday. Mary Dell opened her arms wide, hugging them both at once.

"We were starting to wonder what happened to you," Taffy said. "Hub-Jay called, looking for you. Said he'd tried your cell phone about a dozen times and it kept going into voice mail."

"Oh. I had it turned off. Saving the battery. I'll call him later."

Taffy shook her head and squinted her eyes, as if she was trying to bring her daughter into sharper focus. "You shouldn't ought to be giving a man like that the brush-off, Mary Dell. People say he's as rich as feedlot dirt."

"Momma," she said, pausing at the end of the word, making it a sentence all on its own. "Hub-Jay is a friend of mine. That's all. I'm not interested in him or his money."

"Why not?" Taffy countered. "If you ever hope to put your brand on another man, you need to get a knot in your lasso, and quick. You don't have that many good years left, you know."

Mary Dell arched her brows. "Thank you, Momma. I'll keep that in mind."

The screen door slammed and Linne came running out the door. Mary Dell bent down and scooped her up in her arms.

"Ugh!" she grunted. "What is your momma feeding you, baby girl? I bet you've grown a foot since I saw you last."

"Are you home forever now, Aunt Mary Dell?"

"For good and forever," she confirmed.

It was still early, so Taffy went into the kitchen to make breakfast while Cady and Linne helped Mary Dell unload the car and unpack.

"Momma seems better," Mary Dell said as she piled clothes into drawers.

Cady was unloading a box filled with picture frames, jewelry, and a few mementos Mary Dell had been unwilling to entrust to the moving company.

"She has good days and bad. But more good since she heard you were moving home. I think she missed you. But I made her a doctor's appointment for next week, like you asked."

"Thanks, baby girl. I just want to have Dr. Gillespie give her a once-over."

"Good idea. When will the moving truck arrive?"

"Probably not until this afternoon. I doubt they've even left Dallas yet." Mary Dell shoved a row of dresses closer together, trying to make more space on the rack. "I swear, I don't know where we're going to put everything. I can take my sewing stuff over to the shop, but we'll have to store stuff in the shed until I get it sorted out. But I was thinking we could take my blue sofa and chair over to the rental."

"That'd be nice," Cady said. "The furniture could use some updating."

Mary Dell took some of the pictures Cady had unloaded onto the bed and started setting them up on top of the dresser.

"How's your new renter working out?"

"Fine," Cady said, sounding a little cautious. "Did you know she's your co-host?"

Mary Dell turned toward her. "You're kidding."

Cady shook her head.

"So . . . what's she like?"

"Very nice," Cady replied quickly. "And a real hard worker."

Mary Dell frowned, wondering why or how her niece would have occasion to observe her new co-host's work ethic.

"The thing is," Cady continued, correctly inter-preting the expression on her aunt's face, "Rob Lee called me right after she moved in and asked if I could come over and show her how to do a few things . . ."

"How to do a few things?" Mary Dell's frown deepened. "You mean, like, jiggle the handle on the toilet to keep it from running? Or flip the breakers when the air conditioner overloads the circuits?"

"More like . . . sew." Cady licked her lips, then lifted her gaze to meet Mary Dell's. "She doesn't know how to sew."

Mary Dell's hands dropped to her sides. "You mean she doesn't know how to sew a particular kind of block? Ones with curved piecing or Y-seams? Or . . ."

"I mean she doesn't know how to sew. At all."

Mary Dell's jaw dropped.

"But she's getting better," Cady rushed to assure her. "Really. I've been going over there for a couple of hours every afternoon to help her, but she is stitching from dawn till midnight so she'll be ready in time."

"Wonderful. Just wonderful," Mary Dell said, then clucked her tongue in disgust. "So? What can she do so far?"

"She's got Four Patches and Nine Patches down," Cady replied. "And Rail Fences. Her Snowball blocks are a work in progress."

"You mean that's it? Four beginner's blocks? She doesn't know how to attach a binding, or miter a corner, or quilt a finished top?" Mary Dell tilted her head back, addressing the ceiling. "Why in the world did they hire this girl? Wait. I already know. She's young and gorgeous, right?"

"Uh. I'd say she's definitely . . ." Cady clamped her lips closed.

Mary Dell turned around, addressing Linne, who was sitting on the floor with Mary Dell's jewelry box, putting away her aunt's rings, necklaces, and bracelets, but taking her time doing it, trying on each bauble and bangle before putting it in the proper compartment.

"Linne? Have you met Miss Holly? What does she look like?"

"Like a movie star. She's nice too. She gave me a new horse for my collection! She liked Breyers when she was a little girl, just like me."

Cady pulled another tangle of necklaces from the box and handed them to Linne. "Please, Aunt Mary Dell, don't fire Holly. She's worked so hard. At least give her a chance."

"Bless you for thinking I could, baby girl. I didn't hire her; the network did. I couldn't fire her if I felt like it."

Mary Dell sighed and sat down on the bed, holding a stack of folded tops in her lap. "Guess I'll just have to make the best of a bad situation and get her up to speed as quick as I can. I appreciate you getting the ball rolling, Cady."

"I like her. I bet you will too. Did you know her mother is Rachel McEnroe?"

"Really?" Mary Dell looked impressed. "Then why doesn't she go by McEnroe?"

"Her daddy's name was Silva. I don't think she wants to trade on her momma's fame."

"Huh."

Mary Dell got up, walked over to the dresser, and started putting the tops away, organizing them in the drawers by color and pattern, just the way she did when she organized her stash of fat quarters.

Maybe this arrangement with Miss Holly Silva would work out after all. Or, she thought, remembering those four beginner's blocks, one of which was "a work in progress," maybe it wouldn't.

But Mary Dell would give the girl a chance. She didn't have a choice.

Taffy called out from the kitchen, saying that breakfast was ready. Mary Dell called back to say they'd be right in and put the last of her tops away in the dresser.

"Guess we'd better go eat before the eggs get cold. Hey," she said, frowning, "where's your brother? I haven't seen him at all this morning."

"Probably still in bed," Cady said.

"At this hour? Is he sick?"

"I heard his truck in the driveway around three."

"Three? In the morning? What in the world was he doing out until that hour?"

"Can't say for sure," Cady replied grimly. "But whatever it was, he was probably doing it at the Ice House."

"Excuse me," Mary Dell said, setting her jaw and closing the dresser drawer with more force than was required. "You and Linne go on in and get your breakfast. Tell Momma I said not to wait for me. There's something I need to attend to."

Linne's eyes grew wide as she watched her aunt stride through the bedroom door. The sound of her high heels on the Mexican tile beat out an angry rhythm as she walked down the hall.

"Is Uncle Rob Lee in trouble?" Linne asked her mother.

Cady picked up an empty box and tossed it into the corner.

"I hope so."

Chapter 19

The sound of stomping feet and clucking chickens made Rob Lee stir in his sleep, but it wasn't until someone kicked open the tack room door and snapped on the overhead lights that he truly woke up.

"Dammit, Cady!" he shouted, then grabbed his head with both hands. Eyes screwed shut against the glare of the light, he let out a few more choice words, but in a quieter voice.

"It's not your sister," a forcefully cheerful female voice drawled. "It is I, your loving aunt, coming to make sure you haven't come down with a cold, or bubonic plague. I can't think of any other reason for a working man to be lying in bed at this hour." Mary Dell ripped the blankets off his bed.

"Hey!" he shouted, wincing again at the sound of his own voice as he bolted upright and grabbed the sheet to cover himself.

"When I was walking down from the house, right after I finished inspecting the great big dent in the bumper of your truck—what did you hit, by the way?—I ran into Fred and Cody. They were in the paddock with the vet, all by themselves, helping with the ultrasound and tagging the ewes that are carrying twins or triplets. Said they hadn't seen you yet this morning, that you were probably still asleep."

She barked out an incredulous laugh.

"I told them they had to be pulling my leg. I reminded them that I hired you to manage the ranch, and that, being a member of the family, I knew you'd never, ever dream of letting me down.

"So," Mary Dell said, bending down so her mouth was right next to Rob Lee's ear, "I came out here to ask you one simple question. What in the hubs of hell is wrong with you?"

She shouted so loudly that Rob Lee's head

throbbed like a stubbed toe. He raised his arms to cover his head, thinking how much his aunt had in common with one of the more sadistic drill sergeants he'd had in boot camp.

"Had a rough night," he rasped, then reached down to the floor, picked up his discarded jeans, and started putting them on.

Mary Dell backed off and put her hands on her hips. "From what your sister tells me, you have had a series of rough nights. Rob Lee . . ." She moved her head from side to side, disappointment apparent in her face and voice. "Your dad drank himself into an early grave. Is that what you're planning on doing?"

"I wouldn't say I was planning on it . . . ," he said, his voice acid with sarcasm.

What did she think she was doing, barging in here and trying to tell him what to do? And who did she think he was—Howard? No wonder his cousin couldn't wait to get away from her. Until this moment, he hadn't realized what a bossy old busybody his aunt was.

He yanked his shirt over his head and stuffed his arms into the sleeves. "If I did decide to drink myself to death, why is it any of your business? What do you care?"

"First and foremost because I'm your aunt, I love you, and I promised your momma I'd watch out for you. Also because I hired you to run this ranch, and from what I can see, you're not doing it."

"Hey," Rob Lee snapped, slapping his hands against the legs of his jeans, "if you're unhappy with the way I'm running things, I'll pack my gear and leave. No problem."

Rob Lee backed off toward the other side of the room, but Mary Dell advanced toward him, refusing to break eye contact even when he turned his head away.

"Oh, I see. So now you're going to run away? Where to? Your brother won't have you. You've already burned that bridge."

"What do you care where I go?"

"On the day you were born, your momma put you in my arms and I put Howard, born only hours after you, into her arms. The two of us cooed over each of you just as if the baby in our arms had come from our own body. That's how I felt about you, like I was holding my second son. I always knew that if anything happened to me, Lydia Dale would have stepped up and taken care of Howard. Just the way I've tried to step in for her with you and your brother and sister. I know you're a grown man, Rob Lee, but I love you. And if your momma were here, she'd be standing right here, saying the same things I'm saying. She'd have hated to see you like this."

He turned away again and started picking up dirty clothes from the floor, his walk shuffling and shoulders slumped, moving slowly. Mary Dell stayed where she was, talking to his back.

"I know that you've been through things I can't possibly imagine. I also know you're trying your hardest to forget them but, from where I'm standing, it doesn't look like that's working. You know I'd do anything in the world to help you. So would your sister. But if we can't . . . then please, baby, find somebody who can."

Her voice became even quieter and a little raspy. Even though Rob Lee couldn't see her face, he could tell there were tears in her eyes.

"Nick is dead," she continued. "Nothing can change that. But you're still here, and I think there's a reason for that. Cady needs you, and so does Linne. And, for that matter, so do I. Don't you see? We're family. We rise and fall and get back up together."

Hearing her sniffling as she tried to keep tears back, Rob Lee wished he could cry too. He wished he could hug her, say he was sorry, that it would be all right and that he would do better. But even he didn't believe that.

"The enemy wanted to kill you and failed. Please, don't finish the job for him now that you're home. There's too many people who are counting on you. Too many people who love you."

He felt a hand on his shoulder and knew she was waiting for him to turn around and say something, but he just couldn't.

There was a noise in the driveway, the sound of rubber on gravel.

"Who's that?" he mumbled.

Mary Dell's hand fell away from his shoulder. "Not sure. I didn't think the moving truck would be here for a couple of hours yet. But maybe they got an early start." She was quiet for a moment. "You want to help them unload? We could use an extra pair of hands."

"Sure. I'll be up in a bit."

"All right, then. Grandma's making breakfast if you're hungry."

He shook his head. "I'm good."

When she left, he stuffed his T-shirt into the waist of his jeans, put on a belt and a pair of clean socks, and then pulled on his boots. The tack room didn't have a bathroom, but there was a sink against the wall, and so he brushed his teeth, spat out the toothpaste, then looked into the mirror.

The dead, aged eyes looked strange and familiar at the same time, like somebody he might have known a long time ago.

Rob Lee checked in with the ranch hands and left some instructions about what they were to do next. After that, he stopped by the paddock to say hello to Sarabeth, a patient old palomino mare that had belonged to his grandpa Dutch before he passed. Rob Lee had ridden Sarabeth when he was a teenager and was riding her again now— when he was getting out on the range and doing the job Aunt Mary Dell was asking him to do, which, he admitted to himself, wasn't very often.

He felt guilty about that, and angry at his aunt for pointing it out, but mostly angry at himself for sliding so far that she'd had to. If he wasn't family, she'd have fired him—and been right to do so. A part of him wished she would.

He grabbed a couple of carrots out of a nearby bin, held them out over the top of the fence, and clicked his tongue against his teeth. Sarabeth's ears perked up at the sound. She lifted her head from a small tuft of brown, dry grass she'd been eating and started walking toward him, nearly trotting as she got closer. Considering her age, twenty-one, Sarabeth still had a lot of pep. Rob Lee fed her carrots while scratching her on the forelock, between her eyes and up to the base of her mane.

"You're a good old girl, aren't you? Good girl. Bet you're bored hanging around the paddock. Sorry I've been neglecting you. Don't take it personal; you're not the only one. Tell you what, tomorrow we'll go out for a long ride, stretch your legs, eh? I'll check the fences and you can get some fresh pasture. Sound good?"

When Sarabeth finished eating, Rob Lee headed up to the house, slowly. Contrary to what he'd told his aunt, he really was hungry. Grandma Taffy's scrambled eggs, bacon, and a side of biscuits and gravy would have been the best way to set his queasy stomach right, but he'd rather suffer through nausea than sit at the table, listening to Linne constantly begging him to teach her to ride and feeling his sister glaring at him while he came up with reasons not to.

But he would come up and help unload the moving truck. That was something he could do for his family without actually having to talk to them. He could do a better job running the ranch without talking to them too. He had to stop drinking so much. And he would, he promised himself. Next time he went to the Ice House, he'd have two beers, no more, stay away from the hard stuff, and come home at a reasonable hour.

He could do better. He just had to get hold of himself, try a little harder, and get his act together. And he would. Aunt Mary Dell was right; if his mother were alive to see that face he'd seen in the mirror, that tired old man with eyes like coal pits, it would have broken her heart.

He walked up to the house, wondering what had happened to the movers. He didn't see a truck anywhere, but there was a Jeep parked in the driveway. Somebody must be visiting.

He thought about turning around and going back to the barn, maybe saddling up Sarabeth and riding out to check those fences, but since he'd promised Mary Dell he'd come up to the house, he figured he'd better stick his head in and say hello. Hopefully, they'd all be so busy with their company that he wouldn't have to stay for long.

Aunt Mary Dell and the others were sitting around the kitchen table. Their guest, that girl from the rental, Holly, twisted around in her chair and beamed when he came in.

"Look who the cat dragged in!" Grandma Taffy said, and then, "You want some breakfast, Rob Lee?"

Before he could decline the offer, she was up on her feet, pulling a pan of biscuits from the oven, putting them on a plate, and ladling cream gravy over the top. Not wanting to be rude, he pulled up a chair and started to eat.

"We've been talking about the show a little bit," Aunt Mary Dell said by way of catching him up. "Holly was nice enough to come out here and introduce herself to me before we start filming next week."

Rob Lee bobbed his head and said, "Good idea," because he wasn't sure what else he was supposed to say.

"Actually," Holly said, her expression a bit apologetic, "I didn't realize you were back in town yet, but I'm really happy to see you and start kicking around ideas. But," she said, turning toward the end of the table, "you're the real reason I came out here so early."

Rob Lee heard her words, but since he was sitting hunched over his plate of biscuits, he didn't realize she was talking to him until a long, uncomfortable silence had him lifting his head to see what was wrong and his eyes met Holly's.

"Who? You mean me?"

"Yeah. I've done something . . . well, it's a little crazy. But it's the right thing to do—I'm sure it is. If I don't do it, who will? But I can't handle it alone. I don't have the experience. You're the only person I could think of who might be able to help me. Anyway," she continued, sounding almost breathless as she tried to wrap up her explanation, which, with every word, just left Rob Lee feeling more confused, "I was wondering . . . if you have time, that is . . . would you mind coming with me on a little field trip? I need your advice."

Chapter 20

"I told her she was crazy. Even if she knew what she was doing, which she don't," Mrs. Finley said, talking to Rob Lee, who was standing a few paces back from the paddock, watching Stormy stomp the ground and snort when the trainer attempted to approach him, "it'd still be crazy."

Holly had to fight off the urge to remind Mrs. Finley that she was standing right next to her and could hear every word she said. In another moment, she might have, but then Mary Dell spoke up on her behalf.

"That's why Holly went looking for help. She might not know much about horses, but Rob Lee does. His stepdaddy taught him everything he knows."

"There was no better horseman in the county than Graydon," Mrs. Finley conceded. "Except maybe your husband, Donny. Those Bebee brothers could handle anything with hooves. My Harlan always said so. And Harlan knew horses. And people."

Mrs. Finley swiped her eyes with the back of her hand. Mary Dell put one arm over her shoulder and gave her a squeeze.

"Yes, he did," she said. "He was a fine man. God rest his soul."

Holly was glad she'd invited Mary Dell to tag along at the last minute. She'd mostly done so out of politeness. Mary Dell owned the F-Bar-T and Rob Lee worked for her, so if Holly was going to board Stormy at the ranch and ask for Rob Lee's help with training the horse, assuming he could be trained, Mary Dell would have to approve of the arrangement.

Another reason Holly had invited Mary Dell to join them was because she thought it would make the seven-mile drive out to the Finley ranch less awkward. Rob Lee was a great-looking guy—or had been when she'd seen him at the cottage; right now, he really *did* look like something the cat dragged in—but he sure didn't say much.

It was so weird, because that first time she'd

met him, he'd had plenty to say and he hadn't hesitated to stand up to Rachel. She'd found that pretty intriguing, and after he'd come to her rescue by recruiting Cady to be her quilting coach, she'd hoped they might make a connection. But on the rare occasions she'd seen him since then, when he came over to do a little work on the house or in the yard, he barely said a word to her. Cady said he barely spoke to anyone, so she tried not to take it personally, but the thought of a silent car ride with somebody whose thoughts were impossible to read wasn't appealing.

Mary Dell, on the other hand, had no trouble talking. With Holly at the wheel of the Jeep and Mary Dell riding shotgun, Holly nearly forgot that Rob Lee was in the back. While he stared wordlessly out the window, she and Mary Dell gabbed, marveling again about what an amazing coincidence it had been for them to run into each other in the airport and have had a conversation without ever realizing they'd be working together in just a few months.

"When you walked through the door," Mary Dell said, "I couldn't believe it. I was as surprised as a pup with his first porcupine."

"I know, right? What were the chances?"

"Slim to none. Which means it was just meant to be. It was written in the stars. Or quilted in the stars. Something like that." She chuckled. "Anyway, I've got a good feeling about you."

"Even though I can only sew four beginner's blocks?"

"That's four more than you could sew a couple of weeks ago. Sounds like you're a fast learner." Holly gave her a doubtful look and Mary Dell said, "Listen, baby girl, everybody has something special to bring to the party. Sure, you're a novice, but there might be ways we can use that to our advantage."

Holly cracked out a laugh. "Like how? Film a segment on how not to thread your bobbin?"

"I've got a few ideas," Mary Dell assured her. "Just give me a couple of days to think it through. But you're going to be a good addition, Holly. I'm sure of it."

Holly was sure Mary Dell was just trying to build up her confidence, but she was relieved they were getting along so well. It couldn't have been easy for Mary Dell, having her own son replaced on the show she had created, and knowing that Jason was working against her. Of course, maybe she didn't know.

Holly wondered if she should talk to her about that. But if she told Mary Dell about her meeting with Jason, and the design show he was dangling in front of her, wouldn't that put a wedge between them? Make Mary Dell think she was some kind of double agent? It was probably smarter to keep quiet about it all. But that didn't mean she'd be working against her. She liked Mary Dell. Who wouldn't?

Mary Dell in real life was exactly like she was on those old episodes of *Quintessential Quilting* Holly had watched—warm, funny, self-deprecating, motherly, kind, and in spite of the countrified way she had of speaking, dressing, and acting, very smart. That was the thing that impressed Holly most—it wasn't an act, not any of it. Mary Dell Templeton didn't just play a good person on television; she *was* a good person. She was genuine.

Having grown up in the entertainment business, Holly knew how rare that was.

Rob Lee was standing a few feet off while the women talked, wrapped up in his thoughts, his eyes fixed on Stormy. When the trainer tried to move closer to grab hold of the short lead rope that was attached to Stormy's halter, the horse whinnied and reared up on his back legs.

Rob Lee called out, "That's all right, Bill. Just let him be."

The trainer, Bill, backed off. Stormy calmed down immediately but stayed in the far corner of the paddock, as far from people as possible. Bill quickly hopped over the fence, looking a little relieved.

Rob Lee nodded and said, "Thanks. I've seen what I need to see." Bill returned his nod and headed toward the barn.

"See what I mean?" Mrs. Finley said as Rob Lee walked toward the women. "Can't nobody touch that horse, let alone ride him. You saw how he was with Bill. He could have killed him if he'd a mind to."

"Yes, ma'am. He could have," Rob Lee said, dipping his head a bit. "But he didn't. So that means he didn't have a mind to. Tell me about him. How'd a pissed-off Standardbred end up on a quarter horse ranch?"

"About six years back, we got a call from a horse rescue. You know Harlan did a little work with them now and then, stabling and fostering horses that they'd rescued from livestock auctions until the rescue could find new owners for them. He fostered a few horses over the years. But nobody ever wanted Stormy; he's just too wild. Early on, Harlan tried to gentle him. One day, Lord knows how, he managed to get a saddle on him, but Stormy threw him."

Mrs. Finley clucked her tongue and shook her head. "I told him he was crazy, that a seventy-six-year-old man had no business trying to break a wild horse, but would he listen? No, sir, he would not. He's lucky he didn't break his fool neck," she muttered. "Oh, but he was a stubborn old goat."

"So, Stormy has never been ridden?" Rob Lee asked, ignoring her editorial.

"Oh, no," the old lady replied. "He was a pacer, a harness racer for a few years, but I don't think he ever amounted to much. They retired him from racing and sold him to the Amish and he pulled a buggy for a while. But then, I think it was a year before we got him, he was pulling the buggy and got into an accident. I heard it was a semi-truck, but maybe it was just a pickup; I don't know for sure. Anyway, it was a miracle nobody got killed.

"After that, Stormy wouldn't let them put him in a harness or even touch him. He got sent to the auction and the rescue folks bought him and he ended up here. After that one time Harlan tried to ride him, he just decided to leave him be, let him run with the herd. He kept that rope halter on him with a short lead, so we can grab him in case of emergencies, but that's it. If you're on horseback, he'll let you get hold of the rope and lead him along."

Rob Lee sniffed and pulled at his nose. Holly looked toward him and she could see he was thinking; it was almost like you could see wheels and gears turning behind his eyes.

"So he gets along all right with other horses?" Rob Lee asked.

"Oh, yeah. He likes horses just fine. It's people he can't stand. He won't let anybody on foot get close, and he won't be touched for anything. That's why he looks so scruffy," she said, her voice at once apologetic and defensive. "We can't get close enough to groom him."

"I'm sure you've done the best you could," Mary Dell said, touching the older woman lightly on the shoulder.

"Harlan felt bad for him. So do I. Life hasn't

been too kind to him," she said, turning her gaze to the far corner of the paddock, where Stormy was still standing, looking out toward the road, where, earlier that day and the day before, twelve horse trailers had come and gone.

"Look at him. He's been standing in that corner of the paddock all day. I think he's waiting for his herd to come back for him. Poor old nag." She sighed.

"I tried calling the rescue folks, but they couldn't find anyone willing to take him. And I've done all I can. But I told Miss Holly here unless she could find an experienced handler and a good place to board him, that I flat out wouldn't sell Stormy to her, not for any price."

Holly saw Rob Lee's eyes shift toward his aunt. He sniffed and they exchanged a look; then she stretched her neck and gave a quick, half nod. Rob Lee nodded back and looked toward Mrs. Finley.

"Holly can board him at the F-Bar-T. I'll take care of him."

Mrs. Finley furrowed her brow and clutched at the neck of her flowered blouse. "Oh, I don't know. If something happened to this sweet young girl, or to you, Rob Lee, trying to ride that devil, I'd just never forgive myself. Maybe it'd be better to send him to the auction."

"Oh, don't do that!" Holly exclaimed. "Please, don't. He's not a devil. The buggy accident wasn't his fault. Mrs. Finley, please. I won't try to ride him until Rob Lee says it's safe. Promise." She held up her hand, Girl Scout fashion.

"It won't never be safe to ride him," Mrs. Finley said.

"Then I'll pay for his board and he can live out his days at the F-Bar-T."

The old woman frowned even deeper. "What about you?" she asked Rob Lee. "You going to try to ride him?"

"Not unless I felt sure he'd let me. We'll see how it goes."

"Oh . . ." Mrs. Finley looked down at the ground and muttered to herself. "I just don't know."

"Annie," Mary Dell said, "Rob Lee is a good horseman and a grown man. If he survived Afghanistan, I'm sure he can take care of one old horse. He's not going to take any chances."

Mrs. Finley kept her eyes cast toward the ground for so long that Holly began to wonder if she'd heard what was being said to her. They all stood there, waiting. Finally, the gray head lifted.

"All right. You can have him," she said to Holly, and then to Rob Lee, "You better talk to the vet about tranquilizers. When they brought him here, the rescue people had to sedate him to load him into a trailer."

Rob Lee shook his head. "No, ma'am. I'm not going to put him through that again."

Her wrinkled brow wrinkled even deeper as

Mrs. Finley listened to Rob Lee's response. "Then, how do you expect to move him?"

Rob Lee lifted his chin and narrowed his eyes, looking across the field at Stormy.

"Slowly."

Chapter 21

Three days later, with only five to go before they were to begin shooting, Mary Dell invited Holly to come to the Patchwork Palace for some private tutoring.

When she arrived, Mary Dell was busy going over accounts with Cady and promised she'd only be a minute. But when a customer approached, asking advice about making a baby quilt for a long-hoped-for grandchild, Holly realized this would take more than a minute.

She told Mary Dell to take her time, that she wanted to look around the shop anyway, which was true. Because Cady always met her at the cottage and brought fabrics with her—inexpensive things from the clearance rack that would be fine for practice—Holly hadn't had a chance to spend any real time in the Patchwork Palace or see what all the fuss was about or why quilters came by the busload, sometimes driving hundreds of miles to shop there.

Though Holly was finding her crash course in

quilting frustrating and stressful, as she wandered around the shop she started to see how people could get into it. Walking through the aisles of shelves crowded with beautiful bolts of fabric, stacked like lines of toy soldiers standing at attention, was kind of like taking a walk through a big box of giant crayons. How could you not smile when you were doing it? And how could you not want to reach out and touch the bolts of fabric, or start imagining all the pretty things you could make when you started playing with them?

Turning a corner, she came to the reds and found herself pulled almost magnetically to a grouping that was darker than red but lighter than burgundy, and had maybe just a drop of orange, the same color as the bricks of the old courthouse in the Square. Looking through the stacks of fat quarters, those eighteen-by-twenty-two-inch cuts of fabric, which, according to Cady, quilters collected like baseball fanatics collected trading cards, Holly was drawn to one with a swirling pattern of darker and lighter shades of brick that reminded her of ocean waves hitting a beach. She took it off the shelf, and then, before she really thought about what she was doing, found four more fat quarters of the same color but in different patterns and shades and plucked those off the shelf too. Then, thinking she'd need something more neutral to balance out those rich reds, she found a wall filled with grays and picked out a few of those, from very light, the color of an overcast sky, to a deep charcoal with tiny dots of black and thin stripes of metallic gold. There were ten fabrics in all, each folded into a neat little rectangle and wrapped with a matching satin ribbon, creating packages so pretty that just picking them up felt like she was giving herself a present.

When she walked up to the counter with her armful of tiny treasures, Cady grinned and said, "Uh-oh. Looks like somebody got the bug. Nice choices, rookie!"

Mary Dell, who was bent over a table a little way off, showing the customer who wanted to make the baby quilt how to use a big plastic ruler to make a scalloped border, popped up her head in response.

"Oooh, lemme see," she said, pulling off her reading glasses and walking to the counter, the baby quilt customer following in her wake. "Those are so pretty!"

They were; it was true. Just looking at all those rich reds and cool grays made Holly feel happy, and the fact that Mary Dell and the other women felt the same way only added to the pleasure of the purchase.

"I don't have any idea of what I'm going to do with them," Holly said, the admission making her feel a little foolish, "but I just had to have them."

"A common malady among quilters," Mary Dell

said. "But think of it this way: Does a painter figure out exactly what she's going to paint before going to the art supply store? No. She buys a selection of paints in advance so when inspiration strikes she is ready to capture the vision before it fades."

Cady looked at her aunt with raised brows. "Aunt Mary Dell, that's got to be the most poetic justification for fabric addiction that I have ever heard."

"Thank you," she said with a prim but playful smile. "I've been working on it for about the last twenty-five years. Seriously, Holly, half the fun of quilting comes from finding fabrics you can't live without and then imagining all the possibilities. But," she said, picking up the wavy red that had first sparked Holly's interest, "I think these would work just perfectly for the project I have in mind for our first episode. Just let me finish showing Liz how to make a scalloped border, and then you and I can head upstairs and get to work."

The big classroom was in use, as Pearl was teaching a class on Christmas tree skirts, so they met in the smaller one.

The room was set up with eight workstations: four tables, each with two sewing machines, two padded chairs, and an electrical strip between. There were craft-height cutting tables and ironing stations on each side of the room and a huge design wall at the front, covered in cream-colored felt so quilt blocks could be arranged and rearranged before finally being sewn together.

Mary Dell sat down at one of the tables, motioned for Holly to take the second chair, and then swiveled in her seat so she could face her young co-host directly.

Her expression was uncharacteristically somber, with no trace of a smile on her lips.

"I know that Jason is determined to make sure that the eighth season of *Quintessential Quilting* will be the last," she said with no preamble. "I don't know why he is so set on it, but he is. And he'll do whatever he can to make it happen, including trying to play us against each other. But we're not going to fall for that."

Mary Dell paused. Her gaze was unblinking.

"Are we?" she prodded.

"We're not," Holly confirmed. "Neither of us has anything to gain from that. We'd both end up looking bad."

"Good."

"But I'm starting to think I'm going to end up looking bad no matter what. Just listening to you talk to that lady about bias binding and sewing curves made my head hurt." Holly sighed. "I can't even imagine being able to do that."

"You will, if you keep up with it. You've got more talent than you give yourself credit for. You've got color sense, for one thing," Mary Dell said, nodding toward the bag of brick and gray fat quarters Holly had set down on the table. "Which, I have to say, comes as a relief. I've always relied on Howard to help me with that part. My fabric choices can get a little . . . Let's call them exuberant. That's the word Hub-Jay used once," she said, a small smile bowing her lips. "It sounds more refined than saying I've got no taste."

"Now who's not giving herself credit?" Holly scolded. "I saw you helping that lady pick out the fabrics for her baby quilt. Sure, it was bright and colorful with all that hot pink and lime green, but you didn't go overboard. Bringing in that bright white for the border and then binding it with pink tied everything together. You're good with fabric choices."

"I like what I like," Mary Dell replied, "and what I like is loud and bright. But I have learned to tone it down a little. Howard and Hub-Jay have been good influences. So, how about we both call ourselves a work in progress?"

"Fair enough," Holly said. "I just wish I was progressing faster. Really, Mary Dell, I just don't know how I'm going to keep up with you."

"You can't. Not when it comes to quilting."

Holly opened her eyes, a little surprised by the frankness of her remark.

"That's not an insult," Mary Dell said, lifting one hand. "It's just the way it is. Baby girl, I've been quilting since before water was wet. Two weeks ago, you didn't even know what a bobbin was, let alone how to wind one. If you try to make out like you're ready to play in the same league as me, you'll end up looking foolish. And I'll end up looking mean.

"If we're going to pull this off, we've got to work as a team," she said, leaning forward a little. "I've been mulling it over for the last few days and I think I've come up with a way to make your inexperience work for us."

Holly had real doubts when Mary Dell began laying out her plan, but the more she listened, the more she realized that Mary Dell might be on to something.

"So, what you're saying," Holly said, dunking a peppermint tea bag into the paper cup of hot water Mary Dell had poured her from the dispenser in the corner of the room, "is that we look at the entire next season as a kind of . . . quilter's college, for lack of a better term."

Mary Dell's bright blue eyes lit up. "Miss Holly! That is the perfect way to put it!"

She grabbed a pen from her purse and scribbled a few notes onto a legal pad she'd brought with her, continuing to talk as she wrote.

"This first season will be freshman year. Every week, we'll look at a quilt block, each a little more challenging than the week before. I'll teach you the basic technique for mastering that block, but then we'll show the viewers ways to take that block and work it into all kinds of different quilts, from the most simple to the most complex. Every week will build on the week before. And if we get renewed, next season will be sophomore year—a little more advanced—then junior and so on."

"You don't think your current viewers will be bored by freshman year quilting?" Holly asked.

"Not if we do it right. If we can help novices gain confidence on basic techniques while offering more complex variations and techniques that will appeal to the more experienced quilter, we'll gain viewership. Any quilter worth her salt is going to understand the concept of mastering and building on the fundamentals. It's just like football. Hey, that's good!" Mary Dell started scribbling again. "We should use that. Maybe we could wear football gear for the first show, drive home the point and have some fun. I know I've got a couple of Cowboys jerseys around somewhere."

"Yeah, maybe not. Seems kind of hokey."

Holly wrinkled her nose and Mary Dell looked a little disappointed.

"It's not that I don't think it'd be funny," Holly said, fibbing to spare her co-host's feelings, "but if you're going to establish yourself in the role of teacher, an expert, you need to keep things a little more dignified. Not to say that we can't have fun, but"—she shook her head—"no costumes."

Mary Dell gave an exaggerated sigh. "Fine. I'm not even going to bring up my next idea."

"Which was?"

"Having you dress up as Luke Skywalker and me as Yoda."

Holly grinned. She really liked Mary Dell. "Terrible idea."

"Well, then," Mary Dell sniffed. "Maybe we should just get to work."

While Holly cut her fabric into strips, Mary Dell explained that for the first episode, she'd be making a Courthouse Steps block, all straight lines and patches cut along the grain, with none of the pesky bias stretch that plagued Holly with the Snowballs.

It was a variation on the Log Cabin block, but instead of sewing strips around the center square in a circular motion, for the Courthouse Steps, two patches are added to opposite sides of a center square; then two more strips would be sewn to the remaining sides of the center, and so on, alternating dark fabrics with light to create the "steps" from which the block got its name.

Mary Dell thought it would be fun to film the opening segment of the episode outside on the actual steps of the old courthouse. Holly agreed.

"That's a great idea! We should try to do that whenever we can, you know? Find different locations around town. It'll be a lot more interesting to watch—kind of a little travelogue in addition to the quilting. It'd be really good PR for the shop and the town too."

"Yes, the thought had occurred to me," Mary Dell said, giving her a knowing wink as she picked up Holly's strips and carried them to the sewing machine.

It was supposed to be an easy block, and at first it seemed like it was, just a matter of sewing straight lines. But Holly was tense and anxious, trying to sew a perfect quarter-inch seam, knowing from what little experience she had that failing to do so could ruin the whole block, making it too small or too big.

The trick, Mary Dell told her, was to keep her seams just a teeny bit smaller than a true quarter inch and also to fix her eyes lower down on the arm of the machine when feeding the fabric, rather than staring straight at the needle.

"It's like driving a car," she explained. "You need to look down the road a ways, see what's coming. That way you've got time to correct your course before you crash. Relax! You're wearing your shoulders for earrings." She walked up behind Holly, placed her hands on her shoulders, which were indeed hunched toward her ear-lobes, and then pushed them down into their normal position. "Don't be so anxious, baby girl. Quilting is supposed to be fun!"

Holly took her foot off the pedal and gave her a dirty look.

"It will be eventually," Mary Dell said. "You just need to quit trying so hard. Let's try talking while you sew. That'll distract you from trying to be Miss Patty Perfect and help you master one of quilting's most important skills, the ability to stitch and gossip simultaneously."

Mary Dell sat down at the neighboring machine and started working on a block of her own, sewing much more quickly than Holly. This was supposed to help her relax?

"So, how's it going with the horse? I haven't been able to catch up with Rob Lee. Seems like he's been spending a lot of time over at the Finley place."

"He's been there every day," Holly said, layering a new fabric strip on top of the partially sewn block. "He brought Sarabeth over there on Monday and put her in the paddock next to Stormy's, so they could get to know each other. Then he took the dividing walls out of the horse trailer and left it at Finley's. Tomorrow, he's going to saddle up Sarabeth and see if Stormy will let her lead him into the trailer."

"So, he's going to bring Stormy back to the F-Bar-T tomorrow?"

Holly shook her head, pulled the block out from under the pressing foot, and started sewing another strip on the opposite side.

"He's just going to let Stormy have a look around, spend a little time in the trailer, hopefully get used to it. When he is, then Rob Lee will bring them all back to the ranch. It might take a few days. Oh, I almost forgot, he brought a goat over too, a black-and-white one, and put her in Stormy's paddock."

"Mildred?" Mary Dell asked, raising her voice to be heard over the whir of the sewing machine. "Why'd he do that?"

"Rob Lee says that having another animal around can help a traumatized horse feel calmer. They develop some kind of friendship or connection, I guess. Goats seem to be good candidates for the job. Rob Lee said that, sometimes, the horse can get to be really dependent on a goat."

"Huh. I hope it works out. Mildred's never been good for much besides breaking out of the pen and eating the rosebushes. It'd be nice if she finally came to some good."

Mary Dell pulled a finished block from the machine, snipped off the threads, and carried it to the ironing board. Holly frowned, looking at her own block. She'd started first but was only half-way done. But the seams looked straight, so that was something, and her shoulders weren't tense anymore.

"Sounds like you and Rob Lee have been seeing a lot of each other," Mary Dell said, pressing the iron down on her block.

"Every day since I bought Stormy," Holly said. "I just hang around and watch, hoping Stormy will get used to me. Rob Lee's the one doing all the work."

"That's nice," Mary Dell said. "Rob Lee needs somebody to talk to. Maybe he's like Stormy. Maybe a connection with another creature will help him feel calmer, move past those bad memories."

"He doesn't talk to me much. And mostly just about Stormy, but yesterday, when I showed up in a new pair of white cowgirl boots, he shook his head, said I should have bought some the color of horsesh—" She stopped herself, not sure how Mary Dell would feel about that word, even though Rob Lee had said it. "Of horse manure. And then he smiled."

"He smiled?" Mary Dell stopped what she was doing and turned completely around. "Really?"

"Not a big smile, but . . . yeah." Holly smiled too. From what Cady had told her about her little brother and all he'd been through, she knew that a smile from Rob Lee, even a little one, was a small triumph.

"Dang, baby girl! You might turn out to be more useful than Mildred."

"Hmm. Wonder if I can put that on my résumé. Special skills: can stand in for a goat."

Mary Dell joined in her laughter. "It's good to have you here, Holly. It really is. Other than growing an ulcer trying to learn to quilt, you settling in all right? Too Much is such a small town compared to LA. You're probably bored."

"Not as bored as I thought I'd be," Holly said. "Don't get me wrong, I really wish you had a decent gym in town and maybe a movie theater, but I haven't been bored. Even though she's older than I am, Cady has been great to me, kind of like a big sister. We're going to go off to the Ice House for a girls' night one of these days. Too Much is kind of growing on me," she said, a little surprised to realize she was telling the truth. "So, quilting ulcer aside, things are okay. I do wish I could get hold of my mom, though. She called a couple days after I got to town, letting me know she got to Galveston okay, but nothing since then. I've been leaving voice mails for her for two weeks and she hasn't called me back.

"I'm sure she's fine," Holly said in a purposely practical voice, as if she were trying to convince herself as much as Mary Dell. "I'd have heard if she wasn't. Mom might not be as big a name as she once was, but if something bad had happened to her, the tabloids would pick up on it, and fast. There's nothing they love more than reporting stories about the trials and tribulations of fading stars."

Mary Dell carried her finished block back to the table and sat down at the sewing machine, but didn't begin another.

"And you say she's in Galveston."

"Mexico. She left from Galveston, on a cruise," Holly said, leaving out the part about her doing so with a married man. "She'll be gone for a couple of months."

"Oh, well, that explains it," Mary Dell said, smiling. "Howard and I led a quilting cruise a few years back. Once we hit international waters, my phone wouldn't work at all. I bet she'll call as soon as she's back in port. Don't you worry, baby girl." She leaned over and gave Holly's arm a squeeze, then patted her shoulder.

Something about that gesture, so motherly, made Holly's throat feel thick. She didn't like to admit it, but she really had been worried about Rachel. Not because she thought something had happened to her—the talk about the tabloids was simple truth; if there had been bad news regarding her mom, they'd have tracked her down to the North Pole to get a comment—but because they'd parted so badly. She thought Rachel might not be speaking to her. It was funny, but, until now, she hadn't quite realized how much she depended on her mom for advice. Maybe Rachel was *her* Mildred, the creature who calmed her down. There were so many times during the last couple of weeks when she'd have loved to talk things over with her mom. She'd left six messages without hearing back from her.

But the international waters thing made sense.

When Rachel was back in an American port, she'd call. No matter how they'd left things, there was no way her mom would still be mad at her, not after all those weeks. Was there?

"So," Holly said, finishing up the third round on her block, noticing that the step pattern was starting to show itself, "how are things for you? Is it good to be back home?"

"It is. Not quite as good as I thought it would be. I've been hoping to come home for years, but I always figured Howard would come with me."

"That must be hard. How's he doing?"

"Oh, real well. We talk every day, morning and night. He's taking one class at the community college this term, an art class, just to get his feet wet a little bit. His girlfriend is taking the same class, so he loves that, but it sounds like he's making some new friends too. And he's getting himself to class, making his breakfast and lunch, doing his laundry, staying up too late . . ." She laughed, but it sounded a little hollow to Holly's ears. "You know, being a grown-up. Which is what I always wanted for him, so, of course, I'm proud and happy for him. But it is lonely."

"You've got your family here, though, right? Your mom seems nice."

"Oh, but looks can be deceiving," Mary Dell said, raising her eyebrows to a meaningful arc. "I'm just kidding; Momma's okay. She's no saint, I can tell you, a little self-centered and always was, but she's a good mother. Very protective of her family, always was.

"I'm glad I can be here to take care of her now. She was acting real crazy last week—I found her out in back of the chicken coop wearing a pair of my daddy's old overalls and smoking a package of Marlboros she found in the pocket. When I asked what she was doing, she told me to mind my own gol-darned business, but she said it more colorfully, then called me Florence, accused me of trying to steal her man, and tried to fight me."

"Really?"

The little old lady Holly had met at the ranch, the one who'd filled her coffee cup and called her honey, seemed nothing like the person Mary Dell was describing.

"Really. I thought she'd lost her marbles and we'd have to put her in the loony bin. The doctor said she probably had an infection and prescribed some antibiotics. I've got to take her back in for a follow-up, but she seems fine now."

"It's a good thing you're here to look out for her," Holly said, snipping a thread and preparing to sew another strip.

"It is," Mary Dell agreed. "And, much as I miss Howard, Momma needs me more now. He's doing fine on his own. And I'm glad I can be here for Rob Lee and Cady, too, at least a little bit." She was quiet a moment, thinking, and a little crease of concern appeared between her brows.

"I don't think I'm really helping Rob Lee. He won't talk to me. But at least I can ease Cady's burden a little bit. It was too much for her to try and run the shop all alone." Mary Dell sighed and clucked her tongue. "I sure wish she'd find a nice boyfriend. She's too young and pretty to stay single. When you two go out to the Ice House, see if you can't find some nice man for her to fall in love with. A sober one," she added. "A church-goin' man. Who has a steady job. And doesn't chew. Or swear too much, but that last part would just be icing on the cake. Heck!" She laughed. "If you find a man like that, forget Cady and give him to me! A man like that's as rare as hens' teeth."

Holly took a couple of backstitches in her block and gave Mary Dell a sideways glance, wondering how much she should reveal.

"Cady says you've already got a boyfriend—a secret admirer—and that he sends you flowers every day."

"Oh, hush." Mary Dell flapped her hand dismissively. "That's just Hub-Jay; there's nothing secret about him. And he doesn't send flowers *every* day. More like every other." She smiled a little. "He's just trying to get my attention, but I've got bigger fish to fry at the moment."

Holly pulled the block out from under the presser foot and clipped the threads.

"Any man that sent me flowers every other day would sure have my attention. Other than the corsage I got for prom, I don't think anyone has ever given me flowers."

"What? A pretty thing like you? I can't believe it."

"It's true." Holly shrugged and laid her block down against the edge of a ruler.

"Well," Mary Dell said, smiling a remembering sort of smile, "I can tell you one thing; it doesn't suck. Not at all."

"You know what else doesn't suck?" Holly asked, grinning as she turned her block ninety degrees, confirming her previous conclusion. "This quilt block. It measures exactly twelve and a half inches. Yes!" she cried, and pumped the air with her fist.

"Let me see!" Mary Dell took the block and held it close to her face, examining each seam. "It's perfect. Absolutely perfect. What did I tell you, baby girl? You're a star!"

Chapter 22

Holly opened the paddock gate and walked inside, standing as far away as she could from Stormy. The horse wasn't rearing, which was an improvement, but he was agitated, racing back and forth along the far fence and snorting and tossing his head.

Rob Lee was sitting astride Sarabeth, on the other side of the fence, keeping a close eye on everything. Though this was the third time they'd gone through the procedure of luring Stormy into the trailer, Rob Lee could see that Holly was scared. That was understandable. Holly weighed . . . what? Maybe a hundred and fifteen pounds? Stormy weighed a thousand and was doing his best to remind her of that, trying to look all big and badass so she would keep her distance.

"It's all right," Rob Lee called out, keeping his voice low and calm but loud enough to be heard. "He's all bark and no bite, just trying to warn you off."

Holly looked toward him and nodded, her eyes wide and easily visible even under the rolled brim of her newly acquired straw hat.

She looked good in that hat, he thought. Like she belonged. Definitely an improvement on those white wannabee rodeo queen boots she'd bought. Those were ridiculous. But how could a girl not look cute in a cowboy hat? Or, in Holly's case, even cuter. And the cutest thing of all was that she was spending her money and time to rescue and rehabilitate this horse that clearly scared the crap out of her.

"Okay, call Mildred to you and get the lead on her. Just like before."

Holly took some apple chunks out of her pocket and held them out where the goat could see them.

"Mildred? Mildred, come here. I've got apples for you."

The goat, who had been rubbing her head against the slats in the fence, scratching her face, turned toward the sound of Holly's voice, let out a bleat, and started walking quickly toward Holly, eager to get the treat.

Stormy's ears perked up too. His frantic running slowed to a walk as he watched Mildred cross the paddock. When the goat actually reached Holly and started munching the apple, Stormy stopped pacing entirely and just stood there, watching.

Watching Stormy's face while Holly attached a long lead rope to Mildred's collar, Rob Lee could almost see the tug-of-war going on in the horse's mind, the battle between the instinct to follow his new friend and the need to keep a safe distance from unpredictable humans. In the end, the need to stay safe won. Stormy stood his ground. But, at least for a couple of seconds there, he'd considered taking a chance. It was a start.

After giving the goat another piece of apple, Holly took one end of the lead and passed it over the fence to Rob Lee.

"Okay," he said, wrapping the rope loosely around his hand, "open the gate for me and then hop out of there. You filled up the manger in the trailer, right?"

"Uh-huh. And I put in some oats and the apple

you got from the vet. But I thought you said you didn't want to use tranquilizers."

"This one is very mild. It won't knock him out; just take the edge off the anxiety."

Holly nodded her understanding and swung open the gate. Rob Lee rode through on Sarabeth's back, taking up the slack in Mildred's lead rope as he moved closer and coiling it into a loop over the horn of his saddle.

With the goat in tow, Rob Lee rode toward Stormy. This was the tricky part, getting close enough so he could grab hold of the four-foot-long rope that hung from Stormy's halter. He wanted Sarabeth to approach slowly, as if she were just ambling over to say hello and didn't have a cowboy on her back, getting close enough so Rob Lee could lean down and get hold of the rope without scaring Stormy into backing away or running off.

That was the ideal. But it hadn't worked out like that on their two practice runs. Oh, he'd gotten hold of the rope, but he'd had to chase after Stormy to do it. Today, though, it did work.

Rob Lee squeezed his legs gently against Sarabeth's sides to urge her forward, and then, after a few steps, he tugged the reins a little bit so she'd stop, and they just sat there for a couple of minutes before moving forward again. With each repetition, Stormy moved his feet and sputtered a little, but he didn't back up or run as he'd done in the past. Slowly, they edged forward, a few feet each time, until Stormy and Sarabeth were close enough to touch noses. When they did, Rob Lee reached down to catch hold of the lead and tie the end to a longer piece of rope he had looped over the horn of his saddle.

Once the knot was secure, he squeezed his knees again and Sarabeth walked on while Rob Lee fed out the rope a good two lengths behind, at which point Stormy started following along with Mildred at his side, bleating now and again but otherwise displaying remarkable decorum for a goat.

The little caravan walked calmly through the paddock gate and across the grass toward the open back of the horse trailer. As they approached, Rob Lee hopped lightly off Sarabeth's back and led her up the ramp and into the trailer. Mildred and Stormy followed her in like baby ducks trailing their mother, and Rob Lee made a quick exit through the escape door at the front of the trailer. As soon as he did, Holly, according to plan, closed and locked the trailer's rear doors, and that was that.

Closing the escape, Rob Lee leaned against the metal door for a moment. "Good boy, Stormy," he whispered. "Good boy."

When he walked around the rear of the trailer, Holly was there to greet him. "I can't believe how easy that was!"

"It was easy because we spent five days working up to it, but . . . yeah," he said, "I was kind of surprised myself. He's fussing a little bit now, though; hear it? He just realized that you closed the door."

They were silent for a moment, listening to the sound of Stormy sputtering and testing the trailer floor with his hooves, as well as the sound of steady munching while Sarabeth enjoyed the reward of oats and apples they'd left in her manger. After a few moments the sound of one munching horse became the sound of two.

"Now what?" Holly asked.

"We wait for him to finish eating that apple and make sure he's calm. Then we drive back to the ranch, real slow, maybe five miles an hour. You're going to keep listening to see if he gets agitated. If he does, we'll pull over until he calms down and try again. If he handles it okay, we might go a little faster, but not much."

"Sounds like it could take a while."

"Could be a couple of hours, could be the rest of the day. You got anywhere you need to be?" She shook her head. "Okay, good. I'm going to need you to keep an eye on the side mirrors too. If anybody comes up behind us, you wave them around. But, hopefully, that won't happen much."

"So, what do we do now? Until the tranquilizer has a chance to work?"

"We wait."

They found a spot of shade under a tree and sat down to wait on a patch of parched grass. Rob Lee got a couple of bottles of Dr Pepper out of the cab of the truck and handed one to Holly. She offered him one of the pieces of unmedicated apple she had left over in her pocket.

They sat there eating and drinking silently, lost in their thoughts.

Probably Holly was thinking about something, Rob Lee observed after glancing in her direction. He was enjoying not thinking. It had been a long time since he'd been able to just empty his mind and *be,* and it came as a relief. He'd have been perfectly happy to keep on that way, but now Holly had entered his thoughts, which wasn't necessarily a bad thing.

At first, he'd kind of written her off, figuring she was probably just like that mother of hers: gorgeous, spoiled, and self-absorbed, your typical Hollywood type. Except for that first part, he'd been wrong.

When she'd decided she wanted to rescue Stormy and asked for his help, he'd figured she'd pay the bills and that would be that. He didn't think she'd be out here working alongside him, day after day. Truth to tell, he would have preferred if she hadn't. He was used to being on his own, and God help him but the woman could talk!

But if she wasn't asking questions about the horse and every little detail of what Rob Lee was doing with him and why, she was asking questions about himself and his family. Thankfully, she steered clear of Afghanistan, but everything else seemed to be fair game. And if he didn't answer or kept his answers short, instead of picking up on the hint that he'd rather not talk, she'd rattle off and tell him about her life and family, what it was like to grow up with her famous mother, traveling all over but never really settling down, then about doing that game show, and now Aunt Mary Dell's show.

The first day it seemed like she talked so much his ears might bleed, but on the second day it didn't bother him quite as much, and by the third he started to wonder if it wasn't a case of her talking all that much more than other people but him just not being used to people. Could be.

But she was okay, he concluded. Actually she was pretty sweet, and, yes, real easy on the eyes. He might be depressed, but he wasn't blind. He liked looking at her when she didn't know he was looking. Even more, he liked it when she caught him looking at her and then blushed. That was cute, too, and unexpected. Being on TV and everything, he never imagined she'd be shy or self-conscious. But maybe that was because she'd been so overweight when she was a kid; at least that's what she said. That was kind of hard to imagine, too. When he said so she'd assured him it was true.

"I wasn't just chunky or carrying a few extra pounds; I was fat. I took off seventy pounds in three months, basically starving myself on some liquid diet thing." She shook her head at the memory. "Really, really stupid. When I went back to real food, I gained it all back because I hadn't changed the way I ate; I'd just stopped eating. Anyway, I finally went to see a nutritionist and got a gym membership. The second time, it took me eleven months to lose those seventy pounds, but I kept them off. Of course, I have to work at it every day. I really like working out and eating healthy; I like the way it makes me feel even more than how it makes me look. But"—she grinned—"I'm still subject to occasional lapses. Mocha milk shakes are my downfall—and favorite guilty pleasure."

Yeah, the girl could talk. But she was growing on him. And he liked the fact that everything hadn't come easy to her. She was surprising. In all kinds of ways.

"So," he said, clearing his throat first, kind of priming the pump. "You start shooting day after tomorrow, right?"

"Uh-huh. Just the new opening and some promos. We'll do the first episode next week."

"You still nervous?"

She thought about that for a moment.

"Not like I was before. My quilting is coming

along, and I think Mary Dell's idea for the quilter's college thing will work. At this point, I'm actually kind of anxious to get started."

"Yeah. Sometimes waiting can be the hardest part."

He almost started to tell her about how he felt between deployments, how waiting to get back into combat was almost worse than being in it, and how guilty he felt during those times, knowing that his buddies were still over there while he was home and safe, going to a movie, seeing his family, living a normal civilian life. But he never felt normal, always thinking about the day he'd go back there, because that life, that everyday struggle to survive, had become his normal. He'd lost the trick of living any other way.

But he didn't say that. Because he didn't want to think about it right then.

"You'll do fine," he said instead.

"I hope so."

"You will."

He craned his neck toward the trailer. Everything seemed calm. He got up from the ground and turned to face her.

"I think we ought to head toward home. You ready to do this?"

She grinned. "I am if you are."

He reached out his hand. Holly took it and he helped her up.

Then he smiled.

Chapter 23

For the first day of filming, the cast and crew were to meet at the Patchwork Palace at six a.m., five hours before the shop was scheduled to open. Holly was right on time, eager to get started and to meet their director, Artie Graves.

Despite the early hour, the shop was bustling. There was a big van pulled up to the front. Two men and a woman dressed in black jeans and T-shirts were pulling cables, tripods, cameras, and lighting equipment from the van. Holly was surprised to see them setting up the equipment on the sidewalk. Nothing on the call sheet she'd gotten from the network the day before had said anything about filming the new opening outdoors. Not that that would be a bad thing necessarily; she just hadn't been expecting it.

Now that she thought about it, the call sheet had been kind of vague. It hadn't given any information aside from the names of the cast and crew, contact information for everyone, and the location and time they were expected to show up. Usually the details regarding locations and an outline of what they'd be doing for each specific segment would be spelled out in advance. Holly had heard that the network had hired the new director only the week before . . . after Jason fired the old director.

Maybe this new guy, Artie Graves, hadn't had a chance to hammer out the details yet. They hadn't had any preproduction meetings up to this point, nor had he called to introduce himself to either Holly or Mary Dell. And that was really odd. But, again, he'd only just been hired. He was probably still finding his way. Good thing that Mary Dell had a clear vision for the new season. Her "quilting college" idea really was inspired.

Being careful to step over the tangle of camera cables, Holly said good morning to the crew as she walked up the sidewalk and through the front door of the shop. Things were busy inside too. A man wearing blue jeans and a white shirt was setting up a folding privacy screen in the corner. Two women wearing blue smocks were carting what looked like big fishing-tackle boxes, which Holly was pretty sure contained makeup, up the stairs. A couple of other people, also dressed in the ubiquitous black uniform of film crews, were scurrying around carrying clipboards and looking intense. In another corner of the shop, toward the back, she saw Mary Dell talking to a man wearing a satiny shirt, pink with a black collar and sleeves, with a graphic on the back that said "Bowling Stones" and showed three white pins being knocked over by a black bowling ball.

That had to be the director, Artie. Nobody else

237

on the crew would dare show up looking like that.

He was big and burly, standing six foot five, with a large head that looked even larger because it was covered with an unkempt mass of dull brown curls. He was sucking on a Tootsie Pop but was amazingly adept at talking with his mouth full, moving the sucker from his left to his right cheek as he spoke. But what surprised Holly most of all was his age. He couldn't have been more than a couple of years older than she was.

In fact, as she would later find out, Artie was only twenty-eight, had been working in television for only three years, and had only one directorial television credit to his name, actually as an assistant director, for a program titled *Nudist Colony Wedding Planner*. It was canceled after three episodes.

That wasn't necessarily Artie's fault. Shows got canceled all the time, and it wasn't like he'd come up with the idea. He probably just needed a job, any job. And being young didn't necessarily mean he wouldn't be a good director. But, as she would soon discover, there was more to worry about where Artie Graves was concerned. Youth and a skimpy résumé were just the beginning.

Artie talked a lot, listened not at all, and didn't seem to understand that they were filming an informational program, not a reality show. That was exactly what Mary Dell was trying, unsuccessfully, to explain to him.

Holly stood lingering in the doorway, listening in on the conversation.

"But I don't think you understand the purpose of the show, Artie. We're trying to teach people—"

"Yeah, yeah, yeah . . . I get it." He flapped his hand dismissively. "And maybe that worked back in your day—"

"My day?" Mary Dell arched her eyebrows. "What day was that?"

"The early days of television. You know, the golden years. Hey, not saying anything against them. But let's face it; people would watch anything you put on the box back then. They had to. There were only three channels! I mean, seriously, *Sing Along with Mitch*? People actually sat in their living rooms and sang along with some bandleader! What the hell was that about?"

He guffawed, spread his hands out, and dropped his jaw in disbelief.

"I wouldn't know," Mary Dell said. "I never saw—"

Artie plowed right over the end of her sentence. "But now there are hundreds of channels to pick from, and if you don't keep the audience entertained . . ." He mimed picking up an imaginary remote control and hitting the channel button with his thumb. "Boom! They're off to find somebody who will."

"We've got no disagreement there," Mary Dell said, and Holly could tell from the sound of her voice that she was trying to be patient. "We do have to keep our viewers entertained and engaged, and I have some ideas about how we can do that. But this *is* a quilting show. Our primary purpose is to teach people the art and craft—"

"Yeah, yeah, yeah. I know. And we'll do that. I mean, sure. We've got to show people how to quilt at some point. But let's face it, Mary Dell, your ratings have tanked. If they hadn't, I wouldn't be here. I've been hired to try and bring this show back from the dead. The best way to do that—the *only* way," he added, pushing his face so close to Mary Dell's that she actually took a step backward, "is to create some drama on-camera, a little tension, a story line that'll keep the people coming back week after week to find out what happens next. That's my plan. I am going to turn *Quintessential Quilting* into water-cooler television," he declared.

Mary Dell's eyebrows arched again, this time with skepticism.

"You mean the kind of show that people gather around the water cooler to discuss the next day? Artie, unless those water coolers are located in quilt shops, I don't see how that's possible."

"Yeah, yeah, yeah. I know. But you will." He pulled the sucker out of his mouth and laid a big arm over her shoulders.

"You've got to trust me, M.D.," he said, lowering his voice to a tone that was meant to be soothing but ended up sounding patronizing. "Let me do my job, okay? We're going to breathe some life into this thing, I promise. And just as soon as Holly . . ."

Holly cleared her throat, alerting him to her presence. Artie turned around, beaming.

"You're here! Great!"

He dropped his arm from Mary Dell's shoulder and strode toward her, crossing the room in four huge steps.

"Artie Graves," he said, pumping her hand. "Nice to meet you. Love your work. I'm your new director."

"Holly Sil—"

"Yeah, yeah, yeah. I know all that." He laughed and clapped his hands together once. "So. How about we get started, eh? Let's get you two into hair and makeup; then we'll work on wardrobe."

"Wardrobe?" Mary Dell looked down at her outfit.

She was wearing a bright orange silk blouse over white pants, accessorized with gold hoop earrings and a multistrand necklace of orange, coral, and white beads with gold accent beads. Orange was a good color for her, and the blouse, bright and lacking any visible pattern or design, would read well on-camera.

"I've always worn my own clothes on the show. I called Howard last night and he helped me decide on this. I think it looks pretty good."

"Oh, it does, M.D. But it's not quite right for what we're doing today."

He put the sucker back in his mouth, laid an arm across Mary Dell's shoulders again, took a few steps forward, put the other around Holly's shoulders, and herded them toward the bottom of the stairs, where the women in the blue smocks were waiting.

"You know, getting the opening right is huge. It's your calling card, a chance to hook the audience into that drama I was talking about right from the first. And that's what we're going to do. Trust me. You just go off with Connie and Suze, okay? I've already told them what I'm looking for."

The front door of the quilt shop opened and one of the clipboard-carrying crew members stuck his head in the door.

"Artie? The dog handler called to say he got lost but he should be here in about fifteen, but the guy just showed up with the Lamborghini and the truck. He's unloading the trailer now. Gale wants to know how you want to set up the shot."

"Great!" Artie grinned and clapped his hands together. "This is gonna be awesome!" He headed toward the door with big, clomping steps.

"I do not like that man," Mary Dell muttered after he left.

Holly felt the same way, but it was only the first day and she wanted to stay positive.

"Yeah. He's different. But a Lamborghini sounds promising, doesn't it? And a dog? Who knows? Maybe this will turn out to be fun."

"Maybe," Mary Dell said. "But in my experience, a man who keeps telling you to trust him is a man who can't be trusted."

Quintessential Quilting—Promotional Spot

Shooting in black and white, the camera pans the deserted street of a Western town. A mangy-looking hound dog lies in the middle of the road. He yawns and goes back to sleep. A tumbleweed rolls by. We see a sign. . . .

TOO MUCH, TEXAS
Home of Quintessential Quilting
Population 1,999

Mary Dell Templeton, wearing jeans and a blue-and-white gingham blouse, tight fitting and tied in a knot at the waist and with a "big hair" style, is sitting in a rocking chair with rhinestone cat-eye reading glasses at the end of her nose, hand sewing a quilt.

Cut to the dog, who yawns again. But then his ears perk up. He lifts his head from the ground, alert. He hears something.

Cut to a long shot of a lonely road. There is a cloud of dust at the end of it. The slow and mournful, vaguely bluegrass background music that has been playing up to this point is replaced by the humming of a speeding car engine, the sound melding into a rock riff and building to a crescendo just as a sleek red Lamborghini emerges from the cloud of dust.

Initially, the red car is the only spot of color in the gray landscape, but we soon notice that when the car races through the scene, the landscape it passes is suddenly a riot of color, almost as if the exhaust coming from the vehicle were painting the landscape. It's an effect that continues throughout the remainder of the opening.

The car speeds into town and skids to a stop in front of the porch where Mary Dell is rocking. She removes her glasses, staring at the car. The door of the Lamborghini lifts vertically. Out steps Holly Silva, wearing a red designer dress and looking fabulous—the hair, the clothes, the makeup, the nails, the shoes—she's got it all going on.

Quick close-up. Holly shakes loose her hair and smiles seductively into the camera. Close-up of Mary Dell, who drops her jaw and then her quilt. Holly mounts the steps of the porch—again, the wash of color follows in her wake—reaches down to pick up the old-fashioned, uninteresting quilt, which is transformed at her touch into a beautiful and vibrant masterpiece, and hands it to Mary Dell, who still looks aghast.

Cut to Mary Dell and Holly, who stand on either side of the sign we saw earlier in the shot. Everything is in color now. While Mary Dell watches, Holly takes a bottle of nail polish, the same red as the car and her dress, and applies some to the sign. When she is done, it reads . . .

TOO MUCH, TEXAS
Home of Quintessential Quilting
Population 1,999 + 1

The camera draws back to a wider angle so we see both women—Holly smiling to the camera and Mary Dell glaring at Holly.

Voice-over: *Quintessential Quilting with Mary Dell and Holly:* There's a new sheriff in town. Tuesdays at two and Saturdays at ten. Only on the House and Home Network.

"*That* was miserable," Mary Dell said, and stepped behind a folding screen in their make-shift dressing room.

"Tell me about it. If Artie told me to look into the camera and smile seductively one more time . . ." Holly plopped into a chair and started pulling off her boots. "I wanted to shove his Tootsie Pop right down his throat."

Mary Dell's voice came from behind the screen. "I'd a darn sight rather be asked to smile seductively than end up looking like the biggest clown at the rodeo. That slimy son of a sea slug is trying to make me the butt of the joke. I cannot *believe* that this was his big idea of how to boost ratings! 'Trust me,' " she whined in a nasally imitation of the director.

The Western blouse she'd been wearing came flying up into the air and landed on top of the screen.

"That man is making me look like an idiot! And not just me but the whole town! A dog sleeping in the middle of the road . . . a tumbleweed rolling right down Main Street . . . like Too Much is just some no-account wide spot in the road. And that sign! As of the last census, we've got three thousand six hundred and eighty-nine people living here. More than five thousand if you count the ranches just outside of town."

Mary Dell stepped out from behind the screen, fuming, dressed in the orange blouse and white slacks she'd been wearing earlier that morning, with her hands on her hips.

"Do you know how mad people in Too Much are going to be when they see that sign?"

Holly, upset that Mary Dell was so upset, shook her head and found that doing so made it hurt.

"Very. He's making them the butt of the joke, too, like we're nobodies and that nothing interesting ever happened here until you came on the scene."

"He's a jerk," Holly said. "And you're right. That was miserable."

Mary Dell sat down in front of a small mirror, picked up a brush, and started trying to pull it through the stiff locks of her overly sprayed hair.

"Not all that miserable for you," Mary Dell said bitterly. "He's building you up by tearing me down."

"Okay," Holly admitted, "today was rough. But let's wait and see. Maybe it won't be so bad after they finish the editing. You're nobody's clown, Mary Dell. Especially once you sit down in front of a sewing machine. Once we get to the actual quilting part, you are going to shine!"

Holly got up and stood behind Mary Dell so she could see both their faces reflected in the mirror. She placed her hand on Mary Dell's shoulder and gave it a comforting squeeze.

"Remember what you told me, only a week ago and in this very room? They're going to try and play us against each other, but we weren't going to fall for it."

The angry expression on Mary Dell's face softened a bit and she exhaled a long, deep breath.

"You're right," she said, and reached up to squeeze Holly's hand. "You're right. We're not going to fall for it."

Chapter 24

Sitting cross-legged on the floor of her bedroom, surrounded by piles of blue fabric in every shade of indigo, Mary Dell said, "Now, isn't this better than sitting around feeling sorry for yourself? Of course it is."

This wasn't the first pep talk Mary Dell had given herself that evening. She did feel a little foolish doing it, but there was no one around to hear, so what difference did it make? Rattling around in the big, empty house was the thing that had set her off to begin with, and filling the silent void with the sound of her own voice helped to distract her from her loneliness. So did playing with fabric.

The others, including Holly, had gone to the drive-in.

There was a new animated movie playing, the kind with a spunky but beset singing princess who overcomes evil with good. Linne was dying to see it, and so, a few days before, Cady had suggested a girls' night to satisfy her daughter's wishes and celebrate the first day of filming.

Mary Dell was pleased that Cady seemed to be coming around a little bit. This new friendship with Holly was good for her, and for Rob Lee too. He wasn't exactly skipping around singing

"Zip-a-Dee-Doo-Dah," but he was getting his work done and spending time helping Stormy adjust to his new surroundings, with Holly helping him. That was a lot better than drinking himself into a stupor every night.

Holly was a sweet girl, and Mary Dell had to give her credit for lifting Cady's and Rob Lee's spirits—something Mary Dell had been unable to do.

But gratitude aside, Mary Dell had spent enough time with Holly for now. It took a lot to put Mary Dell in a bad mood, but the humiliation that she'd been put through that day *was* a lot, and so she begged off going to the movie, saying she was tired. They'd protested, urging her to change her mind, but Mary Dell was adamant. Finally, they left, Linne promising to bring her a box of Junior Mints from the drive-in candy counter.

Her relief at their departure was short-lived.

Having married at eighteen, going directly from her parental home to her marital home without living on her own for so much as a day, Mary Dell had never mastered the art of being alone.

Donny's leaving had been hard to endure, but even then, she still had Howard and, for years, continued to live just a stone's throw from the family, in the double-wide she and Donny had purchased upon their marriage. Even in the womb, she'd never lacked for company. She wondered if the intense loneliness engulfing her that night was a consequence of being born a twin, so that having never been alone even before she was born made it impossible to enjoy or adjust to that condition after. Maybe.

Uneasy and unable to settle down, her mind constantly circling back to the degradations she'd been put through that day and how they would be multiplied after the promo spot aired, she puttered around in the kitchen, desperate for something to do.

Wandering through the living room, she spied the bouquet Hub-Jay had sent on Thursday. She carried it back into the kitchen, then threw away the dead blooms and put those that still looked fresh in with the bouquet that had come the day before.

The task complete, she picked up the phone, thinking she might call Hub-Jay to thank him for the flowers, but she changed her mind. She'd been avoiding his calls for days. If she called now, he'd get the wrong idea, assume that she'd been thinking about that incredible, magical night they'd spent together, which was exactly what she *had* been doing.

Every time another vase filled with flowers arrived on her doorstop, every time she felt discouraged, especially today, every time she was being made to feel obsolete and invisible, she thought about Hub-Jay, the way he had seen her and touched her and whispered her name in the darkness.

But she shouldn't.

Jumping thoughtlessly into a relationship with Hub-Jay was not an antidote to loneliness. Or, if it was, it shouldn't be.

She'd done that once before, impulsively accepted a proposal from a man she barely knew because she'd believed, or wanted to believe, that doing so would solve all her problems. Of course it hadn't. And she had only compounded the situation by allowing herself to fall in love. Had she never opened her heart to Donny, she'd never have felt it break when he left her.

She wasn't ready to leave herself vulnerable to that kind of pain, especially not now. She put down the phone, made herself a cup of tea, then picked up the phone again and dialed Howard.

"Hi, Momma."

"Hi, baby! How you doing? How's school?"

She could hear voices and laughter and street sounds in the background, as if he might be walking down a city sidewalk. Howard raised his voice and she was able to hear him better.

"Great. We're learning about pointillism. That's those paintings that just look like little dots of color until you step back and can see the picture."

"Yes, I've seen paintings like that. They're amazing."

"Uh-huh. We've been learning all about it. I'm painting one in class, a sailboat on a lake. Professor Eagan says it's good. I'm going to give it to you for my birthday."

251

Mary Dell pressed her hand to her heart. Lord, but she missed him.

"I can't wait to see it, baby. But you're the one supposed to be getting presents, not me. What do you want for your birthday anyway? Won't be long now, just six more weeks."

"I know! Jenna bought a new dress for the party. She looks pretty in it. Momma? I can't talk. I'm at the art museum. Professor Eagan brought us to see a special exhibit about pointillism."

"Oh. Well. I should let you go then."

"Okay . . . Wait, Momma! I almost forgot. How is the show going? Do you like the new director?"

"Oh, yes," she said quickly. "He's fine. Everything's fine."

He let out a big sigh, obviously relieved by the report.

"That's good. Okay. The tour guide is here, Momma. Gotta go. Love you."

"Love you too, baby. Call me when you—"

He was gone before she could finish her sentence, off on his own adventures.

Pity parties were not Mary Dell's style—never had been—and so, when a teardrop splashed onto her wrist while she was rinsing out her mug, she gave herself a talking-to.

"Oh, you big baby! You brought this on yourself, you know. You could have gone to the movies but you didn't. So snap out of it and go find something to do!"

She felt a little foolish, scolding herself aloud, but it did seem to help. She put her mug back in the cupboard and went back to her bedroom, deciding that she needed a new project—not that she didn't have plenty to work on already, but those were all for the show. Those were work. She needed to do something just because she wanted to, not because she had to.

She'd make Howard a quilt for his birthday. That would cheer her up. Of course, he already had dozens. But could a person ever have too many quilts? Of course not. That would be like saying a person could have too much love. It just wasn't possible. Normally, Mary Dell relied on Howard's judgment when choosing fabrics for a new quilt. But because she really wanted to surprise him, she decided to go it alone this time, promising to rein in her natural exuberance to create a quilt she was certain Howard would love.

The only way she could think to do that would be to severely narrow her color palette, and so she set out to do something she'd never done before: make a two-color quilt.

Technically, it was really a one-color quilt, since white was really a neutral, but her second color was indigo, the color used in blue jeans, and just as there were scores and scores of color variations in jeans—from the palest, most washed-out blue to the darkest, deepest midnight blue—so, too, there were scores and scores of variations of indigo in fabrics.

Mary Dell knew that, of course, but she never truly appreciated how creative you could be even while sticking to just one color, until she started digging through her stash and discovered just how many different indigo fabrics she had collected through the years. This was turning out to be much easier and a lot more fun than she'd imagined.

In fact, Mary Dell was having so much fun auditioning fabrics for Howard's quilt that she didn't hear the doorbell until the third ring. Living so far from town, they rarely had unexpected visitors, especially at night. Mary Dell figured that Cady had forgotten her house keys. She pushed herself up from the floor, groaning because she'd been sitting there a long time and her legs were stiff. She walked through the darkened house toward the door, calling, "I'm coming! Hang on a minute, will you?" because Cady kept ringing the bell.

But when she switched on the light and opened the door, it wasn't Cady; it was Hub-Jay, carrying yet another bouquet of flowers and a suitcase.

"Oh," Mary Dell said, and stood looking at him for a long moment before saying anything else. Even then, all she could think of was, "It's you."

He handed her the flowers, long-stemmed white roses and purple lilacs tied with a white satin ribbon.

"You said I was welcome anytime. Remember?"

She did remember. And at the time she'd meant it. But that was before the night she was trying so hard not to think about. Even then, she would never have figured on him just showing up on the doorstep unannounced.

"It's hard to call ahead and ask if I can come visit when you don't answer your phone," Hub-Jay pointed out. "And if you had answered, would you have said, 'Sure thing. Come on down'? I don't think so."

Of course she wouldn't have invited him to come down. There were very good reasons for that. Mary Dell was sure he knew exactly what they were but began spelling them out anyway.

But she didn't get far, because, just at that moment, a pair of headlights came around the curve of the driveway, shining so bright that she had to shield her eyes. The car parked right near the back porch. Cady, Taffy, and Linne spilled out. Hub-Jay walked over to greet them.

"Oh, I already know who you are," Cady said when he introduced himself. "I've heard a lot about you."

"You have? That's encouraging." He glanced over his shoulder to the porch, where Mary Dell was standing, her arms crossed over her chest. "Depending on what kind of things you heard."

"All good," Cady assured him.

Taffy introduced herself. "We've talked on the

phone," she reminded him, pumping his hand. "A few times.

"Glad you finally decided to come out here and deliver your message in person, seeing as my daughter never finds time to call you back. Though I'll be danged if I can figure out why. The way she's been ignoring your calls, I figured you must be bald or a hunchback, or maybe have one big eye in the middle of your forehead. But look at you!" she said, gazing up at him and letting out a sigh. "You're about as yummy as strawberries picked on the first day of spring."

"Momma!" Mary Dell hissed, wishing the earth would just open and up and swallow her or, better yet, her mother.

Taffy ignored her. "Mary Dell, why won't you return this man's phone calls?"

"I know she's been awfully busy," Hub-Jay said magnanimously. "So I thought I'd come down to discuss the details for Howard and Rob Lee's birthday party and save her a trip to Dallas."

"I don't care if she was as busy as a funeral fan in July; I'd have found time to call you back if I'd been in her shoes. It's too bad I'm not," Taffy said, looking him up and down. "Dang."

Mary Dell closed her eyes and wondered if it were possible for this day to get any worse.

"Are you the man who owns all the hotels?" Linne asked. Hub-Jay bobbed his head. "What's it like? I never stayed in a hotel before."

"No? I've already reserved a beautiful corner suite for you and your momma when you come to Dallas for the birthday party. The bathtub's almost as big as a swimming pool," he said, crouching down so he could look into Linne's wide eyes. "But we've got a real pool, too, so be sure to bring your bathing suit."

"Momma!" Linne squealed and threw her arms around Cady's waist. "Did you hear? A swimming pool! And sweets!"

Cady laughed and smoothed her daughter's hair with her hand. "I think he was talking about a different kind of suite."

"Don't worry, we've got both kinds. The house-keepers leave chocolate truffles in every room when they come to turn down the beds." Hub-Jay lifted himself to his full height and addressed Taffy. "Mrs. Templeton, I hope you're coming to the party. I've reserved a suite for you as well."

Taffy's beady eyes lit up. "Does it have one of those beds with the magic fingers?"

"No," Hub-Jay said slowly, "but would it be all right if I booked you into the spa for a massage?"

Taffy grinned. "Oh, I think I could be per-suaded."

She turned toward her daughter. "Mary Dell, where have you been keeping this man all these years? And why haven't you invited him inside and offered him something to eat?" She clucked her tongue and frowned. "He's going to think I didn't raise you right. How long are you staying with us, Mr. Hollander?"

He glanced at Mary Dell. "Well, I was hoping—"

She interrupted him. "Hub-Jay just happened to be passing through town and stopped to say hello, Momma. He can't stay. He's very busy, running all those hotels. And, anyway, we don't have any empty bedrooms now that I'm home."

"What are you talking about? Nobody ever just passes through Too Much." Taffy swatted away her daughter's explanation. "Don't you worry, Mr. Hollander. You can take Linne's room and she can bunk in with me. Linne, honey, take Mr. Hollander's suitcase inside."

"Are you sure? I don't like the idea of putting anyone out of their room," Hub-Jay said.

Linne grabbed Hub-Jay's overnight bag, clutching the handle with both hands so it banged against her legs when she walked.

"I don't mind. How big is the pool at your hotel?"

"Huge," Hub-Jay replied, then climbed the porch steps, brushing past Mary Dell so he could open the door. "And it has a hot tub."

"A hot tub!"

With Hub-Jay holding the door for them, the women filed into the house. Taffy came right on Linne's heels, grumbling about Mary Dell's lack of hospitality and that it was a good thing she'd made that buttermilk pie the day before. Cady was next, saying she'd set the table and make some tea. Mary Dell followed her, but stopped at the doorway to talk to Hub-Jay.

"Quit charming my family!" she said, her voice somewhere between a whisper and a hiss.

Hub-Jay shrugged helplessly. "I'm a charming man. Ask anyone. And anyway, you're the one I drove out here to charm. Winning over your relatives is just a bonus." He chuckled. "I sure like your momma. She's a pistol."

"Don't I know it," Mary Dell mumbled. "And she's got more gunpowder in her barrel every year."

Chapter 25

Originally, Hub-Jay had planned to stay at the F-Bar-T for three days, but he settled for two, deciding it would be unwise to push Mary Dell too hard or too quickly. Also because he realized that she was under a great deal of pressure. Now was not the time for a hard sell. And that wasn't his style anyway.

Sure, turning up for an overnight visit at Mary Dell's home without her prior knowledge or consent wasn't exactly subtle, but what choice did he have? He couldn't win her if he couldn't spend time with her. But now that he was here, he'd exercise more restraint.

The reason Hub-Jay and, in turn, his hotels were successful was because he had mastered the arts of discretion and observation. The way to win and keep the loyalty of your guests was to pay such careful attention that you knew what they needed and wanted almost before they did, made sure those wants and needs were fulfilled even before they asked, and did so without even a hint of obsequiousness.

If a guest looked at Hub-Jay or his staff as fawning or servile, then they came to see the services rendered unto them as merely something to which they were entitled by virtue of having paid for them. But if that same guest saw the staff as equals, then those same services were viewed as acts of consideration, the kindness of one peer to another, for which no payment was expected or accepted.

People who said that the success of the Hollander hotels lay in their outstanding customer service didn't understand that what Hub-Jay and his staff were doing was not providing a service, but building a relationship. Hub-Jay Hollander genuinely wanted to make his guests happy.

He wanted Mary Dell to be happy, too, only a hundred times as much.

And so, during these far-too-brief two days, he would not press, or push, or make demands. He would listen more than he talked; he would give more than he got. He would bide his time and simply be present for her, so that after he left, she might realize that his absence left a hole in her life, the way her absence had left a hole in his.

At breakfast the next morning, Mary Dell asked him how he wanted to spend the day.

"Whatever you want," he answered. "I'm just happy to spend time with you."

"I was planning to go down to help Cady at the shop, but I don't imagine—"

"Great. What time do we leave?"

Cady made a face. "Oh, you don't want to do that, do you? Aunt Mary Dell, take him on a tour of the town, or out for a trail ride, or go on a picnic. We won't be that busy on a Tuesday. I can mind the store by myself."

"No, no," he said. "I'd really like to go to the shop, Mary Dell. It'll be fun to see you in action."

And it was.

Hub-Jay knew that Mary Dell was successful and that, over the years, she'd taken what was little more than a hobby teaching quilting to a handful of women in her living room and built a thriving business. But he hadn't realized that the Patchwork Palace was so big, or the level of business acumen that Mary Dell possessed in being able to keep the operation afloat.

As soon as Hub-Jay walked through the doors, the businessman in his head immediately began trying to calculate the risks and rewards of the operation. Even though Cady had been managing the store in her absence, when he started quizzing Mary Dell about her carrying costs and returns, she was able to rattle off the figures without hesitation. Cady might be in charge of staffing, schedules, and the like, but Mary Dell was clearly the driving force and brains of the business. She knew, down to the penny, what she'd paid for her inventory of three thousand bolts of fabric as well as threads, notions, tools, pattern books, and such. She also knew exactly what she spent on operating expenses and salaries, what her average per-square-foot sales by year and by month were, and how those sales broke down within the categories of fabric, notions, books, and services, such as quilting classes.

"Wow. You're a going concern, aren't you?" Hub-Jay said.

Mary Dell rolled her eyes. "Might want to do the math again, Hub-Jay. I think you misplaced a decimal."

The point was well taken. While he was genuinely impressed that she was able to keep such a big operation afloat in such a remote location, she obviously wasn't getting rich. She made a decent living, but not a princely one. So what was her motivation for working so hard? It didn't take him long to figure it out.

Mary Dell loved quilts and everything that went into them, passionately. But what she loved most of all was igniting that same passion in others by sharing everything she knew with an open hand and her whole heart. That was her purpose on earth, to teach quilting. Hub-Jay could tell, not just by the way customers made a beeline for her whenever they had a question or problem, but by the way she would drop everything to help them and how her whole countenance lit up when she did.

At those moments, it was clear to Hub-Jay that Mary Dell loved this part of her job. And, even though her words were only positive, from the way that her face fell and the light left her eyes whenever anyone asked how the filming was going for the new season, it was just as clear that, at least at the moment, filming the TV show was a trial.

Interesting.

They didn't spend the whole of his two days in Too Much at the quilt shop, however. When things got slow in the afternoon, Mary Dell decided she wanted to take him on a tour of the town. "That should take all of ten minutes," she joked. But it actually took nearly three hours.

She walked him around the town and the Square, past the Primp 'n' Perm salon, where Taffy had taken her for an emergency intervention after a disastrous attempt at highlighting her own hair when she was twelve, to Antoinette's dress shop, where she'd bought her first pair of high heels, and to Hilda's House of Pie, where she showed him the counter stool that her father occupied during the last years of his life, the place he would drink coffee and swap stories with other gray-headed men whose minds were still agile but whose bodies were breaking down.

They crossed the street to the Square. She showed him the statue of Flagadine Tudmore and took him through the historical society, which her aunt Velvet had run for so many years.

Climbing behind the wheel of her Eldorado convertible, she drove him past the pink cottage that Aunt Velvet had shared with her sister, Mary Dell's grandma Silky, the scene of her first sewing lessons and many of her happiest memories, days spent under the patient and loving tutelage of that worthy old woman. Finally, she took him to the Methodist church, the redbrick building where she'd attended Sunday school and services throughout her childhood and where, barring sickness, she could still be found every Sunday morning.

After she told him about getting her first kiss from the minister's second son during a youth group hayride, they strolled through the adjoining cemetery, where he saw tombstones engraved with the names of her Tudmore and Templeton ancestors, some dating back to the 1800s and some more recent, including those of her beloved aunt Velvet, Grandma Silky, her brother-in-law, Graydon, and her father, Dutch.

"Momma will rest right here next to him," she said, nodding at an adjacent patch of vacant ground. "And I'll be next to her, with Lydia Dale and Graydon."

She crouched down, quiet but not sad, and pulled a couple of scraggly weeds out from the base of her father's grave, then rested her hand on top of the headstone.

"It's a comfort," she said, "knowing where I'm headed."

"Heaven?"

She lifted her face to him, and though he could see the crow's-feet around her eyes, he saw within them the candor and purity of a very young girl.

"Yes. I believe that's my soul's destination, but my bones have to rest somewhere."

She pressed her hand to the ground to get to her feet, but Hub-Jay supported her hand and helped her rise. Eyes still cast down, she brushed the earth from her hands. "It's nice to know that this is my place. Here, with my people."

With the sun low in the sky, they returned to the convertible and drove back to the ranch.

"Now I understand why this place has such a pull on you," he said. "It's not just your home-town; it's your history, the place and people that made you who you are. You must be so happy to be back."

She had been nodding slowly, agreeing with his observations, but stopped when he came to that last one.

"I am," she said, and then, in a voice that sounded almost surprised, "but not quite as happy as I thought I'd be."

"No? Why do you think that is?"

"I don't know." Her brow creased, as if she was trying to puzzle it out, then quickly pushed the question aside.

"It's not important. I'm happy enough."

His last day in Too Much, Taffy prepared a big lunch of sliced ham, potato salad, baked beans, homemade rolls, and fresh peach cobbler. When she apologized for the simplicity of the fare, saying that he was probably used to much fancier food, Hub-Jay replied it was as good a meal as he'd ever had and asked if he could have the cobbler recipe to share with his pastry chef. Beaming, she copied it out for him on an index card with a picture of a sunflower in the corner.

Rob Lee joined them for lunch. Hub-Jay was happy to get a chance to meet him. He was a quiet young man and serious, but they chatted amiably enough. After the meal was done, he volunteered to show Hub-Jay around the ranch while Mary Dell helped Taffy with the dishes.

Hub-Jay stowed his overnight bag in his car, then met up with Rob Lee at the barn.

The F-Bar-T had been founded as a cattle-only operation, Rob Lee told him, but now they raised sheep as well. "It helps spread the risk that way," he explained. "If beef prices go south for a year or two, you might be able to survive on the proceeds of the sheep, and vice versa."

"Good idea. Does it work?"

"Pretty good. Not always. It was my uncle Donny who had the idea. Aunt Mary Dell's husband."

"Ah," Hub-Jay said. "Sounds like a smart guy."

"I wouldn't know," Rob Lee said. "He didn't stick around long enough for me to find out."

While they were on their tour, a Jeep pulled into the driveway and an absolutely stunning young woman wearing faded jeans, a straw cowboy hat, and a pair of dirt-covered boots that looked as if they'd formerly been white came trotting out to the barn. Holly introduced herself, explaining that she'd come to see her horse, as she did every day.

Hub-Jay had heard all about Stormy during the previous night's dinner. He stood outside the paddock, next to Rob Lee, and watched as Holly opened the gate and went inside with Stormy, another horse, and a goat.

"Watch this," Rob Lee said out of the side of his mouth, and then spread his feet a bit and crossed his arms over his chest.

Holly stood at the far end of the paddock with her hands at her sides and clicked her tongue against her teeth. As soon as she did, both horses turned toward her, their ears perked up. The goat bleated and moved immediately toward her with little mincing steps that quickened to a trot. The second horse followed behind at a somewhat slower pace but without the least hesitation. The same could not be said of Stormy, but his reluctance was overcome when Holly pulled three carrots from her pocket.

He approached cautiously, his steps shorter and more static than the relaxed, fluid gait of his stablemate. He stopped about four feet away, watching the goat and the other horse happily munching their carrots while Holly murmured to the other horse and stroked its neck.

"This one's yours," she finally said, lifting one of the carrots up so Stormy could see it but keeping it fairly close to her body. "All you have to do is come over here and get it."

Stormy sputtered, bobbed his head a couple of times, and yawned, making his anxiety and indecision clear. He took one step toward her, then another, and another, until he was standing right next to her. Holly smiled, broke off a piece of the carrot, and held it in her flattened palm. Stormy lowered his muzzle and took the carrot from her hand.

"Oh, what a good boy," Holly said in a soft,

singsong voice. "What a good, brave boy. Want some more?"

She broke off another piece of carrot and repeated the procedure, but this time, while Stormy was eating, she took gentle hold of his rope halter with one hand and lifted the other to his neck and started stroking it, just as she had with the other horse. Stormy flinched a bit but permitted it.

"Will you look at that?" Rob Lee said softly, moving his head from side to side. "Yesterday was the first time he even walked toward her. She had to hold the carrot way out before he'd take it."

"Looks like she has a way with horses," Hub-Jay said.

"Looks like," Rob Lee replied, his admiration obvious.

The show wasn't over yet.

The other horse, who had finished her carrot, walked over to Holly and began nosing her shoulder, hungry for food and attention. The goat was right on her heels, bleating demandingly.

"You want more? Okay, but you're going to have to work for it. Come on, everybody."

She broke off three pieces of carrot, wrapped them in her fist, and walked to the left. The goat and both horses trailed after her. This time, Stormy didn't hesitate at all.

After about fifteen steps, she stopped and administered rewards, then repeated the process, moving to the right and then the left and then the right again, about thirty or forty steps this time, before handing out more treats. Things went on like that for another few minutes, until the carrots were all gone.

"Okay, gang," Holly said. "That's it for today. See you tomorrow."

She walked back toward the gate, but not before reaching out and giving Stormy a farewell stroke on his head. This time, the horse flinched not at all.

Mary Dell came looking for Hub-Jay at about the same time Holly left the paddock. Hearing the report of Holly's progress with the horse, she grinned and said, "Sounds like he's decided you're part of his herd."

"No," Rob Lee corrected, "he's decided that she's the leader of the herd and that he can trust her. That's more important."

Mary Dell asked Hub-Jay if he felt like going for a ride before he left town. He agreed quickly, surprised and encouraged by the invitation. Holly said her good-byes and headed home, saying she wanted to get back and work on her quilt. Rob Lee went to saddle two horses.

"Let's put Hub-Jay on Sarabeth," Mary Dell called after him. "I'll ride Daisy."

They rode toward a ridge that Mary Dell said had a nice view of the stream. Sarabeth, the second horse he'd seen in the paddock, was gentle and surefooted. Hub-Jay didn't have to do much more than hold on to the reins. Daisy, a paint, chestnut with white markings, was equally calm and fell right into step with Sarabeth, making it easy for Hub-Jay and Mary Dell to talk as they rode.

Their conversation was light and largely inconsequential, though Mary Dell did tell him the story about how her ancestor, Flagadine Tudmore, had chosen this particular spot of land after walking the acres and realizing that the tiny "no-account" rivulet of muddy water she'd spied in the heat of summer would swell to a good-sized creek in spring, feeding the ground and ensuring a good supply of grass for grazing cattle. They talked about the party too. Hub-Jay filled her in on how all the plans were proceeding, and she thanked him sincerely, saying she wouldn't have been able to manage it on her own, not from a distance and in the middle of filming.

"But I can't let you give hotel suites to my entire family," she said.

"Sure you can. It's my present to Howard."

"It's too much," she said. "I want to pay for them. I insist."

He put her off, saying it was too nice a day to argue and that they could work it out later.

Mary Dell conceded the point. "But don't think I'm going to forget about it," she said. "Because I'm not."

271

"Fair enough."

When they reached their destination, a rocky outcropping overlooking that creek that Mary Dell had mentioned, they got off the horses and stood silently under the scanty shade of a mesquite tree to look at the view. The rolling hills, carpeted with prairie grass, parched but golden, stretched out to the horizon under a sky as blue as cornflowers and dotted with cotton-puff clouds.

Sensing that the moment was right, Hub-Jay said, "Sorry for showing up unannounced, Mary Dell. I know you've been trying to avoid me, but I had to see you. I can't stop thinking about you."

She turned toward him.

"That's why I wanted to bring you out here. So we could talk about . . . that night. Hub-Jay, I told you before, I'm still married. In all the years since Donny left me, I never . . ." She shifted he eyes away from him, fixing her gaze on the view. Hub-Jay could see a flush of pink paint her cheeks. "I don't want you to have the wrong idea about me."

He was quiet for a moment, marveling at how just the sound of her voice made him feel buoyant, young, hopeful. Happy.

When he was a much younger man, he had sometimes wondered how to distinguish the difference between lust and love. Later, he started to think they were two parts of the same thing, and later still, that love was an idea that women invented and that men bought in to, to make lust more socially acceptable.

What a happy shock to discover, and at this late stage of life, how very wrong he had been.

He cupped his hand over the curve of her shoulder, turned her body toward his, and laid his palm against her cheek. She flinched, ever so slightly, but didn't draw back. He looked in her eyes, leaned forward, and pressed his lips to her forehead.

"I have exactly the right idea about you," he said. "That's why I'm here."

Chapter 26

Holly was anxious about shooting the first episode of *Quintessential Quilting* on Monday, and with good reason. She was worried that Artie, who was clearly more interested in creating a sensation than in filming good content, would end up making a joke of the whole show and driving a wedge between her and Mary Dell.

Though they'd agreed in the dressing room not to let that happen, Holly sensed a slight chill between her and her co-host in the days that followed. Not that Mary Dell was unkind to her; far from it. During the remainder of the week, she was generous in sharing her time and knowledge so that Holly would be prepared and look competent during shooting. She just seemed a little distant.

She smiled and joked with her less than before, and Holly noticed that Mary Dell had stopped urging her to come in for a glass of iced tea and a gab when Holly came by the ranch to work with Stormy, or to stay on for supper after they finished sewing for the day.

Of course, it wasn't required that she and Mary Dell be friends, but Holly knew it would help their on-camera chemistry. More important, Holly liked Mary Dell and wanted to be liked in return. It was a natural enough desire, but as the days ticked off to Monday and the coolness of her co-host continued, Holly feared their friendship had sailed.

If not for Artie, it probably would have.

While the two women were getting their makeup done, Artie came in to inform them he had installed a "confessional corner" with a video camera behind the privacy screens they'd placed in the front of the shop. The idea was that Holly and Mary Dell could sit in front of a video camera at any time and secretly record "private" speeches about their feelings surrounding the show and each other.

It was a cheap ploy from his bag of reality show tricks, designed to create tension and drama where none existed. While Artie didn't come out and demand they go in and trash each other, he was clearly hoping they'd do exactly that.

Mary Dell was having none of it.

"Absolutely not. First off, anything somebody says that gets spilled out into millions of television sets isn't private. Second, anything I have to say to or about Holly I'll say to her face. I'm not a gossip. Never have been. Third, last, and most important," she said, moving her face right up next to Artie's, "the show is about *quilting*. That's what people tune in to see and that's what we're going to give them. Nothing more. And nothing less."

The way she said that last part made it clear that she thought Artie's concept definitely fell into the category of very much less.

Holly backed her up.

"I agree. It's not the right tone for a quilting show. In public or private, the only things I have to say about Mary Dell are good things."

Holly walked up next to her co-host and crossed her arms over her chest. Mary Dell adopted a similar pose, and there they stood, a united front. Artie narrowed his eyes and twirled his ever-present sucker inside his mouth, as if trying to decide how far to push the issue, then skulked off, saying he expected them on the set in fifteen minutes. When he left, Mary Dell and Holly shared a fist bump.

Though the small act of mutiny earned the ire of

the director, it restored the relationship between the two women, and the remainder of the day's filming went according to plan.

The first segment, shot in front of the courthouse per Mary Dell's suggestion, gave context to the episode and the season as a whole. Mary Dell beamed as she told viewers about their new location and welcomed her new co-host. The camera moved to Holly, who said how excited she was to be learning the art of quilting from scratch, and from such a master teacher. Then Mary Dell explained how, as Holly built on her skills week by week, both novice and experienced quilters would have an opportunity to learn techniques that could be adapted to myriad quilting projects, from the simple to the complex. This week, they'd begin with one of quilting's most beloved and versatile blocks, Courthouse Steps. She closed out the segment by smiling into the camera and saying, "Let's get quilting!"

Afterward, they did exactly that: went into the quilt shop turned studio and filmed four more short segments. The first was with Holly alone, explaining how to set up, thread, and clean a sewing machine, as well as check the tension. She was a little nervous, but they got the whole thing in three takes. When she was done, Mary Dell said she'd done a great job.

"You know, I'm almost happy for the ten gazillion times I had to thread and rethread my machine and fight with the tension and untangle the tangles. On that score at least, I actually do know what I'm talking about." Holly laughed and Mary Dell gave her a squeeze.

"You're doing great, girlfriend."

In the next two segments Mary Dell and Holly were on-camera together, working on the block itself and setting the blocks into a quilt. The fourth segment was just Mary Dell, showing advanced settings for the basic block. They came back together for the wrap-up, and Mary Dell signed off by saying, as she had on every episode for seven seasons, "And remember, behind every great quilter is a big ol' pile of fabric. So get to work!"

When the first episode was in the can, they broke for lunch and then went back to work. Because episode two centered on the Flying Geese block, they filmed the introduction at Puny Pond. There weren't any geese in residence just then, only a few ducks, but it was a nice background just the same. Then they returned to the studio, filmed the four instructional segments and the sign-off, and wrapped up by seven o'clock.

It was a grueling twelve-hour day, but after so many weeks of preparation, it felt good to finally get in front of the cameras. Holly was so happy that she and Mary Dell were on the same team again. They started a little game, kind of a secret joke, of putting a hash mark on a piece of paper every time Artie cut someone off by saying, "I know, I know, I know . . ."

By day's end, they'd made forty-six marks and, feeling tired and a little bit punchy, were having a hard time not breaking up with laughter whenever Artie opened his mouth.

Holly gave Mary Dell another hug before departing and said she'd see her around one o'clock the next day, after visiting Stormy, to sew and talk over their plans for the next two episodes, and that, yes, she'd love to stay for supper at the ranch.

Tired but happy, Holly drove back to the cottage, fed the cat and herself, and curled up on the couch under an afghan to watch television. Calypso jumped immediately in her lap, purring his contentment that she was home and, for the first time in days, occupied in the important business of stroking his fur instead of sitting in front of a sewing machine. She was surfing the channels when her cell phone rang.

A youngish-sounding man said, "Holly Silva? This is Brian Kamkin. I'm a producer with *Entertainment 24/7*. I was wondering if you might be willing to give us an interview?"

Holly shifted up on the couch pillows, feeling suddenly alert. Calypso, irritated at being displaced by her movement, put on his Grumpy Cat face and started kneading the afghan, trying to get comfortable again.

"Sure, Brian . . . I mean, I guess so."

She hesitated for a moment, wondering if she ought to refer him to the publicity department. That was the normal channel for booking interviews, and she didn't want to ruffle any feathers at HHN-TV, but *Entertainment 24/7* was a huge national network program, watched by untold millions of viewers. Surely, in this instance, she'd be forgiven for skirting protocol.

After all, how often did an HHN show get the chance for this kind of publicity? And weeks before the new season was set to air. How had *Quintessential Quilting* come onto his radar anyway? Even the promo spot wasn't due to air for another week.

"Great!" the young producer exclaimed. "We're too late for tonight's broadcast, but that's okay. We think it's a story that'll run for a couple of days. If you can get to Dallas in the morning, we'll record the interview at our affiliate. For right now, could you just give me a comment? We've still got time to work it into the script for tonight, or maybe into the teasers for tomorrow's show."

"You need a comment?"

Euphoria gave way to suspicion and then to self-condemnation as she figured out the real reason Brian Kamkin was calling. This was about Rachel. How stupid had she been to think that a national entertainment show would be interested in her? Or her little cable quilting show?

"Yeah, just something quick will be fine," he said.

Holly could hear a click as Brian turned on a recording device.

"We've been trying to track down your mom, but we haven't had any luck yet. I tried reaching her publicist, but she didn't return the call. So, was Rachel surprised when the pageant announced it wasn't going to renew her contract? Or did she know about it ahead of time? As you know, Micah Thomasson, your mother's longtime co-anchor for the Miss Millennia Pageant, was just signed for an additional three years, even though he's five years older than your mom. And Rachel's replacement, Caitlyn Alison, is twenty years his junior. What kind of statement does this make about the double standards for beauty and relevance between men and women in the entertainment industry?"

Oh, no.

Holly closed her eyes. Her heart was pounding. "No comment," she said, making her tone as emotionless as possible.

"Holly, please," Brian begged. "I just want to give you a chance to tell your mom's side of the story. I'm not trying to do anything that would—"

"*No* comment!"

"Wait! Don't hang up! I hear you're doing some quilting show, right? Tell you what: You give me a comment and I'll book you for another interview next month, just about you and the—"

She clicked the "end" button and threw the phone across the room as hard as she could. Calypso let out a startled meow and jumped from her lap.

That jerk! That snake! Was he hatched from an egg or something? Does he not have a mother that he seriously thought I'd sell mine out for an interview on his stupid television show?

Holly howled in frustration and threw a sofa pillow. Calypso bolted from the room and didn't come out for the rest of the night. Holly jumped up from the couch, remembering her phone.

Oh, please! Let it not be broken. What had she been thinking, throwing it like that? She had to talk to Rachel. If the *Entertainment 24/7* people were looking for her, that meant the rest of the media were doing the same thing. Eventually, no matter where she was, they'd track her down. And when they did, if she was discovered in Mexico with Jared Hoffman, a supposedly happily married man with three kids and a wife the public adored, then the two- or three-day story about Rachel's falling star would become a month-long story that would make her the most hated woman in show business.

No matter where she was or what she was doing, Holly had to get hold of her mother. She had to warn her.

Three minutes later, Holly was leaving her mother a voice mail.

"Mom? I heard what happened. Somebody from *Entertainment 24/7* just called me, looking for a comment. You've *got* to call me back." She paused for a moment, feeling her throat tighten. "Are you okay?"

There was a beep on the line, signaling an incoming call. Holly picked it up.

"You heard?" Rachel asked.

"Mom, I'm so sorry. When did you find out?"

"It's okay." She sighed heavily. "I've known for a while. They decided to tell me on the day of the pageant, about two hours before we went on air."

"That long ago? Why didn't you tell me?"

"I didn't want to worry you. And anyway, I was embarrassed."

"Why would *you* be embarrassed? You didn't do anything wrong. I can't believe it! They really fired you right before you went on air? Those rat basta—"

"Holly Silva! Watch your language!" Rachel gasped, feigning shock. "And leave the dirty words to me. I've had so much more practice swearing than you have."

She laughed, but her voice sounded tired and defeated.

"It's okay, honey. Really. I'm over it. I'm just surprised at how long it took for the story to break. Guess the pageant peons decided to delay until they got Caitlyn Alison to sign on the dotted line.

Did you hear? Jordan McHenry put the deal together."

"Your own agent? You've got to be kidding. How can he do that? I mean, ethically. Forget ethically, is that even legal?"

"It was once he dumped me," Rachel said bitterly. "That was about five minutes after the pageant dumped me. I hope he negotiated a better contract for poor Caitlyn than he did for me. She's got enough problems already. Sure, she's gorgeous, but she doesn't have two thimbles full of talent—singing voice of a Schnauzer in heat. Plus, she's got two first names."

"Hang on . . . ," Holly said, trying to cut through Rachel's banter and to the substance of the conversation. "If Jordan's not your agent anymore, then who's representing you?"

"Nobody. For the first time in thirty-six years, I'm a free agent. My publicist dumped me too. Understandable, since there's nothing to publicize."

Holly screwed her eyes shut and shook her head.

"I don't understand. Where *are* you anyway? Is Jared still with you?"

"Oh, honey . . ." Rachel heaved a heavy sigh. "I should have told you. I'm not with him. I never was. I made up the story about the movie and then looking at locations with Jared, and when you jumped to conclusions, thinking I was having an affair with him, I didn't tell you different. It was less humiliating than telling you the truth."

"Less humiliating than letting me think you were having an affair with the married father of one of my old friends? Rachel," she demanded, "where are you and what are you doing?"

"I'm exactly where I said I'd be: on a cruise ship in Mexico. That's where I've been this whole time. Working."

"You mean . . . you're performing? On a cruise line? Oh, Mom . . ."

Holly's jaw went slack. For a second, she didn't know what to say.

Some very talented people work as entertainers on cruise lines. For a young performer, somebody starting out, getting hired to sing or dance on a ship could be a tremendous opportunity, the first rung on the ladder to success. For more seasoned professionals, cruise line work could provide a steady paycheck and a chance to do what they loved year-round, be in front of an appreciative audience.

But for someone like Rachel, a woman who had appeared on television, in movies, and on Broadway, and who had been nominated for a Tony Award, singing for audiences on a cruise line represented only one thing: the last bump on the fall from grace, the ignominious end of a faltering career, an act of personal and financial desperation.

"You could have told me," Holly said.

"Why?" Rachel replied. "What would have been the point? You had enough on your plate, worrying about your new show and moving and all. To tell the truth, I had planned to tell you once we got to Texas. But then we started arguing about Jared and I was kind of ticked at you.

"I know I'm no saint, but really, Holly? Did you honestly think I'd go after your friend's dad? Eileen Hoffman was one of my closest friends when you were little. We baked cupcakes for the damned PTA fund-raiser together! Well . . . okay," she said, dropping her tone into a lower and less irritated register. "I had the house-keeper bake the cupcakes and I just dropped them off at school. Did you really think I was capable of doing something so rotten to a friend? And just to get a part in a lousy movie?"

"I'm sorry," Holly mumbled.

"Yeah. Okay . . . fine. I'll forgive you if you forgive me. Deal?"

"Deal. But, Mom, are you all right?"

"Yes," she said, and then, more firmly, "Really. Of course, now that the word is out about my getting fired from the pageant, it won't be long before the tabloids find out what I'm doing. They'll have a field day with that, I'm sure.

"Aside from that," Rachel said, sounding a little surprised, "it's actually kind of fun. I haven't been in front of a live audience, night after night, for fifteen years. I've been trying out some new

material, working on some different arrangements. The pianist I'm working with is really
talented, such a great guy. Really, it's not so bad.
And until I can sell the condo, it pays the bills."

"You have to sell the house?"

"So what? Big deal. I never liked the place
anyway. Too many windows to wash."

Holly laughed. "You're kidding, right? You've
never washed a window in your life."

"I know," Rachel said good-naturedly, "but the
way things are going, I might have to start. But
I'll survive. If this is the worst thing that ever
happens to me, I'll be a very lucky lady. And I am
lucky. My life hasn't always been easy, but it's
never, ever been boring. Not one day of it."

Holly thought about that night at the pageant,
when she'd gone to the theater seeking Rachel's
advice and stood in the wings to watch her
mother sing. The admiration she'd felt for her
mother that night was nothing compared to the
awe she felt for her now.

In spite of all the anger that must have been
seething inside her, in spite of the pain, rejection,
and doubt she must have been experiencing, the
worries about her future and her finances, Rachel
had gone out on that stage and poured every drop
of herself into that song.

Holly remembered how many people in the
audience, surely feeling as amazed as she had by
the beauty of her mother's performance, leapt to

their feet when the last note faded away, eager to give Rachel the ovation she so richly deserved, and how their demonstration of admiration was cut short when the contestants were rushed onto the stage. Now Holly wondered; was it just a matter of the pageant running long? Or had the organizers done it on purpose, a final slap in the face of an artist they no longer found useful? If they were capable of firing her mother only hours before airtime, they were capable of almost anything.

But whether their cruelty was intentional or accidental, Rachel hadn't let it stop her from giving her all to that audience. Then, without missing a beat, she'd turned around and did it again, this time for her daughter.

Rachel had postponed her own grief and pushed aside her own needs to be there when Holly needed her—encouraging her, cheering her on, telling her that life was full of possibilities and hope at the moment she'd felt most hopeless, urging Holly to go out in the world and find her own way at the moment she'd most wanted to keep her close.

Holly felt tears coming to her eyes, but she held them back. Rachel hated tears, even tears of gratitude.

Instead, she said, "You know something, Mom? When I grow up, I want to be exactly like you."

Rachel never had been the sentimental type, but

287

even so, Holly thought her admission might bring forth motherly tears to match her own. Or, at the very least, an "Awww . . . thank you, honey."

Instead, Rachel laughed. She didn't chuckle or chortle or snicker—she *laughed*. Hard, loud, and long.

And when she finally got hold of herself, taking several big, deep breaths before she could get the words out, Rachel said, "Oh, honey. I don't recommend it. Really, I don't. You can do better. I hope you will. Now, enough about me, punkin. How are things with you?"

Chapter 27

On the following Tuesday, on the outskirts of Alpine, Texas, Donny Templeton walked into his favorite tavern at a few minutes before three and took a seat on his usual counter stool. The bartender brought him a basket of chips and salsa and a bottle of Lone Star, then changed the channel from ESPN to the House and Home Network.

"Rerun?" the bartender asked.

Donny nodded. "The new season doesn't start for a couple of months. I don't mind watching them again, though. Gets to be a habit." He shrugged and took a swig from the bottle. "Gives me somewhere to go."

"It's always good to see you, Donny. Let me know if you need anything."

"Thanks, John."

John went off to check his tequila inventory. Donny ate another chip and waited for the show to begin.

But before that happened, there was a commercial, a thirty-second spot for the upcoming season of *Quintessential Quilting*. Donny had never seen it before. No one had. This was the first time it aired.

Donny recognized the woman in the rust-bucket pickup as Mary Dell, of course, but couldn't for the life of him imagine why the hell she'd done her hair like that. It was so stiff and high it looked like a beaver had been trying to build a dam on top of her head.

The Mary Dell he knew always took care of herself, never left the house unless her hair was looking just so. She could spend an hour and a half locked in the bathroom with a blow dryer and a can of spray. Seeing as the double-wide they'd purchased upon their marriage had only one bathroom, this sometimes caused problems. But it had been worth it to see her emerge at the end of her ministrations looking as pretty as a picture, dressed in something feminine and bright that hugged all her curves as tight as a race car hugs the road.

But now . . . Why was she wearing that ugly gingham shirt tied up at her midriff? She looked like she'd walked off the set of *The Beverly Hillbillies*. Was this somebody's idea of a joke?

When a sleek red Lamborghini drove into the scene and a young woman who wouldn't have looked out of place on the cover of a magazine climbed out of the car and faced off with his wife in a mock duel, Donny concluded it was a joke and that Mary Dell was the butt of it.

That irritated him, but the thing that propelled him off the barstool was the voice that came in at the end of the ad and said, *"Quintessential Quilting with Mary Dell and Holly*—there's a new sheriff in town."

A *new* sheriff? What the hell was that supposed to mean? What was wrong with the old sheriff? And where was Howard? What had happened to his son?

The sound of boot heels against wooden floorboards made John the bartender turn away from his tequila bottles. "Hey, Donny. You need something?"

"No, I'm good." Donny stopped in his tracks, remembering the bill, then took ten dollars from his back pocket and laid it on the bar.

John glanced over to the television. "Your show's starting."

"I got to go and make a call."

"You need a phone? Here." John lifted the telephone from a charging station and held it out to Donny.

Donny shook his head. "No, thanks. I'll find a phone booth."

"A phone booth? Donny, I don't think there's a phone booth within a hundred miles of Alpine."

"I know," he said, and walked quickly toward the door. "That's why I need to get going."

Chapter 28

Dr. Geraldine Gillespie looked up from her tablet computer and smiled. "Everything looks good, Taffy. Blood pressure is good, urine test came back fine, and your cholesterol is down ten points."

"Are you sure?" Mary Dell said suspiciously. "She practically lives on fried chicken and sausage gravy."

"Maybe," Dr. Gillespie replied, "but it doesn't seem to be hurting anything. Taffy's weight is exactly the same as it was this time last year."

"But I've gained six pounds since I moved home," Mary Dell grumbled.

"There is one thing," Dr. Gillespie said, addressing Taffy, who was sitting, fully dressed, with her legs dangling over the edge of the exam table and had just given her daughter a smug look. "I'd like to keep you on a maintenance dose of the antibiotics, at least for the time being. You've had four urinary tract infections in the last year. I'd like to stay on top of that. At your age, those UTIs can really knock you for a loop."

The smirk fled from Taffy's face. "At *my* age?"

"Yes, which is eternally youthful." The doctor closed the lid of her tablet computer and stood up. "Keep this up, Taffy, and you'll live to be one hundred."

"One hundred? Now, why would I want to go and do a fool thing like that?"

Taffy reached for Mary Dell's hand and slid off the exam table. Mary Dell grabbed her mother's purse off the chair, handed it to her, and opened the door.

"Momma, you go on to the waiting room. I'll be along in just a minute."

"Why?" Taffy scowled. "So you can talk about me behind my back?"

"Yes."

"Fine. I'll go see if the receptionist has any of those little Snickers bars left in the candy jar."

After Taffy left, Mary Dell turned to face the doctor.

"She really is fine? All that flirting and outrageous behavior was just because of urinary infections?"

"Well . . ." Dr. Gillespie sat back down on her rolling chair, then took off her glasses and rubbed the lenses with the edge of her lab coat. "Taffy has always enjoyed male attention. As we age, we tend to become more of what we were to begin with, so I don't see her giving up flirting anytime soon. But now that we've got the infections under control, the other stuff—the disorientation, not knowing where she is or what she's doing, forgetting that Dutch is dead and confusing other people with him . . ."

"Stealing pickup trucks and strolling around town half-dressed?"

The doctor nodded. "Shouldn't be a problem. If it happens again, you call me and we'll get her in right away."

"So there's no sign of dementia," Mary Dell said, just to confirm.

"None. But that being said, I am glad you're back home. Medically speaking, your mother is in great shape, but at her age she needs somebody watching out for her. Cady was doing the best she knew how, but she's had her own problems to deal with."

"She said she came in to see you a while ago. Did you give her anything? Because she seems like she's doing better."

Dr. Gillespie smiled. "I really can't discuss that with you, Mary Dell. But you can ask Cady if you're curious."

"Sorry," she said quickly. "I really wasn't trying to pry information from you. I'm just happy she's feeling better."

"So am I," Dr. Gillespie replied, and rose from her chair. "Hey, I saw some folks setting up video cameras out by Puny Pond when I was driving to work last week. And you've got a new co-host, right? That movie star's daughter?"

"Holly Silva. Rachel McEnroe is her momma."

"That's right. The one who just got fired from the Miss Millennia Pageant. Too bad about that. I always liked her. Seems like her daughter is doing all right, though."

"It was rough at first, but Holly and I are getting along fine now. Can't help but wish Howard were still hosting, but," Mary Dell said with a shrug, her tone philosophical, "it was time for him to get out on his own. Did I tell you? He's taking classes at the community college."

"He is?" Dr. Gillespie reflected Mary Dell's smile back to her. "That's wonderful. Good for him! You must be proud."

"I am. Real proud."

"And we're all proud of you. Bringing your TV show home? That's pretty big doings for little old Too Much." She held open the door for Mary Dell. "Looks like you're going to put us on the map."

"Could be," Mary Dell said, "but the jury is still out on whether or not that'll turn out to be a good thing for the town. Or for me."

As they were driving down the road, Taffy looked across the seat at her daughter. "What were you doing in there so long? Making plans to slap me into an old folks' home?"

"As if they'd have you," Mary Dell said. Taffy gave her a smirk. "No, I just had a couple of questions about your medication. And then we got to talking. Dr. Gillespie wanted to know how the show is going."

"I was wondering the same thing," Taffy said. "You sure seemed like you were in a bad mood when you got home last night. Something go wrong at the shoot?"

Mary Dell made a left hand turn. She really didn't feel like talking about it, especially not with Taffy. But she knew her mother well enough to know she wouldn't drop the subject until she got some answers.

"No, the shoot itself went fine. We wrapped up two more episodes. Everything came off smooth as silk. It's what will happen after the shoot that's bothering me. Holly and I can do a great job on-camera, plan out every minute of our presentation, but the director is the one calling the camera shots, and he's the one editing the footage and putting the whole dang thing together. Or, in Artie's case," she said, her eyes sparking with anger, "tearing it apart."

Seeing the look of confusion on Taffy's face, she elaborated.

"He showed us the final cut of the first episode, and it's just a big old mess. He keeps shooting at all these crazy angles. Instead of putting the camera on the sewing machine or the cutting table or somebody's hands, he's focusing the cameras on our faces almost the whole time. Also, he's shooting us in profile, so we're never actually making eye contact with the viewers. It looks like we're just staring off into the horizon. Stupidest-looking thing . . ."

"But that doesn't make any sense," Taffy protested. "How are people supposed to figure out how the quilt goes together if they don't see your hands? You can't learn to quilt by watching somebody's face."

"To be fair, they'll mostly be seeing Holly's face. Artie tends to cut me out of the shot whenever possible. Sometimes even when you'd think it'd be impossible—say, when I'm the only one on-camera."

Mary Dell knew that a lot of what she was saying didn't make sense to Taffy. It wasn't a commentary on her mother's mental acuity; it was just that all this talk about camera angles and editing wouldn't make much sense to anyone who hadn't spent much time in a television studio and didn't understand how much control the director had over the finished product. Even if Taffy had worked in the business, she probably wouldn't have believed how badly Artie had mangled the final edit. Unless she'd seen it with her own eyes, Mary Dell wouldn't have believed it either.

"He cut my four-and-a-half-minute segment down to two minutes. What's left is mostly a slide show of the quilt variations. He sped up the camera and zipped through them so fast it almost made me dizzy. And during the demonstration on making a folded version of Courthouse Steps, he cut out the whole middle part of the instructions. Anybody trying to make that block is going to be confused, or frustrated, or mad—probably all three. And do you know who the complaint letters will be addressed to?" she asked bitterly and rhetorically. "Me, that's who. When that episode airs, I am going to be buried in angry letters from disgruntled viewers."

"I don't understand," Taffy said. "Why would he do that?"

"Oh, Momma." Mary Dell sighed. "You tell me and we'll both know. I'm not sure if he's ruining the show on somebody's orders or if he honestly thinks his way is better. I'm actually inclined toward the latter. I mean, he's so darned excited about it. He actually couldn't wait to show us the edited footage!"

Approaching a stop sign for the lonely stretch of road that led to the ranch, Mary Dell slowed but didn't actually stop, instead glancing quickly to the right before making the turn.

"I think he's trying to be artistic, or cutting-edge. Or some damfool thing. This is a quilting show, not a reality show and not a film school final. We exist to teach people how to quilt—that's it. Hopefully we do it in a way that's entertaining, but if it comes down to a choice between entertainment value and instruction, instruction wins out every time. Artie just doesn't seem to get that. I don't think he's evil or anything, just not very bright.

"But," she continued, her tone more pointed now, "I think the person who hired him knew exactly what he was doing."

The car bumped over the cattle guard that marked the edge of their property and then beneath the big metal arch emblazoned with the F-Bar-T brand.

"That Jason?" Taffy asked. "The man at the network who doesn't like you?"

"That's him. He's the one who hired Artie, and I think he did it on purpose. He hates the show and he hates me. Don't know why, but he does."

They drove the last few hundred feet on the long dirt road that led to the house in silence. Mary Dell glanced quickly over at her mother, who was squinting into the sun and looking out the passenger side window, and wondered what she was thinking. When she pulled up in front of the house and set the parking brake, Taffy let her know.

"I think it's your fault."

"My fault!" Mary Dell choked out an incredulous laugh. "I didn't do anything. How can it be *my* fault?"

"Because this Jason person and that Artie are

your bosses. It's your job to try and get along with them. Not the other way around," Taffy said as she unlocked the car door and climbed out. "That's always been your problem, Mary Dell. No respect for authority."

Mary Dell jumped out of the Eldorado and ran around the front of the vehicle, facing off with her mother.

"That is *not* fair, Momma! And it's not true."

"You sure about that?" Taffy asked, drawing out the question and shooting her a look.

Actually, it was *the* look, the one that all mothers have mastered and all daughters recognize, the look that can make any woman, be she sixteen or sixty, feel put upon and anxious and guilty all at the same time, even if she's done nothing wrong. Especially if she's done nothing wrong.

"Yes, I'm sure! Why is everything always my fault? When I was in the eighth grade Mrs. Caruthers gave me detention for a week, even though Delia Simpson was the one who drew the cartoon of Mrs. Caruthers trying to stuff her big behind into a pair of pantyhose. And when I came home and told you about it, you grounded me for *two* weeks and made me shovel out the barn to boot!"

Mary Dell planted her hands on her hips, daring her mother to deny it, but Taffy didn't even try.

"Mrs. Caruthers wouldn't have punished you if you hadn't done anything wrong."

"I *didn't* do anything wrong. I didn't even know what was on that paper until Mrs. Caruthers opened it and got all red in the face. I was passing it down the row to Lila Jane Meacham."

"And if you'd been paying attention in class instead of passing notes, you wouldn't have gotten in trouble, now, would you?"

Mary Dell threw up her hands and stomped off toward the porch. "You know what? Never mind. There's no point in talking to you."

Taffy shouted after her. "Mary Dell? Don't you dare walk away from me! I mean it. You come back here and talk to me right now."

She stopped at the base of the porch steps and turned around to face her mother. "Why? You never take my side. Never."

"Oh, don't be ridiculous," Taffy scolded. "I'm your momma. I've always been on your side and I'm on your side now. And if you'd listen for a change instead of getting your panties into a twist over something that happened forty-five years ago, you'd realize that I'm trying to help you."

Mary Dell didn't say anything, just stood there with one hand on her hip.

"What I meant to say," Taffy continued in a slightly more conciliatory tone, "was that if these men are acting within their authority, there isn't any point in railing and fussing about it, now, is there? No matter how much you might dislike this Artie fellow, he's the director. So I suggest you start making some effort to get along with him. Then maybe he'll listen to you. You always catch more flies with honey than with vinegar."

Mary Dell puffed in exasperation. "So what am I supposed to do? Send him a fruit basket?"

"Invite him to dinner after the shoot next week," Taffy said. "I'll make fried chicken with all the trimmings. You said he's a big fella. Nothing goes to a big man's heart like a home-cooked meal."

"I don't want to win his heart. I just want to convince him to quit ruining my television show."

Mary Dell felt her jaw clench. She really didn't think inviting Artie home for dinner was going to solve her problems, but at this point, she was willing to try just about anything. Besides, when Taffy made up her mind about something, there wasn't much point in trying to talk her out of it.

"Fine. I'll ask him to supper. But not for Monday. People are too tired to socialize after a shoot, and the crew will all drive back to Dallas that night anyway."

Taffy climbed the porch steps and passed Mary Dell on her way into the house. "Sunday, then. He can have supper and then stay the night."

"You want him to stay *here?*"

Taffy walked through the kitchen and toward the bathroom, ignoring the question.

"Fine," Mary Dell said. "I'll ask him to stay over."

Taffy's voice came from the hallway, asking

what Mary Dell wanted for supper, at the same time the phone started to ring. Mary Dell walked over to answer it.

"You don't need to cook, Momma. Cady's going out and Linne is staying over at a friend's house. Rob Lee's off somewhere too. I'll make us a salad."

Taffy called back from behind the bathroom door, but Mary Dell couldn't hear what she said.

"Hang on a minute, Momma! I've got to get the phone!"

She picked up the receiver, held it to her ear, and said hello. For a moment, all she heard was silence. She almost hung up, thinking it was one of those robotic telemarketer calls. But then a man spoke. His voice was low and gravelly. And familiar.

"Hey, Mary Dell." He stopped, cleared his throat. "I don't mean to bother you. I saw a commercial for the new season today. Howard wasn't in it. Is he all right?"

Mary Dell's hand rose to cover her mouth; she was momentarily dumbstruck. Then she pressed it against her breast. She felt her heart beating hard inside her chest.

"Donny?"

Chapter 29

Mary Dell had started taking Hub-Jay's calls again after he returned to Dallas.

At the end of the business day, it had become Hub-Jay's habit to recline on top of the duvet in his private suite, still dressed except for his shoes, jacket, and tie, and relax while he and Mary Dell talked. The discussion wasn't particularly romantic, just a general chat about their days and respective activities, but Hub-Jay had come to look forward to this as the best part of his day.

Today, she had actually picked up the phone and called him, which meant she was thinking about him. That was progress and reason enough for him to smile. But his smile faded when she told him who had phoned her that day.

"You're kidding," he said, taking his arm from behind his head and sitting up on the edge of the bed. "And what else did he say?"

"Nothing. He just wanted to know why Howard wasn't on the show anymore. I told him that he'd decided he wanted to live on his own and enroll in a program at the community college. He seemed happy about that, but mostly he just wanted to make sure Howard was all right. As soon as I let him know everything was fine, he said good and he was sorry to have bothered me. Then he hung up."

"And that was it? He didn't say anything else?"

"Not a word," Mary Dell replied.

She sounded surprised and a little confused, which was understandable. Hub-Jay was a little confused himself. He couldn't quite think how he was supposed to respond to this situation.

"When's the last time you heard from him?"

"You mean actually talked to him? This is the first time since he left, close to thirty years. I've gotten mail from Donny for years, but he's never called before. When I first opened the shop, he sent a calculator and a note, along with some money. So, somehow or other, he'd kept tabs on us.

"A lot of envelopes with cash or money orders arrived over the years, but I never spent it. It all went into a savings account for Howard, so he'd have something to fall back on if anything ever happened to me. Donny always sends money at Christmas and on Howard's birthday too. I let Howard spend that however he wants."

"Huh. And there was never a return address on the envelopes?"

"No. The postmarks were always from out of state. But yesterday, the caller ID showed a Texas area code. I tried calling back, but nobody answered."

"Huh," Hub-Jay said again, still feeling at a loss

for words and a little bothered by the fact that Mary Dell had tried to call Donny back. Still, he supposed it was a natural enough reaction. Of course she wanted to talk to him, if for no other reason than to get some answers.

"So . . . do you think he'll call again?"

"Oh, I doubt it," she replied. "Otherwise he wouldn't have hung up so quick. He just wanted to make sure that nothing had happened to Howard."

Hearing the certainty in her voice, Hub-Jay felt a twinge of relief. Then, remembering that Mary Dell couldn't obtain a divorce unless she could locate Donny and serve him with papers, relief turned to regret.

It was a missed opportunity. But they'd just have to cross that bridge when they came to it. First, he had to get Mary Dell to agree to marry him.

"Anyway," Mary Dell said, brushing aside the Donny encounter with an ease that buoyed Hub-Jay's spirits once again. "That wasn't the only crazy thing that happened today," she said. "Wait till you hear what Momma's cooked up."

Hub-Jay smiled to himself and lay back on top of the duvet again with a pillow behind his back while Mary Dell related the story of her argument with Taffy, accompanied by many embellishments, editorial comments, and laughter.

When she said, "Hub-Jay Hollander, I tell you

what—I am sixty years old and have more gray hairs on my head than Carter has pills, but every time I get around my momma, I start acting like I'm twelve years old!" Hub-Jay laughed along with her.

He hadn't spent too much time with Taffy, but enough to know that she and Mary Dell were the kind of mother and daughter who were just born to knock heads. They were stubborn, smart, strong-willed women, both of them, and more alike than either of them probably wanted to admit.

Just as Mary Dell finished her story, Taffy called from the kitchen, saying it was time for supper.

"My master's voice," Mary Dell said. "I tried to talk her into letting me make a salad for dinner, but she wouldn't hear of it. She's been in the kitchen for an hour, making meat loaf, mashed potatoes, green beans with bacon, and tapioca pudding. Meat loaf!" She groaned. "It's eighty-five degrees outside and we're having meat loaf."

"Your mother likes to cook. It's how she shows her love."

"Well, if she loves me any more, I won't be able to fit into my dress for the party. Oh, Hub-Jay! Wait till you see it!

"It's red taffeta and very elegant," she assured him, her voice as excited as a young girl's. "I found it online at Neiman Marcus, but I called Howard and got his approval before I ordered.

There's a taffeta bow on the shoulder, so Howard said I should wear just a single strand of pearls. Because anything else would be too much with the bow."

"Sounds beautiful. Can't wait to see you in it."

He heard Taffy calling from the kitchen again, more impatiently.

"Sorry. I'd better run before she blows a gasket." Mary Dell paused for a moment. He could sense the hesitation in her voice. "Can I call you tomorrow?"

"I'd like that. In fact, I might just stay right here and wait until you do."

She laughed and they said their good nights. Hub-Jay hung up the phone, moved his arm back behind his head, crossed his feet on top of the covers, and smiled, feeling happier than he had in a long, long time.

Chapter 30

Holly stabbed angrily at her cell phone before crossing her arms on the bar and flopping her head into them, like a kindergartener napping on her desk.

"They. Just. Keep. Calling," she moaned, her voice echoing inside the cavern of her arms. "Don't they ever get tired of hearing me say I have nothing to say?"

"Why don't you just turn off your phone? Or not answer it?" Cady asked.

"Because it might be my mom," she mumbled, head still down. "The ship is someplace out near Cozumel now, and when she calls from out of the country it doesn't show her number. I have to answer in case it's her."

She felt Cady's hand pat the back of her hair.

"Poor baby. You need a beverage. Hey, can we get a couple of margaritas here? Frozen. No salt for me. Holly, you want salt?"

"No," she mumbled.

"Two, no salt."

Holly lifted her head. "You know what I really hate?" she asked and started ticking off the list on her fingers. "People who post pictures of what they had for lunch on Instagram, people who talk on their Bluetooth in the grocery store, having to watch a forty-five-second ad so I can see a thirty-second YouTube video, cilantro, black licorice, and reporters."

Cady gave her a puzzled look. "How can you hate cilantro?"

Holly elbowed her. "Shut up."

The margaritas arrived. Holly took a sip.

"But do you know what really bugs me? Even though yesterday was rotten . . . well, only after Artie showed us the edited version of the first episode. It's a mess!" she cried and shook her head. "Did Mary Dell tell you?"

Cady nodded and took a medium-sized swallow of her margarita. "She was in the shop this morning before she had to take Grandma to the doctor. She was pretty bummed about it."

"Her and me both," Holly said. "It's so frustrating that we can both work so hard and then Artie just goes in there and screws it all up in the cutting room! And it's not just me and Mary Dell who feel that way. I could see Gina, the assistant director, and some of the crew giving each other looks behind Artie's back. They're not saying anything, but they all know it's total crap."

Holly exhaled a big breath and returned to her point.

"Anyway, what really sucks is that, even with all that going on, until some blogger posted the pictures of my mom singing on the cruise ship and every scuzzball, ambulance-chasing, Dumpster-diving tabloid reporter on the planet started calling and wanting a quote on Rachel's nosedive from diva to aging third-rate lounge act—a reporter actually said that to me! He called my mother an aging third-rate lounge act!"

"Idiot," Cady grumbled, and took another sip of her drink.

"*Until* then," Holly continued, "this started out to be a really great day." She took a sip of her margarita and looked at Cady with a small but victorious smile. "Stormy let me put a riding blanket on his back this morning."

"You didn't tell me that. That's great!"

The two women lifted their glasses and clinked the rims together.

"I know, right? It was so cool. I brought the blanket over, held it up to his nose so he could smell it, then laid it down on the ground and had him walk over it so he could see there was nothing to be afraid of, and after that he just let me put it on his back like it was no big deal. He's really starting to trust me now, you know?"

"That's fantastic," Cady said. "You've done an amazing job with Stormy."

"Oh, stop," Holly said modestly. "It wasn't me. I really had no idea what I was getting into with Stormy, which is probably a good thing. Otherwise I might not have done it. But Rob Lee coached me through everything. It was all him. I just keep doing what he tells me to do."

"But it's still pretty neat," Cady said, putting down her drink and reaching for a nearby basket of tortilla chips, "the way you've gentled him. And, I've got to say, I think you've gentled my brother a little too. He's much less of a grouch than he was even a month ago. He actually took Linne for a ride yesterday. She was so happy I thought she might float away."

"Really?" Holly tipped her head to one side and smiled. "Aw. That's great. But I can't take credit for that either. Rob Lee seems better to me, too, less tense and more talkative. A little bit, anyway.

But I think it's because of Stormy. He's been working with him every day, even when I'm not there, and I think it's sort of . . ."

She paused, looking for a way to explain the changes she'd seen in Rob Lee, but it was impossible to point to one particular thing or moment. It was slow, an inch-by-inch alteration, and, she sensed, far from complete.

"I think he and Stormy just relate to each other somehow. They've both been through a lot, but neither of them can talk about it."

"Maybe," Cady said. "But I think you've helped too. I think Rob Lee likes you."

"Oh, well. I like him too," she said casually. "He's nice."

Cady gave her a chiding slap on the arm. "Oh, knock it off. You know what I mean. I think he *likes* you. Or if he doesn't, he should."

Cady lifted the glass to her lips and, after a sip and a moment of consideration, she said, "Hey, do you want me to talk to him? I will if you want me to. You'd be a great sister-in-law!"

Holly started laughing and nearly choked on her margarita.

"Wow," she said, blinking her eyes. "Where did that come from? Are you sure this is your first drink?"

"First one," Cady said. "I'm a cheap date. That's one of the things Nick liked about me. He said that all he had to do to get lucky was wave a drink under my nose. It kind of runs in the family," she said. "The Fatal Flaw."

"Okay," Holly said, and pulled Cady's glass away. "Then have some more chips, girlfriend. Pace yourself."

"So," Cady said, taking a big breath and then letting it out. "Speaking of Nick . . ."

Holly was quiet, waiting for Cady to go on. When she didn't, Holly repeated, "Speaking of Nick . . . ," and made a circular motion with her hand.

"I have been. Speaking of him."

Cady looked at Holly, waiting for her to connect the dots. When Holly didn't respond, she spelled it out.

"I've started seeing a therapist in Waco. Dr. Gillespie gave me a referral."

"Really?"

Cady bobbed her head, looking a little sheepish about her admission. Holly leaned over and gave her a squeeze.

"That's great, Cady. Good for you."

"Don't say anything to my grandma."

"Okay. But why not?"

Cady shrugged. "I don't know. I don't want to upset her. People here don't go in much for that kind of thing, especially older people. That's why I had to go to Waco to find somebody to talk to. Do you know there isn't a decent psychologist in all of Too Much? Which is pretty bad considering the number of crazy people there are in town. Some of them are related to me."

"Huh," Holly said, a little surprised by this information.

Too Much was a small town, of course. Really small. But Holly had a hard time getting her head around the idea of any town that didn't have at least one mental health professional. In LA there was a shrink on practically every block. When she was in high school, half the kids in her class were in therapy and the other half probably should have been.

"So, who do people go to when they have a problem?" she asked.

"Mostly nobody," Cady said. "A lot of people around here think it's a sign of weakness to have to talk your problems out with somebody and that you should just keep your mouth shut and get over it. Some people even say it's a sin."

When Holly's eyes went wide with disbelief at this, Cady nodded and said, "It's true. I've actually heard people say depression is just a sign of unconfessed sin in a person's life."

"But that's ridiculous!" Holly said. "That's not why you don't want to tell your grandmother you're seeing a therapist, is it? Taffy wouldn't think that about you. She's crazy about you."

"I know. She'd just be worried about me. And Grandma's old-fashioned. In her day, you'd talk to your minister. That's what most people still do around here, if they're really struggling. That's what I did, too, at first. It helped some.

"But you know," Cady said quietly, her eyes becoming shiny, "there's a lot of layers to all this. Reverend Crews was the one who suggested I go and ask Dr. Gillespie for a referral. It's going to take a while to work through it."

"Then I'm glad you did." Holly lowered her head a bit, so she could look into Cady's eyes more directly. "Do you want to tell me about it?"

Cady shook her head. "No, I'm good. I just wanted you to know because I might not have done it if I hadn't met you."

Holly tipped her head to one side and frowned a little. Though she was happy that Cady was getting the help she needed, she couldn't imagine what she'd said or done to propel her in that direction.

"It's just that, having a friend again, but also seeing how"—Cady's gaze floated to the ceiling as she searched for the right phrase—"how enthusiastic you are about life, how brave you are about seeing what you want and going for it, taking chances, made me realize that I'm still too young to be old. You reminded me of how I used to be. Happy."

Cady reached for the glass that Holly had pushed away.

"I decided I want to feel like that again. And I just wanted you to know I've got you to thank for it. I'm glad you came to Too Much."

"So am I. And I'm really, really glad that you've decided not to give up on happiness. But it's all you, Cady. I think you're really brave."

Cady drained the dregs of her melted margarita. "Thanks. I think so too."

She laughed. So did Holly.

"Do you want another one?"

Cady shook her head. "Maybe a Coke this time."

They sat at the bar for another couple of hours, drinking their drinks and sharing an order of fried cheese sticks and Buffalo wings, talking a lot and laughing a little.

Holly politely turned down invitations from two cowboys who asked if she'd like to dance and hung up on four pushy reporters looking for a quote. Cady did have another margarita after her Coke, which left her feeling and acting, not drunk exactly, but tipsy enough that Holly thought it'd be a bad idea to let her drive home.

Just as Holly was trying, not very successfully, to convince Cady to hand over her car keys, Rob Lee came walking through the door of the Ice House.

"Baby brother!" Cady cried out when she spotted him. "Get over here, right now."

Rob Lee walked over to the bar. "Hey," he said, then cocked an eyebrow at his sister's empty glass. "Looks like you're enjoying your margarita."

"Yes, I am," she confirmed. "It's a little strong,

but it's good. You know what else is strong and good? You are. I mean it. It was so, so, *so* sweet of you to take Linne riding. I'm serious. Meant the world to her."

"Good. I'm glad she had fun. So, Sis?" He shot an amused look in Holly's direction, which she returned. "How long have you been here?"

"Couple hours. We're just getting ready to go."

Cady closed her eyes and started humming along with a song that was playing on the juke-box, making no attempt to rise from the barstool.

"Don't worry," Holly said. "I'll drive her home."

"That's okay," Rob Lee replied. "I'll take her."

"Are you sure? You just got here."

"Yeah. I . . . I was actually—" He scratched his ear, cleared his throat, and was interrupted by his sister, whose eyes flew suddenly open as she spun around on the stool to face them.

"Hey, Rob Lee! You know what I was just saying to Holly a while before you came in? That she would be a *great* sister-in-law! Seriously. You two should get married. What do you think?" Cady looked from her brother to her friend.

Holly covered her face with her hand and shook her head. "Wow. That was awkward. Sorry."

"What?" Cady said, throwing out her hands in a gesture of innocence. "You'd be perfect for each other!"

Rob Lee, who was grinning—it was the first time Holly had seen him with a full smile on his face, and she couldn't help but think it made him look even more handsome—ignored his sister and addressed Holly directly.

"Don't worry about it. Cady never could hold her liquor. Nick always said—" He stopped himself. His smile faded, not completely but some. "Anyway, it's okay. My aunt Mary Dell's just the same. Worse. Give her two beers and she starts to sing."

"Really?" Holly laughed. "I'll have to remember that."

"That is not something you want to see. Trust me." He turned toward Cady. "Okay, Sis. Time to go."

"Yeah. I think you're right. You know," she said seriously, "I probably shouldn't drive."

"Good thinking."

He reached into the back pocket of his jeans to retrieve his wallet, but Holly waved him off.

"That's okay, I've got this."

"You sure?" he asked doubtfully.

Holly assured him she was. He shrugged, took his hand from his pocket, and guided his sister toward the door.

Holly was standing at the bar, waiting for her change, and when she looked up she saw that Rob Lee had returned.

"Did she forget something?" Holly asked, her eyes searching the counter and barstools for dropped keys or an abandoned purse.

"No. I just didn't . . . uh." He sniffed, then plunged ahead, as if he'd made up his mind to just spit it out and get it over with. "I didn't have a chance to finish telling you. The reason I wasn't planning to stay is because I only came here looking for you. My aunt is throwing this big birthday party for me and Howard, you know, up in Dallas. And, anyway, I was wondering if you'd like to come with me, be my date."

Holly beamed. She couldn't help herself. When Cady had started in about Rob Lee liking her— even before Cady's clumsy and truly mortifying matchmaking effort—Holly had made little of it because she just didn't think he thought about her in that way. Sure, they had been seeing a lot of each other, but that was because of Stormy. The horse was the only thing they ever really talked about, and she was paying Rob Lee for his training time. She didn't really think he was interested in her, not romantically.

She stopped herself right there, told herself not to get carried away. The man just needed a date for his birthday party. She'd heard Mary Dell talking about it; there was going to be food and champagne and a band, probably dancing. Of course Rob Lee didn't want to go stag to something like that. He was the guest of honor, after all.

Right. It's a date, not a proposal. Don't make a fool of yourself.

She pressed her lips together, trying to moderate her enthusiasm a little.

"Yes. Sure. It sounds like fun."

"Good, then. Thanks. I'd better take Cady home. You coming out to see Stormy tomorrow?"

"I'll be there."

He smiled again and lifted his hand. "Okay. See you tomorrow."

In the parking lot, fumbling through her purse in search of her keys, Holly decided that maybe this wasn't turning out to be such a bad day after all and that she would give Stormy an extra couple of carrots as a reward for his part in making that happen. But then her phone rang yet again and those happy thoughts were crowded aside.

"No," she snapped without even giving the caller time to speak, "for the fiftieth time, I have no comment."

"Then you'd better come up with one," Jason snapped right back in a voice seething with anger, "because you'd better have a damned good excuse for the way you've been acting. You and I had a deal, Holly. Remember? And if you don't start living up to your end of the bargain, not only will I give the design show to somebody more cooperative, I'll make sure you never work in television again.

"So, unless you'd like to see if your mom is willing to put in a good word for you with the cruise line—probably as a cocktail waitress, since you've got more tits than talent—you had better decide right now where your loyalties lie. You got that?"

Chapter 31

It was too late for her to go out to the ranch that night, but first thing the next morning, Holly drove to the F-Bar-T and told Mary Dell everything.

"I should have said something the very first day," Holly said, clutching the coffee mug Taffy had handed her as soon as she sat down at the kitchen table.

"Baby girl, I didn't need you to tell me that Jason was a scheming sidewinder," Mary Dell said with a derisive laugh. "I figured that out about two minutes after meeting him."

"Yeah, but I should have told you that Jason bribed me to sabotage *Quintessential Quilting*. I'm sorry."

"But *did* you sabotage the show? No. Of course you didn't. That's just not who you are," Mary Dell said, looking into Holly's eyes with an almost motherly affection that made Holly feel almost worse—maybe because she missed her own mother.

"From the very first day," Mary Dell went on,

"you gave it your all. Because that *is* who you are—a hard worker and a team player. But I don't blame you for wanting to land that design show, baby girl. Why wouldn't you? There's nothing wrong with being ambitious, not as long as you don't compromise your character in pursuit of it—and you didn't. You and I were pulling in the same direction from the first minute. And I don't blame you for not telling me about Jason's offer right off either. You didn't know me or how I might react to that kind of news. It might have set me up against you and made me distrust you. Sometimes it's wise to hold back a little, until you know who you're dealing with."

Mary Dell reached across the table and curved her hand over Holly's, which was still wrapped around the coffee mug.

"Listen to me; when Jason the Sidewinder said you had to decide where your loyalties lay, that's what you did. You picked the right path, the honest and loyal path. That's the only thing that matters. So quit beating yourself up, all right?"

"Thanks."

Mary Dell gave Holly's hand one more pat and then picked up her own coffee mug. Taffy, who had been shuffling around the kitchen and listening in, refilled both of their cups and set a plate of homemade cinnamon rolls on the table.

"So that nasty Artie has been reporting everything back to Jason?" Taffy asked.

"Uh-huh," Holly said, and after calculating how many extra miles she'd have to run to burn off one of those cinnamon rolls and deciding it was worth it, she took one from the plate. "I can't say for sure, but I bet Jason tried to make the same kind of deal with Artie that he made with me—help him get rid of *Quintessential Quilting* and he'd give Artie a shot at directing something bigger later."

Taffy pulled up a chair and sat down. "So you think he did all that crazy editing on purpose?"

"No, I'm with Mary Dell on that. I think he honestly thinks what he did was cool or edgy or something. He's a terrible director," Holly said. "And an even worse editor. I'm sure that's why Jason picked him, because he knew how bad he was.

"But Artie has definitely been reporting back to him. Jason knew all about how we'd refused to use that confessional camera, and even repeated back exactly what we'd said when we told Artie we weren't doing it. He knew a bunch of other stuff, too, like how I'd backed you up on the idea of shooting the opening segments on location, and how I come over here during the week so we can work together prepping the quilt projects and demonstrations. He knew a *lot* of stuff," Holly said, "and it could only have come from Artie."

Mary Dell, who had been gazing off into the

distance with a kind of bewildered amazement during all this, looked at her mother and said, "So I was wrong when I said I thought Artie just wasn't too bright. Turns out he's dumb *and* evil. You still want me to invite him to dinner, Momma?"

"Of course I do," Taffy said, her mouth half-filled with cinnamon roll. "Nothing has changed, Mary Dell. Artie is still the boss. Unless you're just ready to throw up your hands and let him ruin your show, you've got to figure out a way to either win him over or get around him."

"And you think feeding him a chicken dinner will do that?" she scoffed.

Taffy pushed back her chair, squinting a little as her beady blue eyes bored into her daughter's. "You just do what I'm telling you to and invite Artie to dinner. You hear?"

Chapter 32

If Mary Dell's confidence in the viability of her mother's plan to rescue *Quintessential Quilting* had been plotted on a scale of one to one hundred, the result would have been a negative number. She only followed Taffy's orders because she honestly didn't think Artie would accept the dinner invitation, but, much to her consternation, he did and seemed to enjoy himself immensely, eating more food than Mary Dell could ever recall seeing one person consume in a single sitting.

Watching Artie eat, and eat, and eat some more—the movement of his fork-wielding arm between his plate and his mouth was as constant as the pumping of a piston in a steam engine—was disgusting, but also impressive in its own way, especially since he never, ever, ever stopped talking, not even while he was chewing, which added a whole new dimension to her disgust.

Mary Dell couldn't decide if Artie was the most self-absorbed individual she'd ever met or the most insecure. After a while she ceased to care and just sat there staring at Artie's incessantly moving jaw with a kind of glazed fascination, calculating the odds of him becoming satiated before they ran out of food, deciding they were slim.

Taffy, on the other hand, seemed delighted by Artie's presence, practically simpering as she plied him with compliments and serving after serving after serving of her home-cooked food. Remembering what Dr. Gillespie had said about people who were getting older becoming more of what they'd always been—in Taffy's case, a flirt—Mary Dell tried not to let it bother her, but it wasn't easy. From her vantage point, Taffy's fluttering and fussing over a man who was single-handedly destroying her career seemed like a case of aiding and abetting the enemy.

When Artie finished his second piece of buttermilk pie, saying it was the best dessert he'd ever had in his life, Taffy giggled like a schoolgirl and said she admired a big, healthy man with a big, healthy appetite, and Mary Dell thought she might lose her supper.

"Artie, I am just so delighted you were able to join us tonight," Taffy said as she cleared his plate. "I never realized how difficult it is, directing a television show. The whole thing really rests on your shoulders, doesn't it?"

"Well . . . ," Artie said with a shrug, as if he was too modest to come right out and say that it was so.

"I am truly honored to have someone of your stature sitting at my table," Taffy said, putting the dishes on the counter and walking to the refrigerator. "I hope you saved just a little more room, Artie. Because I made something special, just for you."

Beaming a smile, Taffy set a medium-sized glass serving bowl directly in front of the burly director. "It's my special ambrosia salad. An old family recipe handed down from my mother's mother."

Now Mary Dell really thought she would be sick, and not just from the way that Taffy was sucking up to Artie. The sight of still more food literally made her nauseous.

"Momma, *another* dessert? We're all about ready to burst."

"It's not for you," Taffy replied haughtily before turning her eyes to their guest. "I made this just for Artie."

She batted her eyelashes and handed him a spoon. Artie demurred, saying he didn't know if he could eat another bite, then proved himself wrong by eating the whole thing, even scraping the spoon against the bowl to get to the last bits of the whipped cream and maraschino cherries.

Early the next morning, on her way to the kitchen for breakfast, Mary Dell passed the hallway bathroom and heard the sound of someone being violently and repeatedly sick.

"Artie?" She knocked on the door. "Artie, is that you? Are you all right?"

The noise stopped. She heard the toilet flush and the sound of a man panting, trying very hard to catch his breath and compose himself.

"Yeah. It's me. Oh God . . . ," he said, in a way that sounded more like a prayer for help than an utterance of blasphemy. "God. I've never been this sick. I don't know what's wrong. Must be some kind of bug or—"

Mary Dell heard a groan and the sound of more violent and sustained retching. It was terrible. She actually felt sorry for him.

After another brief conversation through the bathroom door, their exchange cut short by still more nausea, Mary Dell went into the kitchen and found Taffy, already dressed and standing at the stove, frying eggs.

"Poor Artie," Mary Dell said as she poured herself a cup of coffee. "He's in the bathroom vomiting like a volcano. I've never heard anybody throw up that many times. He can't direct the show today; that's for sure. But I'm really worried about him. I wonder if we should call a doctor."

"Oh, he'll be all right," Taffy said breezily. "Must have been something he ate. It'll wear off in a few hours." Taffy scraped her spatula against the bottom of the cast-iron skillet, flipped over the eggs, and started humming a happy tune. Something about the self-satisfied smiled raised Mary Dell's suspicions.

"Momma, tell me you did not poison Artie's dinner."

Taffy put her hand on her hip, offended. "Of course not! The dinner was fine, same thing I served to the rest of the family and ate myself. I was willing to give him a chance, see if there might not be a way to bring him over to your side. But you were right, Mary Dell; the man is dumb as a post and nasty to boot. The more he talked, the more I could see it was a lost cause. There was no help for it," she said. "I had to bring out the ambrosia."

"Oh, my Lord! Momma, you poisoned the ambrosia! You actually did it on purpose?"

"Well, I should hope you wouldn't think I did it

by accident. I'd like to think I'm a better cook than that! Oh, quit looking at me that way," Taffy said, flapping her hand in Mary Dell's direction. "And stop saying 'poison.' Goodness. A little ipecac never hurt anybody. You make it sound like I was trying to kill him."

Mary Dell threw out an arm, gesturing toward the hallway, where the sound of retching could be heard faintly in the distance. "You just about have! Do you hear that?"

Taffy slid the eggs onto a plate, sat down, and started to eat without offering anything to Mary Dell.

"Don't be so dramatic. I told you; it'll wear off. In a while." She paused, fork halfway to her mouth, cocked an ear toward the bathroom, and frowned. "Though I do have to say, I never figured on him eating the whole bowl. Oh, well. Serves him right for being a glutton."

Mary Dell sank into a kitchen chair. "This is terrible. What should I do?"

"What do you mean, what should you do? It's Monday morning. You're going to drive over to the quilt shop and film another two episodes of *Quintessential Quilting*, just like you do every Monday.

"Don't worry," Taffy said, calmly eating her eggs. "I'll be here to keep an eye on Artie. I'll call Dr. Gillespie if it gets too bad. I do think we'll have to keep him here for a day or two, though, until he's feeling stronger. Looks like somebody else is going to have to edit the video footage this week."

Mary Dell stared at Taffy, thinking that Dr. Gillespie must have been wrong about her mother showing no signs of dementia.

"Momma, there's not going to be any video footage this week. We don't have a director, remember?"

Taffy dabbed at her lips with a napkin. "Mary Dell," she said pointedly, "you don't seriously think Artie is such a talented director that somebody couldn't jump in and fill his shoes, do you? I sat there for three solid hours listening to him yammer on about what it is he does, and it didn't sound all that complicated to me. Especially for somebody who's worked on a television show for the last seven years."

Taffy got to her feet and started rinsing her breakfast plate. "Now, go finish getting dressed, honey. You're going to be late for work."

Mary Dell changed her opinion regarding her previous diagnosis. Taffy was definitely not a victim of dementia. Her actions were far too calculated to be caused by any mental deficit or deterioration—quite the opposite. Taffy was far more cunning and devious than Mary Dell had given her credit for. And a part of her kind of respected that.

"By the way," Taffy said as Mary Dell left her

coffee cup on the counter before heading back to her room, "I left some tissue paper outside your door so you can pack your party dress. Taffeta wrinkles so, and if you're going up to Dallas to do the editing anyway, you might as well stay until the birthday party.

"Spend some time with Howard. And Hub-Jay." Her blue eyes twinkled as she smiled. "He is *such* a nice man."

Chapter 33

Before going out to see her horse, Holly stopped in to visit Artie, who was still in residence at the ranch, improved but not quite recovered from the mysterious "flu bug" that had laid him flat two days before.

Mary Dell had sworn her to secrecy regarding the true cause of Artie's illness, but, after hearing the whole story, she couldn't quite believe that Artie hadn't figured it out for himself. However, after sitting at his bedside for fifteen minutes, chatting as a slightly pale-looking Artie consumed a bowl of Taffy's homemade chicken noodle soup, it was obvious that he had no idea that the same woman who had made his soup had also purposely tainted his dessert, or rather, his second dessert.

On the contrary, Artie spoke of how well he was

being looked after in his illness, how Taffy had brought him tea and broth and fluffed his pillows. He spoke, too, in a feeble whisper, of his gratitude to the cast and crew for carrying on in his absence, in spite of the burden this must have placed upon them. Considering the speed with which he was spooning soup into his mouth, Holly found his speech more than a little melodramatic.

Even so, she didn't have the heart to tell him that not only had his absence not been a burden, the crew seemed to be more than a little relieved when they found out Artie was too sick to direct on Monday. Nor did she mention how, with Mary Dell discussing her concepts and desired camera work beforehand and Gina calling the shots during the actual taping, they'd wrapped up filming in record time, or that the entire crew had burst into spontaneous applause when Gina called out, "That's a wrap!" at the end of the day, a thing that had never happened before on the set of *Quintessential Quilting*, at least not since Artie had been directing.

Instead, she smiled with as much sympathy as she could muster and said she'd better let him rest, before tiptoeing from the room, marveling at his utter cluelessness.

But the minute Holly went outside and looked across the barnyard, spying Stormy in the paddock with his ever-faithful friend and mascot, Mildred the goat, by his side, all thoughts of Artie and the show and the gleefully nasty tabloid headlines disappeared. If you believed the papers, Rachel supposedly had a "love child" with a despotic ruler of a banana republic and hideously botched plastic surgery she had undergone in a "desperate" attempt to rescue her flagging career. There were also completely untrue reports about drug and alcohol addictions, angry public meltdowns, and a suicide attempt that, thank heaven, Rachel had called to disprove before Holly heard the story. Even those worries melted away as she walked toward the paddock and she saw her beautiful Stormy, his sleek brown head low to the ground as he calmly munched a tuft of grass.

She remembered being a little girl, desperately begging her mother for a horse, saying how much she loved them, and how Rachel had rolled her eyes.

"Of course you do. But wait till you have to feed, water, comb, and take care of a horse. Wait until it bites you, or rears at you, or throws you. Wait until you've got to shovel out a smelly stall and pay the vet and board bills. *Then* we'll see how much you love horses."

With the exception of being thrown—something that might well still occur—Holly had experienced every one of the situations her mother had listed, and it hadn't diminished her ardor in the least degree. She couldn't say for sure if she loved all horses, but she did love Stormy; of that she was certain. And more and more she believed that Stormy felt something for her too.

Not love, at least not yet, but perhaps . . . trust? Maybe.

Today would be the test, and an important one, because as everybody knows, trust is the place where love begins.

With Rob Lee watching from his usual spot about ten feet back from the fence, Holly entered the paddock and clicked her teeth with her tongue.

Mildred, who was standing right next to Stormy, trotted toward Holly, eager for a snack. There was nothing unusual in that—Mildred was a bottomless pit, with an appetite nearly as big as the hapless Artie's.

What was unusual was that Stormy was leading the way.

He walked right up to Holly, nosed her shoulder in greeting, inviting and allowing her to scratch his forelock.

"Hey, sweetheart. Did you miss me? Yes? I missed you, too."

She reached into her pocket for a piece of carrot, holding her hand flat while Stormy picked it up, mouthing her palm with his velvet lips, ignoring the goat's insistent bleating until Mildred started butting her head against Holly's legs.

After tossing a carrot butt to Mildred, who gobbled it greedily, Holly turned her attention back to Stormy, stroking her hands along his neck, then working her way down past his shoulders to the gentle bow of his back, laying her head sideways against his body and resting there for some long moments, breathing in the earthy scent of hair and flesh and sweat that was his particular perfume, then closing her eyes and feeling the heat and life of his body and a sensation like being adrift on a summer day in a small boat, rocking on the waves of a gentle sea, as her head rose and fell with each breath he took.

It was such a calm feeling, so peaceful, that she might have stayed much longer, perhaps even fallen asleep resting against him, but she and Stormy had more to accomplish that day, or so she hoped.

Holly attached the long lead to Stormy's rope halter. It was the same lead she had introduced him to many days before, having let him sniff and mouth it before she laid it over his back and then moved it back over his rump, then drawn it forward in the opposite direction all the way to his neck so he understood it was nothing to fear. With the lead attached, she reached for the green saddle blanket, showing it to Stormy before settling it evenly across his back, then took a gentle hold on the halter rope and walked confidently ahead of him, knowing that he would follow her left and right and left again, anywhere in the paddock, trusting Holly to safely lead him.

She did this for some minutes, talking softly to him all the while, until, feeling the time was right, she brought him to the center of the paddock and signaled him to stop and to stand. He did so, readily. Holly stroked his neck again, then walked around to his side and reached up and took hold of his mane, as she had on previous occasions, holding the hair tight in her fist and tugging a bit.

But then she did something she never had before. After saying, "Are you ready, Stormy? Good boy," she pulled harder on his mane, grabbing hold of it as if grabbing a length of climbing rope, using the leverage she gained to propel her body forward, up, and over, onto Stormy's back.

Over many days now, she had dreamed of doing this—days, not weeks, because when she first laid eyes on Stormy, fearsome and frightening all at once, she had not dared to dream that such a day might come. Her only thought upon buying Stormy was to rescue him from slaughter, to keep him safe, bring him home, and give him as much peace and happiness as he might accept.

And even now, after the weeks of patience and presence, letting him slowly, slowly get to know her and, even more slowly, to believe that what she did for, with, or to him would bring him to no harm, she had not been entirely sure Stormy would permit her to ride him. As she made the attempt, every muscle in her body and thought in her mind was on high alert, ready to abort the action or jump clear of danger should Stormy begin to buck or bolt.

But he didn't. Not at all.

Yes, he gave a sputter of surprise, feeling her weight on his back. He jerked his nose up, startled, and took two short steps to the side, as if trying to regain his balance, but then, as Holly settled into the center of him, Stormy settled, too, standing quiet and still, waiting for what came next.

At first, she just sat there, grinning and so enjoying the moment that she almost feared risking more. But finally, deciding there was nothing to lose, Holly leaned down low to grab hold of the lead rope, using it like a rein, then sat up again and squeezed her legs firmly but gently around his girth.

Stormy walked forward without hesitation, his gait easy, moving around the paddock to the left or to the right, responding to Holly's gentle pressure on the reins as if it were the most natural thing in the world for him to do. He seemed utterly relaxed.

So did Holly, from outward appearances, but inside, her heart was doing cartwheels. And when she looked out over the top of the paddock fence and saw Rob Lee standing where he always stood, with his feet planted wide and his arms crossed over his chest, the way they always were, but with the widest, brightest smile she had ever seen on his handsome face, it was all she could do to keep from whooping for pure joy.

If there was ever a time when Holly had been happier with the world or herself, she couldn't remember it. But the day wasn't over yet.

After five trips around the paddock, Rob Lee, still grinning, shifted his stance and moved from his accustomed spot, walking around the short end of the paddock and then climbing up three slats of the pasture fence before swinging his legs over the top and jumping lightly down to the ground.

"What are you doing?" Holly asked, careful not to raise her voice too much, as Rob Lee approached the paddock from the pasture side.

"What do you think?" he called back, reaching for the latch and then letting the paddock's back gate swing wide.

"Horses are meant to run. Let's see what he's got."

Never having had a horse of her own before now, Holly's opportunities to ride at more than a walk had been few and far between. At this point, she wasn't even sure she remembered how to gallop and was almost afraid to try.

There was no reason to worry.

After exiting the confined regions of the paddock and entering the open pasture, Stormy was more than ready to stretch his legs. With an encouraging click of Holly's tongue and a slight pressure from her legs, Stormy transitioned easily from a walk to a trot and, after a few minutes, from a trot to a canter, warming up nicely as horse and rider found their balance. And when, at last, Holly sensed his eagerness and confidence and felt confident herself, she gave him his head and allowed him to full-out gallop.

They practically flew across the fields, up, over, and down the gentle slopes and hills, with Holly angling her torso lower but keeping her back strong, moving her body forward, down, up, and back in a steady, rolling rhythm that matched the drumbeat pounding of Stormy's hooves across the open prairie. They moved like one being, single of mind and purpose, exhilarated and free, for a long time.

And when they became tired, both rider and horse, gallop became canter, became trot, became walk, as they returned to the gate, where Rob Lee was waiting. And though Holly's body was tired, her mind and heart were still doing cartwheels.

Reining Stormy to a standstill, she felt no less exhilarated, or less free, than she had in those minutes before, flying at full gallop across the field, as happy as she could ever remember or imagine feeling, until she dropped Stormy's rope and slid from his back into Rob Lee's embrace.

When his mouth pressed to hers and she parted

her lips, Holly understood that happiness is not measured by or limited to what you have known in the past but by what you will allow yourself to experience in the present and risk for the future.

Chapter 34

It had been a good day for Mary Dell. A challenging day to be sure, but a good one— partially because it *was* challenging.

Mary Dell had always loved learning new things. That was part of the reason she loved quilting so much, because it constantly provided new opportunities to stretch herself, master new skills or refine old ones, and express her creativity in new and different ways. Because of that, some of her quilting experiments turned out better than others and there had been more than a couple of notable disasters, but over the years, Mary Dell had come to realize that she could learn as much from her failures as from her successes. That knowledge helped her to become fearless in her willingness to tackle new quilting challenges, a quality that often spilled over into other areas of her life.

However, in spite of what Taffy had said about the job of directing and editing a television show not being all that complicated, Mary Dell approached the task of overseeing the editing for the two episodes of *Quintessential Quilting* she had helped to direct with a degree of trepidation that was not unwarranted. Though seven years of standing in front of the cameras had given her a pretty accurate sense of what did and didn't work when it came to content, presentation, timing, and camera work, when it came to editing and directing, there was a world of technical knowledge that Mary Dell simply did not possess.

The edit suite of the Dallas studio really wasn't much more than a big desk in a windowless room, but on that big desk was a computer with an enormous screen with graphs, tabs, displays, and tools that could be used to edit, add, or alter sound and lighting levels, video and audio effects and transitions, and much more, all done by operating the tabs and buttons on a special color-coded editing keyboard loaded with buttons and dials that bore no resemblance to anything Mary Dell had on her home desktop.

The whole thing reminded her of an airplane cockpit, and upon sitting down in the edit suite, Mary Dell felt nearly as nervous and intimidated as if she'd been asked to land a plane single-handedly and without benefit of prior instruction or access to an operations manual. Fortunately, Mary Dell was not alone.

Gina, the quiet but capable assistant director, was there by her side, just as she had been on the set, and Mary Dell wasn't too timid to ask for her advice, nor too proud to follow it. Working side by side for three days straight, the two women pulled together two finished episodes they could be proud of. It was a truly successful collaboration.

At the end of the third day, as they were going through the credits that came at the end of the programs, Mary Dell gave her collaborator one final instruction.

"Okay, stop right here," she said, standing behind Gina and peering over her shoulder.

Gina pressed some buttons. The screen froze.

"Good. Now click on the directorial credit." Eyes glued to the screen, Gina complied. "And type in your name."

Gina's head snapped to the right. "No, Mary Dell. You don't have to—"

"Oh, yes, I do," she insisted. "You're the one who deserves the credit for pulling this whole mess together, and I want people to know it. So do as I say: List your name as the director and me as the assistant. Go ahead."

"All right," Gina said with a reluctant shrug.

She typed in the changes. When she was finished, she said, "Thanks, Mary Dell. I gotta say, this is the first week since I started working on this show that I've felt good about an episode. If you took a poll, I'm pretty sure the rest of the crew would say the same thing. It's been a real pleasure working with you. Hope we get to do it again sometime."

Gina stuck out her hand. Mary Dell gripped it.

"Thanks. I hope so too."

Mary Dell was in excellent spirits when she met up with Howard and Hub-Jay at Habanero, her favorite Mexican restaurant, and proudly handed each of them a DVD of the two completed episodes.

"Wow, Momma!" Howard said, gazing at the disc with wide eyes and a kind of reverent fascination. "You're a director now?"

"Not quite." She laughed. "Gina did most of the heavy lifting, but I sure learned a lot in the last few days. It was really fun."

"I'm very impressed. Can't wait to watch it," Hub-Jay said, and then, without preamble or permission, leaned in and kissed Mary Dell on the cheek.

His kiss would have landed on her lips had not Mary Dell, surprised by Hub-Jay's gesture and that he would do it in front of Howard, twisted her head just as Hub-Jay made contact.

Howard, watching this awkward interaction, looked at Hub-Jay with raised eyebrows and said, "Are you Momma's boyfriend?"

Mary Dell stammered and started to answer, but Hub-Jay beat her to it. "I'd like to be, Howard. Is that all right with you?"

Howard's forehead furrowed momentarily as he considered the question. "Yes. That's okay with me. Momma's been alone too long. And I like you, Hub-Jay."

"I like you too, Howard."

Hub-Jay reached under the table for Mary Dell's hand. She let him take it.

The dinner passed quickly. The food was delicious and they had so much to talk about.

Hub-Jay shared more about the plans for the birthday party and told funny stories about some of the more eccentric hotel guests he had encountered during his career. Mary Dell filled Howard and Hub-Jay in on all the goings-on in Too Much and with family, and told them more about her experiences as a substitute television director, leaving out the part about Taffy's role in making the substitution necessary.

But for the bulk of the evening, the podium belonged to Howard. He filled them in on his daily routine and how he had mastered the use of public transit, meaning he no longer had to ask for a ride if he wanted to go somewhere, and how he had taken the bus to a fabric shop on the other side of town and purchased four yards of chenille in various colors, as well as several yards of cording, which he was using to make pillows for the sofa in his little apartment.

"Jenna's momma asked me to make two more for her. She's paying me sixty dollars plus the fabric!" Howard exclaimed, his expression glowing with pride as he shared the news.

Mary Dell was proud too. "That's wonderful, baby!"

"You know," Hub-Jay said as he folded a spoonful of melted queso fundido into a home-made flour tortilla, "you might have the beginning of a nice little business there, Howard."

"I thought about that," Howard said. "I like sewing pillows for a hobby, but I want to do something bigger. I've decided to be a fabric designer."

"You have?" Mary Dell asked.

Howard bobbed his head. "Uh-huh. I'm going to take two classes next semester—computers and digital photography. There is this software now that lets you load your pictures or art onto a computer so you can print it onto fabric.

"Jenna and I have been talking about it. Her sunflower painting would be pretty as fabric. I could design a fabric panel of the whole painting, and then some yellow, gold, and green solids, plus a blender fabric with the leaves, another with the seeds, and a border print with little sunflowers. We could make a whole collection. If people buy it, I could design more fabric from paintings by artists with Down syndrome and donate the money to help other people with Down syndrome."

"You've really spent a lot of time thinking about this," Mary Dell said, sincerely impressed by his determination.

"Uh-huh. I already thought of a name for the company," Howard reported. "Down Home Fabric. Get it? It's like Down syndrome."

"I like it!"

"Me too," Howard replied.

The Habanero restaurant was located in the Arts District. Their original plan for the evening had been to walk from the restaurant to the Meyerson Center for a special screening of the musical *West Side Story* with the Dallas Symphony Orchestra performing a live accompaniment of the movie score.

However, just as their dessert was being served, Howard seemed to run out of steam and asked if they'd mind if he skipped the movie and concert. Mary Dell was worried—he did look a little pale—but Howard insisted he was fine, just tired. "Going to college is a lot of work," he said seriously.

Howard said he'd take the bus back to his apartment, but it was late and dark, so Hub-Jay made a call and asked one of the hotel drivers to pick him up. Mary Dell stood on the curb, watching Howard waving excitedly from the window of the sleek black limousine as Hub-Jay stood next to her with his arm around her shoulders.

When the car disappeared around the corner, she turned to him and said, "I have a feeling he won't be quite as enthusiastic about taking the bus after tonight."

The movie was wonderful, one of Mary Dell's favorites. Having a live orchestra play the score only enhanced the experience. But Mary Dell was uncharacteristically quiet when she and Hub-Jay walked back to the hotel. The night was cool but temperate. The sound of their footsteps made soft echoes as they traversed Dallas's darkened streets.

"Is something wrong?" Hub-Jay asked. "You haven't said a word for three blocks."

"That's probably a record," Mary Dell replied with a laugh that softened into a reflective sort of smile. "I'm fine. I was just thinking."

"About Howard?" Hub-Jay guessed.

"He was so talkative tonight," she observed, sounding excited. "So full of plans and hopes for the future. He's never been shy, but whenever we're together, I do most of the talking. I thought it was because he was just naturally a little quiet, but I just realized that maybe it was because he didn't think he had anything much to add. His whole life has always been wrapped up with mine, you know? I always used to say that we were two sides of the same coin—which was true.

"After Lydia Dale died, Howard stepped into her shoes and started picking out the fabrics for my quilts and helping me decide what to stock in the shop." She laughed out loud. "Heck, I can still barely dress myself without Howard's help."

Hub-Jay slowed his pace and turned his head toward Mary Dell, making a show of looking her over.

"He didn't dress you tonight, did he?" Mary Dell shook her head. "There you go. I think you look lovely. You know, leopard print is really starting to grow on me."

Mary Dell gave him a good-natured elbow in the ribs. Hub-Jay put his arm more closely around her shoulders as they continued walking.

"My point," she continued, "is that Howard has something to say for himself now. He has his own plans and life. He's not just another side of me anymore. He's his own person, an adult."

Mary Dell stopped abruptly in the middle of the sidewalk. "I did the right thing, letting him go."

It was a declaration, not a question.

Hub-Jay turned to face her directly, tilting his chin lower so he could look her in the eye, and taking hold of her two hands. "You did a lot of things right where Howard is concerned."

"I did," she said, her voice choked with emotion. "And I'm so, so proud of him. But it's hard to think that he doesn't need me anymore."

"Howard is *always* going to need you. Maybe not in quite the same way he did before, but nothing and no one will ever change what you are to each other."

Hub-Jay stood there and just looked at her, smiling, for such a long and silent moment that Mary Dell couldn't help but smile back, and then laugh.

"What? You look like the cat that ate the canary," she said.

"Well . . . yeah. I was going to wait until the party to do this . . . I had a whole plan and a speech. But this thing has been burning a hole in my pocket for more than a week. I just can't wait anymore."

Hub-Jay reached into the pocket of his jacket and took out a small box of black velvet. He placed it in her hand and, in the still street of the silent city with tall sentinel skyscrapers standing witness, sank down on one knee.

"Howard isn't the only one who needs you, Mary Dell. I do, very much. And if you'll just give me the chance, I know I can be the man that you need too."

Chapter 35

Back in Too Much, on the night before he was to drive to Dallas for his thirtieth birthday party, Rob Lee dreamed about Nick and the bombing.

It was the first such dream he had had in three weeks, almost the same dream he'd had before—on patrol with Nick and the others, spotting someone walking down the road, the hesitation at recognizing the enemy, the blast, heat, and fire, the screams that went unheard. But on this occasion when the figure walking down the road turned quickly toward him, the face that made him hesitate a breath too long and confused his loyalties belonged, not to the enemy, but to Holly.

And in an exquisitely appointed hotel suite in Dallas, Mary Dell went to bed quite alone and dreamed she was already at the birthday party, wearing her red taffeta dress, gliding around the dance floor in Hub-Jay's arms while the Dallas Symphony played "Tonight," her favorite song from *West Side Story*. But when she lifted her head from Hub-Jay's shoulder to tell him how happy she was and how much she loved him, she found herself looking into Donny's face.

A hundred miles distant one from the other, aunt and nephew each woke with a start, sat straight up in their beds, and took in long, ragged breaths, trying to separate themselves from their dreams and understand what they meant.

Chapter 36

Hub-Jay had gone off in search of a bottle of sparkling cider to serve to Linne, so Mary Dell stood alone to greet her guests in the foyer of the Jacaranda Suite, one of the Hollander Grand's largest and the only one that boasted a rooftop garden.

Nearly one hundred people attended the celebration, family and old friends from Too Much and Dallas, a couple of Howard's new friends from college, and quite a number of the old friends he'd made through the Down Syndrome Association programs and events. Most of Howard's friends were accompanied by parents, but one or two who, like Howard, were capable of living independently arrived on their own. All of them were dressed in their best.

Howard's oldest friend in Dallas, Sawyer Hill, came in white tie. He beamed when Mary Dell said, "Sawyer, you look about as handsome as a handful of spades! Promise you'll save me a dance later, will you?" But if anybody had been taking a vote, the award for Best Dressed Party Guest would have gone to Luke Hayden, a Marine and friend of Rob Lee's who was home on leave and came to the party wearing his dress blues.

Mary Dell was so happy to see Luke. In comparison to Howard, Rob Lee had so few friends in attendance. Since his return to Too Much, Rob Lee hadn't reconnected with his old high school classmates, and most of his Marine Corps friends were either still deployed or, sadly, had never returned from combat.

Observing his serious expression and the tentative way he entered the room, Mary Dell correctly sensed that Luke was a shy young man and possibly struggling with some of the same kinds of adjustment issues that Rob Lee had experienced upon returning stateside. With that in mind, she purposely reined in her natural effusiveness and greeted him warmly but in a quiet voice, saying how handsome he looked and how glad Rob Lee would be to see him. Craning her neck in the direction of the dance floor, Mary Dell caught her nephew's eye and waved him over. Rob Lee lifted his hand so his friend could see it and began wending his way through the other dancers with Holly in tow.

Seeing how lovely Holly looked in a simple ivory shift with a bit of beading at the neckline and the way Rob Lee clung to her hand, Mary Dell couldn't help but smile. Rob Lee was a different young man than he'd been when Mary Dell confronted him that day in the tack room. He'd stopped drinking and he worked hard—in fact, the ranch was running more smoothly than ever. Most important of all, he was happy.

Mary Dell was under no illusions that the talking-to she'd given him had been the catalyst for such change. The credit belonged to Holly and Holly alone. And to think she had once resented this girl. Holly Silva might not be the best quilter Mary Dell had ever seen, but she had turned out to be just what they needed at the moment they needed it most.

It was like Mary Dell always said: God was in the business of just-in-time inventory.

Rob Lee grinned when approaching Luke, and the two friends embraced in one of those deeply felt but understated macho boy-hugs, a single two-handed pound on the back followed by a tight embrace that extended to a beat of one, two, three, before the men took a step back and looked at each other.

"Wow," Rob Lee said in an appraising tone of voice, his eyes moving up and down over Luke's impeccably pressed uniform. "You look terrible."

Luke's smile made the corners of his eyes crinkle. Rob Lee released his hold on Luke's shoulders, spreading his hands.

"Seriously, dude. You look like a recruiting poster."

"Thanks. Hey, happy birthday, buddy. Thirty, huh?" Luke shook his head sorrowfully from side to side. "Man, that's old. But you haven't changed a bit. You look just like you did. Like a complete pile of sh—"

Luke stopped himself midsentence, looked at Mary Dell, and turned a little pink.

"Pardon me, ma'am."

"Don't worry, Luke. I've heard worse."

"Hey," Rob Lee said, tugging on Holly's hand to pull her forward, "I'd like to introduce you to my girl."

Taking note, Mary Dell, without Rob Lee seeing her, tossed a quick, "Oh, yes?" sort of look in Holly's direction. Holly said nothing, but her smile said it all. Something had definitely happened with these two in the last few days, and Mary Dell couldn't have been happier.

"C'mon, buddy," Rob Lee said after Luke and Holly exchanged greetings, putting his arm over his friend's shoulder and reclaiming Holly's hand. "Let's get you a beer."

Most everyone had arrived by that time, but Mary Dell was still waiting to greet one more guest. She remained at her post but turned around so she could watch the goings-on.

The party was definitely in full swing. The dance floor was packed with young people jumping, twisting, and bouncing to the music. Most were paired up, but Mary Dell noticed that a cluster of women, including Cady and four of Howard's girlfriends, were dancing as a group, forming a little sisterhood of singles. They looked like they were having more fun than anyone. Judging from the size and enthusiasm of the crowd, the DJ must have been a good one, but the music was mostly unfamiliar to her and a little loud for Mary Dell's taste.

Apparently, she wasn't the only one who felt that way. Peering through an open pair of French doors, Mary Dell saw that most of the people over forty had migrated to the roof deck, where potted trees and shrubs decorated with strings of tiny white lights created a magical if somewhat more sedate setting.

Taffy and Linne were sitting at a candlelit table in the corner with Reverend Crews and his wife, talking and sipping glasses of something golden and bubbly—somebody must have located the sparkling cider after all. Howard and Rob Lee were the first babies Reverend Crews had baptized upon taking his pulpit in Too Much. It meant worlds to Mary Dell that he and Mrs. Crews had come all this way for the party, even though they would have to drive back home the same night in order to be home in time for Sunday services.

Mary Dell was also touched that Pearl, Pauline, and their cousin Sweetums, the first three women she had ever taught to quilt, were there, too, along with their husbands.

It was wonderful to look around the room and see so many familiar faces, people who had loved and supported her and her family through triumph, tragedy, and everything that came between. She was so happy to see that everyone was having fun. They stood in little clumps and clusters, holding conversations among themselves and flutes of champagne in their hands as waiters in white coats circulated among them, offering appetizers of shrimp, beef tenderloin, chicken skewers, and a special pimento cheese spread on toasted slices of brioche. So sweet of Hub-Jay to include that. He knew pimento cheese was her favorite. It was a wonderful party, thanks to him.

One thing was bothering her, though. She couldn't see Howard anywhere. He wasn't on the dance floor or the roof deck. Where could he have gone?

She was just about to go in search of him when she noticed him sitting in a corner with Jenna at his side, holding his hand. He must have needed a break. He'd been dancing all night. Mary Dell frowned; she didn't like his color. Maybe he was overheated.

She was about to go over and suggest he go out on the deck to cool off when Hub-Jay arrived, looking triumphant and clutching a bottled of sparkling cider in his hand.

"Found it! Finally!"

Mary Dell gave him an apologetic look. "One of the waiters beat you to it."

"You're kidding," he said. "Where were they hiding the bottles?"

Before Mary Dell had a chance to answer, the door opened and the person she was more anxious to see than all the others entered the room.

"Evelyn!"

Mary Dell threw her arms wide, tottered across the marble foyer in her stiletto heels, and hugged her beloved friend as tight as she could.

"I am so, so, so happy you're here!"

"Me too! I'm sorry we're late. There was some kind of air traffic control issue in Chicago and . . . Never mind." She dismissed the subject with a wave of her hand. "We're here. That's what matters."

"Charlie," Mary Dell said warmly, embracing Evelyn's husband. "Thank you for coming. I know how hard it is for you to leave the restaurant on the weekend."

"Wouldn't have missed it for anything," Charlie replied, his Irish burr just as prominent as it had been when he immigrated to America four decades before.

"Besides, I consider it something of a business trip—research." He grinned and extended his hand to Hub-Jay. "Evelyn says you started out in the restaurant business."

"True," Hub-Jay said. "I started busing tables at seventeen, worked my way through the ranks before opening my first hotel. Aside from dealing with temperamental executive chefs, the restaurant is still my favorite part of the business."

"Bunch of prima donnas," Charlie said, nodding deeply. "My chef just had a three-day pout because I wouldn't buy him a six-thousand-dollar espresso machine. No appreciation of what it takes to run a business."

"I can tell you two are going to have a lot to talk about," Mary Dell said. "Hub-Jay, do you want to get Charlie a drink and some food? Watch out for him, though, or he'll steal your recipes."

"I don't mind. Professional courtesy. Charlie, want to go talk some shop?"

"We'll be right there." Mary Dell grabbed Evelyn's arm. "We've got to run to the powder room."

Dragging Evelyn off in the opposite direction,

Mary Dell called out over her shoulder, "Charlie, be sure to try the pimento cheese appetizers. Heaven!"

Mary Dell pulled Evelyn into the powder room and locked the door behind them.

"This looks serious," Evelyn said. "What's up?"

Eyes sparkling, with her lips pressed tight together, as if trying to keep back a possible explosion of words, Mary Dell spread out her right hand and twisted a platinum band on her ring finger one hundred and eighty degrees, revealing a stunning and very large cushion-cut diamond, surrounded on four sides by a row of smaller but no less brilliant diamonds.

Evelyn gasped and her hand covered her mouth.

"Mary Dell! Oh, it's beautiful! But"—she frowned a little and looked at the ring more closely—"it's an engagement ring. Shouldn't you be wearing it on your left hand?"

"I can't. Not yet." Mary Dell bit her lower lip. "I'm still married. I never divorced Donny."

Evelyn's mouth dropped open as she tried to process this information. "What! Never? Even after all these years? I always assumed that after he left . . ."

Mary Dell shrugged, looking almost apologetic. "I know. For a long time, years and years, I kept thinking he'd come back. By the time I finally accepted the fact that he wasn't, there didn't seem to be any point to it. For one thing, I didn't know where he was. Besides, I had no pressing reason to divorce Donny. I wasn't interested in marrying again. I had Howard, my family, my career— I couldn't imagine ever needing or wanting anything more."

"But Hub-Jay changed your mind?"

"He did. And it's just so . . . it's a wonderful feeling. I'm in love! Really and truly in love!" Mary Dell laughed, displaying both delight and shock that she had uttered those words aloud. "I never imagined feeling like that again. Maybe that's why it took me so long to figure it out. Hub-Jay too. We'd both given up on love."

"Oh, Mary Dell. I am so happy for you." Evelyn hugged her friend in a tight and sincere embrace. "But if you feel that way, why are you hiding your ring? This is such wonderful news. I'd think you'd want to shout it from the rooftops."

"Oh, believe me," Mary Dell said, nodding and taking a step back, "I do. I've just about bit a hole in my tongue to keep it to myself. But today is Howard and Rob Lee's big day. I don't want to steal their thunder. But I also don't think it would be right to make our engagement official yet. Not until I can get a divorce."

Evelyn frowned. "But how are you supposed to divorce someone you can't even find?"

"I've talked to a lawyer. First, I have to make a

real effort to locate Donny and convince a judge of that. You know, he actually did call a few weeks ago. He saw the promotional spot and was worried that Howard wasn't in it. First time I've heard his voice in thirty years," she said. "So strange. He sounded just the same; I knew it was Donny the minute he said hello. But he hung up before I had a chance to ask where he was. I wish I'd known then that I would need to find him now. Anyway, if he can't be found, I have to fill out paperwork and put an ad in the paper saying I'm filing for divorce. It's doable but complicated and will take at least a few months. Until then . . ."

She fingered her diamond, gazing wistfully at the shimmering stone, before finally twisting it back toward her palm. "I'm so happy I just about dropped my harp through the clouds. It's been so hard keeping quiet," she said. "But I had to tell you. I couldn't keep it from my best friend, now, could I?"

"I should hope not!" Evelyn grinned. "Don't worry. Your secret is safe with me. But I really can't wait to tell Abigail and Margot and all the rest of the gang. They'll want to throw you the biggest bridal shower *ever*. You know that, right?"

There was a knock on the door and Cady's voice said, "Aunt Mary Dell? Are you in there? It's time for the cake."

"Be right there, baby girl!"

●●●

The pastry chef, Vivian, had outdone herself, baking two beautifully decorated triple-layer cakes; chocolate with hazelnut filling for Rob Lee and lemon with raspberry filling for Howard. Waiters wheeled both cakes, topped with thirty blazing candles, out onto the roof deck and placed them in front of the guests of honor while everyone sang "Happy Birthday."

At the end of the song, everybody clapped, and Mary Dell, who was standing off to one side with Hub-Jay's arm around her waist, called out, "Make a wish, boys!"

Rob Lee glanced quickly to his left, where Holly was standing, grinned, and blew out the blaze in one big breath. Howard took a breath at the same time but managed to blow out only a third of his candles. Mary Dell, still smiling but concerned, moved to his side.

"Here, baby. You want some help? Let's do it together." On a count of three, mother and son took in a big breath and, together, extinguished the remaining candles.

Ten seconds after that, while the guests were still applauding, Howard's eyes rolled to the back of his head and he passed out cold.

Chapter 37

After he'd regained consciousness, which occurred even before the ambulance arrived, Howard seemed more or less back to normal. He complained of fatigue and a headache but didn't seem to be in any significant pain. Even so, Mary Dell was happy when the emergency room doctor decided to admit him for observation and testing.

Three days in, however, Howard was irritated that he was missing class and Mary Dell was anxious for answers. Dr. Ted Brewer, the hospital nephrologist, a middle-aged man of middling height with heavy black eyebrows and a serious demeanor, came into Howard's room late on Tuesday to introduce himself and give them a surprising diagnosis—Howard was in end-stage renal failure.

That word, "end-stage," struck fear into Mary Dell's heart, but she held her emotions in check. She had to, for Howard's sake.

"Don't worry. Howard is in no immediate danger, but he is suffering from autosomal dominant polycystic kidney disease," the doctor said by way of explanation, even though the string of multisyllabic words meant nothing to Howard or Mary Dell. "Basically, it's an inherited type of kidney disease."

"Inherited?" Mary Dell frowned. "From who?"

"Either you or your husband."

"It can't be me. I feel fine."

"A person can be a carrier, or even have a mild form of the disease, without ever displaying any significant symptoms. We'll want to schedule you and your husband for testing as soon as possible."

"My dad left when I was a baby," Howard said matter-of-factly from his hospital bed. "We don't know where he is."

"All right. Then we'll start with you, Mrs. Templeton. If your results don't show ADPKD—that's the shorthand term for this type of kidney disease—then we'll know that Howard's father was the carrier."

Mary Dell screwed her eyes shut and lifted her hand, feeling overwhelmed and wanting to get back to what really mattered.

"What does this mean for Howard? Are there medications or treatments that can help him?"

"In the earlier stages of the disease, yes. But ADPKD can be very hard to detect early in its progression. Many patients, like Howard, don't display any significant symptoms until reaching a fairly advanced stage. The good news is that, aside from a slightly elevated blood pressure, which we're going to treat with diet and medication, Howard is in fairly good health. His heart looks fine. The bad news is that Howard's kidney function is at twenty-seven percent and it will continue to decrease. When it falls below twenty percent, he'll have to go on dialysis."

"What's dialysis?" Howard asked, repeating the word slowly.

Dr. Brewer looked at Mary Dell and lifted his brows, as if asking for her permission or guidance on how to proceed.

"Howard's an adult," she said, slightly irritated that she even had to point this out. "He has a right to understand what is happening to his own body."

The doctor nodded and, in relatively uncomplicated language, went on to explain what dialysis was, how it was necessary to clean waste and impurities from the blood that Howard's kidneys were no longer able to filter, that Howard would have to go for dialysis treatment three times a week, for three to four hours each time, and that, given his age and general state of health, there was every reason to think he could continue to live a long time on dialysis.

"These days, with the advances in technology, it isn't uncommon for people to survive twenty or thirty years on dialysis."

Howard's eyes went wide. "Thirty years! I just started college. Someday, I'm going to have my own fabric company. I don't have time to go to the doctor three times a week forever. I already missed my art class this week. That was bad enough!"

The doctor smiled sympathetically. "I understand your feelings, Howard. You're not at the point of needing dialysis yet, and it could be a long time before that happens. But when we get to that point, it will likely be the only means we have of keeping you alive."

Howard went a bit white and Mary Dell grabbed his hand.

"I assure you," the doctor went on, "people can live long and productive lives while on dialysis. We can try to schedule your dialysis sessions around your other activities. In certain situations, dialysis can even be performed in the home. After some intensive training, your mother could learn to—"

"I don't live with my mother," Howard said, his voice uncharacteristically testy. "I have my own apartment. I like it and that's where I want to stay."

"Ah. I see." Dr. Brewer shrugged helplessly and looked at Mary Dell. "As I said, we'll do our best to work the appointments around Howard's schedule."

"What about a transplant?" Mary Dell asked.

"Yes," the doctor said slowly, in a way that made Mary Dell think he was somewhat reluctant to answer. "That is sometimes an option. But there are a number of factors that we have to take into consideration before we decide if a person would be a good candidate for a kidney transplant— age, general health . . ."

"Howard is young, and you already said that his health was good."

Dr. Brewer nodded empathetically and, once again, answered slowly. "That's true. But we would also need to take into consideration the patient's ability to follow through with the required medical protocols. Transplant patients have to follow very strict dietary and lifestyle guidelines—no soft cheeses or deli meats, no sushi, no eating at buffets or salad bars, fresh vegetables must either be avoided or carefully washed, no use of hot tubs or steam rooms. That's just a partial list. The biggest issues post-transplant would center on medications. Patients take a variety of medications, upward of a dozen pills per day at twice-daily intervals. Forgetting to take those medications can put the transplanted kidney at serious risk of rejection."

The doctor was quiet. Mary Dell sat there for a moment, waiting for him to go on.

When he didn't, she said, "So are you trying to say that someone with Down syndrome isn't capable of following the doctor's orders or taking medication on time?"

"I am saying," he replied in a measured and careful manner, "that kidney transplants are expensive and complicated and that to be a good candidate for a transplant, we would need to be certain that the patient had the intellectual and emotional capacity to follow all the protocols."

"I see." Mary Dell set her lips, her gaze all but boring a hole through the good doctor, before turning toward Howard, who was observing this exchange from his hospital bed.

"Howard, explain to Dr. Brewer what your schedule is like."

"On what day? My art class is on Monday, Wednesday, and Friday. But I go to my old program at the Down syndrome center on Tuesday and Thursday. And on Sunday I go to church and volunteer in the nursery during Sunday school. But on Saturday I just hang out with my friends."

"Oh, you don't need to explain all of them," she replied. "How about just the days you go to college?"

Howard complied, explaining his routine for rising at six-thirty, cooking breakfast, cleaning his apartment, and doing a load of laundry before catching the bus, which involved one transfer, to get to the campus of his community college, then taking his class, perhaps spending time in the art studio or meeting with his adviser before making the return trip, stopping at the transfer point, which was close to a shopping center, to buy any groceries or anything else he needed, before heading home for the evening, eating dinner with the Morris family, and then either watching television, talking with his mother on the telephone, spending time with his girlfriend, or working on a sewing project.

"Thank you, baby. Now tell Dr. Brewer all about your plans for your fabric company," she said, sounding more than a little smug, "and your pillow business."

"The pillows are just kind of a hobby," Howard said, then launched into a description of where he liked to buy his fabric, how much he needed for each pillow, and what fabrics worked best.

That was as far as he got before Dr. Brewer, who had been listening carefully, smiled and lifted a hand. "Thanks, Howard. I get the general idea."

He turned to Mary Dell. "Your point is well taken, Mrs. Templeton. Howard is obviously a high-functioning and capable young man. If you could arrange to be in the area on a regular basis during the early phase, just in the first few months of recovery, and to be sure that the medication routines were well established, I'd have no problem recommending Howard as a transplant candidate."

"Thank you," Mary Dell said, her words clipped but her expression pleased.

"Even so, I have to point out that the waiting list for donor kidneys is years long and that patients whose lives are in immediate danger have highest priority. Any way you look at it, Howard will probably have to go on dialysis for some length of time before he would be eligible to receive a donor kidney."

"He can have one of mine," Mary Dell said

without a moment of hesitation. "A person only needs one kidney to live; isn't that right?"

"Yes," the doctor confirmed. "But your kidney would have to be a good match for Howard's, and while close relatives are usually the best candidates—for example, a parent has a fifty percent chance of being a good match—in your case, Mrs. Templeton, we'd have to rule out any possibility of kidney disease in your own body before considering you as a potential live donor."

"Fine. Let's do it."

"All right. I'll order the tests tonight and we can start in the morning. We'll need blood work, urinalysis, and a CAT scan to begin with. If those are clear and there's no sign of ADPKD, I'll order more tests to see if your kidney is a good match."

"Thank you, Dr. Brewer."

The doctor rose from his chair, said he'd see them both the next day, and headed off to check on his other patients.

"Oh, Howard," he said, pausing at the door. "Those pillows you make. Do you think I could order two for my wife? Her birthday is coming up."

"Well," Howard said seriously, "I can't until you let me out of the hospital, and I do have another order ahead of yours. Would the middle of March be soon enough?"

"Perfect. I'll ask Karen what colors she likes and tell you tomorrow."

The deal having been made, Dr. Brewer said farewell again and left the room. Mary Dell got up from her seat to rearrange the blankets on Howard's bed.

"I'm okay, Momma. I'm not cold."

"I know," she said. "But it gives me something to do. Makes me feel needed."

Howard reached for her hand. "I always need you, Momma. You know that. But are you really sure you want to give me your kidney?"

"Baby, I'd not only give you my kidney, I'd give you my heart." She smiled. "That is, if you didn't already have it."

She squeezed his hand. Howard frowned curiously, then twisted her right hand so it was facing palm up. His eyes bulged wide.

"Momma! Where'd you get that diamond? It's humongous!"

Mary Dell blushed, took the ring from her finger, and slipped it into her pocket.

"It's not important," she said, and tucked in his sheet. "The only thing that matters to me right now is helping you get better."

Chapter 38

Rachel sat drinking unsweetened iced tea at an aged and slightly gouged wooden table that Holly, trying to keep herself busy in Mary Dell's absence, had sanded and painted a light aqua color earlier in the week.

"So you don't know when she'll be back?" Rachel asked. "Or if she'll be back?"

"Not exactly. But Howard is out of the hospital now. I'm sure she'll be back as soon as she can."

"Yeah, but how many weeks are you behind with filming—two? Maybe they need to look for a replacement. Or," Rachel said in a considering tone, before taking another sip of tea, "maybe they should just let you take over the whole thing."

Holly barked out a laugh at the very idea.

"First off, nobody can replace Mary Dell. She's one of a kind—a complete original. Second, even if there was somebody who could step into her shoes, it's definitely not me. I don't suck at quilting anymore. In fact I'm actually starting to enjoy it. But that doesn't mean I'm ready to carry the whole show on my own. Mary Dell will be back as soon as she can. We've got plenty of time to catch up on filming."

Rachel opened her mouth to speak and Holly held her hand out, traffic-cop flat, in front of her mother's face.

"No. Don't even start."

Rachel shrugged. "Fine. Guess I'm not exactly in a position to offer career advice."

Holly, who was standing at the kitchen counter, making their lunch, dipped her head, feeling guilty for being hard on her mother. Rachel had had a rotten year, as rough as any in her career, which was saying a lot.

The tabloid furor over Rachel's "nosedive" had died down considerably in recent days. Maureen Gilronan, an actress whose star had reached its zenith in the early 1960s and who was penniless after years without work and because of exploitation at the hands of unscrupulous managers, had been found dead in her small apartment in one of Hollywood's more unsavory neighborhoods. Now the tabloid and entertainment news was all Maureen Gilronan, all the time. No detail of the woman's private life was too ghoulish to be shared, including the fact that her refrigerator was empty of all food, aside from a jar of expired pimentos, that she had supposedly been found lying next to an open scrapbook of her old press clippings, and that no one had seen her for more than a week before thinking of knocking on the door to see if she was okay.

The coverage was macabre and revolting and

sad, but Holly couldn't pretend she wasn't relieved that the stories about Rachel, though they hadn't disappeared completely, had migrated to the back pages.

Holly finished slicing a ripe nectarine and tossed it into the salad bowl together with some spring greens, goat cheese, and slivered almonds.

"Now that the cruise gig is done, are you going to start looking for a new agent?" Holly was working hard to sound more nonchalant than she felt. She knew that Rachel's finances were a mess and that, so far at least, no one had made an offer on her condo. "You know, if you need some money, I've got—"

Rachel's laugh stopped her from finishing the sentence.

"Oh, honey. You're sweet, but don't think of lending me money, seriously. History has proven that I am a very bad investment indeed. You've always been so good with the financial stuff, never lived beyond your means, putting part of every paycheck into savings. In other words, doing exactly the opposite of everything I ever did. Can't imagine where you got it from; your dad wasn't any better at handling money than me."

Holly didn't point out that the reason she was so careful about money was precisely because Rachel wasn't and that this particular quality, along with a few others, came as a result not of following her mother's example but of looking at Rachel's life and figuring out exactly what she *didn't* want to be when she grew up. Still, Rachel had done the best she knew how. She wasn't a conventional mother, but she was a good one, and without her, Holly wouldn't be who she was.

"I appreciate your concern, honey. But, seriously, save your money. Besides," Rachel said, getting to her feet and pulling two plates out of Holly's cupboard, "things are looking up. I've got a new gig starting next week. That's why I have to leave in the morning."

"Really? Where? Doing what?" Holly was smiling as she gave the white balsamic vinegar and oil dressing another quick whisk and poured it over the salad.

"You won't believe it." Rachel chuckled. "It's actually kind of embarrassing. But, hey, a girl has to work, right? I called up Mikey."

"Mikey Grainger? That Mikey?" Holly's brows shot up; she really didn't believe it. For years now, she'd heard the story of how her ex-stepfather, Mikey, had "insulted" Rachel by booking her into the casino lounge instead of the big room.

"That Mikey," Rachel confirmed. "Honestly, I wasn't sure he'd take my call. But he did and signed me to a three-month contract. And, before you even ask—yes, I'll be performing in the lounge."

"Oh. That's really . . ."

Holly wanted to say that it was great, but, given Rachel's history with Mikey, she wasn't sure if this was the correct response.

"It's a good thing," Rachel said as Holly placed a generous serving of salad onto each plate. "I'll have a very nice suite in the hotel, seven hundred square feet, which sounds like the Taj Mahal after living in that closet of a stateroom they gave me on the boat. The money is better than the boat too. I'll be able to pay my bills, as well as some of the money I owe the IRS."

"Mom!" Holly gasped. "You're in trouble with the IRS? Why didn't you tell me?"

Rachel spread out her hands. "Why didn't I tell you? Because of this! Because I knew this was exactly how you'd react."

Holly gave her mother a disapproving stare and carried the plates to the table. Rachel refilled the iced tea glasses.

"Anyway, I'm telling you now. Everything is fine. This gig at the casino means I'll be able to catch up for the rest of this year. So don't lecture me, okay?"

Rachel sat down and so did Holly.

"Sorry, I wasn't trying to lecture you. I just worry about you. I just wish you'd told me; that's all. Maybe I could have helped."

"That's very sweet, but I'm the one who got myself into this mess and I'm the one who has to get myself out of it. And I will. Mikey and I had a long talk—he really is a nice guy. If I hadn't been such an idiot . . ."

Rachel rolled her eyes and sighed. "Anyway, water under the bridge. After I get to Vegas, Mikey is introducing me to a money manager he knows. Hopefully the gig at the casino will lead to other jobs and I can dig myself out of this hole. We'll see." Rachel took a bite of her salad. "Honey, this is really good."

"Thanks. New recipe," Holly said absently. "Listen, Mom. If you ever are in trouble, you know I'd help you, right?"

"And I appreciate that. But you need to look out for your own future, Holly. This is a very insecure business." Rachel sighed again and speared a slice of nectarine with her fork. "Sometimes I think I should have listened to my dad and become a PE teacher."

"A PE teacher? You?" Holly laughed. "Yeah, right. You could never have been anything but a singer and actress, and you know it."

"You're probably right. The only reason to be an artist is because you can't not. If you can think of any other way to be happy, then do. Really. Speaking of being happy—have you been in touch with Jason? Any word on whether or not they're going through with the design show?"

Holly was glad her mouth was full of salad so she didn't have to actually lie to her mother out loud. This way, she could just shake her head, which didn't seem quite as bad. The truth was that, at the moment, the only person Jason disliked more than Holly was Mary Dell, something that didn't bode well for her future at HHN-TV. But why worry Rachel about that?

More and more, Holly was beginning to wonder if she even liked doing TV. *Quintessential Quilting* was definitely more fun than doing the game show, but it still wasn't as fulfilling as she'd hoped. And she wasn't sure the design show would be any better. Working in television had its moments, but could Holly say that she was in the business because she couldn't imagine not being in it? Definitely not. But she didn't feel that way about anything else either, and television did pay the rent, at least for now.

"How else are things going?" Rachel asked after Holly finished swallowing. "How's the horse?"

"Stormy? He's great!"

Holly's face lit up as she told Rachel about Stormy's progress, the bond of trust that had formed between them, and the thrill of riding over the fields at a full gallop, as well as the various training techniques and goals she was working toward. After about six minutes, Rachel held up her hand.

"Honey, you lost me at dressage. But I get the general idea—you're crazy about Stormy."

"I am," Holly said. "Spending time with him is the best part of my day."

"And what about your cowboy? Still like spending time with him?" Rachel asked, and then, seeing the way Holly's expression transitioned from glowing to bemused, she said, "Or has that burnt itself out already?"

"I'm not sure it ever really caught fire. I thought it did, but . . ." Holly shrugged. "Ever since the birthday party it feels like maybe I was wrong. Or maybe I did something wrong? I mean, one day he wouldn't let go of my hand and introduced me as his girl, and the next day it feels like he's avoiding me. I don't get it."

"Fear of commitment," Rachel said without hesitation.

"You think?"

"Absolutely. You got too close, too fast. It scared him. Just hang back a little bit, don't push. Let him come to you. If he doesn't, then he wasn't the man for you anyway.

"Of course," Rachel said as she speared the last bites of salad with her fork, "this is advice I have never, ever been able to follow in my life. Not once. But, personally, I think that's a pretty good indicator of just how good it is. Do as I say, sweetie, not as I do. You'll be a lot happier."

Chapter 39

Hub-Jay was in a meeting with David, catching up on a few staffing issues that had come up during the course of David's recent vacation. After working through the agenda, Hub-Jay had planned to tell David that he was considering him for the general manager position at the Fort Worth property, set to open the following spring, and wanted to move him into an assistant manager role at the Hollander Grand as soon as possible. But their conversation was interrupted when Hub-Jay's assistant rang in, saying that Gloria Benavides, his attorney, was on the line.

"Do you want me to step outside?" David asked, rising halfway from his seat.

Hub-Jay waved him back into his chair. David was his right-hand man and as discrete as the day was long; that was one of the reasons for the promotion. Hub-Jay knew he could trust him not to repeat anything he heard.

"It's all right. This shouldn't take long."

Hub-Jay put the receiver to his ear and punched a button on the phone. "Hey, Glo. Thanks for calling back."

"Sorry it took so long. I was in depositions all morning. What can I do for you, Hub-Jay?"

"You know that other matter we discussed before?"

"Trying to track down Mary Dell's husband so she can serve him with divorce papers? I thought you said that she said she wanted to put the wedding plans on hold until she was able to get her son through this kidney thing. Did Mary Dell turn out to be a good donor match?"

"No," Hub-Jay answered. "The kidney disease definitely comes from her. Sounds like she got it from her father, since her mom is fine. The doctor even speculated that her dad's aneurysm, the one that caused the car crash that killed her sister and brother-in-law, might have been a result of undiagnosed kidney disease. Apparently, that's one of the complications."

"That's terrible. Is Mary Dell all right?"

"Absolutely fine. She'll need to be monitored from here on out, but, as of this moment, she's not suffering from any symptoms. But this knocks her out as a donor."

"Oh, the poor thing. She must be so upset."

"She's pretty torn up. I think a part of her feels guilty, you know, because she was the carrier."

"That wasn't her fault," Gloria countered. "She didn't even know she had it."

"That's what I keep telling her. Anyway, the only thing that will help right now is to find a kidney donor for Howard. I'm getting tested to see if I'm a match, and so is about half the town of

Too Much. But the chances of finding a match among relatives is much more likely, the closer the better."

"And so you want me to see if I can find Howard's father?" Gloria asked, connecting the final dots on her own.

"Yes, ma'am."

"All right. Give me his name again and anything else you know about him."

Hub-Jay pulled a legal pad off the desk, spun around in his chair so he was facing the window, and read the notes that he'd jotted down in anticipation of Gloria's question.

"Donald Hobart Bebee, goes by Donny. Six foot two, blue eyes, age sixty-three, which means his hair is probably gray. Occupation, cattle and sheep ranching, but that was thirty years ago. At this point, he could be doing just about anything and living just about anywhere. He did send a few cards with cash or money orders over the years, but there were no return addresses."

"Postmarks?"

"Out of state—Arkansas, Oklahoma, New Mexico. Almost always states bordering Texas. But he did call recently, first time in thirty years. There was no caller ID showing, but it was a four-three-two area code."

"So, somewhere in West Texas. Do you have the rest of the number?" Hub-Jay read off the numbers. "Okay, I'll see if we can trace it. What else?"

"That's all."

Gloria made a sputtering sound with her lips. "We'll do our best, but I'm not going to lie to you; this won't be easy. It's not much to go on, and after thirty years."

"I know, but I have to try."

"Okay, I'll get right on this. But, Hub-Jay?" She was quiet for a moment. "Are you sure you want to bring this guy back? I mean, he's been working hard to stay lost for a long time. Suppose he is a match but doesn't want to give up his kidney? It's not like he's ever been there for his kid before; why would anybody expect that to change now? Or," she said, in her best law school hypothetical voice, "suppose he *is* a match and is willing to give up his kidney for his son. I can't think of a more certain way to rehabilitate a deadbeat dad into a returning hero. Are you sure you want to give this guy that kind of credibility? Especially since Mary Dell still hasn't announced the engagement?"

Hub-Jay worked his lips as he listened. Gloria was an excellent attorney, determined and relentless. If anybody could track down Donny, she could. It was her job to advise him of all the possible legal, financial, and emotional facts and complications of any given transaction. But, sometimes, he wished she'd be just a little bit less craven.

"We're talking about possibly saving a human

life here, Gloria. And not just any life, but Howard's, the young man who I hope will be my stepson someday. So, I have to say, I'm not real concerned about how this affects me right now."

"Sorry," she said quickly, hearing the irritation in his voice. "I was just trying to—"

"Just find him, Gloria."

"Yes, sir. I'll start working on it now."

"Thank you."

Hub-Jay spun his chair back toward his desk, put the phone down a little harder than he'd intended to, and looked up at David. He'd almost forgotten he was sitting there.

"Sorry about that. I didn't plan on it getting quite that involved. Now, David," he said, clearing his throat, "there was one more thing I wanted to talk to you about. Good news, I think. For both of us—"

David scooted forward in his seat. "Mr. Hollander, I'm sorry to interrupt, but I couldn't help but overhear your conversation. I didn't realize that Miss Mary Dell's son was so sick. He needs a kidney? And you're trying to find his father?"

"That's right."

David licked his lips. "Mr. Hollander, I can help. I think I know where to find Donny Bebee."

Chapter 40

Standing at the stove, Taffy dipped a spoon in a stockpot, brought it to her lips, and made a face.

"Still too bland," she said as Mary Dell entered the kitchen. "You really don't realize how much salt you use until some doctor comes along and says you can't. But it's worth the trouble just to have you and Howard home again."

She poured some dried oregano into her palm before tossing it into the pot.

"I know he's still upset about not being able to finish his art class this semester. Maybe a good dinner will help cheer him up." She tasted the dish again. "Which, so far, this isn't. Oh, well, there's always dessert. That doctor didn't say anything about him having to cut back on sugar, did he?"

Getting no answer to her question, Taffy turned around.

"I said, what did the doctor say about . . ." The glazed, almost slack-jawed look on her daughter's face stopped her in mid-sentence.

"Mary Dell, what's wrong? Who were you talking to on the phone?"

"Jason Alvarez."

Taffy curled her lip. "Oh, that little worm. What did he have to say?"

"I'm fired."

• • •

On the other side of town, Holly was equally shocked at hearing the same bad news, in this case, from her agent.

"But, Amanda, I don't understand. How can they cancel us? The first episode hasn't even aired yet."

"They can. Shows get canceled all the time; you know that. And your buddy Mary Dell made it easy for them, canceling out on two weeks of filming, leaving them four episodes behind schedule."

"Oh, come on! Her son was in the hospital. What was she supposed to do?"

"She was supposed to go to work," Amanda said without hesitation. "Flood, fire, famine, divorce, even death—unless it's your own—you show up for work. That's the way this business is. And you know that too."

Yes, she did.

Because of the business, Rachel had had to miss Holly's piano recitals, soccer games, and even her high school graduation. And when Holly got sick, a babysitter or housekeeper had been the one to take her temperature and bring her chicken soup, usually out of a can.

Holly didn't fault Rachel for that—that *was* the business, and Rachel was the sole bread-winner. But she didn't fault Mary Dell for having different priorities. In her shoes, Holly hoped she'd have done the same thing.

"But there was still time to make up the schedule," Holly said. "We were all set to do it this week. Mary Dell and Howard came in from Dallas yesterday. We were going to film every day this week and wrap up the rest of the season. Jason didn't have to cancel the show—he wanted to."

"Yes," Amanda replied, "and Mary Dell gave him just the excuse he was looking for. Now he can get rid of her without paying any penalty because she was in violation of her contract."

Holly, who understood what could happen when you were found in violation of contract, bit her lower lip, worried for her friend.

"You don't think they'll fine her, do you?"

"They could," Amanda said, the harshness in her voice indicating that she might have, had she been in charge, "but I doubt they will. The circumstances are a little bit dicey. There'd definitely be a lawsuit, and the public relations fallout that would come from firing and fining a mother for taking care of her sick, special needs son wouldn't be pretty. I imagine they'll leave well enough alone."

"That's good at least."

"You know," Amanda said, her irritation obvious, "I wish you'd take as much interest in your career as you seem to be taking in Mary Dell Templeton's. Can we discuss your future now?"

"Right. Sorry. So, what's going to happen?

Do they have to pay me a kill fee or anything?"

"No. Nothing beyond what they've already paid out. Which means that you got your last paycheck two weeks ago. And, judging from the fact that you didn't ask about the design show, I am guessing you know Jason dislikes you only slightly less than he loathes Mary Dell Templeton. So, we can kiss that one good-bye. I thought I told you to be nice to him and play ball."

"Yeah, well. I couldn't seem to do that without losing my self-respect or my soul. So I didn't."

Angry as Amanda was about this whole debacle, and knowing that at least part of her blamed Holly for not doing more to prevent it, Holly half-expected Amanda to tell her she needed to find a new agent, especially after that last little piece of lip. But instead, Amanda surprised her. She laughed.

"Listen to you! You've grown a spine since the last time I saw you. All this time in Texas must be toughening you up, which is good. Jason is a slimy spawn of Satan; there's no doubt about it. So, I forgive you. Just don't make a habit of pissing off programing execs, okay?"

Holly smiled. "Okay."

"Good. And speaking of advice, which I hope you didn't ignore—have you been doing what I said about paying yourself first?"

"I've got some savings," Holly said. "About eighty-five thousand dollars."

"Good girl! And you don't own a house so you don't have to worry about paying a mortgage. That'll help. How much is your rent there?"

"Cheap. Six hundred dollars a month."

"Six hundred dollars a month! You can't rent a parking space in LA for six hundred a month. And Too Much is only a two-hour drive from the Dallas airport?"

"Uh-huh. Why all the questions?"

"Because I think that, for the moment, you just ought to sit tight and stay in Texas. I'm putting out some feelers, trying to get you auditions for a morning show in Little Rock and a spokes-model job at the SATC network."

"The Shop Around the Clock channel? Amanda," she moaned, "not that. I'd have been better off staying at the game show than going to SATC."

"Yeah, I know," Amanda said testily, "but there aren't going to be a lot of television auditions until later in the season. So you can't afford to be quite so picky. After all, a girl's got to work, doesn't she?"

"I know," Holly replied glumly. "Sorry."

"It's okay." Amanda sighed. "This hasn't been my favorite day either. Anyway, I think the best thing for you to do right now would be to stay in Too Much. You'll go through your savings slower there, and if I need to send you to an audition, you can fly out of Dallas as easily as LA."

"Oh, I . . . I don't know. Maybe I could stay at

my mom's place. She's in Vegas for the next three months and her condo hasn't sold. I could stay there for free."

"Yeah, but what about the horse? You can't exactly keep a stallion in a condo."

"Stormy is a gelding."

"Okay, and if I knew what that meant I'm sure I'd care, but you still can't keep a horse in a condo in LA. Besides, I thought you liked Texas."

"Oh, I do," she said sincerely. "It's just that . . . things have gotten a little complicated."

"Uh-oh. What'd you do? Fall in love with a cowboy or something?"

"Something like that," Holly admitted.

Amanda clucked her tongue chidingly. "Big mistake. Men always are. Doesn't have to be a cowboy. Mine was a shoe salesman, until he let me work my butt off putting him through law school so he could dump me for some chick who sells jewelry on Etsy. The jewelry he bought from her was supposed to be for me, I might add. Now she lives in my old house."

"That's terrible. You never told me that. And he got your house?"

"Uh-huh. He specializes in divorce law. Turned out to be very good at it. Anyway," she said dismissively, "that was a long time ago. You can't let men make you crazy. Let them buy you dinners and jewelry, use them for sex, but don't let them get to you. They're not worth it."

"Might be too late for that," Holly said. "But I'll try."

"Listen, I've got to go into a meeting, but I'll call you in a couple of days—"

"Yeah, but!" Holly interjected, afraid Amanda was about to hang up. "Wait a sec! What am I supposed to do until then?"

"Do? Go for a run, read a book, ride your horse. Relax! You've been working like a dog trying to become an expert quilter in less time than it takes to grow tomatoes. Now you've finally got a chance to kick back. Enjoy it while you can, because I'm sure it won't last long. After all, a girl's—"

"Got to work," Holly said. "I know."

Chapter 41

On a sunny Tuesday afternoon in March, on the outskirts of Alpine, Texas, Donny Bebee tilted his gray Stetson a little lower on his gray head and crossed the street to the tavern.

It took a moment for his eyes to adjust from the bright sunshine to the dim lighting of the bar, so at first he didn't see that someone was sitting in his usual spot, near the far end of the bar and right under the flat-screen TV. When he did realize that a man about his same height and age, wearing a light gray sports jacket and the whitest shirt he'd ever seen, was sitting on his barstool, Donny cast a look in the bartender's direction, figuring that John would ask that man to move to another spot.

Instead, John looked at him and said, "Hey, Donny. Like to introduce you to a friend of mine. Actually, he's a friend of David's, my little brother."

"The one who came to visit a couple weeks ago?"

"That's right. This is David's boss, Hub-Jay Hollander. Owns the hotel over in Dallas."

Donny was confused about what a man who owned a fancy hotel in Dallas would be doing all the way out here in Alpine, sitting in his seat, but he was too polite to come right out and ask, and there were still eight minutes until the show started, so he inclined his head and said, "Pleased to meet you."

"Same here," Hub-Jay Hollander replied. "I was wondering if I could buy you a drink."

Donny frowned and looked at John again, but the bartender shifted his shoulders and tilted his head to one side, silently indicating that everything was okay, so Donny sniffed and said, "I'll have a Lone Star."

"Sounds good. Can we make it two?" Hub-Jay looked at John, holding up two fingers.

Donny sat down, feeling awkward. The stranger sitting in his seat didn't say anything until John set the two open bottles in front of them, then walked off to the far end of the bar and started polishing glasses.

Donny glanced at his watch. Six minutes left. Why hadn't John turned on the TV?

"I realize I'm interrupting your routine," Hub-Jay said. "And I apologize. But I need to talk to you about something concerning your son, Howard."

Donny frowned. "How do you know Howard? Is he all right? Did something happen to him?"

"Howard's fine," Hub-Jay assured him. "At least for right now. But he's sick. He has polycystic kidney disease. His kidneys are only working at twenty-seven percent of their normal capacity, so he gets tired easily, sometimes feels dizzy. It's affected his blood pressure too. He's had to drop out of his college classes for the time being."

Donny frowned. "How do you know all this about Howard? Are you some kind of doctor? John said you own a hotel."

"I do. I'm a friend of Mary Dell's." Hub-Jay paused for a moment, and looked like he was trying to decide what to say next. "Mary Dell and I are engaged."

"Engaged? I don't think so. Last time I checked, Mary Dell was still married to me."

Donny narrowed his eyes, taking in the starched white shirt and the even more starched white handkerchief that peeked from the pocket of Hub-Jay's gray jacket.

"You don't look like Mary Dell's type to me."

"You know, let's just forget about that for now." Hub-Jay spread his hands a little and made a single, short chopping motion, like he was trying to sever the words he'd just uttered from what he said next. "I shouldn't have brought it up. What I came here to tell you is that, in a while—could be a few weeks or could be a few months; there's no way to know for sure—Howard's kidney function is going to drop below twenty percent. When that happens, he'll have to go on dialysis."

"That's where they hook you up to all those tubes and stuff, don't they? To clean out your blood?"

"I don't know too much about how it actually works, but that sounds about right. He can live on dialysis, even for many years, the doctors say. But there are still some risks, infections and such, and it would radically alter Howard's life. He'd have to go for dialysis three times a week for several hours each time."

Donny's expression was perfectly still and unreadable as Hub-Jay spoke, but his mind was reeling. It was a lot to take in at one time, especially since the news was being delivered by a man he'd never laid eyes on before, who purported to be engaged to Mary Dell. But he couldn't let himself get sidetracked by that right now. He needed to understand what had happened to Howard.

"What about a transplant?" Donny asked. "They do those for kidneys, don't they?"

"Yes, but the waiting list for donor kidneys is years long. Howard's best bet for getting a kidney before he has to go on dialysis would be to find a live donor whose kidney is a good match. The best chances would be a parent. Mary Dell isn't a candidate because she carries the disease herself."

Donny was quiet for a moment, trying to sort through everything he'd just heard. "Did Mary Dell send you out here to look for me?"

Hub-Jay took a quick swallow from the beer bottle and shook his head. "I decided to come out here on my own. She's going through a lot right now and I didn't want to get her hopes up unnecessarily."

Donny's gaze drifted past Hub-Jay's right shoulder where a neon sign blinked blue and green, declaring that it was five o'clock somewhere.

"Look, I realize this has come out of the blue. You disappeared a long time ago. Probably you had your reasons." Hub-Jay reached into the pocket of his jacket and pulled out a business card. "Maybe you want to take some time to think it through and get back to me. Nobody is saying you have to do this . . ."

That final sentence severed Donny's reverie.

"What the hell are you talking about? Howard is my son. If he needs my kidney, he can have it."

Donny stood up, pulled a five-dollar bill from

the back pocket of his jeans, and tossed it onto the counter next to his untouched bottle of Lone Star.

"I can buy my own beer."

When Donny stalked past, John looked up from his glass polishing. "Your show's about to start. Where you going, Donny?"

"Dallas."

Chapter 42

During the week it would take to complete the testing, Donny and Hub-Jay developed a relationship of sorts, more than an understanding but less than an alliance.

They decided not to alert Mary Dell or Howard to Donny's presence in Dallas, agreeing that, until they knew for certain if Donny's kidney would be a match, this information could only increase the anxiety in an already anxious situation. Hub-Jay offered to put Donny up in the Hollander Grand while he was undergoing tests, but Donny said he'd pay his own way, thank you very much. However, he didn't object when Hub-Jay made some calls to friends and found Donny a reduced rate at a clean, quiet motel that was close to the hospital. The two men had no reason to like each other and didn't, but their mutual concern and connections allowed them to put those feelings aside in the interest of helping Howard.

But Mary Dell didn't know any of that. She was in Too Much.

Mary Dell's original purpose in returning to the ranch and bringing Howard with her, over his protests, was so he could rest under Taffy's watchful eye while Mary Dell completed a marathon filming session, catching up on the days she'd missed. But even though the show had now been canceled, she didn't feel she could leave Too Much just now. As if she didn't have enough to worry her, Rob Lee had chosen this moment to revert to his old behavior. He was moody, silent, indifferent to his work, and borderline hostile in his dealings with both the ranch hands and the family, and he had started spending evenings at the Ice House again.

"I just don't understand how so many things can go wrong at once," Mary Dell said during one of her daily phone conversations with Hub-Jay. "A month ago, I was flying high. Apart from Jason being hit by a bolt of lightning, I'd have been hard-pressed to think of a way my life could be any better. And then, poof! Everything went to hell in a handbasket. And the worst part is, there's nothing I can say or do to change any of it."

Hub-Jay murmured sympathetically. He understood how she felt.

"I tried to talk to Rob Lee the other day—he's so depressed—but I might as well have tried talking to a wall," Mary Dell continued.

"Howard's mad at me too. He wants to go back to Dallas, but I'm afraid to leave him on his own right now. He's so tired all the time. His skin itches all the time and he's getting headaches. I don't know if this is all new, or if he's getting worse, or if he was just masking the symptoms before, afraid I'd be worried."

"And you would have been," Hub-Jay said. "Just like you are now. But the doctors are on top of it. And you'll both be up here next week for your appointment with Dr. Brewer, right?"

"Right," Mary Dell said, her voice conceding the logic of his reasoning. "And I'm sure he's fine. It's just hard to wait. If I didn't feel like I had to keep an eye on Rob Lee and try to pick up his slack here, I'd put Howard in the car and drive to Dallas right now. I miss you."

"Miss you too," he said. "I wish I could come down there right now."

"So you can hold my hand? Don't be silly. You've got work to do."

She laughed, but not convincingly, and in her voice Hub-Jay thought he heard a silent accusation. But that might just have been the voice in his own head.

He felt the same way he'd felt on that day when she'd told him she was leaving Dallas, the day that he'd come to understand that he was in love with her and not just because he suddenly realized how much a part of his life she'd become. No, the moment he understood the depth of his feelings for Mary Dell was the moment she first came under attack from that weasel, Jason. When she'd told him about the disrespectful, contemptuous way she had been treated, Hub-Jay had instantly and instinctively been overcome by an almost violent compulsion to defend her honor, to protect and care for her, accompanied by a maddening frustration at his inability to do so.

Hub-Jay liked to think of himself as sophisticated and reasonable, a gentleman. But when it came to issues of Mary Dell's happiness, safety, and honor, there was no doubt in his mind that, should the occasion arise, he'd tear off his coat, roll up his sleeves, and beat the crap out of any man, anywhere, who even dared to speak ill of her. That was how he knew he loved Mary Dell. Because he'd never in his life felt the urge to throw a punch on behalf of any other woman.

In fact, when he'd returned to Dallas and gotten word that Mary Dell had been fired, his first instinct was to go to the corporate offices of HHN-TV, track down Jason, and kick him so hard his cousin fell down. But during the drive between the hotel and the HHN headquarters, Hub-Jay experienced a brief moment of clarity. That was when he remembered that, as satisfying as it would be to beat the stuffing out of Jason Alvarez, a man in his position had a much more effective and potentially lethal weapon at his disposal—his Rolodex.

Of course, he shouldn't tell Mary Dell about that yet, though he very much wanted to. He hated the idea that she was down there in Too Much all alone, suffering and sad and under the impression that he didn't care enough to put business aside and come to her aid, if for no other purpose than to stand by her.

When Mary Dell was explaining to him how humiliated she felt when people came into the shop, asking when the new season would begin, and she had to tell them she'd been canceled, he wished he could share what he was up to, or at least hint at it, so she would know that he wasn't just sitting on his hands while she was being attacked.

Just as he was about to give in to that urge, Mary Dell asked if he could hold on for just a moment. Fred, one of the ranch hands, had come in wanting to talk.

Fred had a tendency to mumble, so, at first, Hub-Jay couldn't hear everything he said, but he understood that Fred was unhappy, threatening to quit because he and Rob Lee had exchanged words when Fred had expressed his unhappiness at having to do Rob Lee's work in addition to his own.

"Hub-Jay, I've got to go," said Mary Dell. "There's some kind of problem with Rob Lee. But

I'll call you later," she said, and hung up before Hub-Jay could say good-bye.

"I know you got problems right now," Fred continued. "I don't like to bother you, but things are pretty bad. I don't appreciate being cussed at just for telling what's true and trying to do my job, or having to carry somebody else's weight. It ain't fair. I'm not the only one who feels that way, Miss Mary Dell. Cody's about ready to quit too."

"That's all right, Fred. You did right in coming to me. I'll talk to Rob Lee," she promised. "And I'm going to make sure you and Cody get a bonus next payday to help make up for all the extra work you've been doing."

"It ain't the money or work so much, Miss Mary Dell. It's the respect."

"I know," she said soothingly. "And I'm sorry. You know I appreciate you and Cody, couldn't run the place without you. Tell you what; why don't you two go home early today. I'll find Rob Lee and tell him he's got to finish up your chores."

"You can't do that, Miss Mary Dell. Rob Lee ain't here."

"Where'd he go? Into town?"

"No, ma'am. I don't know where he's gone off to. I come into the tack room looking for him this morning, around about ten o'clock. He was dressed, sitting on the edge of his bed, but he looked like holy hell. His eyes were bloodshot and his hair was a mess and he was just staring off into space. Made me wonder if he'd ever been to bed.

"I stood at the door, waiting for him to notice me. When he didn't I finally asked if he'd ordered new barbed wire so we can fix that spot on the fence where the cattle broke through. He just started going off on me! Things heated up pretty quick. He took a swing at me, but I dodged it. Then he jumped in the truck and drove off so fast the wheels were spittin' gravel. Ain't seen him since."

"Oh, no. Fred, I am sorry. You all right?"

"Yes, ma'am. Like I said, I dodged the punch. I know Rob Lee's had a hard time since he come home from the war, and I've made allowances for that, but there comes a point—"

"I know, Fred. I'll take care of it, all right? One way or the other, I will."

"All right. Thank you, ma'am. Hate to bother you."

Fred ducked his head and backed out of the room, closing the door behind him. Mary Dell picked up her phone, thinking she ought to call Hub-Jay and apologize for being so abrupt, but changed her mind and hung up before the call could connect.

She would call Hub-Jay, but later. Right now, she needed to find her nephew.

Chapter 43

After going out to the barn to make sure that Rob Lee hadn't returned while she'd been talking to Fred, Mary Dell went up to the house to get her car keys.

It was only four o'clock in the afternoon and Rob Lee was a grown man. Aside from short-changing his work duties, if he felt like disappearing for a few hours on a Friday afternoon, there was no reason he couldn't. But something about the story Fred told her, his description of how Rob Lee had looked, plus the way he'd been acting ever since the party, combined with an overall sense of anxiety that Mary Dell couldn't quite explain, made her decide to go looking for him. After telling Taffy that she was going out and not to hold supper for her, Mary Dell backed the Eldorado out of the carport.

Before Mary Dell could pull out of the driveway, she met Holly pulling in, coming for a late afternoon ride. Mary Dell got out of the car to ask if she'd seen Rob Lee anywhere.

"Not since Tuesday," Holly replied. "I mean, I knew he was here on Wednesday and Thursday—I saw him saddle up Sarabeth and ride off—but he didn't say a word to me. Seems like he's been going out of his way not to."

Mary Dell could see Holly was upset, but at that moment, Rob Lee was her biggest concern. Something wasn't right with him. Maybe Holly knew what it was.

"Did you two have a fight or something?"

"No. Or if we did, then he didn't tell me about it. But then, Rob Lee isn't much of a talker."

"He wasn't always like that," Mary Dell said. "When he was a little boy he could talk the paint off the walls. Such a prankster, always getting in trouble at school. But Rob Lee never cared. He'd take his detention like a man and spend the time planning his next practical joke."

"Really?"

"Oh, yes. He was a scamp, but such a good little bad boy that you couldn't stay mad at him for long. Devoted to family too. The kids in school knew they'd better not say anything mean to Howard unless they wanted to deal with Rob Lee. He was real close to Howard when they were growing up, being born on the same day and all, but not as close as he was to his momma.

"Lydia Dale's death was hard on him. Graydon's too. Rob Lee never knew another father besides Graydon. Of course, we were all broken up after the accident. I lost my father, my sister, and my best friend in one day. Taffy lost her husband and daughter. Jeb and Cady were orphaned too, but I think Rob Lee took it harder than anybody. The light just started to fade from him after that.

And going to Afghanistan, that bombing . . ." Mary Dell shook her head sorrowfully.

"I know," Holly said. "Cady told me about it. I can't imagine. So awful. There've been so many times, especially lately, when I thought he was finally starting to trust me. I wanted to talk to him about it. I thought maybe it'd help if he could share that with me, you know? But every time the conversation got within a million miles of Afghanistan, he'd change the subject.

"Except for the night of the party," Holly said slowly, in a reflective tone of voice. "He and Luke didn't talk about anything *but* Afghanistan. They talked about all the guys in their unit, the tough spots they'd been in, the bad food and the heat and cold, one of the officers who sounded like a serious jerk. I didn't say anything, because, you know, what could I say? I didn't mind. They had lots of catching up to do. But after a while, it was like they forgot I was even there.

"When Luke started talking about a firefight he'd been in, Rob Lee let go of my hand and leaned in, staring at him. Luke was telling him how he'd been ambushed and got trapped inside this house with a couple of other guys. They were trying to radio for help, but there were insurgents all through the area, so it took almost two hours before they were rescued. One of the guys didn't make it. I think it was somebody Rob Lee knew."

"Did he say anything else about that later?"

"No. It was time for the cake and then Howard passed out. Rob Lee went off to the hospital with Cady and Taffy and Linne. He didn't say good-bye, but I didn't think anything about it at the time. Everything was so confused. I thought about going to the hospital, too, but I figured you probably didn't need any more people in the way. I mean, I'm not family or anything. But I was really worried about Howard. I'm so glad he's doing better. Any word on a kidney?"

"Not so far," Mary Dell said, "but it's early days yet. Cady's not a match, or Rob Lee either. Of course, Taffy's too old to give up her kidney. But there's a lot of people in town who volunteered for testing. I'm just praying that one of them turns out to be a good match."

"Me too."

"Listen," Mary Dell said, her face apologetic, "I've been meaning to come over and talk to you. But things have been so crazy. I'm really sorry about what happened with the show. I never thought there'd be a problem just doubling up on the filming schedule. I even checked with Artie first, and he said it was fine. If I had realized that Jason would use that as an excuse to cancel the show—"

Holly raised her hand to stop Mary Dell's apology. "It's okay, really. You were exactly where you needed to be. If I were a mom, I'd have done the same thing. It's not your fault that Jason is a slimeball. And anyway," she said with a little smile, "I don't think that season eight of *Quintessential Quilting* was going to do a thing to help either of our careers."

Mary Dell let out a regretful chuckle. "You're probably right. But the two episodes we got to do without Artie were pretty good."

"They were *great*. That day was the most fun I've ever had in front of a camera. I felt really proud of what we did. Well," Holly said with a shrug, "it was really you. But it was still fun to be part of it. I was so excited to see the way the editing turned out. But you didn't really think that Jason was going to let those episodes go on the air, did you?" Holly tilted her head to the side, raising her brows to a skeptical arch.

"It was kind of a Hail Mary pass," Mary Dell admitted. "I was hoping that they might slip by without him seeing them, or that if he *did* see them, maybe he'd be so impressed that he'd finally forget about the bee in his backside and decide to redo the whole season with a good director in charge."

"You really thought that could happen? I mean, you've *met* Jason, right?"

Mary Dell threw out her hands and bowed her head, a mea culpa gesture. "I know, I know. I'm a very optimistic person. I really do believe that things work out in the end, somehow." She smiled.

"But then, I'm also not one hundred percent sure that Santa Claus isn't real."

Mary Dell laughed and Holly grinned.

"I'm just sorry that you got caught up in this mess."

"What mess? I had fun," Holly insisted. "I got to see Texas and I got a horse, the best horse in the world. It's my childhood dream come true."

"And you got your heart broken," Mary Dell said, making her voice a question.

"Maybe a little," Holly admitted. "But I hear people recover."

"They do," Mary Dell said. "Eventually."

"See?" Holly said, blinking quickly. "I'm going to be fine. All I need now is a job. My agent's already working on it. That's why I'm happy I ran into you. I've got to fly to Nashville for an audition tomorrow. I probably won't get it," she said modestly, "and even if I did I'd have to come back to get my stuff and figure out how to get Stormy out to Tennessee. But in the meantime, if Howard gets a kidney or something . . . I just wanted to make sure that I got a chance to say good-bye. And to give you something."

She opened the door of her car and reached inside to retrieve something from the passenger's seat, then handed the package, a thick, soft square wrapped in three layers of red tissue paper, to Mary Dell.

"It's a quilt," Holly said, in case there had been any doubt.

Mary Dell eagerly ripped through the layers of tissue, grabbed two corners of the fabric, and, with all the panache of a magician removing a silken drape during a particularly spellbinding trick, shook out the folds to reveal a lovely brick red and gray Courthouse Steps lap quilt.

"Oh, it's beautiful! I love it!"

"Are you sure?" Holly deadpanned. "Because I was afraid you might already have a quilt."

Mary Dell laughed and hugged her young apprentice. "I don't have *this* quilt. And I'll always cherish it, Holly. And the time I got to spend with you. Forgive me if I sound too much like a momma, but I'm so proud of you. Thank you, baby girl."

"Thank you," Holly said. "I'm going to miss this place and you. A lot."

Mary Dell squeezed Holly yet again, as tight as she could.

"Now, you listen to me, Holly Silva. This is not good-bye. Not yet. One way or another, you are going to have to come back to the ranch for dinner before you go. Momma would never forgive me if I let you slip out of town before she had one more chance to try and fatten you up. Cady and Linne would be heartbroken too. Promise me that you'll call as soon as you're back from your audition, all right?"

"All right. Promise."

"Good."

Mary Dell loosened her grip and took a step back. "I wish I could invite you in right now," she said, "but I need to track down Rob Lee."

Holly gave her a quizzical look. "You're really worried about him, aren't you? Do you want me to help you look?"

"Oh, it's all right. He had a run-in with Fred; I'm sure he's just off pouting somewhere," Mary Dell replied, but her dismissive words couldn't mask her concern. "And anyway, you came out here to ride Stormy."

"I can ride tomorrow. Stormy will probably be happy to take a day off anyway." Holly opened her car door and climbed back in. "Where do you want me to start?"

"He could be anywhere," Mary Dell said. "I'm going to go over to the quilt shop and see if Cady's seen him. While I'm doing that, would you drive by the Ice House?"

"I'm on it," Holly said, and turned the key in the ignition.

Chapter 44

Rob Lee was not at the Ice House.

After the altercation with Fred, he got into his truck and drove as fast as he could, like something was chasing him. And it was.

Until that morning, he'd been able to stay ahead of it, but only just barely and only by piling up obstacles, leaning in as hard as he could to barricade himself from the emotions and condemnation that had pursued him for three long years.

For a while, he'd thought he could outrun it or at least increase the distance between him and his pursuer enough so that he could relax a little, catch his breath. Holly had made him think that it might even be possible, someday, to quit running and find a way to live again.

Though doubts and dreams had already begun to plague him, seeping out in odd places and at unexpected moments like leaks in a carelessly constructed dam, it wasn't until the party that he understood how foolish he'd been, trying to take shelter behind something so flimsy.

When Luke had started talking about Afghanistan and the guys in his unit, the daily deprivations, the cruelty and madness of that life that was not life but a fight for survival in a land where nothing made sense, where the man who served you tea one day could make a bomb to kill you the next, Rob Lee realized that his war wasn't over and never would be. What right had he to happiness, to love and desire, or to forget his mistakes in the arms of a beautiful girl, while the friends he'd left behind were still in that place, running for cover and battling to stay alive? How did he have the audacity to weave plans and hopes for the future when the lives of three good men who counted on him had been cut short because of his inability to recognize the enemy, falling short in his loyalty to his brothers and making them pay the price for his failure?

He didn't. He couldn't.

And so he had pushed Holly away and started running again, faster than before, racing to stay ahead of the demons that were closing in on him step by step and day by day.

When his cell phone rang that morning, rousing him from the fog of a fitful and brief alcohol-induced sleep, and he heard the choked voice of Luke's father, telling him that Luke had shot himself only the day before, Rob Lee knew it was over. He could drive as far as he wanted and as fast as he could, but there was no escape. The barricade had crumbled.

Sometime after dark, he stopped for gas and whiskey in a town whose name he didn't know, then turned the truck around and headed back to Too Much. He parked at Puny Pond, but far down the road and behind a little scrub of mesquite, just in case anybody came looking for him.

He hiked over a small hill, tripping once when a cloud blocked the moon's light, and sat down at the water's edge to drink and beg forgiveness from the ghosts of the betrayed. When the bottle was empty, he drove back to the ranch, driving slowly with the headlights off, careful not to wake anyone inside the house.

After walking through the barn, where horses, hens, and lambs dozed in innocent sleep, he went into the tack room, turned on the light, and sat down on the edge of the bed. He wondered if he should leave a note or something, some kind of explanation. After a few minutes' consideration, he decided that there wasn't much he could say that would make sense to anybody but himself. He tore a sheet of paper from a notebook he kept in the second drawer, wrote out a single sentence, then folded the paper into thirds and left it on top of the dresser.

Squatting down next to the foot of the bed, he reached beneath the mattress to retrieve a present he'd bought himself the day after his party, a Beretta M9 semiautomatic pistol. It was the same type of gun he'd used in the service, the standard sidearm for Marines.

The gun was already clean and loaded—he'd seen to that the day he purchased it—but the safety was on. He laid it on top of the bed while he tucked in the sheet and quilt and straightened his pillow, then put away a few things he'd left lying around, making sure the room was tidy. When he was finished, he walked back to the bed, picked up the Beretta, and clicked off the safety.

There was a squeak, the sound of the door opening. His muscles went instantly taut and he spun toward the noise, pistol braced in two hands, shouting unintelligibly.

Cady shouted too. "It's me! It's only me!" Her hands flew up over her head, palms out and empty, concealing nothing.

Heart still racing, Rob Lee dropped his arms to his sides, though the gun was still clutched tight in his hand, and his shoulders drooped. He closed his eyes, breathing heavily, realizing how close a thing it had been and trying to block out the image of his sister's blood splattered on the floor and walls.

"God, Cady," he said, his voice rasping. "God. I damned near . . . What are you doing here?"

Her eyes, mirrors of grief and fear, scanned the room, her brother's face, the pistol in his hand.

"What are *you* doing here?"

"Nothing. Cleaning my gun. You just startled me is all. I'm fine. You can go now, Cady."

She pressed her lips together and shook her head hard, like a stubborn toddler. Rob Lee felt his jaw set, angry that she was interfering with his plans, making a hard thing even harder.

"You need to go, Cady. You need to leave now."

"Okay, fine," she said. "But you have to come with me. Either you or the gun. Because I'm not leaving the two of you alone."

Rob Lee scowled, clicked the safety on the Beretta, and dropped it onto the bed.

"There," he snapped. "You happy? I told you, I was just cleaning it."

Cady crossed her arms over her chest. "Cleaning a gun. Drunk and at three in the morning. Why do you even have a gun?"

Rob Lee made an incredulous face and spread out his hands.

"For protection. For fun. It's Texas, Cady. *Everybody* has a gun."

She shook her head again, that same stubborn look on her face, the look that said she wasn't buying his story.

"Shotguns. For hunting and sport, but not one like that. That's a combat pistol, a gun designed to kill people. Or yourself."

"Go back to the house, will you? Just leave me alone."

"I won't." She walked into the room. "Not until you tell me why you want to die."

He knew from the look on her face that she was absolutely serious, that she was not going to budge so much as an inch until he explained himself. Cady was stubborn. And smart. She wouldn't be fooled by fabrications or half-truths.

Hoping she would come to see that this was the only option left to him, or at least to accept the fact that he would not be dissuaded, he told her. All of it. He held nothing back.

He told her about Holly and the sin of being happy while his brothers in arms were under attack; he told her about the dreams and depression and how there was no place for him in this world; he told her about Luke and watched her face crumple in grief and tears fill her eyes as he said the words; and then he told her about the day Nick had died, about the bomber who had served him tea, how he had ignored the rule of combat that anyone who didn't wear your uniform was a threat, and how his hesitation in judgment had killed her husband and the father of her child.

He told her the truth as he saw it, that it was all his fault and that he deserved to die, that his death was the only way to balance the scales.

Cady listened. Even when his words brought her to tears, she listened, without comment or correction, until he came to the end of his explanation. Only then did she speak.

"It wasn't your fault."

By this time Rob Lee was sitting on the edge of the bed again, pistol still within reach, and he dropped his head into his hands and groaned.

"Cady . . ."

"It *wasn't* your fault," she repeated, forceful to the point of exasperation. "I never, ever thought that, and I still don't. You know why? Because it was mine."

Rob Lee lifted his head and looked at his sister, thinking this was some kind of sick, twisted teasing, but her expression was absolutely serious.

"Nick re-upped his enlistment without asking me; did you know that?"

Rob Lee shook his head.

"Well, he did," Cady said. "When we got married, he promised me that he'd get out after eight years. He was already three years into his first four-year contract when we got married, so I figured, okay. Five years, not so bad. I could handle that."

She let out a laugh, eyes sharp and bitter.

"But that was before I understood what those five years would be like; that was before I knew what a troop surge was and that my husband, and my baby brother," she said as her voice caught in her throat, "would be deployed four times in those five years—four times—and that the old rule of seven months' deployment followed by fourteen months' in garrison just wouldn't apply anymore.

"Do you know how much time Nick and I actually got to live together during our marriage? Nineteen months. Of course, we didn't quite make it to the five-year mark, so maybe it would have been more if he hadn't died. But I have to say, little brother, it wasn't enough. Nineteen months with my husband in four and a half years of marriage wasn't nearly enough. At least not for me."

Cady was crying now; tears fell from her eyes and rolled down her cheeks like rain rolling down a windowpane during a thunderstorm, liquid fury over the happiness she'd been denied.

"Even when he was home it was hard, because I kept feeling like a part of him wanted to be back there, like he'd rather be with you and Roger and Jeremy and all his Marine buddies than home with his wife and baby."

Rob Lee shook his head. "It wasn't that. He wanted to be with you, but it's hard to be back. You feel guilty about being home and safe when you know the job isn't finished, that other guys are over there and in danger while you're going to the mall or eating pizza. It just feels wrong," he said. "You forget how to be normal. Nick loved you, Cady. He talked about you and Linne all the time, every single day."

Cady bobbed her head slowly, like she wanted to believe him, but from the way her lips contorted and the muscles in her throat twitched as she swallowed back more tears, he could tell that she didn't.

"On the day of the bombing," she continued, "he called me on the phone and told me he'd extended for another four years. It just came out of the blue! We never discussed it at all; he just did it. And I was so, so, so mad at him."

Saying the last sentence, she clenched her fists and teeth so tight that getting the words out seemed to require a monumental effort, like squeezing half-set cement from a toothpaste tube.

"His excuse was the bonus they were offering. He said it'd be enough we'd be able to make a down payment on a house. But I didn't want a house. I wanted a husband!" she cried, leaning urgently toward her brother.

And then, in a voice suddenly soft, she said, "But he didn't want me. That's what it felt like. We had a fight, said terrible things to each other. Before we hung up, I told him I wanted a divorce."

Though Rob Lee had been sitting perfectly still while his sister talked, he couldn't keep his brow from furrowing when she said this last bit. He remembered introducing Nick and Cady, how he had insisted that Nick come home to Too Much over the Memorial Day weekend, thinking all along that he might be the perfect guy for his sister. He never told either of them what he was up to, though. He just put them in the same room and waited to see what would happen, kind of like the way he used to play with his chemistry set when he was a kid. He'd pour something blue into the test tube and then top it off with some red, shake it up, and wait to see if anything happened.

He didn't have to wait long when it came to Nick and Cady—the spark between them was instantaneous and obvious. Chemistry, pure chemistry. They were practically glued together that weekend.

When everybody went swimming at Puny Pond, Cady splashed Nick to get his attention, which she already had; then he pretended to dunk her and she pretended to scream, but they were both grinning. They sat next to each other under a tree at the picnic, ignoring everybody else, eating chicken and potato salad and talking seriously. The next day, they went off by themselves for a walk. When they returned, Rob Lee noticed Cady had grass in her hair and that her shirt was buttoned wrong. Grandma Taffy noticed too. As Nick and Cady were walking up toward the porch, both looking happy and a little flushed, Taffy mumbled, "Uh-oh. Looks like the Fatal Flaw has struck again. I sure hope that boy does right by her."

He had, and willingly.

Seven months later, only eight weeks before the battalion left for another deployment, Nick and Cady were married. Rob Lee was best man. Cady teased him, saying that she'd have asked him to be a bridesmaid if Nick hadn't nabbed him first. They were so happy that day. And later too.

Rob Lee remembered how excited Nick had been when he found out Cady was pregnant, how upset he was when he learned that they were to be deployed yet again when Cady was in her sixth month and so he wouldn't be home for the birth.

But he remembered, too, the day Linne was born.

He and Nick were sitting in front of a computer when Cady Skyped from the hospital. When she held the tiny little bundle with the pink hat up to the computer screen and said, "Linne, meet your daddy and your uncle Rob Lee," his own eyes had gotten moist, but Nick had sobbed like a girl.

Rob Lee had never seen Nick cry before, not once.

No matter how much Cady might doubt it, Nick really did love her and Linne. He wanted to be with them. Why wouldn't he? It was the most natural desire in the world.

But, for a soldier, doing what comes natural isn't always easy. War complicates a lot of things that ought to be simple.

"Did you mean it?" Rob Lee asked.

"About wanting a divorce?" Cady's gaze drifted off to a spot on the far wall and rested there.

"At the time, I think it was just something I said to hurt him. I was so angry. I felt betrayed. If I had realized that was the last time we would ever talk, I know that I wouldn't have said it. But if Nick had lived, would I have followed through with it?" She paused. "I don't know."

Her voice was so tired and worn that he knew she had spent many hours wrestling with this question but never finding an answer. Rob Lee knew what that felt like, the obsessive examination of the past and your part in it, sifting through each word and action, trying to pinpoint your mistakes, because inside every grown-up is a little child who wants to believe that saying "I'm sorry" will wind back the clock and make everything the way it was before.

"We never did get to finish that fight," Cady continued. "He had to go on patrol. I honestly don't know what might have happened if we had. All I know is that when he got off the phone, he was still angry and really upset. And I'm sure it affected his judgment. It had to have," she mused. "It *had* to. If we hadn't left things the way we did, he would have noticed that something wasn't right; he'd have seen the bomber or the bomb in time. But he didn't. He was too busy thinking about all the terrible things I'd said."

Cady pulled her gaze back from the memories of what might have been into the world that was. She looked at her brother squarely, her eyes dry again.

"You didn't kill Nick," she said. "Because I did."

"Cady, stop it. That's crazy."

Cady raised her brows, silently nudging him to the next logical step, to sort out why her conclusions were any less sane than his. Rob Lee wasn't sure.

But what he did realize was that Cady was a casualty of war, just like Nick, and that if this was true, then maybe he was as well. The difference was that, unlike Nick, he and Cady might yet survive. Maybe.

At that moment, he wasn't sure he wanted to survive. It was too soon to tell.

Cady walked across the room, sat down next to him on the edge of the bed, and held out her hand.

"Is the safety on?"

He nodded and handed her the gun.

"Thanks. Before you ask, I'm already getting help, and it's . . . helping," she said, smiling a little at the inadequacy of that description. "Nothing about this is easy, but I'm going to be okay. You will too. Promise.

"Tomorrow, I'm going to drive you to Houston. Actually, today," she said, acknowledging the hour, "but after it's light. I found a nonprofit residential program for veterans with PTSD."

"Cady, I don't think I need—"

She lifted the pistol off her lap. "Little brother, no disrespect intended, but your best thinking isn't that good right now."

He was quiet. She might be right.

"Just give it a try for thirty days, all right? If it's not helping, you can come home. If it is helping, you can stay and finish the program in ninety days."

"Three months? Cady, I can't be gone for three months. Lambing season is only a month off. We've got more than one hundred ewes ready to deliver and lots of multiples this year. Fred and

Cody can't handle it. Fred's too lazy and Cody's too apt to listen to Fred."

Cady drew her brows together into a scowl. "Okay, hang on. Five minutes ago you were going to blow your brains out. Who would have delivered the lambs then?"

She shook her head and he looked down into his lap, embarrassed.

"Look, sheep are just sheep. We'll figure out a way to take care of them. But you're my baby brother, the only one I've got. I can't take one more loss in my life, Rob Lee. First, Momma and Graydon and Grandpa. Then Nick. I can't lose you too. I just can't. So please, Rob Lee, just try. For me."

Her expression was so pleading. A fresh wave of shame passed over him, thinking of how close he had come to causing his family even more undeserved pain.

"Okay," he whispered.

Cady moved the pistol from her lap to the floor and wrapped her arms around him.

"Thank you."

Rob Lee started to cry, and then to sob. His shoulders shook and his body convulsed. Groans and apologies and cries for help poured out, just the way they did in his dreams, only this time, someone heard him.

Cady didn't say anything. She didn't shush him or try to tell him that everything would be all right, but for the first time in forever, he didn't feel alone.

After a long, long time, Rob Lee was finally able to stop crying, steady his breath, and release his desperate hold on his sister.

"Sorry," he mumbled and swiped his hand across his face.

"It's okay. Come on. Let's go up to the house. I'll make breakfast."

She picked up the gun and started walking toward the door. Rob Lee wasn't hungry but followed her anyway, knowing she wasn't going to leave without him.

Spotting the folded piece of notebook paper on top of the dresser, she frowned. "What's that?" she asked. "Suicide note?"

"Kind of."

"What's it say?"

"It says, 'None of this was your fault.' "

"Really?"

Cady grinned, and even though he felt stupid, Rob Lee did the same.

"Good note," she said. "You should hold on to that."

Chapter 45

After hours of fruitless searching for Rob Lee, Mary Dell had gone to bed reluctantly and slept fitfully. It wasn't like this was the first time her nephew had disappeared without telling anyone, but she couldn't shake the feeling that something was very, very wrong with him.

She woke abruptly around four-thirty and sat up in her bed, listening for noises. When a slice of light appeared suddenly beneath her bedroom door, she knew someone was in the kitchen, so she got out of bed, put on her bathrobe, and went to investigate.

Cady was standing at the counter, cracking eggs into a bowl, and Rob Lee was sitting at the table.

Mary Dell said good morning, but the relief she'd felt to see Rob Lee safe dissipated when Cady grabbed a dish towel and threw it over the top of something sitting on the counter, a handgun. Sleepy as she was, Mary Dell didn't have to work very hard to put the pieces together, but she didn't say anything about it.

"I was just getting ready to make a pot of coffee," Cady said. "Want some?"

"Please. Eggs, too, if you don't mind. I think there's some of that cinnamon bread left over. Rob Lee, you want some cinnamon toast?"

He nodded. "Sure."

Cady cracked two more eggs into the bowl and beat them with a fork. "I know Howard has that doctor appointment in Dallas today, but can you find somebody to fill in for me at the shop and pick Linne up from her piano lesson? I'm driving Rob Lee down to Houston. He'll probably be gone for a while."

Mary Dell had to clench her arms tight to her body to stop herself from putting her arms around her nephew, the poor, sad, confused boy. But she knew Rob Lee well enough to know he wouldn't welcome any emotional displays just then.

Instead, she pushed the lever down on the toaster and said, "Not a problem. Fred can cover things for a while." Walking past Rob Lee's chair to get the plates and set the table, she paused briefly and squeezed his shoulder. She couldn't help herself.

It was a surprising and emotional start to the day, but there was even more to come.

Eight hours later, having juggled myriad scheduling, logistical, and personnel details, as well as an unexpected traffic snarl, Mary Dell and Howard made it to Dallas just in time for their one o'clock appointment with Dr. Brewer.

It was supposed to be just a regular appointment, the standard round of testing to measure Howard's kidney function or lack thereof. So she was surprised when Dr. Brewer, normally a circumspect man, walked into the exam room with a broad grin on his face and said, "You two have the best timing in the world! Absolutely the best!"

Mary Dell's pulse picked up, correctly interpreting the reason for the good doctor's elevated spirits.

"You found a donor?"

"We did! I got the test results less than an hour ago. Howard," he said, turning from Mary Dell toward the exam table, where Howard was sitting, "Your dad's kidney couldn't be a better match."

"I won't have to go on that machine? That . . ." Howard frowned, trying to summon the word.

"No dialysis for you," the doctor confirmed. "We won't perform the transplant yet, not until the kidney function deteriorates to a point where—"

"Wait." Mary Dell lifted her hand, cutting him off in mid-sentence. "Donny is the donor? You found him?"

"I think it was more a case of him finding us," Dr. Brewer replied. "And it's a good thing he did. Howard has an unusual blood type. Most of the candidates were eliminated before we even got started. But Donny is in excellent health, a near perfect match, and a very willing donor. I told him the news not five minutes ago, and he's thrilled."

"Donny is here? In this office?"

Dr. Brewer nodded. "Three doors down and on the left. I just left him to come talk with you."

Howard's face split into a grin. "My dad is here!"

He slid off the table, wobbling a little on the landing because he was too impatient to bother with the step, and all but ran from the room.

Mary Dell followed, calling his name, begging him to wait a moment, but Howard either didn't hear her or didn't care. By the time Mary Dell caught up with him in the other examining room, Howard was in Donny's arms.

"Dad! I am really happy to see you!"

"Me too, son."

Chapter 46

Holly sat on top of the checkout counter at the Patchwork Palace, waiting for Cady to finish totaling up the day's receipts before locking up.

"You're kidding!" Holly exclaimed. "After all these years he just shows up and offers Howard his kidney?"

"Not quite like that," Cady said. "Hub-Jay tracked him down. He and my uncle agreed that they wouldn't say anything to Howard or Aunt Mary Dell unless he turned out to be a match."

"Wow." Holly picked up a basket full of odd buttons, marked ten cents each, and started sorting through them. "But she's happy, right?"

"Sure. But, honestly, I don't know how I'd feel if I were in her shoes. I mean, are you grateful because he comes to the rescue? Or angry because it took thirty years for him to do it?"

Holly thought about this. "Both, I guess. How does Howard feel about it?"

"That's the funny part," Cady said, putting a rubber band around a stack of twenty-dollar bills and placing them inside a red zippered bank bag. "Aunt Mary Dell said he acts like Donny's just been away on a long trip or something. He's happy to see him, not the least bit resentful. That's why they're staying in Dallas for the rest of the week—because Howard wants to spend time with his dad. For Howard, it's like nothing ever happened. I don't think he understands."

"Maybe," Holly said. Inside, however, she wondered if perhaps Howard understood things that other people didn't.

Maybe, having had to struggle with his own natural challenges and limitations, as well as those imposed upon him by a world that has little patience or tolerance and is quick to assign blame and presume motive for actions it knows nothing about, Howard had already mastered a lesson that few ever grasp. Maybe he knew that most people are doing the best they can with what they have and that nobody is really in a position to judge anybody else.

Holly scooped up a handful of buttons and let

them pour from her fist into the basket, enjoying the slippery feel of the plastic and metal against her skin and the *rat-a-tat* sound they made as they fell.

"I talked to Rob Lee last night," Cady said.

Holly picked up more buttons, keeping her eyes on the waterfall of colors.

"He said to tell you hello and that he's sorry he didn't have a chance to say good-bye before he left."

"That's okay," Holly replied, pouring more buttons.

Truth was, he'd left without good-bye or explanation weeks before, and left a hole in her heart that still hurt. She wished he'd told her before what was really going on instead of leaving her to believe that he'd withdrawn because of something she'd done or said.

But he couldn't help it, she reminded herself. Rob Lee was like Stormy, wounded but unable to speak, and so frightened by the world that he fought to keep it at a distance, terrified to let anyone get too close.

"I just want him to get better," she said.

Cady hadn't painted a full picture of the events that had precipitated Rob Lee's sudden departure, but she'd said enough so Holly understood that he'd faced a true crisis and that it was very much mixed up with his experiences in Afghanistan. But that was all she knew. Someday, if she saw him again, Rob Lee might tell her himself. And if she never saw him again . . . she still wished him well.

"He is," Cady said. "It's only been a few days, but he's already called to say that he wants to stay for the whole course of the program, the full ninety days. After that, they'll pair him up with a mentor closer to home so he can have somebody to talk to who understands what he's been through."

"That's great," Holly said sincerely.

"He asked if it would be all right to call you after he finishes the program. He's just dealing with a lot of stuff right now," Cady said, almost apologetically.

Holly put the button basket back on the counter. "Sure, anytime. I mean, I don't know if I'll still be in Too Much by the time he comes home, but he's got my cell number."

"Oh, that's right. I forgot to ask how the audition went. Did you get the spokesmodel thing?"

"Uh-huh," she said. "And already turned it down. Amanda is really pissed at me. Mom was too, at first. But then she calmed down. I just didn't want to do it. Of course, I have to do something eventually. But I think . . ."

She hopped off the counter and then brushed her palms together. The buttons had left them feeling dusty.

"Life is too short to spend it doing something you hate, especially if it doesn't add anything to the world. I know I'm never going to win an Oscar or find a cure for cancer or anything, but I hope I can do something besides sell things nobody needs to people who already have way too much stuff, you know?"

"Makes sense to me," Cady said.

She put the bank bag in her purse, then picked up a pile of bolts from the counter and carried them to the shelves for restocking. Holly grabbed what Cady couldn't carry and followed her around the shop.

"Me too. But then I say stuff like that and Amanda says, 'Fine, Mother Teresa. Then tell me what you want to do.' And, of course, I have no idea. Which makes her crazy. But don't you think it's a good idea to take time to figure it out?" Holly asked, then answered her own question. "I do. At least a little while."

"Just tell her to cool her jets for a couple of months."

"Amanda's all right," Holly said, shoving a bolt of pink paisley into an open spot on a shelf. "She's just doing her job. And she cheered up when I told her I'm making her a quilt."

"You are?"

Holly nodded. "A House block pattern, all solids but kind of scrappy. Every block is a different color. She told me her rotten ex-husband got their house in the divorce, so, I don't know, this just seemed like a kind of good idea."

"She'll love it," Cady said, sliding her last bolt,

a blue-and-red windowpane check, onto a shelf of Americana fabrics. "Let me know if you need any help.

"Hey, remember that first day we met? When you had that bobbin so tangled up I had to use an X-Acto knife to cut through the threads? And the time you sewed that wonky Snowball block to your sleeve? Did you ever think then that you'd actually make a quilt voluntarily?"

Holly grinned. "Never."

"Neither did I. But I'm glad you stuck with it, glad things worked out. You know, a lot of things are working out," Cady said, sounding a little surprised.

"Sure, it really sucks that the show got canceled. I have no idea how we'll hang on without the publicity. But I'm doing better now and so is Rob Lee. Linne seems happy, horse-crazy as ever, but happy. Even Grandma seems to be in her right mind. Most of the time," she said. "When she's not poisoning people's food."

"Hey, that was totally justified," Holly said. "Artie had it coming to him."

"Maybe, but I'll still think twice before ever eating her ambrosia. Anyway"—Cady shrugged—"things are okay. Howard found his father and a new kidney all in one day. Of course, Aunt Mary Dell is dealing with a lot of stuff, but I could hear how relieved she was to know that Howard would be okay."

"Me too," Holly said.

"My only big concern, at least this week, is dealing with Fred." Cady walked to the back of the store and started turning off the lights. "I thought that Fred was always griping because Rob Lee wasn't doing his job, but now I see that Fred is always griping because he's a griper. I'm glad Aunt Mary Dell is coming home soon. Then she can deal with him.

"But I really don't know what we're going to do about the lambing season. It's always a crazy hard time, everybody taking shifts, working around the clock for about two weeks. But you really need somebody dedicated and experienced to be in charge, and I'm not sure Fred is the man for the job. Things can go very badly, very quickly if a ewe has trouble during labor, and since income from the quilt shop is bound to sink once *Quintessential Quilting* goes off the air for good, we can't afford to lose a single lamb."

"If I'm still in town by then, I'll come and help," Holly said. "I don't know anything about sheep, but if you need an extra pair of hands, count me in."

"Thanks. I might take you up on that." Cady started walking through the shop, turning out lights as she went. "Rob Lee is definitely where he needs to be right now, but the timing couldn't be worse. Fred is so lazy. Always complaining about something. I can picture him upping and quitting just when the ewes start to pop. Oh, well. No point in worrying about it, but it's hard not to. I just wish we had a manager we could count on."

Before turning out the last light, Cady shouted, "Linne! We're ready to go! Are you coming or not?" She waited a moment. "I'm counting to three. One! Two!"

The pounding of feet on the wooden floor of the upstairs classroom and down the stairs sounded like a stampede.

"New cowboy boots," Cady explained. "Birthday present. She had to have white ones, just like Miss Holly's."

"Not too practical," Holly said, grinning as Linne came bounding down the stairs, "but super cute."

"Did you turn off the lights and the DVD player?"

"Uh-huh," she said, then turned to Holly. "Can we go for a ride later?"

"Not tonight," Cady said, answering for Holly. "It'll be dark by the time we get home. Besides, we're supposed to be having a girls' night, remember? Miss Holly is sleeping over. Grammy is making hamburgers and hot fudge sundaes and then we're going to watch a movie."

"Your mom is right," Holly said, seeing Linne's disappointed face. "It's too dark tonight, but we can go for a ride in the morning, okay? Right after breakfast."

"Okay!" Linne exclaimed, happy once again.

She grabbed hold of Holly's hand as they walked through the door. Cady bent down to put the key in the lock.

"Good, now that we've got that settled, what movie are we going to watch?"

Linne grinned mischievously and Holly winked at her.

"*National Velvet*!" they chorused.

Cady covered her face with her hands, groaning and laughing at once.

"No! Not again!"

Chapter 47

"Come on, Momma. Please?" Howard begged. "Just one more time."

Mary Dell shook her head.

Normally, she found it impossible to refuse Howard anything. If that weren't the case, she wouldn't have been at the amusement park on a hot afternoon in early April, on the final day of a very strange weeklong tour of Dallas's major family-friendly attractions that had included the Dallas Zoo, the World Aquarium, the botanical gardens, the Museum of Natural History, the Frontiers of Flight Museum, and the Fort Worth Stockyards. But after seven days of enforced family togetherness, Mary Dell had had about all she could take.

She was amazed that Howard's stamina had held up so well this week. Yes, he slept in the mornings and she made sure he was in bed by nine, but he had much more energy than before. Donny's return seemed to have affected him like a shot of adrenaline, and Mary Dell was happy to see him enjoy himself, but even so, she was counting the hours until they could return to Too Much.

"Baby, I can't," she said wearily. "Three roller-coaster rides in one day is two more than my limit. Besides, my feet hurt. Y'all go on without me. I'm going into this café to get myself a Dr Pepper. I'll be waiting right here when you're done."

Howard looked disappointed, but he ceased his pleading. "All right, Momma. We'll see you in a little bit. C'mon, Daddy."

Donny pushed his Stetson back on his head a little and wiped his forehead. "Think I'll sit this one out too. You and Jenna go on and have fun. I'll be right here, keeping your momma company."

Before Mary Dell had a chance to lodge a protest, Howard grabbed Jenna's hand and walked off toward the end of the line for the Judge Roy Scream roller coaster. Having already ridden the coaster twice that day, Mary Dell knew they wouldn't return for at least half an hour, which meant that she would now be forced to do the thing she'd been trying to avoid all week: spend one-on-one time with Donny.

Wonderful.

The café was crowded, as lots of people had decided to take a break to escape the heat and enjoy a cold drink, but they were fortunate to spot a family getting up from a table on the patio, located under a blessedly shady tree. Mary Dell sat down, laying claim to it while Donny went off to get their drinks. He returned a lot quicker than she'd hoped.

"Here we go," he said, removing the big paper cups from the tray and setting them on the table. "I asked for extra ice in yours."

Mary Dell smiled woodenly and took a sip, wondering if he expected her to give him a gold star for having remembered that she liked her drinks cold.

"Bet I know what you're thinking," Donny said. "You're thinking, 'Dang. I was just inches from a clean getaway.' "

He smiled and Mary Dell smiled back, partly because he was right but mostly because that's what she'd been doing this whole long week, smiling and trying to go with the flow.

There was a lot at stake here, and as much as she found the events of the prior week, particularly Donny's suggestion that they take a "family vacation" together, bizarre in the extreme, she was trying not to rock the boat.

She'd tried to explain this to Hub-Jay only the evening before, while they were having dinner at the hotel after Mary Dell and Howard had returned from their "family outing" to the stock-yards. Hub-Jay wanted her to ask Donny for a divorce, but Mary Dell insisted that she couldn't until after the transplant. Howard's kidney function was nearly unchanged since their last appointment. Until it slipped below acceptable levels, Dr. Brewer would not perform the operation.

This meant that they were all stuck in an uncomfortable limbo, waiting for Howard's health to deteriorate to the point where the operation was required and they could all resume their regular lives. It might take a month or it might take a year, maybe even two. There was no way to know for sure, but until it did, Mary Dell was loath to do or say anything that might make Donny change his mind about giving Howard his kidney—nor did she appreciate being pressured to do so.

"Come on," Hub-Jay had protested. "You don't seriously think he'd renege on the kidney just because you want to remarry, do you?"

Maybe not. But if you'd asked her thirty years ago if Donny would have been capable of deserting his wife and his baby, she'd have said no, absolutely not. But he had. Which only went to show you—men were capable of anything. And since she didn't know what to make of Donny's sudden reappearance any more than she'd known what to make of his disappearance all those years before, and since Howard's health and life hung in the balance, it was wiser to not take any chances.

Donny took the plastic top off his soda and took a long drink. "Thank you for putting up with me this week," he said. "I know it's been awkward for you."

"Well." She paused a moment, trying to think what she could say that was true but innocuous. "Howard was glad to get a chance to get to know you better. And I am grateful to you for what you're doing for him. It can't have been easy for you."

Donny shook his head. "You're wrong. Nothing was ever easier. I've been waiting for a chance to do some good for Howard for a long time."

Mary Dell pressed her lips together so hard they went white as she swallowed back a bitter retort, stopping herself from pointing out that if Donny had really wanted to do something for his son, he might have started by not abandoning him.

Her attempts at disguising her emotions didn't seem to be working, because Donny said, "I know you're mad at me, Mary Dell. There's no need to bite your tongue in half, trying to pretend you're not. I don't blame you for not believing me. If I were you, I wouldn't believe me either, but I'm telling you the truth."

Donny curled his two hands around the base of his soda cup and looked down at the table.

Droplets of condensation dripped down the sides of the cup and onto his fingers.

"I did want to help Howard. From the day he was born, I did. But I just didn't know how. And you were so busy reading all those books and articles about Down syndrome, articles with words I couldn't even pronounce let alone understand, and spending every waking minute taking care of Howard, talking to him and doing those exercises . . ."

Donny was right about the way she'd been trying to keep the peace all week pretending she wasn't angry with Donny. But that wasn't anything new.

For years that stretched to decades, Mary Dell had told herself she'd forgiven Donny, that he just wasn't as strong as she was. Perhaps there was some truth in this last part, but the assertion that she'd forgiven him was a myth of the first magnitude, even though she'd actually convinced herself it was true.

Had Donny never returned, had Mary Dell never been forced to look him in the eye again or listen to the sound of his voice, she might have carried on like that, year after year, painting over the black fury of betrayal with layer upon layer of whitewash and rationalization, a protective coating against emotions too frightening to face, a makeshift patch job to fill in the cracks and hold together the pieces of her broken heart.

But Donny had returned, riding in on the white charger of his perfect kidney to save the day and Howard's life from the genetic misfortune that Mary Dell had passed on to their son. And now that he was here, spouting nonsense and excuses, Mary Dell couldn't live with the lie of feigned forgiveness, not for one more hour, not for one more breath.

"Stop right there," she snapped. "Don't you dare sit there and tell me that the reason you left was because I wasn't paying enough attention to you, Donny Bebee. Don't you dare! I had a baby to take care of; a sickly baby, born a month premature and with Down syndrome. Yes, it's a big word—Down syndrome. And when the doctor came and started talking all that medical jargon about chromosomes and genetics and intellectual deficits and shortened life expectancy and I don't know what all, I was just as terrified and confused as you were. I didn't know what it all meant or how I was supposed to deal with it. But I did, Donny. I figured it out. Because somebody had to! Because that's what parents do!

"So I'm sorry if Howard didn't live up to the ideal of whatever it was you thought your son ought to be, but guess what? It wasn't about you. It was about Howard, the baby we both prayed for. Do you remember that, Donny? Do you remember all the years of heartache and infertility? The eight miscarried babies I bore and buried and mourned? Do you remember how we used to lie in bed at night, holding hands on top of the quilt, and prayed for God to give us a baby? Because I do. We prayed for a baby, a healthy, living baby.

"And so when our child was born, I loved him with all my heart. Because Howard wasn't just a baby. He was my baby, *our* baby, the gift God meant us to have, a sweet, loving, beautiful boy who happened to have Down syndrome and deserved every ounce of love, strength, intellect, and effort I could muster.

"And if cherishing and caring for that precious gift, giving him the attention and time he needed to grow up to be the man he is today, meant that I didn't have time to cook your damn supper, or wash your damn clothes, or stroke your damn ego—well, forgive me, Donny, but I really don't give a rat's rear end!"

Mary Dell was not normally given to profanity of even the mildest sort, nor to making scenes in public. Yet she'd done both, speaking so loudly that two families sitting nearby hurriedly gathered up their food and went in search of someplace else to sit. Mary Dell didn't notice or care. Three decades of suppressed fury, betrayal, fear, denial, and heartbreak poured from her mouth in a white-hot stream.

Once she'd let it loose, there was no stopping it, not as long as she remained in Donny's presence, and so she got up to leave so abruptly that the chair she'd been sitting in tipped backward and to the side, blocking her exit.

Mary Dell bent down and grabbed the chair, trying to pull the obstacle from her path, which gave Donny time to intercept her. He begged her to stop and listen to him just for a moment, but she didn't want to hear anything else he had to say.

He clutched her arm, but she jerked away from his grasp, then hauled back her arm and let it fly like a catapult loosed from its tether, slapping him so hard that the ever-present Stetson fell off his head.

The crack of her hand striking Donny's face and the sight of the angry red mark on his cheek brought Mary Dell back to her senses somewhat. The fight-or-flight response Donny's words had summoned from her quelled slightly as she remembered that Howard would be returning to this spot looking for her before long. She realized she couldn't just run away before Howard returned, but that return to clarity didn't mean she had regained control of her emotions.

"How could you do it?" she asked, tears streaming down her cheeks. "How could you leave us? How could you leave *me?*"

And there it was, at last.

The question she had never dared to voice until now, because she already knew the answer. She had heard the malevolent whispers in her mind for years now.

Donny left because he didn't love her. Because she was unlovable. Aside from Howard, no one loved her. No one could.

This was what she had always known in her heart but never dared to admit, even to herself. This was the belief that made her barricade her heart behind the excuse of a marriage that had ended in all but name, preventing anyone else who might hurt her from getting too close. Until now.

Before Hub-Jay came along, keeping suitors at bay had been a relatively easy task, partly because she had found such fulfillment in her son but mostly because she'd never encountered a man of Hub-Jay's caliber before, someone so fine and loving and good that he made her consider lowering her guard.

But that was before Donny's return, before she remembered how much it had hurt when he'd left, recognizing once again the hole he'd left in her life and how close she'd come to disappearing inside it. She couldn't take that kind of risk again; she couldn't endure that kind of pain.

That was why, on the previous night, when Hub-Jay had pressed her to ask Donny for a divorce and the conversation between them became heated, she had taken the ring from her finger and given it back, saying that she should never have accepted his proposal, that it had been a mistake.

"How could you do that to us? How could you

leave me all alone? I hate you, Donny! I really hate you!"

He took a step toward her and gathered her in his arms. She didn't draw back or resist, but laid her head on his shoulder and gave herself up to the flood of emotion as the man who had been her husband held her close and whispered, "I know you do, Mary Dell. Sometimes I hate me too."

Chapter 48

Mary Dell cried for a long time, and Donny let her, ignoring the whispers and stares of people who walked past gnawing on turkey legs and carrying cheap stuffed animals, holding on tight while she undammed years of pent-up resentment, recrimination, doubt, and despair, until she was spent and dry and finally able to hear what he'd come so far and waited so long to say to her.

"Let me talk for three minutes," he said when he finally convinced her to sit back down. "Let me say my whole piece before you make up your mind about what you think I said, all right? That's all I ask."

The way she crossed her arms over her bosom, something that wasn't all that easy for a woman as buxom as Mary Dell, didn't quite convince him that she was approaching this with an open mind, but Donny forged ahead just the same, knowing this would be the only chance he had to explain himself and get her to agree to the proposal he had thought long and hard about.

"What I was trying to say before, obviously not real well, was that after Howard was born, I was drowning. For the first time in my life, I didn't know what I was supposed to do. You were one hundred percent right in what you said about me—I had a set idea of what our son was supposed to be. It wasn't that there wasn't room in my mind to let Howard be his own person. He could have been an artist or an athlete, a bookworm or a bodybuilder, but that our child might be born with Down syndrome, or any kind of physical or developmental problem—it just never crossed my mind. I was sure that our baby, whatever his personality, would be perfect."

"But he was perfect!" Mary Dell protested. "And he still is. Howard is the most perfect Howard on the planet, exactly who he was meant to be."

"You're right," Donny said, ignoring the fact that she hadn't lasted even a minute before interrupting him. "I can see that now. Back then I couldn't. The only thing I could see, or hear, or think, was that Howard had a problem, a problem that I couldn't fix. So I felt useless and guilty. But you seemed to jump right in and deal with it," he said, amazement still evident in his voice, even after all these years. "You pulled up your socks and sprinted right down the road, leaving me in the dust.

"No, let me finish," he said, lifting his hand to ward off another interruption. "I'm not saying that with any kind of bitterness or blame. I didn't feel it then and I don't now. What I felt was in the way, like I was dragging you both down. You can credit that or not, but it's God's honest truth, Mary Dell. At the time, I truly felt like you'd be better able to give Howard what he needed if I was gone.

"That's why I left, because I thought you two would be better off without me. I'm not saying this because I want you to feel sorry for me or to excuse what I did—I'm just saying how it was. I didn't leave because of anything that was wrong with you, Mary Dell, but because of the things that were wrong with me."

He stopped for a few seconds to give her time to let his words sink in; also because he needed to take a breather. Once upon a time, Donny had been known as a talker, but living by himself for so long, enduring decades of a self-imposed exile in the remotest part of Texas, where the most intimate relationship he had was with a bartender he saw once a week, had left him a little out of practice when it came to expressing himself.

But the one thing those years in West Texas had given him was time to think, to retrace the map of his life and see all those times he'd made a wrong turn or circled around the same route, again and again, getting nowhere, wasting time, energy, and opportunity. He was sixty-three years old. The docs at the hospital said he was in real good shape for his age, but he knew there were more days behind him than ahead, and he was tired of wasting time.

"I failed you both so badly," he said. "And I am sorry for that. But there was never a day when I didn't care about Howard or you. I kept tabs on you both for years. Of course, that was easy once the show started to run. I don't have a TV, but I go to a bar in Alpine every Tuesday to watch."

"You do?"

"Yes, ma'am. I've learned enough about quilting in the last seven years that I've almost been thinking about taking it up myself." He smiled at his own joke, hoping she might do the same and so lighten the mood a bit. When she didn't, he went on with his story.

"But I found other ways to check in on you before that. Got myself a subscription to the *Limestone County Gazette*. That's how I knew you were opening the quilt shop. Later, when computers and the Internet came along, I started going to the library so I could read the Methodist church newsletter. Sometimes they'd show pictures of the Christmas pageant, and there you'd be. When Howard got confirmed, they put in that picture of him, standing next to the minister."

Donny shifted his weight forward and reached

into the back pocket of his Levi's. Opening his battered wallet, he pulled out a newsprint photo of Howard and the Reverend Crews, covered with clear plastic laminate.

Mary Dell's hand rose to her throat. "You've carried that with you all these years?"

"I was real proud of him," Donny said, bobbing his head as he slipped the picture back into his wallet. "Proud of you, too, Mary Dell. You raised him right. Howard's a good man, better than I could ever hope to be, and you're the reason."

Mary Dell's eyes were shiny. For a moment, Donny was afraid she might start to cry again, but when he started to speak once more, she collected herself and listened.

"The church newsletter was how I heard about the accident—"

"You sent flowers," she recalled. "Three sprays of yellow roses."

He nodded. "One for Dutch; one for Graydon; one for Lydia Dale."

"But you didn't come to the funeral," Mary Dell said. "I really thought you might. Your own brother—"

"I know," he said, dropping his gaze. "I wanted to. I nearly did. But you were already dealing with a world of heartache. I thought my showing up would just make things worse. That's what I told myself anyway."

"You might have been right," Mary Dell

conceded. "I don't know if I could have taken one more shock that year."

"Maybe. There's no way to make up for the things I did before, but I'll tell you something true; when Dr. Brewer came in and told me that my kidney was a match for Howard's, I bawled like a calf. I did," he said, countering the doubt he saw in her eyes. "I was so happy, because after all these years, I can finally do something for my son."

Mary Dell nodded slowly. "You are. You're giving him a chance to really live his life and reach for his dreams. I'm grateful to you for that, Donny."

"I'm the grateful one," he said. "I can't make up for what's passed, but I'm getting a chance to redeem a piece of the time and opportunities I wasted where Howard was concerned. And I'd like to do the same for you. If you'll let me."

As he'd been talking, Donny noticed that Mary Dell's posture had relaxed and she'd leaned toward him, just a little, but now her shoulders tensed again and she shifted back in her chair, the suspicion his words had awakened in her mind evident in her body. Donny rushed ahead to explain himself.

"I wasn't eavesdropping," he said, "but your voice kind of carries, Mary Dell. It always did. There was no way not to hear all these conversations you've been having with Cady the last few days. I know that Rob Lee is going to be gone

450

for a couple of months yet and that the hand you've got running things isn't up to the job, especially not during the lambing season.

"I'd like to come down and help you out for a few weeks," he said, opening his hands a little, as if wanting her to understand that he wasn't hiding anything, "just until Rob Lee is ready to come home. I know you're worried about what's going to happen with the quilt shop once the show goes off the air for good. I can't help you there, Mary Dell, but I can make sure that you get a good lambing season, and that'll give you some breathing room so you can focus on your other problems. I know as much about sheep as any man in Texas," he said. "You know it's true. I started that herd. You won't be able to find anybody one-half as good to fill in while Rob Lee's gone, especially not on short notice."

Her face was set like a flint when he began to talk, but as he neared the end of his speech, for a moment that was as quick as the flicker of a candle flame, he saw her resolve waver. But then, just as quickly, the suspicion returned to her eyes.

"Why are you here, Donny? You come back on the scene as quick as you ran from it, disappearing and reappearing like the rabbit in a magician's hat, and you expect me to act like nothing ever happened." She made an incredulous noise, some-where between a cough and a laugh. "What is it you want? Do you think that a

451

trip to the zoo and the amusement park and a couple of rides on a roller coaster makes you a father again? Makes us a family?"

"No," he insisted, moving his head from side to side. "That's not what I think. I won't lie to you, Mary Dell. When I saw you in the doctor's office, there was a part of me that thought I could come back. But it didn't take me long to figure out that was just me wishing for something that can never be. We're different people than we were. You especially. You're not a wide-eyed child who falls head over heels because the moon is full and a cowboy thinks her dress is pretty. You're a woman now. You're smart, determined, and more beautiful than ever. You make your own decisions and you don't take no for an answer. You amaze me, but you intimidate me a little too. I couldn't make you happy now, Mary Dell. You're beyond me. I know that.

"But that doesn't mean you're beyond love." Donny looked down at the empty finger on her right hand. "Where's your engagement ring?"

Mary Dell's eyebrows arched in surprise.

"Doesn't matter what hand you put it on," he said. "Right or left, I knew what it was first minute I saw it. I might be dumb, Mary Dell, but I'm not stupid.

"But you will be if you run from love because you're scared of getting hurt again. There's no guarantees in this world, but I'll tell you something true: Hub-Jay Hollander loves you. If not, he wouldn't have come looking for me.

"Don't get me wrong; I'm not saying I like him. He's not the kind of man I'd want to take on a roundup, but he's a good man. He'll make you happy if you let him. And you'll make him happy too. Hell, you already do." He shrugged. "I've been watching this last week. I've seen the way he looks at you, like you're a treasure. A precious treasure."

Looking over Mary Dell's shoulder into the distance, Donny saw Howard and Jenna come around the corner, still holding hands and grinning. He returned Howard's wave before turning his eyes back to Mary Dell.

"Don't be so dang stubborn, woman. Let me help you with the sheep. You don't have to pay me, or feed me, or even talk to me. You can go right on hating me if you want to; I'll understand. All I want is the chance to help . . ." He paused for a moment, searching for a word, smiling when he found it. "A lost love. I've got no ulterior motive," he said, getting to his feet. "I'll prove it."

He reached into the front pocket of his shirt, pulled out a stack of folded papers, and handed them to Mary Dell.

"What's this?" she asked.

"Something I should have given you a long time ago. Your freedom. And another chance at happiness."

Chapter 49

Mary Dell didn't think she should just walk into Hub-Jay's office unannounced, as she might have before the argument that had resulted in her returning his ring. When she got to the hotel, she walked up to the front desk to ask one of the clerks to let Hub-Jay know she was in the lobby, and was surprised when a door behind the desk opened and David came out, dressed in one of the blue blazers that all the hotel clerks wore.

"What are you doing behind the desk? Did you quit the restaurant?" she asked him.

"No. Just expanding my horizons. Mr. Hollander wants me to learn hotel management."

"I see. Would this have anything to do with the new property in Fort Worth?"

"Well," David said with a modest smile, "it would be premature to say. I've got a lot to learn yet."

"I'm sure you're catching on quick," she said.

"Thank you. I hope so. Miss Mary Dell, are you sure you don't want to go right up to the third floor? I'm sure Mr. Hollander will be happy to see you."

"No, thank you. I'd rather wait down here. By the way, I didn't have a chance to thank you for helping Hub-Jay find my husband. You may have helped save Howard's life."

"I'm glad everything worked out. I didn't like to presume on anyone's privacy, but in this case, I thought it was the right thing to do."

"It was," Mary Dell replied. "For all kinds of reasons."

David picked up the phone to call Hub-Jay. Mary Dell went to stand next to the stairs and wait, thinking about the night when their friendship had turned to something more, how he had offered her his arm and escorted her up the staircase for the dinner he had planned in such detail.

She thought, too, about the flowers and the phone calls, the gentle but persistent way he had pursued her, making her feel desired and special, awakening desires and emotions she'd never imagined experiencing again.

When she was younger, she doubted she would have found Hub-Jay attractive. But she wasn't young now. She understood things she hadn't at twenty, thirty, or even forty—the value of steadiness and patience and humor, and that kindness trumped looks any day of the week. Fortunately, Hub-Jay had both. She understood, too, the value of a man who was not threatened by female intelligence or ambition, a man who was comfortable in his own skin and didn't demand that you turned yours inside out for him.

But more than all that, she understood the thing

she had always known, even in her youth: that real love is rare. If you're fortunate enough to find it, you need to hang on tight, because if you let fear dissuade you from taking the chance, you might never get another.

David took the phone from his ear and said, "Mr. Hollander said to tell you he's finishing up a conference call and will be down in just a few minutes."

Mary Dell thanked him and walked across the lobby, her heart beating a little faster. She took a seat in a white upholstered chair to wait, hoping her second chance at happiness hadn't already passed her by.

Three minutes of waiting always feels like ten of doing almost anything else. Mary Dell became more anxious as the seconds ticked by. Her cell phone was stowed in the outer pocket of her purse and set to silent. When she felt the vibration that signaled an incoming call, her nerves were so taut that she let out a startled little gasp.

Like mothers everywhere, Mary Dell checked her phone no matter where she was or what she was doing, in case Howard needed her. At that particular moment, apart from Howard, she would have ignored almost any caller, but when she saw HHN-TV on the screen, curiosity got the best of her.

When she picked up the call a female voice said, "Ms. Templeton?"

"Yes. This is Mary Dell."

"Please hold for Mr. Frankel."

"I'm sorry . . . ," Mary Dell stammered. "Do you mean Bernard Frankel? The chairman of the network?"

Mary Dell was still on the phone, pacing back and forth across the lobby, when Hub-Jay arrived. He hung back a few feet, waiting for her to finish her conversation.

"Absolutely," she said. "Anytime next week is fine with me. Yes, sir. All right. Thank you, Mr. Frankel."

She pressed the "end" button on her phone and spun around to face Hub-Jay. Her eyes were dancing and her mouth hung open in an expression somewhere between utter shock and sheer delight.

"You will not believe who called me!"

"Bernard Frankel, head of HHN."

Mary Dell's brows shot up. "How did you know?"

"You called him Mr. Frankel. I can't think of a lot of other Mr. Frankels you'd be this excited to hear from. What did he want?"

Mary Dell sank slowly into a chair, as if she needed something solid under her. Hub-Jay sat down in the seat across from hers.

"He wants to offer me a new contract, two seasons guaranteed with an option for two more after that."

"Four more seasons of *Quintessential Quilting*?"

"No. Four seasons of a whole new show," she said, looking off into the distance, as though she was trying to put together the pieces of some mental puzzle. "*The Quilter's College*. Somehow, he got hold of those two episodes we shot without Artie. He's crazy about our idea to have an older, more experienced quilter mentor a novice, taking her from ground zero to expert over the course of several seasons. We're going to work out the details, but he wants to give me a free hand in developing the content each season. He's going to give me a say over the hiring of a new director and list me as executive producer in the credits.

"Oh, and get this!" she exclaimed, turning her gaze back to Hub-Jay's face. "Jason Alvarez is fired! Mr. Frankel saw a couple of the other episodes too, couldn't believe how terrible they were, and gave him the boot.

"I can't believe it," she breathed. "This is just . . . I can't believe it. How did things go from rotten to fabulous in the course of one day?"

"Maybe it's like you're always saying—every time the sun comes up, you might be about to have the best day of your life."

"Maybe," she said, still sounding a little dazed. "Whatever it is, I'll take it."

"I'm happy for you, Mary Dell. And so glad

that you came over to share the news with me," he said. "I hope that means we're still friends."

Hub-Jay's words and the look on his face, wistful and a little sorrowful in spite of his smile, snapped her back to the present moment and place, reminding her why she'd come looking for him.

"Oh, Hub-Jay." She pressed her hand to her mouth for a moment before lowering it to clutch at her throat. "I am so sorry. I don't know what's wrong with me or why I couldn't figure it out on my own. I've been such an idiot. I don't want to be your friend anymore."

The light of hope that had begun to flicker in Hub-Jay's eyes when Mary Dell began to speak was doused. He rose from his seat and stood ramrod straight, as if trying to steel himself for whatever came next.

"Oh. I see. I'm sorry you feel that way—"

"I'm not," Mary Dell said quietly, rising from her chair. "I'm only sorry that it took me so long to figure it out. I really don't want to be your friend anymore, Hub-Jay. But if it's not too late, I'd like to be your wife."

Mary Dell had never been petite, not even in her youth, but Hub-Jay, tall, strong, and pulsing with joy, was not in the least daunted by her height and fulsome figure. Nor was he embarrassed by the looks he got from hotel guests and employees when he squatted down and grabbed Mary Dell, wrapping his arms just below her backside, and lifted her into the air, making her squeal with delight and demand that he put her down before he hurt himself.

"No, ma'am!" he cried. "Now that I've got you, I'm never letting go. Point me to the nearest threshold and I'll carry you over it right now."

Laughing, Mary Dell repeated her demand. "Put me down! I'm serious, Hub-Jay. No bride wants a groom with a hernia!"

Grinning as wide as the Rio Grande, he lowered her toward the ground, sliding her body along his until their lips met in a kiss, as the hotel guests, desk clerks, and David broke into a round of applause.

"David!" Hub-Jay shouted joyously across the lobby. "Send a bottle of champagne up to the private dining room, please."

"Right away, Mr. Hollander. What vintage?"

"Whatever is sweetest," he said, and looked into Mary Dell's eyes with pure, unfiltered, hundred-proof love.

Hub-Jay put his arm around Mary Dell's shoulders as they ascended the staircase.

"I almost forgot! Donny has filed for divorce, so we can get married anytime we want. But I guess we'd better make some plans first," she said in a kind of coming-back-to-reality tone. "I mean, are we going to live in Dallas? Or Too Much? I don't want to leave Momma alone again, and Mr. Frankel wants us to keep filming in Too Much, so that'll be good for the town. But you've got your business to attend to, and not just in Dallas. You'll need to spend time at the other properties too."

She furrowed her brow, realizing that this was going to be complicated. "I'm not sure how we're going to figure this out."

Hub-Jay shrugged. "We could retire. Take up golf or tennis or bridge."

Mary Dell looked at him, aghast, and he laughed.

"Just kidding. I know you've got to work, and so do I. Not just for the money, but because that's who we are. We love what we do. Don't worry. We'll figure out a way to love our work and each other at the same time. As long as I've got a good phone and Internet connection, I can work any-where. And I'm sure Bernie Frankel will let you set your own schedule. He was so anxious to get you back that I think he'd agree to just about anything you ask for—"

"Bernie? Wait a minute!" Mary Dell exclaimed. "You sent those DVDs to Mr. Frankel! He's a friend of yours, isn't he?"

"He wasn't before," Hub-Jay replied. "But after the restructuring at HHN, Bernie and all the rest of the management moved to Dallas. Turns out Bernie is a sailor and wanted to join the yacht club."

"And you're on the membership committee," Mary Dell said, finishing his sentence for him, shaking her head in amazement. "Hub-Jay

Hollander, you are the most wonderful man."

"It was a lucky coincidence," he said modestly. "Good timing. I know some people who know some people."

They reached the top of the stairs. Hub-Jay turned toward Mary Dell, took hold of both her hands, and then lifted them to his mouth as if to kiss them, but stopped short, frowning.

"Hang on. Something's missing."

He reached into his pocket, pulled out the black velvet box containing Mary Dell's engagement ring, and opened the lid.

This time, she put it on her left hand.

Chapter 50

The visitors' lounge at Camp Courage reminded Holly of the common room in a college dorm. There was a Ping-Pong table in one corner, a couple of vending machines in another, a television, a shelf filled with paperback books and board games, and several oak-framed chairs and sofas upholstered in navy blue with red and white throw pillows, a nod toward the veteran status of the residents.

She sat down on a sofa and waited for Rob Lee, who looked surprised to see her. He also looked better than the last time she'd seen him, she noted. His eyes were clear and his skin was less sallow. He'd shaved, which Holly thought was an improvement. Not that she had anything against facial hair, but she didn't like that scraggly in-between stubble that Rob Lee had going after the party. That look always made her think a guy just didn't care, which, in Rob Lee's case, had been true. This was definitely an improvement.

"I thought you were Cady," he said after taking a seat in a nearby chair.

"Disappointed?"

"No, no. Just surprised. I thought you were Cady," he said again.

Things were obviously awkward between them, and small talk wasn't going to change that, so Holly decided it would be best to get to the point. Before she could, Rob Lee cleared his throat, as if looking for some way to fill the silence, and asked her how things were going. How was the job search? How was Stormy?

"Good. All good," she said, bobbing her head. "I got a job offer, a couple of them, actually. And Stormy's doing great. We went on a trail ride with Linne and Cady just yesterday, to see the bluebonnets. The hills are carpeted with them," she said. "Just gorgeous."

Rob Lee opened his eyes wider. "You actually got my sister on a horse?"

"It was Linne. She is one persistent kid. But it did the trick. I don't think Cady's going to be entering a barrel-racing competition anytime soon, but she survived. I think she even had fun. At least a little."

"That's amazing. She's always been scared of horses. Well, not always, just since she got thrown that time. Good for her."

"Yeah. Linne was pretty excited. Now she's got a new obsession." Holly smiled. "She thinks Mary Dell and Hub-Jay should be married on horseback. And that the wedding party and guests should be riding too."

A light came into Rob Lee's eyes, the same kind of light she'd seen on that day when she'd first ridden Stormy, and he laughed. Really, it was more of a chuckle, but it reminded her of how he'd been before, during that brief period of time when he'd finally warmed to her, just about the time she'd started to think that maybe, just maybe . . .

She stopped herself. There was no point in going there. If he'd looked happy to see her when he'd first entered the room, that might have been one thing. But he hadn't. That was fine. Just because she'd gone and gotten a crush on Rob Lee for a few weeks didn't mean they couldn't do business together.

"Knowing Linne," Rob Lee said, still chuckling over his niece's antics, "I wouldn't be surprised if she got her way. She's like a dog with a bone when she gets her mind set on something. Stubborn," he said admiringly. "Nick was the same way."

Holly lifted her brows, surprised to hear him speak of Nick, especially with nostalgia instead of anguish. He'd always avoided doing so before. Whatever it was he was doing here, it seemed to be helping him face his demons and reclaim his past, the good along with the bad. Good. She was happy, for his sake.

"Listen," she said, anxious to return to the business at hand, "about Stormy."

"It's fine," Rob Lee said. "He can board out at the ranch for as long as he wants. My uncle Donny'll keep an eye on him until I get back, and then I'll take over again. I don't mind at all."

"Oh. No." Holly gave her head a quick shake. "That's not what I meant. I'm actually planning to move him."

"Oh?" Rob Lee looked a little disappointed. "There's a stable near your new job?"

"Kind of. I was offered two jobs—one as a spokesmodel on a home shopping channel and one hosting a new design reality show on HHN-TV."

"The one Jason offered you? You got it?"

Holly nodded. "Uh-huh. The network fired Jason, but they liked the show concept and offered me the host slot. But I turned them down. I turned down the spokesmodeling gig too."

Rob Lee gave her a quizzical look. "But I thought you really wanted the design show."

"So did I. But, the more I thought about it, the

465

more I realized it wasn't for me. Don't get me wrong; it's going to be a great show. I'm looking forward to watching it someday. When I was talking to Mr. Frankel at the network, I realized my first instincts about that show were right—it's going to be a big success, and by the second season, the host's name will be a household word. But the thing is," she said, tilting her head to one side, "I don't want to be a household word. I know what that world is like. I see what it's done to my mom, and I just don't want that, not for me."

"Okay. So what do you want?"

"To be happy. To have a normal life," she said, laughing a little. "Whatever that means. Maybe have a family someday, kids and all. Try not to screw them up too much. But in the meantime, I'd like to do something I love. And the truth is, I don't love television. I like it all right and I'm good at it, too, but it isn't the thing . . ." She paused, trying to figure out how to explain herself. "It isn't the thing I would do because I can't *not* do it.

"That's why I went to see Mrs. Finley yesterday. I made an offer on her ranch."

Rob Lee frowned, and his brows drew together almost into a single line as he realized what she was getting at.

"You're going to raise horses?"

She grinned and his mouth went slack.

"Holly, do you have any idea how hard it is to make a living raising horses?"

"Very. Especially since I have so little experience. I mean, rehabilitating one emotionally damaged gelding doesn't exactly make me an expert, does it?"

"No," he agreed. "It doesn't."

She bobbed her head and continued to grin. She was enjoying this.

"I know. And since I plan to devote about thirty percent of my stall space to fostering rescue horses, horses like Stormy, I'll probably be lucky just to break even."

"I'd say." Rob Lee gave a little grunt of disbelief and tugged at his nose. "So tell me again how this is a recipe for happiness? I like horses as much as anybody, probably more than most. They beat the heck out of raising cattle or sheep; that's for sure. But I like eating regular, too, and being able to pay my bills. I assume you had to take out a mortgage to buy the place?"

"Uh-huh. The mortgage is a hundred and sixty, but I'm putting forty thousand down. That leaves forty-five in my savings to buy breeding stock and hay and"—she shrugged—"whatever else it is I'll need."

"Tack, a truck, a trailer, oats, fencing." Rob Lee was counting this all off on his fingers, shaking his head from left to right while he did, as if he was trying to clear water from his ears. "Not to mention payroll. Holly, you can't run a horse ranch alone. You're going to have to hire some help."

"Right," she said. "That's where you come in. Your uncle Donny seems like he's settling in at the F-Bar-T; he handled the lambing season just fine—I know because I spent a lot of time out there helping out. Oh! And get this!" she exclaimed, leaning in to share the news that she still had a hard time believing and probably wouldn't if she hadn't seen it with her own eyes. "Even Hub-Jay was helping out! Thank heaven Mary Dell made him change into jeans and a regular shirt before he did." She made a face. "Delivering lambs can get kind of messy."

"Yeah. I know," Rob Lee said. "I've done it a few times. Is there a point to this story?"

"Yes. Okay. Sorry." She took a big breath and started again. "Anyway, Donny is working out fine at the ranch, and I think he wouldn't mind staying, as he'd get to see Howard more often that way. And now that Mary Dell and Hub-Jay are engaged and happy, she seems okay with having him around. Anyway, I was thinking that if Donny stayed on at the ranch and worked with the cattle and sheep, which he really seems to like, then you could come and work at my ranch with the horses, which *you* really seem to like."

She stopped, waiting for him to respond. When he didn't she said, "What do you think?"

"I think that by the end of the year, probably sooner, you'll be out of savings and I'll be out of a job. Seriously, Holly, tell me this is a joke. You didn't actually make an offer on the Finley place, did you? Is it too late to get your deposit back?"

"So," she said, making her eyes as wide and innocent looking as possible, "what are you saying? You don't think it's a good idea?" She blinked twice, her face becoming a mask of disappointment and confusion.

"No!" he barked, his tone making it clear that the answer should be obvious. He threw out his hands momentarily and then grabbed hold of his own head, almost as if that's what he had to do to keep from shaking her. "Holly, do you have any clue how hard it is to—"

Holly smiled, then giggled, then laughed out loud. Seeing her response, a slow smile spread over Rob Lee's face.

"You *were* joking." He punched her in the shoulder. "Jerk."

She took a breath, letting laughter fade to a smile. "I was starting to wonder when you were going to figure out that I was messing with you. Really, how dumb do you think I am? Don't answer that," she said with mock seriousness. He smiled at her and rolled his eyes.

"And actually, I wasn't joking. Everything I told you was true; there was just one part I left out. HHN offered me two jobs: the design show gig as well as a chance to co-host with Mary Dell on her new show. That job, I accepted. It's not as much money but, after all, a girl has to work. And if I'm going to do television, there's nobody I'd rather do it with than Mary Dell. Plus, quilting turns out to be kind of fun. Not as fun as horseback riding, but still.

"Anyway," she continued, "I sat down and did the projections—your uncle Donny and the county extension agent helped me. I can show you the figures, but the bottom line is this: the commercial horse operation should make enough to pay for foster horses as well as the mortgage, so I can live off my HHN check."

"Wow," Rob Lee said, his tone respectful, "you've really spent some time on this, haven't you?"

"I have," she said, feeling proud of herself. She pulled a sheaf of papers out of her purse, the financial figures she'd mentioned, and laid them on the coffee table in front of Rob Lee. "So, now what do you say?"

Rob Lee picked up the papers and flipped through the pages, studying the figures, far too slowly to suit Holly. More than a minute passed and he still hadn't said a word.

The way they'd been laughing and teasing, she'd started to feel like things were thawing between them and that he'd jump at her offer. But now, as one minute stretched to two, she was feeling awkward again and was certain he was going to turn her down.

Finally, he laid the papers back down on the coffee table and let out a breath.

"Yeah. You know, this all looks good and everything, seems like it should work. But"—he looked down at his lap—"I'm not sure I'm the right guy for the job."

He raised his head once again and looked her in the eye, his expression serious.

"I've been doing a lot of thinking while I've been here, about the war but about a lot of other stuff too. Kind of like you, trying to figure out what I really want out of life. I'm still working on it, but I've definitely made some decisions about what I want to do when I'm finished here. I was actually going to call you and talk to you about that in a couple weeks. That's why I was so surprised to see you today."

Holly clutched her hands together in her lap. She could not figure out where he was going with this, but from the way he was talking, she had the terrible feeling that he might have decided to leave Too Much for good. As she considered this possibility, she started to realize that at least part of her decision to buy the Finley farm was based on a hope that she hadn't dared admit, even to herself—that by living in Too Much, she'd likely run into Rob Lee on a regular basis.

"The thing is," he said, "I'm not sure how you'd

feel about having your boyfriend working for you."

Holly blinked. "My boyfriend?"

Rob Lee bobbed his head and looked down at his lap again, almost as if he was embarrassed. "Yeah. We've been working on some stuff, goal setting and all. One of my goals—top of the list, actually—is you."

Holly felt her eyes fill. "Oh."

Rob Lee cleared his throat, sounding nervous. "I don't know how good I'm going to be at this. Another thing I figured out while I was here is that I really have a lot of stuff to work out. My mom dying. My stepdad. My relationship with Cady. And my brother, Jeb. Bunch of stuff.

"Let's face it," he said, letting out a self-deprecating chuckle, "I'm kind of a mess. It could take a while before I'm ready for . . . anything more. But maybe? If you're willing to give the whole boyfriend-girlfriend thing a try?"

He lifted his eyes, full of hope and uncertainty, to hers.

"I am," she said softly.

His face lit up in that way she loved, steady and warm as fire glow on a cold night, and he reached for her hand.

"Me too," he said.

Chapter 51

On a picture-perfect morning in June, Mary Dell stood at the bathroom mirror, putting on a pair of earrings.

"Honey," she said when Hub-Jay entered the room, "I can't reach the zipper. Can you help me?" Mary Dell pulled her hair up off her neck as he came behind her to raise the zipper on the pink dress and button the lace-overlaid bodice.

"When I was single, do you know how many pretty dresses I had to take a pass on because I couldn't do up the back by myself? One of the benefits of married life."

"One of the many," Hub-Jay said, smiling at her reflection in the mirror before lowering his lips to her bare neck and kissing a line down her throat.

Mary Dell laughed and tried to pull away, but he looped one arm around her waist, pulled her to him, and reached up with his free hand to try to undo the button he'd fastened only a moment before.

"We don't have time," she protested laughingly, and slapped his hand away. "The wedding starts in less than three hours. Rachel and Mikey will be here any minute, and I still need to hang up flower baskets on the patio. Rachel felt so bad that she wasn't able to come up earlier to help,

473

but how could she? She's so busy rehearsing for her new show."

Mary Dell grabbed a tube of pink lipstick off the counter and started applying it as Hub-Jay continued nuzzling her neck. "Tell you what," he murmured, "how about I help you hang up the baskets and you help me—"

"Aunt Mary Dell?" Linne's voice came from outside the bathroom door. "Granny said to come tell you that Holly has something old, new, and blue, but she still needs something borrowed. And Uncle Donny wants to know where you want him to set up the bar."

"Okay, baby girl! Tell them I'll be right there."

Hub-Jay groaned and dropped his head on Mary Dell's shoulder as she disentangled herself from his grasp.

"I love your family. I really do," he said. "But there are times when living with the in-laws gets a little inconvenient."

"Which is why it is so nice that we have our own suite at the hotel," she reminded him. "Splitting our time between Dallas and Too Much lets us keep tabs on Howard, Momma, and the rest of the family but still gives us plenty of private time."

"Yeah," he agreed, and heaved a dramatic sigh. "But a suite in Dallas isn't doing me much good right this minute in Too Much."

Mary Dell laughed. "Hub-Jay Hollander, we have been married for one year, three months, two weeks, and two days . . . when do you plan to quit acting like a love-struck groom on his honeymoon?"

"Never."

"Good."

She turned toward him, kissing him lightly on the lips.

"Tonight, I promise. After the guests have gone. It'll be worth the wait. I was going to surprise you," she said, adding a tantalizing note to her voice, "but when I took Holly to Neiman's last month to pick out her bridal lingerie, I picked up a special garment for myself that I think you'll enjoy."

Hub-Jay grinned. "Any chance of a preview?"

Linne's voice came from the hallway. "Aunt Mary Dell?"

"Coming!"

She kissed him once again, letting her lips linger long.

"Tonight," she repeated, her voice a whisper, her words a promise to herself as well as to her beloved.

Two hours later, the wedding guests began to arrive. Howard and Jeb, dressed in their groomsmen's attire, matching tan summer suits with bright blue neckties the same shade as the delphiniums and hydrangeas Holly was to carry in her bridal bouquet, directed everyone out to the back of the house.

The design and construction of the new patio and pool had been supervised by Hub-Jay and finished just in time for the wedding. He had created a true backyard oasis, surrounding the patio with big trees to provide shade on hot days, building an enormous pergola of rough-sawn wood and a large outdoor fireplace and barbecue made from stone that matched the patio pavers. The new pool sat a few yards distant, at the bottom of a rolling hill planted with prairie grasses and native plants, the dark black bottom and stone edging creating the impression of a natural pond fed by an underground spring.

It was the perfect setting for a small, intimate, casual wedding, which was exactly what Holly and Rob Lee had wanted. Though both Rachel and Mary Dell had offered to help pay for the wedding, Holly and Rob Lee said, "Thanks, but no thanks," believing that at their ages, nearly twenty-eight and thirty-three, they should pay their own way. However, that meant keeping a lid on the budget and guest list.

They could have afforded a larger celebration—under Rob Lee's management, the horse farm, now named Stormy's Refuge Ranch, was actually making a profit even while continuing to foster abandoned animals—but they were thinking ahead to the end of Holly's contract with HHN and the time when they hoped to start a family. To that end they were saving up to build more stables and a bunkhouse and planning to open a riding academy specializing in weekend workshops for novice riders in the hopes that it would replace Holly's television income. With that goal before them, they were perfectly willing to forgo a large wedding.

But the bills for even a small wedding could mount up quickly, and so when Mary Dell and Hub-Jay suggested they have the wedding on the new patio, they immediately said yes. They were also delighted to accept Donny's offer to grill steaks and chops for fifty guests and Taffy's proposal that she prepare all the side dishes— baked beans, potato salad, coleslaw, and homemade rolls. She had wanted to make her special ambrosia salad, too, but Mary Dell absolutely forbade it. A small argument ensued, but it blew over quickly, and after that, every detail of Holly and Rob Lee's long-awaited day had gone smoothly—until now.

Holly, hair still in hot rollers but dressed in the simple, floor-length white gown that Cady had sewn and she had personally embellished with a star pattern of silver bugle beads along the neckline, stood at the window in Mary Dell and Hub-Jay's bedroom, nervously peeping through a small gap in the drawn curtains, scanning the faces of the arriving guests.

"Where are they?" she moaned. "We're supposed to start in forty-five minutes."

Holly was thrilled that her mother's fortunes had changed. Who could have predicted it? Two years ago her career was in the toilet, and now she was married, once again, to Mikey, the man who had always loved her. On top of that, in just three weeks she would be headlining in Las Vegas, with the first two weeks of her run already completely sold out. But this success and the demands of rehearsal made it hard for her to get away from Vegas, even for a day. But Holly wished they had booked an earlier flight.

Cady pulled a roller from Holly's hair, careful to keep from burning her fingers, and set it on the dresser.

"They'll be here any second. You know how the traffic can be from the airport. If they were going to be late, they'd have called. Ouch!" she cried when Holly moved her head unexpectedly, craning her neck to see if a couple walking across the lawn from the driveway might be Rachel and Mikey. "Will you hold still! I almost singed my hand."

"Sorry," Holly said, and let go of the edge of the curtain. "I'm just nervous. What if they don't get here in time?"

"Then we'll open the bar early and let everybody have a drink until they get here. Really, it's going to be fine. Just calm down. One way or another, by this time tomorrow, you'll be Mrs. Holly Benton. And my sister-in-law. Which is an even more important title," she said, cracking a wry smile.

Cady reached into her pocket and pulled out a slip of paper. "I caught Rob Lee skulking around the kitchen. He wanted to come down here and see you, but I said he couldn't so he wrote you a note instead. Here," she said, handing it to Holly. "You can read it, but don't cry. Your mascara will smear."

In spite of Cady's commands, Holly's eyes did tear up as she read the words of love written by the man who held her heart in his. Holly sniffled and Cady took another piece of paper from her pocket, a tissue, and handed it to her.

"Feel better now?" Cady asked.

Holly nodded and pressed the tissue delicately under her bottom lashes.

The bedroom door opened a crack. Taffy stuck her head into the room. "How are things coming in here? The minister just arrived."

"I'm not ready! Mom and Mikey aren't here yet. I can't get married without them. Mikey is supposed to give me away."

Cady rolled her eyes and pulled the last curler from Holly's hair.

"We've still got forty-five minutes," she reminded her. "And if we start a little late, then we do. Seriously, Holly, take a deep breath and calm down. If you start sweating it'll stain the satin."

The door opened wider and Mary Dell stepped into the room, carrying a can of hairspray.

"Found it!" she announced triumphantly. "I don't care how much times change, when you need your hairdo to hold up, nothing does the job like a good coat of Aqua Net. What's the matter?" she asked, her brow furrowing with concern when she saw the troubled expression on Holly's face.

"Rachel and Mikey still aren't here," Cady said, answering for the bride.

"They will be," Mary Dell said, setting the hairspray on the dresser, then quickly combing through Holly's curls with her fingers. "I put Linne on lookout in the driveway. She'll let us know the minute they pull in. Now close your eyes and hold your breath. This stuff smells kind of strong."

Mary Dell was so enthusiastic in her ministrations that even after she finished, the air was still clouded with the acrid alcohol and perfume scent of Aqua Net. When Holly took in a deep breath after the hissing of the spray can finally ceased, she started coughing so hard that her eyes watered. Mary Dell and Taffy started pounding her on the back and Cady ran to the bathroom to get some water just as Linne bounded into the room shouting, "They're here! They're here!"

Barely a minute later Rachel entered the bedroom, panting for breath because she was wearing heels and had run from the car, into the house, and down the hallway.

"I'm so sorry!" she puffed, addressing Cady, who was standing nearest the door. "Our luggage got lost and my phone ran out of battery and I forgot the charger and . . ." She waved her hand. "Anyway, we're here."

"Mom! I was so worried!" Holly exclaimed, walking toward her mother.

Rachel lifted her head, turning toward her daughter with a look of surprise, as if suddenly remembering what this was all about. "Oh, punkin. Oh. You are so, so beautiful," she breathed, then pressed both hands to her breast and burst into tears.

In spite of the drama surrounding the last-minute arrival of the mother and stepfather of the bride, the wedding went off without a hitch, and it was beautiful, as are all such occasions that celebrate the joining of two people who are truly in love.

But for Mary Dell, the real beauty of the occasion emanated not from the flowers, or the music, or the surroundings, but from the faces of the people, this gathering of the people who made her heart tender and her life meaningful.

There was Rob Lee standing at the front of the aisle, a man who had been to hell and back and emerged transformed, whole and happy at last, the entirety of his love and devotion to the woman he loved shining in his eyes, perfectly reflected back to him in the mirror of Holly's face. She was so fresh and hopeful, so breathtakingly beautiful and young. She was also strong, loyal, and wise, qualities that had made Mary Dell come to love her like a daughter as well as a friend.

They would do well, Rob Lee and Holly. In the years to come, life would surely buffet and batter them, as it does everyone, but, together, they would endure whatever troubles might befall them. Mary Dell was sure of it.

That was the trick of life: to cling to family and the people you love. People, Mary Dell had discovered, far more than any particular longitude or latitude, were the anchors of the heart's true home. This gathering was proof of it.

Standing next to Rob Lee was Jeb, the best man, the title a testament to a broken relationship between brothers that had been repaired and renewed. At Holly's side stood Cady as matron of honor. She, too, had been transformed in these last two and a half years, finding the peace that had eluded her. She was happier now but also confident, able to roll with the punches and handle whatever setbacks might come. When the time came, Cady would be ready to take over the reins as matriarch of the Tudmore-Templeton clan, ensuring that the family name would continue, carved deep into the life and landscape of this corner of Texas that had shaped and defined Taffy, Mary Dell, Cady, and all those who had come before, the women upon whose shoulders they had stood, generation after generation. Mary Dell hoped that, somewhere along the way to fulfilling that role, Cady might find genuine and lasting love again, just as she had.

Mary Dell glanced to her right and spotted Matt Pallow, Cady's date. He was an old high school classmate she had reconnected with at last year's Christmas Ball, and seeing the way he looked at Cady, Mary Dell couldn't help but think that her wish for her niece might come true.

Her wishes for Howard certainly had. Mary Dell had never suffered from a want of optimism, but even she could not have predicted the wonderful future that had awaited her son.

Nearly two years after the kidney transplant, Howard was in excellent health, more energetic than ever. The operation had had the unexpected effect of transplanting Donny back in all their lives too. And that was good. Howard loved his daddy and Donny loved Howard; they were part of each other's lives in the way they always should have been. Seeing them reconciled made it possible for Mary Dell to reconcile her own relationship with Donny, too, to genuinely and finally forgive him for what he could not be, a true husband, and embrace him for the lifelong bond they shared as parents, lost loves, and old friends.

Hard and painful as the road had been, there was something beautiful in all that.

Mary Dell saw Jenna sitting in the second

row, gazing at Howard with pure adoration, and wondered what the future might hold for her son and this dear, talented young woman. Together, Howard and Jenna had given Rob Lee and Holly a sunflower quilt made with the fabrics based on Jenna's painting, fabrics from the first collection in Howard's Down Home Fabric line. The initial collection had raised more than sixteen thousand dollars to benefit the National Down Syndrome Society and had been followed by a second just-as-successful collection, also inspired by one of Jenna's paintings, with plans for more in the works. But that wasn't the only thing keeping Howard busy these days.

While recovering from the transplant, he had started sewing decorative pillows and selling them on Etsy. People snapped them up, and so Howard, after seeking some guidance and a small loan from Hub-Jay and Mary Dell, had opened a small company, Down Home Interiors, to manufacture pillows for sale in gift and home-accessory shops. The company employed three part-time workers with Down syndrome who helped with sewing, stuffing, packing, and shipping and some clerical work. Things had gone well. The com-pany was on schedule to pay back the loan and Howard was already talking about hiring more workers.

He was a happy and entirely independent man, capable of caring for himself and for others, making the world better by being exactly who he was and fulfilling every ounce of his personal promise.

What more could she have wanted for him or for herself? Yet beyond all that, she had found the other half of herself, Hub-Jay, a man she could love fully and trust completely, who made her feel alive to life's possibilities. She could not believe her good fortune, and the way Hub-Jay's face lit up whenever she entered a room made her know that he felt exactly the same.

Holly and Rob Lee joined hands and repeated their vows. A soft breeze rose from the west, bringing with it the scent of earth and stone, juniper and mesquite and grass, the incense of the prairie come to bless the union of two who had decided to make their lives there. The mossy hanging baskets of flowers Mary Dell had hung with Hub-Jay's help swayed gently. The purple faces of pansies nodded ever so slightly, as if to say, *Amen and amen, so say we all.*

As they did, Mary Dell felt the presence and approval of the great cloud of witnesses, those who were loved no less dearly for being long departed: Grandma Silky, Aunt Velvet, Dutch, Graydon, and Lydia Dale.

Sitting at her side, Taffy reached for her daughter's hand and in a voice choked with tears whispered, "How I wish your daddy and sister could have been here to see this."

Mary Dell squeezed her hand.

"They are, Momma. They are."

Even at her age there was nothing Taffy liked more than cooking for a crowd, and so they had far more food than was required for fifty guests. Still, the fare was so delicious that people lingered at the reception, eating and talking and refilling their plates again and again. It was a lovely day, and no one, except the bride and groom, was in a hurry to leave.

Linne, just as horse-crazy as ever, had campaigned for a wedding on horseback, arguing that because Stormy was the one who had brought the couple together, he should definitely be included in the wedding party. Her idea was rejected, but even so, Stormy did get a chance to play his part in the ceremony.

When it was time for Holly and Rob Lee to depart, Stormy, handsomely groomed, with blue and white ribbons braided into his mane and tail, came up the driveway pulling the black two-seater horse cart, driven by Donny, that Rob Lee had given Holly as an engagement present.

After giving the reins to Rob Lee, Donny handed Holly up into the cart, making sure her train didn't get caught in the wheels. When she was settled safely, dress tucked up into the cart, Rob Lee clicked his tongue against his teeth and Stormy walked on.

While the wedding guests applauded and whooped, Holly threw her bouquet over her shoulder. Somehow, the ribbon holding the flowers came loose and the bouquet split into two bunches. Cady caught one half, and Jenna, showing surprising speed and agility as she sprinted past a determined Taffy, caught the other half, waved it triumphantly over her head, and then looked at Howard, whose face split into a grin.

After that, everyone returned to the party, but Mary Dell, with Hub-Jay's arm around her shoulders, stood on the porch watching and waving as Stormy carried the newlyweds home to begin their new life together.

When they finally disappeared over the crest of a hill, Mary Dell laid her head on her husband's shoulder.

"Hub-Jay, do you know what I love about life? Do you?"

"Tell me," he said, and kissed the top of her head.

"Everything." She sighed. "Just everything."

Gentle Reader,

Mary Dell Templeton, who first made a cameo appearance as the best friend of Evelyn Dixon in my 2008 novel, *A Single Thread*, the first book in my Cobbled Court Quilts series, quickly became one of my favorite characters. I enjoyed her humor and sass and admired her optimism as well as her inner strength. Fortunately for me, readers felt the same way and wrote myriad letters saying they'd like to hear more from Mary Dell. In fact, it was a letter from a reader that convinced me to give Mary Dell and Howard a book of their own.

Joyce Ely, the mother of Sara Ely, her beautiful and capable adult daughter who has Down syndrome, sent me a truly heartwarming note, one I will never forget, thanking me for my work and saying that few novels ever presented characters with Down syndrome as having "something to offer."

Reading her words compelled me to write my previous Too Much, Texas, novel, *Between Heaven and Texas*, which tells the story of Mary Dell's early history and of Howard's birth. If you haven't yet read that book, I hope you'll get an opportunity to do so.

Readers responded so positively to *Between Heaven and Texas* that I knew they would be eager to read a second book about Mary Dell and Howard. However, I was a little nervous about writing a follow-up, afraid it might not measure up to the original. But Mary Dell and Howard came through for me once again, revealing their hopes, dreams, and fears to me and showing me how greatly they had each matured in the thirty-year span of time that had passed between the story told in *Between Heaven and Texas* and *From Here to Home*.

I do hope you enjoyed reading *From Here to Home* and that, like me, you found yourself laughing, cheering, and occasionally tearing up as you walked alongside Mary Dell, Holly, Howard, and the other characters, coming to think of them as dear friends, as I do.

While we're on the subject, I think of my readers as friends, too, and I so appreciate the encouragement and support that so many of you have shown me over the years. I love hearing from you, and the Internet makes it easier than ever for us to connect.

Follow me on my Facebook fan page and on Twitter:

www.facebook.com/mariebostwick
www.twitter.com/mariebostwick

Or send me an e-mail through my Web site:

www.mariebostwick.com

Of course, if you prefer to use regular mail, you may do so by writing to this address . . .

Marie Bostwick
P.O. Box 488
Thomaston, CT 06778

Another great way to keep up with all my books, travels, appearances, and such is by registering as a Reading Friend on my Web site:

www.mariebostwick.com

Just click on the log-in/registration link in the upper-left corner to get started, and please make sure you are registering from a desktop computer or laptop, as it may not work from tablets or mobile devices.

When you register as a Reading Friend, your e-mail address will be added to the distribution list for my monthly newsletter, filled with all kinds of articles, links, contests, recipes, and other information I think you'll enjoy. Also, as a registered Reading Friend, you'll be able to log in and down-load free companion recipes and quilt patterns from my books—six so far!

As of this writing, I'm not yet sure if or when we'll have a new pattern to go with *From Here to Home*, but I do have some ideas along those lines, so hopefully there will be time to put those ideas down on paper and then translate them into fabric and thread.

Some of the quilt patterns you'll find on my Web site were designed by me, but most were created by professional designer and my dear friend Deb Tucker. In addition to the free downloadable patterns, Deb has also created a number of truly spectacular companion patterns to go with my books that she offers for purchase on her Web site:

www.studio180design.net

Be sure to check them out.

Thank you so much for reading *From Here to Home*. Life is so very busy for everyone these days that I am deeply cognizant of the honor you do me by spending some of that most valuable currency, time, in reading my books. I hope you enjoyed the journey and that we will have a chance to meet again, very soon, in the pages of another of my novels.

Until then . . .

Blessings,

Marie Bostwick

Discussion Questions

1. *From Here to Home* opens with a scene about Donny. How do you feel about this man who walked out on his wife and son thirty years prior? Do you feel angry with him or do you feel sorry for him? Can you think of a choice you made long ago that you now regret?

2. Mary Dell Templeton has known her share of tragedy, and yet she believes that "Every time the sun comes up, you might be about to have the best day of your life." How do you think she has been able to maintain an attitude of optimism in spite of the hardships and challenges she has faced? Is this a motto you might like to adopt for yourself?

3. In *From Here to Home*, we see a few mother-daughter relationships: Rachel and Holly, Taffy and Mary Dell, Cady and Linne. Can you relate to any of them? If you are a mother and/or a daughter, what is something you wish you could have handled or done differently in that relationship? What is something you think you got exactly right?

4. Howard is thirty now, a young man with plans and dreams, yet Mary Dell still calls him

"baby." Did you feel frustrated by Mary Dell's dependence on, care of, and attention to him? Or were you impressed with her dedication? How would you have dealt with raising a child with Down syndrome? If you're the mother of a grown child, what challenges did you face when your fledglings flew the nest? If you're a mother of young children, are you dreading the day when they go out on their own? Looking forward to the freedom of the empty nest? A little of both?

5. In Chapter 14, Holly had not yet met Linne, but "she knew how it felt to be fatherless, adrift and unclaimed, like a piece of lost luggage with no label, nothing to explain where and to whom you belong." Do you ever feel like this? Some of the characters didn't have a father. How does this affect their lives and the story?

6. Rob Lee bears terrible emotional scars from his experiences in Afghanistan. Do you know anyone like him? What can or should communities, societies, or individuals do to support veterans or other public servants who have been through traumatic experiences and are suffering in the aftermath?

7. When Mary Dell confronted Rob Lee, she said, "We rise and fall and get back up

together." That seemed to click with him. Can you relate to her statement? If so, how? Do you have a family motto?

8. Hub-Jay turns out to be Mary Dell's knight in shining armor. Were you rooting for Mary Dell and Hub-Jay's relationship? Or do you think Mary Dell should have given Donny another chance?

9. In *From Here to Home*, the author writes, "Trust is the place where love begins." Do you agree? Why or why not? Discuss which characters found this to be true. What actions or attitudes helped them to gain trust?

10. Cady and Holly form a friendship. Mary Dell and Holly have a special bond. Discuss friendships between women. Do you have a best friend? If not, would you like one? What three qualities do you think are most essential in a lasting friendship?

Center Point Large Print
600 Brooks Road / PO Box 1
Thorndike, ME 04986-0001 USA

(207) 568-3717

US & Canada:
1 800 929-9108
www.centerpointlargeprint.com